The
ICE MASTER

Other Books by James Houston

JAMES HOUSTON

The ICE MASTER

A NOVEL OF THE ARCTIC

Canadian Cataloguing in Publication Data

Houston, James, 1921 –
    The ice master

ISBN 0-7710-4207-8

I. Title.

PS8515.079122   1997   c813'.54   C97-931483-6
PR9199.3.H68122   1997

Set in Goudy by M&S, Toronto
Printed and bound in Canada

The publishers acknowledge the support of the Canada Council for the Arts and the Ontario Arts Council for their publishing program.

This is a work of fiction. Names, characters, places and incidents either are the product of the author's imagination or are used fictitiously, and any resemblance to actual persons, living or dead, or historical events, is entirely coincidental.

A Douglas Gibson Book

McClelland & Stewart Inc.
The Canadian Publishers
481 University Avenue
Toronto, Ontario
M5G 2E9

2 3 4 5   01 00 99

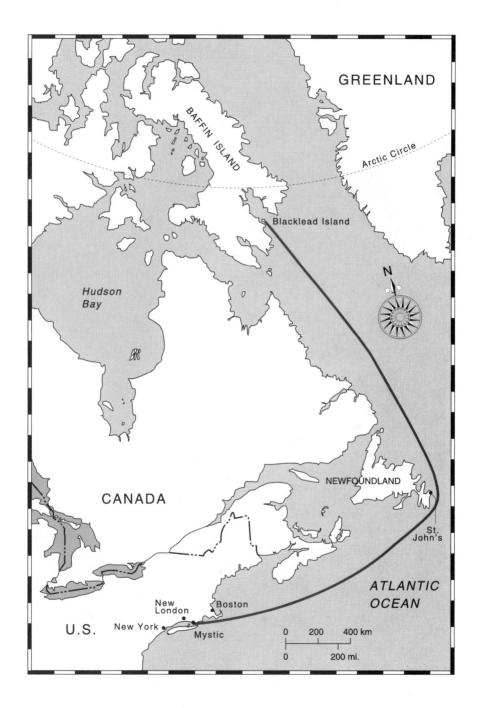

GREENLAND

BAFFIN ISLAND

Arctic Circle

Blacklead Island

N

Hudson
Bay

CANADA

NEWFOUNDLAND

St.
John's

ATLANTIC
OCEAN

New
London   Boston

U.S.   New York

Mystic

0	200	400 km

0	200 mi.

For Alice

Ayü, Ayü, Ayü.
I wish to see the musk ox run again.
It is not enough for me
To sing of the dear beasts.
Sitting here in the igloo,
My songs fade away,
My songs melt away,
Like hills in fog.
Ayü, Ayü, Ayü.

Inuit song

Chapter 1

"Ice master?" Caleb Dunston snorted. "What the hell's an ice master?"

"It's what our Whale Fisheries discovered that he is, that's what!" Amos Peapack shouted across the partners' table.

"Never heard of such a rank," growled Dunston as he rose, scraping back his chair. The four partners sat and stared at him.

"I don't give a sweet goddamn what you've heard or haven't heard. This Thomas Finn is a qualified ice master and he's going north to Newfoundland with you," Peapack replied, his face flushed. "The doctor says he's well enough to travel. You're going to set him safely off at St. John's harbor or Heart's Content. That's an outport he calls home."

"You're determined to rope me into this scheme, are you? Demanding that I go zigzagging all over the goddamned North Atlantic doing foolish little favors for you, Peapack. Why?"

"Because one of the vessels from this ice master's sealing company took hellish risks to go in close and help the *Hattie B.* when she was foundering three years ago off the coast of Nova Scotia in that awful blow. You were away in the Arctic, Dunston, safe in your frozen ignorance. That's why all this means nothing to you. But it meant one helluva lot to the crew of the *Hattie B.* and it saved one of our best vessels from destruction. Remember that, Dunston. You hunt whales and sail for us, that's all!"

"I'm going to quit right after this voyage," shouted Dunston. "I'm sick to death of dealing with the likes of you."

"Well, hear this, Captain," Peapack snapped at him, "this man, Finn, is a ship's master and this Fisheries is going to treat him fair!" Peapack flung his cigar butt into the brass spittoon. "Any other business to address, gentlemen?"

Dunston turned, strode out, and slammed the door. The partners shook their heads, then followed him, leaving Peapack to drum his heels and fume.

"Thompson, get your arse in here!" Peapack bellowed.

The door opened gently and the pale face of a Fisheries accountant peered inside. "Just look at that goddamned brass spittoon, will you, man? It hasn't seen a lick of polish in weeks. You find a man who can keep this room shipshape or you'll find that it's you, Thompson, who's doing the dirty work around here!"

"I'll see to it, sir." Thompson quietly closed the boardroom door. Then, opening it just a crack, he said, "Your nephew, Captain Kildeer, is here to see you, sir."

"Jesus, what a morning," Peapack groaned as he watched the cold rain slanting across the windowpanes. A tall young man appeared in the doorway. "Come on in, Titus, sit down. Over there in that corner chair. What the hell's wrong with you today?"

"Nothing, sir, nothing," Titus answered cautiously, having heard his uncle's ruckus with Caleb Dunston. "I've come to ask about that ice master, Thomas Finn. I've heard he's going north aboard our ship – well, my ship, *Lancer*."

"You're damned right, he's going north with you as far as St. John's, Newfoundland, or Heart's Content. Look that place up on your charts. Those are my orders, Titus. Don't let Dunston change them. I hate that horse's ass! If that pirate-rich wife of his didn't hold a partnership in this Fisheries, I'd haul Dunston back in here and fire him. By God, Newfies, Brits, colonials, whatever the hell they are, I'm going to send word north to their seal fishery in St. John's and return their ice master with my own personal letter of gratitude. Now, tell me this, Titus, is *Lancer* ready to set sail with *Sea Horse* on Wednesday's morning tide?"

"Ready she is, sir. *Lancer*'s old, but we've got her shipshape now."

"Since you haven't met Tom Finn, march yourself over to the Captains' Rest and get acquainted with him."

"I'll do that, sir. But it was about Kate Dunston that I've come to see you."

"That can wait, Titus. I'm trying to get an Arctic whale hunt under way. Head out, Titus, get your arse over to the Captains' Rest. You can tell me later what you think of Finn after you've heard what that man's been through."

Titus leapt up, grateful for the excuse to leave. He would try to talk to his uncle later when he was in a calmer mood.

He turned up the collar of his oilskin as he hurried along New London's waterfront in the foggy rain, smelling the seaweed mixed with dead fish that lay exposed in the harbor's ebb tide. "Captain Titus Kildeer," he said to himself and grinned. "I'm twenty-two, and I'm on my way."

"Congratulations, Titus," said the steward at the Captains' Rest when he opened the door. "I heard yesterday that you got your captain's papers and you'll be mating north on *Lancer* this voyage with Captain Dunston." He made an awful face, then laughed. "I hope he drowns his furies and allows you home alive."

"Oh, I'll make it." Titus grinned again. "Remember, I've served three years before the mast, rounded the Horn, and worked up to mate, sealing and whaling in the Pacific for more than a year."

"Well, good luck to you, Captain Kildeer," said the steward. "I've known you since you were no taller than my knee, and look at you now." He shook his head. "Anyway, I'd guess you're here to visit Captain Finn. He's looking a good deal better today. I've been trying to fatten him up on ale and suet pudding. He's out there on the back porch, taking his rest. He got rained out on his walk this morning. I'm proud of the way he's doing. He hardly needs his cane."

Titus walked through the dark hall and opened the screen door. "Good morning, Captain Finn. I'm Captain Kildeer," he said.

Finn stopped rocking and turned. "Did I meet you earlier when they first brought me in and I was . . . kind of off my head?"

"No, no," said Titus. "We've never met before."

They shook hands, and Titus sat down.

"I'll be giving you a passage back to St. John's, Newfoundland, aboard my ship, *Lancer*. We'll be leaving Wednesday morning on the tide. Are you feeling up to sailing north?"

"That I am," said Finn as he resumed his rocking. "I'd get too fat lolling around here, enjoying this steward's cooking. He's a companionable sort of man. Have you ever heard him make a banjo sound like wind singing through the rigging?"

"No," said Titus.

Finn turned his head and stared at the mist rising over Long Island Sound while Titus eyed him carefully. Finn had large, work-hardened hands with long, powerful fingers. He was tall and lean. Was that by nature, Titus wondered, or was it that this stranger had nearly starved to death? Finn's nose was long, his cheeks still hollow in an almost handsome face, its upper half tanned and weathered beneath dark hair that matched the color of his chestnut rocking chair. From beside Finn's nose two deep channels ran down to tighten his mouth, then lost themselves in the jutting boldness of his chin. Titus noticed that Finn's eyes were a faded, penetrating gray and had a look of desperation in them. But most of all, Titus was taken with Finn's sense of calm understanding, as though he had peered into some future place that normal humans never see.

"Most here wonder," Titus continued, "what happened that got you into such a fix."

"We just went out for cod," answered Finn, "and now I've forgotten much of it myself. I suppose I should be grateful for that." He paused. "I'll try to tell you what I can remember, if you care to hear it."

"I would," said Titus.

Finn stopped rocking and hung motionless in the chair. "*Huntress* finished her spring season in the ice," he said. "Eighteen seventy-five has turned out to be the best year for sealing in this century. When I got her fully loaded back to port, I was done with my duties as ice master. Henry Horwood is the captain who takes over on her for the longer part of the year."

"Hold on," said Titus. "What is an ice master? Lots of sailing folk along this Sound are asking that same question."

"An ice master," Finn replied, "is a captain who takes his vessel into ice during the early spring season. *Huntress*, a brigantine, is plying the West Indies now, trading off barrels of our salt cod for sugar, cotton, coffee, Barbados rum, and spices . . . items we need around Newfoundland and on the Labrador, especially the rum. Near the end of winter, the ice comes in and the seal hunt begins. That's when I take over from Henry, in March, and become ice master aboard *Huntress*. I take the hunters out searching for those big, solid moving ice floes – seal meadows, us Newfoundlanders call them – and they start their search for seals. *Huntress*'s crew does little of the hunting. But the others, the sealers, they jump down onto the ice and spread out. They do the killin', then drag the hides back to the ship."

"Our New London Fisheries crews do the same," said Titus, "but they do their seal hunting on the Falkland Islands and Patagonia near the south polar ice. Besides the oil, they're after hides of the big elephant seal, good leather to cover trunks and make sturdy footwear."

"When the hunt was over in late spring this year," said Finn, "during the first cod run, I had nothing much to do, so me and my cousin, Darcy, who was my same age, being twenty-five . . . we decided to sail around from our family's outport. That's Heart's Content, on the east arm of Trinity Bay. Darcy was eager as me to go cod jigging again, the way we two had done since we were boys. Our uncle offered to hire us on for serious cod fishing aboard his schooner off the Grand Banks, so we said fine. He puts out five dories, two men to a boat, hoping for big takes of the cod. Two men with any luck can take in a thousand pounds a day.

"Me and Darcy had taken nothing much this whole day," Finn added, "when we ran into one of those quick storms out on the Banks and our dory was driven beyond sight of my uncle's brig. It was one of those wet-snow breezes that come sweeping out of the west at the end of springtime, thrashing the waters like Satan's tail and scaring both of us to death." Finn frowned. "Darcy and me, we set the long oars and rowed for our bloody lives. We had quite a few big cod in the dory, and at first they acted like ballast. But when it got really wild out there, we began taking a lot of water and the cod were slipping and sliding around, greasing the bottom boards beneath our feet. So we returned almost all of those fishes to the waters, but, Lord Jesus, it hardly helped at all. Darcy was rowing all hell hard to keep the dory straight into the wind, and I was busy pitching out the bilge, using my oilskin hat and the wooden bailer. I remember me and Darcy trying to sing some hymns together and him saying prayers to all the saints because he'd quit our family's Anglican Church to get married to a pretty girl from Fogo, they're the other side. I don't know whether him doing that had helped or hurt us. Anyway . . ." Finn paused, "I'm the one, not Darcy, that's here talking to you now."

Finn told of how, on the next day, the wind had shifted around to the southwest, driving them north and east. As night came down, they took to shivering in the darkness because of their near- ness to a giant iceberg they couldn't see. Then, at dawn, the wind had switched back into the northwest and it blew deadly cold and drove them further out over the Atlantic. By and by, that wind had begun to drop away. Their heads dipped off to sleep, though they were soaking wet and shivering like half-dead dogs. When they awoke, there was nothing but fog around. Gray ghost fog, Finn called it, the kind, he said, that makes a man worry that a big, square-rigged clipper ship will come and run a dory down before she even sees it. Darcy had flown his undershirt from the top of an oar, hoping some vessel might see it above the low sea fog that kept the dory hidden.

"Me and Darcy held some shouting and whistling contests," Finn said, "sung hymns again until night came down. The two of us had spent lots of our lives on dories and I don't ever remember being scared. But, Lord Jesus, it was bad out there with all our drinking water gone and nothing but that one small cod that we had kept.

Even our two jig hooks were washed over and Darcy's shirt had blown away. The weather cleared for a bit, then the wind kicked up an ocean chop, the only good part being that it dried our clothes. But we began to suffer from a terrible thirst and hunger. Each of us ate half the fish and shared its blood. There's not too much blood in fish," said Finn. "But anything at all does help a soul that's feeling down. We drew our canvas-oiled coats round us and slept again. Next day, it was clearer, better weather. We set up a watch, but saw nothing, just the heaving gray Atlantic. I started taking catnaps and having ghastly dreams."

As Finn told the story, he explained to Titus how they had lost all track of time. He told of how on the seventh or eighth day, maybe, Darcy had seen a sail on the far horizon, but by evening it was gone and a new and colder wind began to drive them north. Darcy had talked to Finn of old times, had cracked some outport girlie jokes, and they had had a laughing fit, followed by a lot of crying. They had slowly licked, then ate the eyes and head, and sucked the fins of their last cod.

"Darcy was always a stronger boy than me," Finn said, "when we were growing up together. But we were suffering in that dory and Darcy was shivering harder and going down faster than me. 'You can start looking north for Greenland, or maybe east for Iceland,' Darcy calls to me through chattering teeth. 'We'll never lay our eyes on dear old Newfoundland again.' Next night," Finn shuddered to think, "it was deadly cold and at dawn Darcy was so weak and hungry with salt caked around his mouth that he couldn't shiver any more. Worse, he had stopped praying or even speaking about the girl he'd married 'cause he had started to drink the salt water. I couldn't stop him, and after that he fell silent. Next morning, I was weak, but I said to him, 'Stay where you're to and I'll come where you're at.' I crawled back to his end of the dory and felt him. He was cold. He was dead.

"What I judged was that our dory had been blown north, downwind of Funk Island, because the stink of bird shit is strong around there. I tried to roll poor Darcy overboard, but I got scared to be alone. It wasn't hard to get the coat off him, for he had only wrapped it round himself before he died. I took it from him to lay over me for warmth. It helped.

"The gulls began hovering above our boat. Soon one herring gull came down and landed on Darcy's head and began to peck at him. Then others landed and I was too far gone to stop them. One of those hungry devils ripped a strip off Darcy's face. It landed on me. Oh, I was starving, and I'll tell you I was tempted, but what I did was this: I drew his coat up to hide like a hunter in a duck blind and I held that bit of flesh between my fingers stuck up behind my head. A big, black-backed gull landed on the bow," said Finn, pausing to catch his breath, "and before it took a second peck of Darcy's meat, I grabbed it by the throat, hauled it in, and wrung its neck. Oh, Jesus, let me tell you, gull is warm and good to eat and drink – yes, drink. I caught one more next day. But the gulls had grown wise to me and I never caught another. Later I was having dizzy spells and visions, awful visions. If you've not been starving you've no idea how it feels. I lost all track of time."

Dory

Finn admitted he didn't remember seeing the Yankee bark when it hove to and picked him up. He couldn't remember being wrapped and fed split pea soup and rum.

"When we arrived in New London" Finn said, "the doctor, then the steward here, started caring for me. And, well sir, here I am."

Titus shook his head. "What a terrible ordeal you went through. You're a lucky man to be alive."

8

"It's all fading away from me now," said Finn. "Going hazy like a dream where you open your eyes in the morning and the last of the images are just escaping from you, fading into blue and gray. I've heard that your Fisheries captain gave a proper Bible reading and buried at sea what was left of my dear cousin, Darcy."

"They say he had nothing to identify him," said Titus, "but that you were wearing a brass belt buckle."

"That's true." Finn drew down the wool blanket that partly covered him and showed the buckle to Titus. "My uncle was one of the Royal Marines who fought in the Crimean War that ended in 1856. Before that, he had been apprenticed to a watchmaker for a year in London, then ran away and took the Queen's shilling and joined the army. During his apprenticeship, he'd learned to use engraving tools. Later, because he was proud of me becoming ice master, he engraved my name, rank, ship, port and colony on his Royal Marine buckle and gave it to me for my birthday."

"Our New London Fisheries inquired and discovered that your buckle read true," Titus told him, "for they know sailing men in Westerly, Rhode Island – that's a town just three leagues east of Mystic – who have been aboard your same brig, *Huntress*, when she was trading down in Spanish Town, Jamaica. They had been drinking with her other captain, Horwood. He told them all about you being the ice master of that brig."

Finn nodded, felt his fresh-shaved chin, then stroked his throat. "I feel myself sometimes and wonder if I really am alive."

"Oh, you're here alive, all right, and the doctor says you're on the mend. I'll tell you what I'll do," said Titus. "I'll come over to this wharf with a whaleboat and some oarsmen. We'll row you out to *Lancer* on Tuesday after you've had supper. And we'll pick up the new sea chest that the steward at the Captains' Rest has packed for you to replace your gear. I've got a kind of private cabin for you aboard. It ain't much bigger than a cupboard, but I guess it will suit you well enough from here to Newfoundland."

"Thank you." Finn smiled.

9

Chapter 2

Dawn was breaking out in front of Topsail House when the tall front door flung open. Captain Caleb Dunston, always jumpy as a cat before a sailing, stormed out across the porch and tried to read the morning sky as it spread its wings above the town of Mystic. He brandished his long glass like a weapon in his hand while tight against his chest he clutched a leather chart case full of secret Arctic soundings.

"Samson, get your arse out here," yelled Caleb. "Bring my sea chest with you. Move, man! Move!"

Inside the large white house, three whale-oil lights were burning, one upstairs, others in the front hall and in the breakfast room. Topsail's lawns had turned rich green and the pungent scent of blooming lilac was heavy in the early summer air.

Samson and his eldest son eased the captain's large sea chest aboard the cart. Topsail's chief maid, Nellie, scurried out onto the drive and placed a wicker hamper in the cart.

"Nellie," the captain shouted, "you tell Mrs. Dunston and our daughter to come along behind me in the buggy. Samson's boy will drive them. Can you feel that wind arising, girl? You warn them, Nellie, that *Sea Horse* and *Lancer* are sailing on this tide."

A captain's widow peering through her window across the street watched Dunston hop up onto the cart seat next to Samson.

"Get going, man," he growled, then leaned forward and slapped Windy on the rear.

The cart swayed and clattered over Mystic's rough-stoned streets before it turned onto the softer, gravel coast road that led west toward New London's massive harbor. Caleb lit a short Brazilian cigar and sat studying the array of morning clouds now fanning out like rising geese across Block Island Sound.

Caleb Dunston was a middle-sized, broad-shouldered man of forty-seven years, with gray piercing eyes, a short, straight nose, and dark hair now mixed with gray. His sideburns covering his ears were almost white. Dividing his face was a compass moustache pointing due east and west. It had been carefully waxed this morning. Caleb and his present wife, Arabella, had both lost their marriage partners in an epidemic of flu. She was a descendant of a family that had garnered a fortune during the War of 1812 while mastering a fast topsail schooner engaged in privateering through the British blockade of Long Island Sound. But Dunston, too, had been successful, making his money just as dangerously in the whaling trade. To prove his success, he wore an Alaskan watch fob of a gold bowhead whale at the end of his vest pocket watch chain. Dunston was a sort of bull-headed man. It was rumored that Topsail House turned hellish for his equally strong-minded wife when he was at home.

Slowly, Caleb's mind began to settle as he left the house and town behind him. He began to concentrate on that poor, benighted bastard, Willie Kinney, his first mate. What a rotten break he'd had. Would Willie be aboard by now, he wondered, or still lying drunk in the Cock and Spur. How could he sail north without Willie? Had that unlucky bugger really caught the rabies? Caleb had demanded that Fisheries delay the sailing for a week while waiting to hear the doctor's fresher judgment of Willie's health, but all the partners — even his high-and-mighty wife, Arabella — had refused to alter the sailing date. All this because that weird son-of-a-bitch who lived below the Mystic bridge had told the watchman that he'd seen a crazed raccoon bite the town whore in the leg and Willie in the arm when Willie tried to defend her.

Dr. Greeley had told the New London Whale Fisheries that Willie must not be allowed to sail, saying that if he had indeed caught rabies, he would go absolutely frothing mad at sea and bite his fellow crewmen, who would in turn bite others. Times had been hard during this last depression and the partners knew that the failing numbers of whales could ruin their already risky gamble to profit from this mating voyage. Willie swore to them that if he felt or showed the slightest signs of rabies while at sea, he would jump overboard. But still the partners would not allow Willie Kinney to go north in 1875 as master of the whale ship *Lancer*. In his stead, Fisheries was sending Board Chairman Peapack's twenty-two-year-old nephew, Titus Kildeer, with the ink still wet on his captain's papers. This did not sit well with Caleb Dunston.

Caleb's anger began to build as he struck a sulphur and relit his cold cigar while striding up and down the short deck of the Groton ferry. Through its smoke, he caught first sight of *Sea Horse* waiting for him by the Fisheries dock among a forest of masts and yards and slack sails on vessels at the wharfs.

Out in the harbor, the whale ship *Lancer* lay at anchor, an ancient, oversized tub that had not sailed in nine years. Fisheries had had *Lancer* newly painted black to try and hide the fact that she had been built before the Revolution, was ninety-eight years old, oil-soaked, and rotted far beyond any serious repair. All Caleb and the partners wanted was for that creaking hulk to stay afloat. Every last man in both these crews had his mind set on cramming both ships' holds with all the whale oil and bone that they could carry, then on how they would divide out the profits or "share the lay." Dunston planned to deck-load these two vessels with thousands of pounds of drying baleen bone from the mouths of the Arctic bowhead whales, called right whales, then to mate north close enough to guide ancient *Lancer* home again on this, her last voyage. With a lot of luck, Caleb reckoned, she could make him a rich man.

As for *Lancer*'s new, young skipper, Titus Kildeer, he had abandoned his education at Yale at age eighteen and sailed to the sperm whaling grounds in the Java Sea, and had there risen to a mate's position. This was, Caleb believed, because their ship had had four boats broken and had lost the captain and first and second mates. It wasn't brains, but sharks, that had caused his rise. Caleb Dunston had predicted whilst drinking at the Captains' Rest that Amos Peapack's nephew, who had yet to see an Arctic right whale, would prove as useless as tits on a boar.

After landing from the Groton ferry, Caleb's blood rose as he heard his cart's wheels rumbling over the hollow, wooden dock. Samson pulled up the mare in front of *Sea Horse*'s gangplank. When the mates spotted Dunston in front of the companionway, they started yelling, and the action aboard his ship increased to a feverish pitch.

Caleb roared at all of them, then turned to oversee the unloading of his sea chest.

"You there, you donkey's dick leaning useless on that monkey rail, get down that gangway and take a two-handed grip on that sea chest of mine. The mate will show you and Samson where to store it in my cabin. Do you hear me, man?"

Once aboard, Dunston paced back and forth on *Sea Horse*. Her deck had been scrubbed and sanded down until it was clean as bleached bone.

"Stow those fresh food bags and boxes by the cook shack," Caleb shouted. "Jump to it. This whale ship's looking like a goddamned garbage scow."

His newly promoted first mate, Dougal Gibson, sprang into action, whispering out of the side of his mouth to Mario Fayal, *Sea Horse*'s second mate, "Just knowing Willie's not going with us has set the old man in a rage this morning."

"Has Willie come aboard?" Caleb shouted to Gibson.

"He's aft in your cabin, Captain. I'd judge you'll find him snoozing hard by now."

Caleb marched astern, clumped down the narrow stairs, and unlocked the door. Willie was curled up on the horsehair settee sound asleep. "Come alive, mate," Dunston yelled as he slapped Willie hard across the butt.

"Oh, there you are. You finally made it, did you, Captain?" Willie swayed when he sat up, then winced when his bandaged arm touched the back of the settee.

"I need a drink," said Caleb, "and I guess another one among the many won't sink you."

"'Twill save my life," said Willie, holding out his mug with a trembling hand. "Pour a good one, Captain! I crept aboard and tried to stow away before dawn. But that sharp-eyed little bastard, Mario, was on watch. He's the one that stuffed me in your cabin and locked the goddamned door. I must have nodded off for a minute."

Caleb poured Willie half a cup of rum and filled his own. "Every one of those prick-headed Fisheries partners is dead set against you coming north with me. I made them promise to find a decent job for you whilst we're away. I trust, Willie, that you've got brains enough not to go traipsing south with the first New Bedford sperm whalers who offer you a mate's berth."

Together, they downed their cups and had a double fit of coughing.

"Is young Titus hereabouts?" asked Willie.

"He'd better be out there on that old hulk and ready to sail," Dunston grunted. "He's taking that lost Newfoundlander back home. I'd have a lot better feeling in my gut if you were mastering *Lancer*."

"Kildeer's all right. He's young, but he'll be mating close to you. You'll show him the ropes," said Willie. "I'll pour this next rum for both of us."

"Keep your gorilla's fist off that bottle, Mate. I'll handle this." Caleb gave his ex-mate a half-cup of rum and himself another whole one.

It wasn't long before Willie broke into song.

"Oh, stow that," Caleb grunted. "Lie back on that mothering settee and finish off your nap. I've got to check these lists that useless Fisheries agent left for me. Who've we got for crew?"

Willie handed Caleb a sheet of paper, and the captain scrutinized the list of crew members in silence.

SHIP *SEA HORSE* – CREW LIST & LAY
Departed New London, Conn. – Wednesday, June 9, 1875

NAME	RATING	LAY
Caleb Dunston	Master	1/12
Dougal Gibson	Mate	1/20
Mario Fayal	2nd Mate	1/50
Jack Shannon	3rd Mate	1/55
Ricardo Moniz	Boat Steerer (Starboard Boat)	1/75
William "Bill" Shelley	Boat Steerer (Larboard Boat)	1/75
Alfonso Fernandes	Boat Steerer (Waist Boat)	1/85
Ezra "Hoops" Morse	Cooper	1/50
Nate Carson	2nd Cooper	1/110
"Needles" Wiggins	Sailmaker	1/130
Edward "Chips" Bell	Carpenter	1/95
"Hammer" Haden	Ironsmith	1/140
Rudi Haas	Steward	1/175
Domingo Pulvur	Cook	1/115
Israel Steiner	Seaman	1/125
Robin Crooks	Seaman	1/120
Orval Windtree	Seaman	1/130
Seth Baker	Seaman	1/130
Randall Martin	Ordinary Seaman	1/175
Charles Flender	Ordinary Seaman	1/175
Lemuel Smalley	Landsman	1/180
Jesse Big Man	Landsman	1/180
Rafael Costa	Landsman	1/220
Alden "Buffalo" Munro	Landsman	1/190
Jose Pasco	Ship's Boy	Food & clothing only

Caleb mumbled to himself, "For *Sea Horse* and for *Lancer*, each ship to be supplied with the following, enough for thirty men for thirty-four months," and began reciting the ship's list of provisions:

90 barrels	Salt Beef	800 pounds	Coffee
120 barrels	Salt Pork	2 boxes	Tea
50 barrels	Flour	8 barrels	Vinegar
4,000 pounds	Pilot Bread	30 bushels	Corn
1,200 pounds	Medium Bread	2 tierces	Rice
8 hogsheads	Molasses	5 barrels	Dried Corn Meal
7 barrels	Sugar	1,000 pounds	Pork
2 barrels	Salt Mackerel	4 barrels	Pickles
8 quintals	Salt Cod	15 bushels	Beans

And on and on . . .

"I'm not going to read any more. Jesus, Willie, that bastard of an agent has short-changed us on the pickles again. This gang will gobble these down afore we even get to Baffin Bay. Goddamnit, I'm not going to read this whole provision list right now."

A little later, *Sea Horse*'s ship's boy, Jose, came and tapped on the cabin door. His young voice sounded nervous and excited. "Two fine ladies coming aboard, sir, and two men carrying whalebone canes, and Captain Kildeer. They're halfway up the gangplank, Captain." He counted on his fingers. "There's five of them."

Caleb Dunston rose and heaved himself up the companionway for a better prospect forward along his starboard deck, then ducked back down quickly. "Rise up, Willie, the bunch of them is heading this way. God, I wish I was a whole lot drunker than I am. Go visit the harpooners, Willie. Comb your sideburns, man. You look like a dockside bum. Oh, I'll miss you, Mate."

Willie rose, and spread his arms like an evangelical preacher. "I'm up, Captain. Don't worry about me."

Dunston stepped out and made his way unsteadily along the deck. He saw that on the dock, a small crowd of relatives stood watching, waiting to say good-bye to their friends or kin aboard. He gave Amos Peapack and the other senior partner a dirty look before he turned to stare at his wife and stepdaughter, then glowered at young Titus Kildeer.

"Kildeer, can you find nothing at all to do out aboard *Lancer?* Are you so heart-and-soul bound to the state of Connecticut that you cannot bear to leave her shore?"

The young captain looked nervously at the partners, then at Kate as he said awkwardly, "I had the agent's boat row me ashore, sir. I've got Ice Master Finn in a cabin aboard. I'll go out again soon. I wanted but a moment or so to say farewell to my parents, my Uncle Amos, and to Mrs. Dunston, and to your daughter . . . Ka . . . Kate." Titus seemed to clamp his lips around Kate's name, reluctant to let it go as the handsome Kate made cow eyes at him from beneath her flowered bonnet.

Arabella, Captain Dunston's wife, was garbed totally in black from her somber bucket bonnet to her tight-laced boots. Her tall, ample body was draped with a long black cape. She had pinned a cameo at the throat of her high-necked blouse and wore a bustled skirt that with the help of whale baleen had utterly reshaped her stern. She looked like an admiral in a full-dress cape. She stared hard at the boylike Captain Kildeer before she shifted her gaze aloft to *Sea Horse's* rigging with its pennants blowing in a fare-well flutter. She searched for clues as to her husband's plan to set *Sea Horse's* twenty-seven sails. Who could forget that Arabella Dunston was a granddaughter of the owner and master of the famous topsail schooner *Lightning*, a fast and deadly privateer, American-designed to raid against any merchant vessel, English, French or Spanish, that dared to try to resupply the British ships that held the blockade of Long Island during the War of 1812 to 1815. It would have been a whole lot kinder of God, some of her sewing circle members whispered, if He had just gone ahead and created Arabella Dunston as a man. It was agreed in Mystic that she looked and acted like a hard ship's captain, with her dark, wild-eyed stare and deep, trumpet-sounding voice that would cause any man or woman to jump.

It was also agreed in Mystic that her handsome daughter, Kate, was utterly different from her mother. Kate was gracefully formed and greyhound lean, with a fine-drawn face kept fashionably pale. She had large, Spanish eyes and chestnut hair.

Kate gathered up her nerve, and said, "Father, Mother, could I be allowed to go aboard and view *Lancer* with Captain Kildeer? He has invited me out to bid farewell."

"I want Willie to go with you," growled Caleb, "and don't you dally, Kate. This fair wind is rising."

Kate's mother nodded, then frowned. "You heard Captain Dunston's orders, Katherine. These ships and men are outbound."

As he passed a greenhand, Willie said, "You're lucky, lad, to be heading north into Arctic waters where it's nice and cool. This ship will smell as sweet as a nut up there, not like one of those sperm whalers that must hunt their blubber in the tropic sun and stink to high hell all the while."

Titus, Kate, and Willie were rowed out toward *Lancer*.

"I've got my master's papers," Titus explained to Kate, "and my uncle assured me that my *Lancer* captaincy is exactly equal to your stepfather's. You can count on it, Kate, I'm not letting him run my life for me. Oh, I'll mate close enough to *Sea Horse* because I'll welcome his advice in ice. Your stepfather understands the different ways of bowhead whales and heavy Arctic ice, but . . ."

"Titus," Kate interrupted, "you'll do fine. Just don't let his ways upset you. I've heard he's judged to be a hard man at sea, and I know just how he is at Topsail House, but he's a successful whaling master. You try your best to learn from him."

Titus twitched when he heard Kate's stepfather bellowing at them through his gamming horn. "Kildeer, cut your long-winded farewells. This wind is rising and we must avail ourselves of it. You there, Willie, see that Kate comes swift off *Lancer* – and be damned quick about it!"

Willie did not turn, but waved his arm above his head in the fashion of a drunken boat steerer.

Titus stared at Kate, and when she glanced at him, he nodded toward *Lancer*. "You'll see my ship's a bit sea-whacked, ice-gouged, and worn beneath her coats of paint. And I hardly know her crew. But you can bet your boots, dear Kate, that, God willing, I will fill her hold – which is the size of a New York hay barn – and I'll jam her with casks of oil, load her deck with corset bone, and bring *Lancer* safely back to port for you, Kate, for both of us."

Kate stared tearfully at Titus.

"You keep a sharp eye on that crew," Willie called from the stern. "I don't know where the Fisheries agent found that bunch you've got aboard. They look to me like a shiftless gang of bad hats, but you'd be a better judge of sperm whalers than I would. If they give you any sass, Titus, you and the mates come down on them hard, then use your gamming horn and call Kate's old man to help you."

"Captain Kildeer knows that right well," Kate answered huffily, for she could see that Willie was still drunk, held upright mainly by the steering oar.

"Having Jeff Johnson as my chief mate is what I count on," Titus answered.

"Count on yourself, lad." Willie's voice was slurred. "It's up to you to master that ship and crew. Stay mating close with *Sea Horse*, hear me?"

The whaleboat pulled into *Lancer*'s bulging shadow as the summer wind was kicking up a pretty chop, making the water shine like shattered bits of mirror.

"Well, here we are," sang Willie. "She's not as new or fine a ship as *Sea Horse*, but God knows she's got an elephant's belly of a hold. With all those signal flags and Fisheries pennants flying from her rigging, you can tell *Lancer*'s glad to be putting out to sea again."

When the boat's bow touched *Lancer*'s hull, crewmen lowered the boatswain's chair. Titus had to help Willie stumble into it. Kate watched him protecting his bandaged arm as they hauled him up, then heard him joking with some harpooners as they hauled him aboard. They lowered the chair a second time for Kate. She had trouble stepping into it while holding down her long, bustled skirt, which ballooned out like a jib sail. Titus hurried up the swaying ladder.

"Whale ships are built for men," said Kate to *Lancer*'s first mate as he helped her onto the deck. The tops of her high-buttoned boots and white stockings had showed well above her knees to an ogling swarm of crew.

"Kate, have you met Captain Finn?" Titus explained, "We're giving him passage back to Newfoundland after his ordeal."

"No, I've not had the pleasure of meeting Captain Finn, but, of course, I've heard of him."

Tom Finn bowed and touched his hat.

"Kate, do you remember my first mate, Jeff Johnson?" Titus asked.

"I don't think I've ever met Mr. Johnson. You take good care of Capt –" Kate felt Titus nudge her side. "Of course, I mean all of you return home safely with tons and tons of bone and oil."

Jeff smiled and nodded. "We'll do our best, ma'am."

The wind was chafing noisily at *Lancer*'s half-reefed mainsail.

Kate looked up and said, "Your ship looks very grand, Titus."

They could hear *Sea Horse*'s bell clanging across the water, then heard Dunston's voice on his gamming horn. "The tug's got *Sea Horse*'s hawser. She's in tow, Kildeer. Haul your blasted anchor, man. Get *Lancer* under way."

"Jump to it, men," Titus bellowed in a voice that Kate had never heard him use before. "Chase those seamen and those farmers' sons round that capstan, Otto. Move them! Hear me? Move!"

"I take it you are Captain Dunston's stepdaughter," Tom Finn said to Kate as he safely led her to the ship's side, away from the burst of activity.

"Yes, oh, yes, I am, sir, and I'm pleased to see you so well and sound, Captain. We were all appalled to hear of your terrible . . . that's not the word, may I call it your brave victory against the sea."

"Thank you, ma'am, I am all right now," he said. "And since I'm parting, may I be allowed to say, Miss Dunston, you're a very beautiful young woman."

"Oh, sir . . . ," said Kate, "how kind of you to say."

They both turned and looked forward to watch sixteen men working like mules as they pushed on the capstan bars, slowly hauling up the anchor.

"Work!" yelled the third mate, Otto Kraus. "Work, you blue-balled bastards! *Raus, raus*, you drun –" Kraus turned, remembering Kate, looked pained and touched his cap.

"Those two hampers are for you, Titus." Kate nodded to them weakly. "Just some cakes and pies that I thought you'd enjoy . . . and I'm sure you'll wish to share with Captain Finn." She looked at this stranger again, more closely this time.

Willie came along the deck behind them, calling out good-byes to many of his friends, then used his left hand to shake farewell with Finn.

"Kate, I'll ride down first," said Willie. "When you come down, I'll give you a hand." He looked straight at Titus. "Jesus, man, you should be staying right here getting married. I'd give anything to be going north instead of you." He handed Titus a small object wrapped in a red bandana kerchief. Willie's face screwed up and his eyes began to fill with tears. "You ask for Nowya when you get there, Titus. Remember her name, Nowya. It means sea gull. Tell her . . . it can't be helped about my missing the voyage because of this." He held up his bandaged arm. "Tell her I don't know as I'll ever get back north to see her again. You tell her that for me, Titus, tell her I said she ought to marry that young Inuk hunter from the north camp . . . you tell her *tavvauvutit* for me." He winced in pain as he forgot his arm and tried to shake hands hard with Titus.

Kate watched as the seamen helped Willie out of the boatswain's chair below. "Good hunting, Titus," he called. "And steer wide of that son-of-a-bitching . . . sorry, Kate, I mean, Titus, steer clear of heavy ice."

"Who was he asking you to deliver that present to?" Kate whispered. "'Nowya.' Is that some woman's name?"

"I guess so," said Titus. "He was just talking about someone who lives up north, someone who's out of his life for now . . . maybe forever."

"Oh, Titus," Kate gasped, "you stay safe. And you, too, Captain Finn."

In the distance, they heard the bell from *Sea Horse* clanging.

"Our anchor's up," Titus said. "And the steam tug's got our hawser. Kate, we're moving. *Lancer* is under way. You've got to go now." Titus kissed Kate's cheek, but closer to her lips than he had ever dared before.

"The Lord protect you, Titus," she whispered in his ear. "May God watch over all of you." Kate gazed tearfully at Finn, then, holding down her skirt, stepped into the boatswain's chair.

Willie helped her into the agent's boat, and they drew away from *Lancer's* side. Titus started to wave and call something to her, but in the middle of his first hand motion, *Lancer's* mainsail rumbled out above his head like a heavy clap of thunder. Titus disappeared as half a dozen seamen scrambled into the rigging, letting out more sail. Standing quietly by the rail, the ice master, Finn, made a farewell sign to Kate.

Sea Horse *under sail*

Chapter 3

"Reset sails, Kildeer, do you hear me? Come about, man!" Dunston hollered through his horn. "Set my same tack . . . north by northeast, staying well outside Nantucket's shoal . . . I'll chart another tack for you . . . tomorrow morning."

"Your words were heard, Captain," Titus answered on his horn. "Christ!" he said to his mate, Jefferson. "Is this the way it's going to be, with him bellowing at me the whole way north?"

Titus marched forward on the deck and, leaning over, looked down at the figurehead on the bow of *Lancer* with its broken harpoon. He grumbled aloud, "I hope your wooden ears can't hear that son-of-a-bitch."

With a good sea running beneath *Lancer*, her deck planks groaning, and her new hemp lines creaking as they stretched and strained, Titus made a signal to the wheelman and *Lancer* heeled to larboard in the breeze. Titus grinned triumphantly at the thought that the ninety-eight-year-old ship was all his. "Oh, God," he prayed, "please hold her together. Let me jam her holds with casks of oil and corset bone and let me bring her safely back to home port and Kate."

Leaning against the starboard monkey rail, Titus watched *Sea Horse* heeling, lunging forward like a minke whale heading into the wind. No square-rigger could head straight into the wind, but *Sea Horse* was making a spectacularly close tack, a zigzag course northeast. Every time she changed, it would take fourteen minutes to come about with the old man bellowing to those aloft to let go sheets and haul on braces as they pivoted the great yards. The sails flapped and boomed until the wind came over the opposite bow, and they were headed on a new tack. *Sea Horse*, with *Lancer* off her stern, would make many hundreds of such tacks on her long journey north into Arctic seas. These rugged whale ships had been built with hulls as blunt as warehouses, which is what they were. They were not meant to sail like privateers, but to carry great cargo and make fortunes for their partners and captains, their wives and children and grandchildren as yet unborn.

A flock of gulls hung screaming in *Sea Horse*'s wake. She was capable of greater speed, and could easily have outdistanced *Lancer*, but Titus knew that the old man had eased sail so they could continue mating. Caught in the light of the setting sun, the lead ship's canvas, he saw, had taken on the mellow tint of weathering. Titus planned to study the old man's tactics, for Dunston was famous as a whaling master who understood the art of setting sails. Near the mouth of the Sound off Newport, they saw the whale bark *Morgan* and the schooner *Hero* both on southern headings.

That night when Johnson was on watch, Titus sat at mess with his second mate, Chris Acker, his third mate, Otto Kraus, and Finn, the gaunt outsider, who remained silent. Titus had sailed with Acker in the southern whaling trade and trusted him. He believed that he would also come to like the big, square-jawed Otto with the walrus moustache, but, as yet, he scarcely knew him. Otto was the bronco, fierce at keeping order. Whenever either of these two mates called him captain, Titus Kildeer felt a flush of pride.

When the old man began his new sail set next morning, Titus stepped back to check *Lancer*'s steering, then walked forward along the rain-slick deck. It was a dreary day off the coast of Massachusetts of a kind that made Titus flop down on his bed and console himself by trying to imagine that he was for the first time naked in the arms of Kate, and that she lay trembling beside him.

During the following dawn watch, *Lancer* was still in easy sight of *Sea Horse*, though both ships were running in and out of shrouds of fog and driving rain. Working together with Jeff and the ship's keeper, Noah Anderson, he planned their own first independent ocean tack. Titus was proud to see how closely it matched *Sea Horse*'s course.

"Noah's getting kind of old," said Jeff, "but it's good to have his experience aboard."

Noah, like so many in the whaling trade, had started young as a cabin boy, then climbed through every rank until he reached ship's master. But a lack of skill or luck had meant that he had fared badly in the hunt. He'd returned home to port nearly empty after two separate voyages. No whale fishery would stand for that. So Noah became a mate again for a number of years, retired awhile, then came aboard *Lancer* as ship's keeper, with only a small share in the lay.

"Noah knows a lot and he speaks some Eskimo," said Otto Kraus. "Strange to think that you, a captain, at twenty-two years, and Dunston, at forty-seven years, are both called 'the old man' on these Yankee ships and old Noah, he's over seventy, is called 'ship's keeper.' Well, American is kind of a crazy language anyway."

Finn leaned against the rail and studied the three whaleboats hanging on their davits on *Lancer*'s port side, their bows brightly painted red and blue and green so that each boat could be recognized from a distance. The captain's boat hung alone on the starboard side, its bow painted a golden yellow. Above him stretched a web of rigging and of shroud lines, vastly more than any ship he'd traveled on.

Inside his master's cabin tween decks aft, Titus studied his crew list, trying to memorize the names of the twenty-four men and the ship's boy aboard:

25

SHIP *LANCER* — CREW LIST & LAY
Departed New London, Conn. – Wednesday, June 9, 1875

NAME	RATING	LAY
Titus Kildeer	Master	1/17
Jefferson Johnson	Mate	1/22
Chris Acker	2nd Mate	1/50
Otto Kraus	3rd Mate	1/65
Noah Anderson	Ship's Keeper	1/75
John James	Boat Steerer (Starboard Boat)	1/75
Samuel Douglas	Boat Steerer (Larboard Boat)	1/75
Angelo Daluz	Boat Steerer (Waist Boat)	1/85
Lester Lewis	Cooper	1/50
Everett Roberts	Carpenter	1/95
Noel Wotten	Carpenter	1/110
Bob Norris	Ironsmith	1/140
Antoine Carpentier	Steward	1/175
Elvara Caldari	Cook	1/115
Jesse Mako	Seaman	1/120
Clarence Walker	Seaman	1/130
Josh Greene	Seaman	1/130
Abel Valso	Seaman	1/130
Calvin Jackson	Ordinary Seaman	1/175
Abraham Bellows	Ordinary Seaman	1/175
Jacob Tyler	Ordinary Seaman	1/180
Charlie Zinkos	Landsman	1/180
Henny Norwalk	Landsman	1/180
Horatio Abbott	Landsman	1/220
Antonio Lacardo	Ship's Boy	Food & clothing only

Plus Captain Thomas Finn, ice master, authorized passage to St. John's, Newfoundland, or Heart's Content.

He rose and studied his own boyish face in the small wall mirror. "Old man," he said aloud, then tried to look mean, hoping that the men aboard would not consider him a boy. He read his crew list again, checking each man's share of the lay. He stared at the bottom of the list at the words written in pencil. Titus wondered what that quiet Newfoundlander, the ice master, who was carefully keeping out of the way as the ship settled into a routine, thought of him as captain of this vessel.

The fair wind held for them and their northern tacks seemed endless as *Lancer* doggedly pursued her mate, *Sea Horse*. Now, for the first time this voyage, they began to sight small ice, worn-out growlers that had turned pale blue from rolling in the heavier, southern salt water on their way to disappearing in the warm Gulf Stream.

Titus stood with Finn by the port rail, both studying the ragged southeast coast of Newfoundland with the long glass, observing an old panoramic drawing with care, for this was a region where weather could slow their progress. Both Finn and Titus noticed that Caleb kept *Sea Horse* never far off coast.

That day, the two ships drew close enough again for the old man to shout across on his gamming horn. "My lookout's seen some ice ahead and there'll be more that's hidden in this damned sea fog. Look sharp, Kildeer!"

"Following you, Captain!" Titus hollered back. "I'm in your wake."

Next morning early, the man in the crow's-nest atop the main-mast hollered, "Ice off the port and starboard bow."

"How much ice?" Titus shouted up to him.

"Looks like slob ice, sir, stretched in skeins across our course. It's clear beyond," the lookout answered.

"There goes our last chance of a quick delivery home of Finn, and a clear passage north," said Johnson.

Titus watched as *Sea Horse* slacked sail, then moved cautiously through the rain squalls toward the only opening in the long, shifting fields of withering white. Titus did the same, carefully imitating the old man's sail set.

"It's them rotting bergie bits that I hate," said Otto, standing midships. "They don't look too bad from here. But they're the

27

devil's helpers, waterlogged, they are, with only a white bit showing on top and maybe a thousand tons of ice hiding just below. One of them struck us off south Greenland five years back, tore open the whole belly of our ship! We lowered the chase boats and jumped in to watch all that oil and money bone go plunging down like tons of rocks."

"Stay well away from them," said Finn. "They're the worst thing in this bloody ocean."

"Captain, how long do you figure to stay up north?" Henny Norwalk, the landsman, had appeared behind them, his oilskins slick in the steady rain.

"Only as long as it takes to load these two ships," said Titus. "The more oil and bone we take, the sooner we'll sail home and the agent will give you cash for your fair share of the lay."

"That means we may be two winters over?" other greenhands grumbled. They had come closer to listen along with Norwalk.

"*Hush dein Mau, schweinehunde.* Get back to work," roared Otto.

After they had moved along the deck, Titus lowered his voice. "Mr. Johnson, we must watch those men. I don't like the cut of their jib." He looked ahead again. "The old man's resetting *Sea Horse*'s sails 'cause that damned breeze is failing us. It's calm ahead, then there's ice as far as the eye can see. Mr. Kraus, get a fresh, sharp pair of eyes up into that crow's-nest. We're looking for an island called Twillingate."

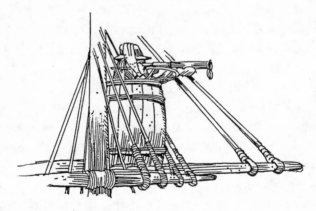

Man in crow's-nest

He watched the new man climb up the shrouds to take his post, then noticed a little knot of sailors on the deck by the cookhouse. From them a rough voice shouted, "Captain, can you hear me? You got this rotting hulk going north instead of south. Put about now, Captain, while you can. This ship ain't going north, it's turning south, you hear me? That lyin' fuckin' agent swore that *Lancer* was hunting south with *Sea Horse*. And the foredeck of this old bucket leaks already. My goddamned bunk's awash."

Titus gripped the rail and glared at them. "Who said that?" he demanded.

There was silence.

"If any of you men has a problem, like sea water in your bunk, you make your complaint to Mate Kraus. You understand me? Where this ship is heading is my business, the Fisheries' business, not yours."

At that moment, Otto Kraus, the bronco, came along the deck, wearing his oilskins with his weather hat tipped forward.

"We've got a bad problem, mate," one seaman sneered. "I drew a top bunk in this old hulk and my mothering straw tick and my blankets are afloat."

"Come on, show me your bunk right now," said Otto Kraus. "If there's just a pissy splash of rain in there, I'll knock your front teeth right down your goddamned throat. And hear this, you sons-of-bitches, I'll break any man's back that I hear giving the captain, or us mates, your kind of lip."

Later, Kraus came back to Titus who stood with Noah by the port rail. "*Ja*, it's true. They took some water in their bunks and this new rain's still drooling in on them."

"Do the old trick," Noah suggested. "Get two or three spare lugsails from our sailmaker. Let the crew stretch them overhead and run the drippings into barrels."

Finn, who stood near Titus, nodded, but said nothing.

After a few more hours of dead calm, *Sea Horse* and *Lancer* lay less than a cannon's shot apart. Leaving Jefferson in charge, Titus, with Acker and the two carpenters, scrambled down *Lancer's* larboard side and into the captain's whaleboat. When they reached

29

Sea Horse, some crewmen on her deck leaned down and gave them a hand up over the side.

"Well, Kildeer, here you are close enough for me to look you in the eye again." The old man nodded at Titus, Acker, and the visiting carpenters. "We've run out of wind today. It's unusual for this time of year. Come back to my cabin, we'll have some coffee. Let me see . . . we've been nine to ten days mating since I've had a chance to talk to you without racking my throat on that damned gammer!"

Jose Pasco, the old man's cabin boy, brought in coffee, then closed the door behind him. Caleb sat in his lashed-down desk chair and Titus perched himself on the captain's Windsor chair attached to the lower deck with rope and ring.

"We had fair winds until we ran into this calm. How's *Lancer* holding up?" asked Caleb. "And how's the health of that poor bugger, Finn?"

"Both are doing well enough," said Titus. "Her fo'c's'le's leaking through the deck and Finn's eating everything he can get. But, well . . . there's some grumbling from the crew."

"Grumbling?" Caleb frowned. "Don't you take any goddamned nonsense from those sperm whalers. Do you know any of them?"

"Not a one," said Titus.

"Well, they're probably testing you because you're young and they know you're green at captaining," the old man snorted. "That ignorant son-of-a-bitch of a Fisheries agent should never have signed on that bunch of South Sea hula dancers who can't wait to get their arses back to those Maori girls."

"I know," said Titus. "They swore to me that they'd have jumped ship if they'd known we were heading north. There's no doubt I've got some real bad hats aboard. My other problem," said Titus, "is that I have to put four hands on the Yankee pump at every watch and it just barely holds its own against the leaks that *Lancer*'s springing every day."

"Don't worry," Caleb laughed, "she'll tighten up. She won't sink now. Her hull's so soaked with rancid whale oil that she's like a mother duck." The old man tongued his moustache points. "Don't sink yourself in gloom, lad. Just pray she makes it to the Blacklead Island station. You can tighten the old bitch up before we try to sail her south again. Remember, Kildeer, even if her bottom opens up and she drops her keel, all those empty oil casks we've had your cooper set up tight inside her hold will float her like a cork. Getting caught in a crushing ice floe is what you've got to set your mind against."

When Titus did not answer, Caleb rambled on like the Fisheries doctor. "Your problems, lad, are normal except for a few bad hats, and they'll settle down, or you'll have to knock them down. Our meat aboard is getting high in all this summer weather, but I tell my greenhands it's high-class, just like eating Hudson River caviar or cheese with blue mold in it." He looked at the walls. "Let's have some rum, lad. The dirty weather outside has given this cabin of mine the icy sweats."

Later, Caleb stepped out on deck and Titus followed. "When I'm back on *Lancer*," said Titus, "I'll keep a sharper eye on the crew."

Mario Fayal shouted for *Lancer*'s carpenters, who came up out of the fo'c's'le after losing two games of checkers and headed down into the captain's whaleboat.

"Lord, God, it's like a friendly kiddie's party over in *Sea Horse*'s fo'c's'le after trying to sleep in our damned snake pit," said Noel as they started back. "*Lancer*'s got a real bad bunch of bastards, troublemakers, especially that Jesse Mako. Being becalmed near this ice has got our crew in a goddamned flurry."

"Yeah," Everett agreed. "We've got a hornet's nest in our fo'c's'le, Captain."

Back on *Sea Horse*, Caleb spoke to Dougal. "Most of those southern flying fish on *Lancer* have never seen a piece of ice before. We'll have to go over and straighten them out for young Kildeer. I wish that ice master was in better health. He looks like somebody who could be of a lot of help. Dougal, you, Mario and Buffalo Munro stay ready at all times."

That night at mess, Finn listened as Noah warned Titus and his three mates about being quick in squashing anything that could turn into a mutiny. "Everett says he overheard Jesse Mako telling some of those island-hopping bums in our fo'c's'le that he roughed up a ship six years ago while whaling off Madagascar. He says it was dead easy – first to take the vessel, then kill the old man, cast off the mates and a few loyalists in a whaleboat, with no water, nothing, then sail south to the tip of Africa. They sold the ship and oil on the docks at Cape Elizabeth. They shared the money and separated, signing on to four different ships. Mako swears that not a single one of them got caught. He's guaranteeing those who will join him that it will be easier to take old *Lancer*. He says that the first with him will become rich men when he takes this ship, turns her, and sails to Rio, where he'll sell her. Then they'll stay on the beach awhile, drink rum, and sand-roll with the local girls."

"We've got to prepare ourselves for trouble," Titus said as Antonio, the cabin boy, cleared away the dishes. "They'll get stinking mad when they have to pay out from their future share to buy cold-weather gear from *Lancer*'s slops chest. Antoine tells me our slops chest hasn't been able to charge out a single piece of clothing to those beach lizards, though they're shivering half to death with cold. Have you seen them wearing those thin canvas trousers, flimsy cotton shirts, and ten-cent Panama hats? Those southern men have separated themselves from our decent seamen. But they're working on the greenhands to join them. They're shivering like men who've caught malaria."

On *Sea Horse*, Captain Dunston unlocked the magazine closet and its bottom drawer and took out what was called an Apache revolving pistol. It was stubby, with no barrel, loaded with five bullets that fired directly from their chambers. It had a short, folding dagger and a set of heavy iron knuckle dusters instead of a pistol grip. Dunston placed this weapon in his side pocket and hid a heavy sealer's knife in his belt beneath his vest.

"Dougal, here's the Colt revolver for you. Mario, you can take this scatter gun. Don't use it till you're close, and give the boat steerers these three carbine rifles. Take extra cartridges in your pockets. This Winchester repeating rifle belongs to Buffalo Munro."

Alden Munro nodded. He had a thick Midwest accent, having

worked on river steamboats. Aboard *Sea Horse*, Munro was well known as "the Buffalo."

Caleb explained, "Buffalo got my permission to bring aboard this rifle. Keep it out of sight, Buffalo, but close by you. I trust you know how to use it! I've got a feeling that *Lancer's* going to be in trouble and I don't trust young Kildeer to handle it alone."

At dawn, both ships were mating close. When Mario Fayal stepped outside his cupboardlike cabin space to pull on his trousers, he saw the first bad signs aboard *Lancer*. He stopped and stood dead still. Then, reaching back, he found his long glass and examined a knot of men gathered on *Lancer's* foredeck. The man named Jesse Mako was doing most of the talking. Mario couldn't hear his exact words, but saw Mako point several times at Kildeer's cabin while angrily punching his clenched fist into his other hand.

Mario crouched down and ran to Caleb Dunston's cabin. Opening the door, he whispered, "Captain, wake up! I've been watching *Lancer's* deck and there's a bunch of bad hats stirring up the greenhands, brewing up trouble over there. That bugger Mako's the ringleader."

Caleb, who was fully dressed, swung out of bed and followed Mario outside.

They heard the cabin door slam over near *Lancer's* stern and saw Kildeer, Jeff Johnson, and Otto Kraus go marching forward with determination. Big Otto pushed in angrily among the eight men who were gathered abaft the foremast.

"What in the devil's name is going on?" Otto yelled as he forced his way among them, violently shoving Mako out of his path.

Mako was a big, wild-haired man whose face flushed red with anger as he had to be steadied by those behind him.

"I ordered you useless bastards to sand down this deck, not to stand around here brewing rat turds. If you *Dummkopfs* are looking for trouble, I'll give you trouble." Otto shook his heavy fists in their faces.

Abel Valso frowned, hawked, and spat on *Lancer's* deck, then yelled and doubled over as Otto drove his knee into the seaman's groin.

"Wait. Let them have their say," Kildeer shouted. "What's bothering the lot of you?"

"Your agent told us this ship was heading south," yelled Mako, "and sure as hell you're going north. But not with us, you ain't."

At that moment, Mako gave a signal and two greenhands and Kildeer's ship's boy came running forward along the deck, their arms loaded with all the muskets stolen from *Lancer's* armory cabinet. The ship's boy had a pair of pistols dangling from his hand while powder horns and cartridge pouches hung across his back.

The mutineers clustered around the mast had grabbed the muskets and cocked them, leveling them at *Lancer's* mates and crew before they could react.

"Well, little boy captain . . ." Jesse Mako smiled and raised the pistol he'd just been given. "Get down on your knees right here in front of me. I've got a little job for you to do."

Kildeer stood motionless.

"I'll put you to your knees, dear boy," said Mako, and he shot Titus through the throat.

As the captain sank to the deck, blood spurting fore and aft, Mako shouted, "Fling the little bastard overboard!"

Two of the mutineers who stood with Mako dragged Titus across the deck and heaved him over the side, his blood staining the rail and his choking sounds silenced only by the splash below.

On *Sea Horse*, a double stone's throw off *Lancer's* after quarter, Dunston whispered, "More sail, more sail. Larboard, rudder, larboard. They've forgotten us. Get your pike poles ready. We're going to try and board her."

Mario leapt to the task.

"We're almost on them now, sir," Shannon said.

"Have crew get the plank. Nice and quiet, though," growled Dunston.

As they drifted nearer to *Lancer's* stern, they could hear other shots and shouts from the mutineers.

Suddenly, the ice master, Finn, rose near the stern and cast them a spring line.

"Grab the hawser. Haul on it. Haul, boys, haul," whispered Dunston, pulling as hard as he could.

"Ten of them, eleven with the boy," gasped Dougal. "That's half of *Lancer*'s crew. They're the troublemakers."

They heard Mako yell in alarm, "Look out for *Sea Horse!*" He fired a pistol at the group now hauling on the short rope hawser drawing the ships together.

"Ezra, Chips, Haden, keep below the rail. Creep forward," Dunston ordered. "Take the long gaffs. Dougal, Mario, Buffalo, are you ready?"

As they waited for the chance to board the ship now tight beside them, Dunston saw *Lancer*'s mate, Jeff Johnson, make a move and a mutineer shoot him in the chest. The bullet spun him round and sat him hard on deck.

"Now!" the old man shouted.

Buffalo Munro rose up near the bow of *Sea Horse*, leveled his repeating rifle, and shot Jesse Mako squarely through the center of his forehead.

When the greenhand, Tyler, tried to pass out the last of the stolen rifles, Buffalo shot him through the heart. He fell against Antonio, the ship's boy, who let out a wail and went scrambling aft with the powder horns and bullet pouches flying out behind him. When the boy realized that the hatches were closed, he leapt to the monkey rail, then began bounding up the rigging of the mizzen-mast near *Lancer*'s stern.

Old Noah Anderson was one of the few who turned to watch the boy make his panic-stricken upward flight. When Antonio reached the level of the top gallant sail, his bare foot slipped in the rigging. Noah saw him try to grab a ratline, but, heavy-laden, he missed it, arched back, and fell. He made no sound except the awful thump of his head when it struck the rail. His lifeless body fell in off the stern. Noah jumped when he heard more shots.

"Who wants this one?" Buffalo yelled at the mutineers. "Who's next? Any of you bastards moves a muscle, and I'll drop you on that warped old mother's deck."

Meanwhile Dunston and his party had come leaping aboard and

35

now dashed forward and joined the melee. They stood among the mutineers.

"Drop your weapons or you're dead men!" Dunston rasped.

The cook, who had shot down the mate, was trembling so hard that Dunston thought he'd fall. But instead, he lurched toward *Lancer*'s cook shack, grabbing a meat axe and a long carving knife. Finn took him on. He ducked under the stroke of the meat axe and, rising, struck the cook with a blow from a belaying pin that sent him rolling unconscious into *Lancer*'s scuppers.

Buffalo eyed the remainder of the mutinous men as he reloaded. "Get your hands up and drop your knives or by the living God I'm going to kill you now!" He leveled the rifle at them again.

Muskets, pistols, knives, and belaying pins went clattering to the deck as the mutineers still on their feet thrust their hands up high. The mutiny was broken.

Caleb looked down at Johnson, whose face had turned deadly pale. The fact that dark artery blood was still pumping from his wound and spilling across the deck was the only sign that the first mate remained alive. "Mario, strip off your shirt and hold it at his neck to staunch the bleeding," Caleb ordered. "You, Shannon, grab that long gaff. Dougal, help him fish up Titus before he sinks."

"Imagine this young captain murdered by these crazy, god-damned hooligans," Dougal growled to Shannon, as they hooked the gaff beneath the captain's belt. They hauled him up, then drew him carefully over the rail, which was still smeared with his blood. Titus's face had locked itself into a cold, blue-gray mask.

"Lay that canvas over him," the old man said.

"But first you look at him, you filthy scum," Otto Kraus shouted at the mutineers. "I should run this Apache shooter down every one of your *schweinehund* throats and pull this fuckin' trigger."

"Hold off, mate," called Caleb. "I have other plans for these bastards."

The two ships had been lying side by side, touching, rubbing, moaning like a pair of mourners, but now they were slowly beginning to drift apart.

36

Caleb turned and looked over to Buffalo Munro. "We all owe a lot to you, Munro, and that fancy rifle of yours. Without your help, I believe we would have lost *Lancer* and maybe many more men. And we owe much to you, too, ice master. If you hadn't known to throw us that spring line, we might have been too late."

Finn inclined his head, but did not speak.

"Well, no use waiting. I've got to decide right here what we're going to do with the rest of this bloody trash. Go ahead, Mr. Acker, get your crew list and check off these bad hats for me, both those living and those dead."

Acker finally named each of the nine surviving mutineers.

"Ironsmith, bring me any leg or wrist irons you can find."

Their search turned up only three sets.

"We'll put them on the worst ones, then we'll figure out about the other six."

"Oh, Jesus, not the irons," said the tall one when he was dragged forward by the hair. "They'll freeze our feet off."

"Shut your murderous mouth," yelled Bob Norris. "If your talking makes me nervous, I'll break your goddamned leg." He arranged his small anvil and with his ball-peen hammer pounded the cold rivets into place.

The next two men were silent, afraid to look at the enraged crewmen who stood angrily packed around them.

Now the old man said, "You three animals, get your arses up the rigging of this mainmast. When you reach the cross stay of the fore-sail, Angelo and Billy will tie you tight and cinch the knots. Buffalo, you cover them. Bring me that length of cod line," Caleb called to his ship's boy.

Jose ran and jerked a cod line from the cook-shack wall.

"*Corre! Sobe! Sobe!*" Mario Fayal shrieked in Portuguese at one mutineer who still refused to move.

Buffalo stepped forward, leveling the rifle at him.

"Get your arses up there fast," yelled Caleb as they ran to the rails. "If you're not monkey quick at climbing up them lines, I'll have Buffalo shoot you down!"

When the three mutineers were firmly tied spread-eagle in the rigging, the old man relaxed.

"Dear God, that wind is cold up there," said Angelo Daluz as he regained the deck, grinning.

"What about these last six?" Dougal asked. "What the hell do we do with them?"

"Where's the cooper?" the old man called.

"Right here behind you, Captain," said Ezra Morse.

"You go with Lester Lewis into the forward hold and bring up some of those knocked-down shooks, enough to build up six new barrels. The forty-two-gallon size should fit these buggers fine."

"Is he going to set them adrift in barrels?" young Jose whispered.

"Who knows?" said Rudi Haas. "I've been a ship's steward for years, but I've never seen a fix like this."

When both coopers returned, they had their arms full of oak barrel staves and iron hoops. Lester had his box of tools.

"Knock together the butts. Set them in a circle," Caleb ordered. "You," he said sternly to a man who had helped throw Captain Kildeer overboard, "you stand steady right there on that butt."

Jack and Ricardo had to force the man to keep his place as the cooper unbound his bundles of shooks.

"Now squat," the captain ordered.

Ezra spun the killer's straw panama hat overboard, then forced the mutineer to hug himself while he measured the length of the shook against the man. "It's going to be snug, but you should fit. Now get your ugly feet off that butt," growled Ezra. "I'm going to set your barrel in order."

When he had hammered the two lower iron hoops around the barrel, he stood back and said, "Hop in there and crouch, you murdering bastard." He waved his hammer. "Crouch!"

The man climbed in and folded himself down inside the barrel, encouraged by a couple of taps with the hammer to the top of his protesting head.

"He fits in there like this cask was made for him," Ezra told the old man.

"Good!" Caleb said. "Set up the other five." When Ezra finished, Caleb yelled, "Snap to it, the bunch of you, hop inside."

"That longer bugger, he's going to be a snugger fit," said Ezra.

"I'll make him fit," the old man shouted. He put his hand on the tall man's skull and forced him down. "Now, cooper, set your barrelheads!"

Casks

Ezra drove all the lids in place amidst a lot of yelling, then jammed the top hoops tight. One of the barrels lurched over from the violent action inside and began to roll.

"That's the way to do it," Dunston told the crew. "Topple the other barrels, roll them into place, and lash the lot of them to the foremast. Dougal, you go and see if there's anything more we can do for Jeff Johnson. Put some extra blankets on him and offer him rum so he doesn't catch a chill. See if the bullet went right through him or do we have to try and take it out. Jesus, I hate to do that sort of thing." He paused. "We're grateful to you, Ice Master, for your fast spring line," the old man said, "and you, too, Munro. That fancy repeating rifle certainly saved the lives of a lot of decent men. You two won this day for us."

Chapter 4

Next morning when dawn watch came, the two vessels were well within earshot.

"Ahoy, *Sea Horse!*" Chris Acker shouted on the gamming horn.

The old man emerged on deck and took his horn off the wheelhouse wall. "How's Johnson?" he called.

"He's doing poorly, sir," was Acker's answer. "He's breathing bad."

"I've been awake and worrying over our troubles most of the night," Dunston shouted. "You can't go on with no captain over there, and your first mate's barely alive with a bullet in him."

"We're not too far off St. John's, Newfoundland, sir. Our passenger, Captain Finn, says he knows the best doctor there."

"Good," Dunston shouted. "When this wind picks up, we'll head on in. I'm coming over now to say the service and give your ship's master a decent burial. And besides that, I want to talk to Finn."

"We'll slack sail, sir," Acker shouted. "We heaved that pair of mutinous buggers' carcasses down through the slob ice last night."

When the old man and Dougal climbed up over *Lancer*'s rail, the crew was waiting for them. "How are those bastards in the rigging doing today?" He looked up, eyeing them disdainfully.

"Angelo climbed up to check them this morning," Chris Acker reported. "They're all right, meaning they're still alive. Jose ladled

40

some warm water into their mouths. That one with his head hanging down on his chest, he's just trying to look bad. He didn't move or answer when I hollered up to him. He's a stubborn son-of-a-bitch."

The old man went forward with the bronco, who kicked all the barrels. They listened until they got a grunt or groan from each.

"I'm glad they're alive," said Caleb. "I don't want to take the responsibility of hanging them out here . . . or even setting them adrift. We've got to get rid of all of these mutinous bastards somewhere. If you look at the chart, the closest landfall is . . . Funk Island. But there's been a lot of criticism in the Senate and Congress and in the press complaining about American whaling captains dealing out brutal penalties to their crews, and you'll notice the Seamen's Union is getting stronger, gaining a lot more say. If I shove them off on Funk Island, they'll accuse me of marooning them there to freeze or starve to death." Caleb frowned. "I'd a helluva lot sooner throw them into the St. John's jail. The Boston and the New York papers can't holler too much about that."

"Well, we sure can't take them north," said Chris.

"Not to Blacklead Island. They could break out of any of those flimsy wooden shacks we've got up there. And none of us would sleep a wink with those murderous bastards roaming loose. Goddamnit," Caleb growled, "they've kicked my plans into a cocked hat. Master Finn, come back to the captain's cabin and we'll look at the charts."

Finn paused beside the ship's rail. "Do you see that, Captain Dunston?" said Finn. "That southwest breeze is ruffling up the waters near that slob ice. When that breeze turns into a wind, it will carry us into St. John's harbor."

Dunston looked pained. "Jeff Johnson's got to have a doctor's help, but I don't like to run the risk that those colonial customs officers will demand a court of inquiry about the mutiny and maybe impound both my ships."

"I might be able to talk them out of that," said Finn. "St. John's is home port to me, and the British Navy's North Atlantic squadron is based there."

"Well, then, I'll take the chance," said Caleb. "We're twelve men shorthanded. We can't go north the way we are, and Acker doesn't have the experience to master this ship – and remember, I've got forty pairs of eyes eager to report to the Seamen's Union on every goddamned move I make. Will you take *Lancer* into St. John's for me – as her master, I mean?"

Finn thought briefly, then nodded. "That I will," he said.

When they regained the deck, one of the mutineers called down to Caleb, "My feet are freezing off, Captain. My hands have turned blue, sir, and my fingers, they're dead white."

Caleb's voice was icy. "We've got this ship's master tween decks lying dead on the mess-room table, getting wrapped in shrouds. His hands and feet have turned deathly pale because you stinkin' bilge rats did that to him." He turned. "Acker, while we're waiting for the wind out here, we'll lend you a couple of seamen and two green-hands. We'll send Rafael Costa to wrestle up the grub, because Finn had to belay that so-called goddamned cook . . ."

Sea Horse's No. 3 whaleboat was rowed over, carrying five men with their sea chests. When the transfer had been made, Caleb read the service, ending with the words, "I bet he wished he'd stayed to finish his schooling at Yale. Amen."

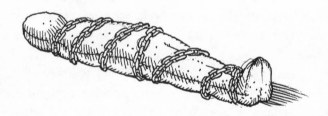

Body wrapped in chain

Sad eyes watched as the board was tipped and young Titus Kildeer's body plunged out from beneath the flag, straight down into the deep.

Two days later, the ships were mating close once more off the wide mouth of Conception Bay with only scattered ice around. As they approached St. John's harbor, they saw the light off Signal Hill, and when dawn came, they watched brigs and schooners setting out, their decks laden with two-man dories ready to go jigging off the Grand Banks for cod. Caleb hauled down his distress signals, the American flag flown upside down from the fore- and mizzenmasts, then ordered the three mutineers rope-lowered from the rigging and put in barrels.

"Are your colonial customs inspectors the world's worst?" Dunston called across to Finn.

"That they are," Finn answered. "Warn your crew, sir, not to volunteer a single word about our troubles."

Apart from Finn, not a man aboard had ever put into port at St. John's, and they were all surprised at the grand size and protection it afforded. Sailing through the narrow mouth of the harbor entrance, they saw its many cannons thrust out through the stony fortress walls and its military barracks looking down on them. There were a dozen types of vessels at anchor – ships, barks, brigantines, and schooners – but what caught Caleb's eye was the brightly painted Royal Navy frigate, H.M.S. *Firebird*, her gun ports gaping open while her crew scrubbed the cannon barrels.

"Prepare to lower away, Mr. Gibson," Caleb called. "No, hold on. Wait. They're coming out to board us."

As he strode back to midships, he saw those of the crew who were aloft staring down at him. The old man made a stitching motion across his lips in a hand sign, warning them all to stay close-mouthed and silent, for Caleb knew all too well how clearly voices carried over dead calm, foggy waters.

The old man lowered his voice to Dougal. "A British court of inquiry could hold us up for God knows how long. I'm going to tell them we've come in to try and find a doctor for a mate who accidentally got shot, and at the same time try with Finn's help to pick up some crew."

Dougal nodded in agreement.

Two customs officers boarded *Sea Horse* to make their routine search. They were accompanied by six quick-marching Royal Marines, each wearing varnished, hard black hats, scarlet tunics and chalk-white Red Cross belts and dollar-sized brass buttons polished brighter than the sun. Each bore a short naval musket. When they were done with their inspection, they went and boarded *Lancer*, and when her inspection was completed, the chief customs officer returned, saying to Captain Dunston, "Show me your crew lists again."

The old man grunted as he handed them over.

"Who was Captain Titus Kildeer, and why is his name struck?"

"Died," the old man said, "lost overboard, drowned."

"And Tyler, what happened to him?"

"Same thing. Both went over the side. We've suffered some mighty boisterous weather off the coast."

The customs officer demanded that they return to *Lancer*. "Line up your crew, sir. I wish to make a head count."

Caleb ordered, "Muster every man!"

Even with those borrowed from *Sea Horse*, Dunston knew *Lancer* would be in trouble.

The customs officer squinted at the line of men, then at Caleb suspiciously. "You're short too many men, Captain. What happened to this crew?"

When Caleb failed to answer, the customs officer ordered his second officer, "Mr. Ryan, take the Marines with you and do a thorough search of the ship's hold and fo'c's'le."

When they were below, the officer stepped closer to Caleb and said, "I've been aboard a dozen Yankee whalers. I've seen oil barrels deck-loaded going south, but never when they're going north to hunt. The slightest sea would set those heavy barrels a-rolling on this deck and killing sailors. And there's a nasty, pissy smell coming off those barrels."

He gave the nearest barrel a kick. There was no sound. He moved forward and gave the second barrel his boot, and from inside heard a tapping and a groan. He looked cautiously along the deck. The harbormaster and marines were down below. "Do you have men in all those barrels, Captain?"

"Yes, there is a man in each of them – and for a damned good reason."

"Good Lord!" said the customs officer. "You must have had a hellish pile of trouble."

"We had a full-blown mutiny aboard this ship a week ago. They killed *Lancer*'s captain and put a bullet into his first mate's chest. I thought instead of hanging them, I'd do the decent thing instead. I mean, sail back here and ask your judge to jail them."

"These . . . ah . . . mutinous men inside the barrels, could they be called experienced seamen?"

"Oh yes, you'd have to call them that. But they're a rough, dangerous bunch, most of them accustomed to sperm whale fishing in the southern oceans. They're what we call palm tree lovers. When they saw the first bergie bit of ice as we were heading north, the cocky bastards started screaming, 'Captain, take a different tack, head south.'"

"By George!" said the customs officer, looking along the deck again to make certain they were still alone. He lowered his voice. "These might be just the handy kind of seamen who could benefit the pair of us!"

"How's that?" Dunston asked.

"See that frigate *Firebird* anchored over there? She's sailed up here from Virgin Gorda, where they ran into cholera. She's desperate now for any kind of crew that she can catch – drunk, sober, drugged, or blackjacked by her press gang. Of course, *Firebird*'s recruiters are looking for experienced seamen, but they'll take pimps, bums, fishmongers, grave diggers . . . nine, ten-year-old boys are fine with them. *Firebird* will take anyone today. She received orders three days ago to make full sail to Gibraltar, where she will join the royal fleet. But," said the customs official, "what should interest you and me is that *Firebird*'s naval commander is willing to pay a guinea each for any able-bodied seaman, even Scotchmen or Yankee whalemen. Nine," he counted again, "and two guineas extra if there's a real seaman in every one of those barrels who can still stand up."

"Maybe," said Caleb, "two of them are only strong greenhands we hired on to work the pumps. They're all scum, but I would judge that a bit of Royal Navy discipline might shape them up."

"This could prove a moneymaking scheme for both of us." The customs officer leered and fingered his hairy side chops. "If you agree, I'll alert *Firebird*'s recruiting sergeant. He'll come over here with me. Not now, but during your night watch when things quiet down around the harbor. Both of us will be out of uniform. Let's see. Your crew will take up those nine barrels in your net sling and offload them onto a Royal Navy workboat that will pull alongside. Then with you and me and your first mate, if you wish, we'll accompany them and transfer your cargo onto the deck of *Firebird*, where the Navy will open up the barrels and examine the goods, making sure that they're all alive. Does that sound like a sensible plan to you, sir?"

"It does not." Caleb snorted. "Do I look that stupid to you?"

"No, Captain Dunston, you do not. Have you a better suggestion?"

"Yes, you bring half the money – that's five guineas – to pay me in advance for half the men. Only after that will we take all nine barrels aboard the frigate, where you will immediately pay me the remainder if the contents can stand."

"Have you a second copy of this crew list, Captain?"

"Yes," said Caleb. "Mr. Gibson made one, though his handwriting is not so fine as mine."

"May I borrow this list to help convince the Royal Navy that they're receiving living, breathing qualified seamen? Would you please put a check by the names of those men in the barrels? Don't be shy about upgrading your greenhands."

When Captain Dunston was finished, the customs officer nodded and signed both ships' papers. "*Sea Horse* and *Lancer* are now cleared through customs, unless, of course, that sister vessel happens to have any other seamen whom you would wish to export."

"No." The old man shook his head. "We're shorthanded as it is.'

"I'll be back," said the customs officer, "at twenty-three-hundred hours."

At eleven o'clock, St John's harbor was only faintly lit by moonglow when the Navy workboat pulled alongside *Lancer*. Ten oarsmen, most of them mere boys, had rowed her over very vigorously. One of *Firebird*'s midshipmen stood in her bow and a rugged-looking boatswain's mate stood steering the tiller with one massive brown hand.

The midshipman and the customs officer climbed aboard *Lancer*. The old man already had the nine barrels in the rope net of her cargo sling.

The customs officer tapped each one and listened for some sound. "Captain, may I see you in the cabin?"

Once inside, the customs man handed Caleb an envelope that contained half the total sum in U.S. federal dollars. "Our paymaster thought you might prefer them to British currency."

"I would," said Caleb as he turned up the lamp wick and carefully backlighted every bill, then had Dougal double-check them. "Seems right enough. I'll order my men to lower the sling."

When they arrived on *Firebird*'s deck, Dunston and Gibson pretended not to be impressed, but neither of them had ever been aboard a British fighting ship. *Firebird*'s deck was sanded white as a field of snow, and her brass fittings twinkled in the lanterns' lights. Red-coated marines and neatly suited sailors with their wide-brimmed hats stood rigidly at attention.

"Quarters!" a sharp voice commanded.

The sailors and marines took one pace back, then turned smartly and hurried away.

The barrels were rolled into place, then heaved upright on *Firebird*'s deck. The cooper, who had come over with the old man and Dougal, watched for the word, then began knocking away the top hoops and flipping off the lids. The smell that rose was awful. One by one, seven mutinous crewmen appeared, rising slowly, their cramped limbs almost immobile. From two of the barrels, pairs of feet arose, waving stiff as lobster claws. The Navy boatswain intervened with a kick that overturned each barrel.

"Get them out of there and strip these stubborn creatures down," shouted *Firebird*'s boatswain. "Throw every stitch of their filthy clothing overboard."

The commander of *Firebird*, holding a linen handkerchief to his nose, walked past them as a bullet lantern light was cast over each of the naked mutineers.

"Spread your legs," the officer ordered. "Turn smartly, damn you," he threatened. "Put your arms above your heads. Turn to face me. Do you speak and understand the Queen's English?" he shouted in each man's face.

Each of them answered, "Aye, sir!" realizing now that they were possibly going to remain alive.

"They'll do. We'll take them all," said the commander. "They'll need a bit of discipline, I'd judge, but we know how to handle troublemakers aboard *Firebird*. Captain, you've solved nine urgent problems for us. Good fishing and goodnight."

He turned on his heel and strolled back along the deck toward his cabin, where he was entertaining the Governor General and his wife along with a few other leading residents of the town.

The second envelope of money was handed to Captain Dunston. He and Dougal counted its contents.

The nine naked seamen were standing in a shivering line when the old man, Gibson, and the cooper reached the frigate's gangway. The mutineers cursed and hollered at them, "Goddamn you! Now you've thrown us to this lime-sucking navy!"

"Shut your Yankee mouths," the huge boatswain bellowed at them as he struck the nearest man a casual backhanded blow that broke his nose and dropped him to the deck. "Get your filthy carcasses into those scuppers. We'll brine you and have you scrub each other down with pig-bristle brushes and horse-tar soap. When you're spanking clean, we'll issue you a hammock, skulker hats, and a proper British seaman's rig. You'll be free men in seven years." He laughed. "Unless some Frenchman tears your guts out with a boarding hook."

At dawn next day, Caleb and Dougal leaned against the monkey rail and watched the royal frigate ease out through the narrow harbor's entrance, towed by thirty sailors rowing in three longboats to a drum beat that kept each man in stroke. *Firebird's* enormous pennants, flags, and sails hung sodden after a cold night's rain.

"There they go, those mutinous bastards," Caleb snorted. "Now, let's row ashore and buy some fresh supplies. I've heard the market here sells a box of good salt cod for a single penny. Out there on the Grand Banks, Tom Finn says you can damn near walk across the water on the backs of cod. But don't you ask him after that horror story he went through cod fishing out there."

Caleb turned toward the whaleboat. "We'll go out for a hearty midday meal. The customs officer told me of a first-rate eatery. We can drink a bit and stuff ourselves and yack together. I've been wondering if Finn would take the job of mastering old *Lancer*."

In the mid-morning, Caleb left Dougal and went wandering along the harbor docks examining the vessels that had tied up there, noting the unusual way that some were rigged. One of the larger topsail schooners had deep ice cuttings on her hull and bore the name *Kigulik*. It was surely an Eskimo word, thought Caleb, as he racked his brain to remember. It was a word Nilak had taught him. Yes, he was getting it now – a seal, one of the four kinds. Ah, oh yes – a harp seal. *Kigulik*. That was it.

A man Caleb judged to be the cook came to the stern of this hard-used vessel and threw a pail of fish guts to the gulls.

"*Comment ça va?*" he called to Caleb, who only nodded since he understood no foreign languages except maybe a few words of Portuguese.

"*Très bon* day, very good weather." The man jerked his thumb east toward the sun that was rising through the fog. "You want to see one helluva great lobster, sir?"

"Sure," said Caleb, whose favorite food was lobster.

The cook reappeared at the vessel's gangplank holding by far the biggest lobster Caleb had ever seen. Caleb went up the plank to examine this monster more closely.

"They took it out of a net this morning, must weigh forty pounds. You hold it. Tell me." The cook handed it to Caleb, its huge plugged claws waving like a windup toy.

"Can I buy this from you?"

"Sure, I guess you can," the cook answered him. "It will cost you a shilling and that's a fair price. Big lobsters, they don't get tough, you know, they taste just as sweet as the littler chicks."

When Caleb reached the ship, Dougal said, "I'm sorry to tell you, Captain, poor Jeff died ashore this morning just as the church bells were ringing eleven. The doctor says you should make arrangements to have him buried. Finn knows a deacon who will help."

That night, Dunston was host to the ships' mates at dinner at the Crow's-Nest Tavern, a small, softly lighted tavern with old-fashioned leaded diamond panes for windows. On the first round of rum, they stood to bid a sad farewell to Titus Kildeer and his first mate, Jeff Johnson.

"We've arranged to have Jeff Johnson buried tomorrow morning in St. Thomas's Anglican churchyard here because his family was Episcopalian. The minister says he'll hold a service for him at ten o'clock. Old Noah and Everett are building him a coffin tonight. I'm going to write to Kildeer's uncle and Jeff Johnson's father, letting them know what happened. I've already started my letters."

The burial was over by eleven, with most of both crews there at the graveside. Later, Caleb felt a sense of loneliness engulf him as he wandered by himself along the dockside. Had he been too harsh on young Kildeer? And now, a few weeks out of New London harbor, Titus had been murdered, sent into eternity with his mate, Jeff Johnson. He shuddered to think how much that would hurt poor Kate. There was so little time to write, and the nearest telegraph between St. John's and Halifax was out of order, as often happened.

Caleb returned to the Crow's-Nest Tavern. As he stepped down inside the half dark, he recognized Finn.

"I've got a table for us over here," said Finn.

"Good," Caleb grunted. "Have the barkeep bring us a round of his best rum, Barbados if he's got it."

"When do you plan to leave?" Finn asked.

"Oh, in a day or two," said Dunston. "That part may depend on you. Let's have a drink or two while they cook up the victuals. Smells to me like they're baking a shepherd's pie."

In the lamplight, Caleb could see that Finn must have been in some kind of a recent fight. His lip was split at the corner of his mouth, and a dark purple proud mark was starting to show around his eye. Wondering if Finn had won or lost the battle, Caleb roared, "Barkeep, what's holding up the rum?"

The tavern keeper hurried over. "We've got beef, and potatoes, and fresh mutton pie, salmon steaks, and cod tongues and cheeks taken this day with buttered mashed potatoes and green peas."

"Mutton pie sounds fine to me," said Caleb, "and send along another pair of rums. Now, Finn, how are we going to get some crew?"

"I know some good sea hands fresh in from the Magdalen Islands on this morning's tide. Ice hunters, they are, with nothing now to do and looking for a vessel."

"Are you looking for work yourself, Finn? Would you be willing to go north with us yourself as captain of *Lancer*? You've got the papers, Fisheries told me."

"Well, maybe I would, sir, if I could replace *Lancer*'s mutineers with good men like the ones just in from the Magdalens." Finn paused. "I'd like to talk to you about my fair share of *Lancer*'s lay. It's well known here that Yankee whale ships do pay well. I'd want the same part of the lay that your Fisheries agreed to share with Captain Kildeer, God rest his soul. When do you plan to sail?"

"Day after tomorrow on the tide, if we've got the men. We'll both need another drink," said Caleb. "It's a helluva lot of rank and pay for a man who's probably never even seen a bowhead."

Finn rearranged his length on the tavern chair. "It's all or nothing with me, Captain. I'll master *Lancer* only on her captain's share of the lay."

Caleb shook Finn's hand. "It's a deal, Ice Master."

Finn stood up. "I'll go net up those eight Magdalen seamen for you while they're sober enough to understand. I'll offer them a bunk aboard *Lancer*, same crew's lay shares as are on her list."

"They must be aboard tomorrow."

"I've got to run, Captain, and leave this pie. I'm off to find those Magdalen men." Finn finished off his rum and hurried out the door.

"That Captain Finn's a scrapper," said the barkeep. "But he's well admired by the fisher folk around this town."

Next morning, Jose, the ships' boy, rapped on the old man's door. "Captain, Mr. Finn's pacing up and down the dock, waiting to see you. He's got a flock of seamen with him talking French, and Newfoundland. I can't understand one word from any of them."

"Stand clear of that door, lad. I'm coming out!" Caleb stamped into his boots and pulled up his suspenders, then walked fast to the main gangway. "Ice Master Finn, come aboard. We'll talk. Tell your men to hold there a minute."

Finn hurried up the gangplank.

"Dougal, you come with me and Finn. I want you to witness all of this."

Inside his cabin, Caleb squinted his eyes, then blew his nose. "You say those men down there with you are seamen, not just a bunch of greenhands?"

"Seven real seamen, sir, and two of them only once or twice out. That's the God's truth. I've sailed with every one of them myself."

"Good men, are they?"

"Yes, sir, as good as you'd be likely to find," Finn answered.

"Fair enough!" the old man said. "Dougal, send a man along to *Lancer* and have him ask Chief Mate Acker and Mate Kraus to come aboard *Sea Horse*. I'll tell them they'll be working under Captain Finn and with these new men. Finn, will you have a belt of rum with me?" asked Caleb.

"As you probably must know, Finn, we two ships have been mating north together on this voyage. I, being the senior captain, am in charge of both vessels."

"It doesn't say that on *Lancer*'s list," said Finn. "Does it say that on yours?"

"Well, say it or not, I am," Caleb frowned.

Finn looked hard at the old man, then at Dougal. "Is *Lancer* to be under my command or not?"

There was silence.

"I'm only giving you the choice," the old man growled, "to sign that paper or not to sign. We've got no time to bugger around. We're late ten days already. As it says in *Lancer*'s list, you'll get the full share of *Lancer*'s captain's lay."

Finn sucked in his breath and stared back hard at him.

"Oh, I'll sign, all right, but you and your mate must sign as well, agreeing to the change in captains and men, but no change in the shares."

Caleb thumped his fist on *Lancer*'s crew list. "Sign the son-of-a-bitch," he said, "then give me the goddamned pen." He dipped it in the ink pot.

Finn signed on as *Lancer*'s captain, then the other two witnessed with name and date. Caleb noticed that Finn's hands were over-sized and scarred from too much work – or was it fights – at sea.

"We'll have a drink on that," said Dunston, looking at this ice master with new eyes. His trousers and once-blue naval jacket, stiff with salt, had faded to a monkish gray, its brass buttons murky green like the changing color of his black eye. He had picked up a naval plug hat which he had set squarely on his head. In Boston or New London on a Saturday night, thought Caleb, that hat would have been a screaming invitation for some dockside tough to knock it off.

Finn tossed down the rum and hurried out to shout down to the nine men who were pacing back and forth on the wharf.

"Jesus!" said Acker as he stepped back out of earshot to whisper to Dougal. "What about this new bunch? Where did Finn ever find them?"

When the new men with their sea chests had made their "X" on the new crew list and been shown their bunks in *Lancer*'s fo'c's'le, the old man heaved a sigh and went ashore with Finn, Dougal, Acker, and the stewards from both ships to buy supplies. They didn't stint on these, first and foremost because they wanted to set sail with fresh and tasty victuals, hoping that would spark good feelings between *Lancer*'s crew and the new Canadians and Newfoundlanders.

Thomas Finn led them to the largest English ship's chandlery in St. John's and showed them many expensive seagoing tools. Then when Captain Dunston was about to start buying, Finn whispered something in his ear. They left and walked a block away to a dockside street and another chandlery where the quality was just as good and every item was selling at about half the price.

"Wonderful!" said Caleb, taking out his list.

When he was done, Finn said, "I'd like to buy a new Swedish pump. I saw one working in an old vessel off Newfoundland's south coast and it was performing wonders. I noticed that *Lancer* was taking on more water than her pump could handle in a storm. I'd like to add this new model so *Lancer* could have two pumps. I'll talk to the owner here and see if I can get a special price."

Finn did. They bought the pump and all the other items they required.

"A profitable morning for us," Caleb said as he told the stewards to hire a wagon and take their purchases to the ships. The old man pointed at a tavern across the lane. "Come on. I'll stand a drink all round."

"Not that tavern, Captain. This one around the corner's better," Finn suggested. "Doesn't water down the rum."

Once inside the tavern, Finn bent close to the mates and said, "Since we're shipping out together on Thursday's tide, I'd like to ask you if you'll join me after sundown. I'd like to show you the town."

"I'm on!" said Dougal, and Acker smiled and nodded.

Next morning, Dougal and Acker returned to *Sea Horse*.

"You look like you had a good time," the old man said. "Do you like that ice master?"

"We sure do!" Acker laughed. "There's a wild side to this town you'd never believe. I mean, just look at all those church spires up from Water Street. They hide more fancy whoring than ever I've seen."

"Will Ice Master Finn get himself back here before our sailing?"

"You're damn right, he will," said Dougal. "He's dead keen on going north with us. I think you'll come to like him. He's a wild-eyed bastard and he sure showed us a good time. There's a helluva lot more to St. John's than seal flipper pie and those cocky Navy blokes, as Finn loves to call them. That's where he got the fat eye and the split lip."

Dunston had no knack for writing, but finally his two brief, formal messages were done, almost word for word the same. He informed the New London Whale Fisheries and Jefferson's family of the two officers who died in the mutiny, giving few details, in short, dead, cold sentences.

> Mutiny aboard *Lancer*, June 23, 1875. . . . Captain T. Kildeer and Chief Mate J. Johnson murdered. . . . Three mutineers killed. Nine mutineers turned over to naval authorities St. John's harbor. Have engaged Thomas Finn, who holds captain's papers, to master *Lancer*. C. Acker now first mate. Nine new crewmen signed on here to replace the dead and mutinous men of *Lancer*'s crew. . . . Captain Kildeer buried at sea. Chief Mate Johnson buried in Anglican churchyard, St. John's, Newfoundland. Both vessels will continue north, departing July 15, 1875.

> Regrets to families,

> Caleb Dunston, Master of New London Fisheries
> Whale Ships *Sea Horse* and *Lancer*

On Thursday morning, Dougal asked him, "Did you post your mail, Captain?"

"Dear God, I all but forgot! My mind's been in a devilish flurry." Caleb hauled from his side pocket the letters, each one sealed with wax, and said, "Give them to that man who's leaning on the monkey rail and doing bugger all." He hauled out his turnip timepiece. "The post office is open and it's right there on Water Street." He pointed. "You can see its roof from here."

"I wouldn't trust that wharf rat, Smalley, with a letter," Dougal said. "I'd send Seth Baker."

"Well, he's aloft," said Dunston, "helping to get this vessel under way. Hey, Smalley, can you see that postal office with its green copper roof?"

"Aye, I sees it, sir," Lem Smalley answered.

"Well, you take these two letters – hold them tight 'cause they're important – and you run up and post 'em."

"He'll need money for the posting, sir," said Dougal.

"How much?" said Dunston.

"I don't know how much these colonials will charge."

Caleb fished around in his change purse and drew out one silver Spanish dollar. "This will be more than enough," he said to Smalley. "You get those letters posted and get back here quick with all my change. You hear me, Smalley? Get up there and post these letters and get back here goddamned fast. We're sailing on this tide, Smalley, keep that in your mind."

Smalley scurried down the ladder and into a harbor workboat. They watched him reach the dock and run up the cobbled street.

More than half an hour passed as the crew began to come down from the rigging and the tug caught hold of *Sea Horse*'s main hawser and prepared to haul her out to sea.

"Where is that devil, Smalley? How long does it take that goddamned fool to post two letters?" Caleb roared. "After all our troubles, I don't want to sail north short a man and I won't risk sending a mate to haul him back. Cast off lines, Mr. Gibson!" Then he bellowed through the gamming horn, "Cast off lines, Ice Master. Do you hear me, Finn? Get *Lancer* under way."

"Where is that little son-of-a-bitch?" yelled Shannon.

"Well, we can't hold up for him."

"There he is, sir," a seaman called down from *Sea Horse*'s foremast. "Smalley's out in front of that tavern arguing with someone."

"Smalley," the old man bellowed through his gamming horn. "You get your arse back here, man, fast! Run, run! Fast!"

56

Smalley started running toward the ship, slipping and sliding along the wet, rough-cobbled street, not so much running as shambling, waving his arms out like a man who'd just won a drinking contest.

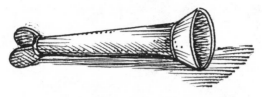

Gamming horn

"Look at that useless, drunken prick," roared Dunston. "Spent all the change from my Spanish dollar. He'll drown when he tries to get in that boat, Dougal. How can we snare that little bastard without using a harpoon on him?"

"He's coming, sir," said Dougal. "We'll haul him aboard and search his pockets for your change."

"Hurry, man, look at *Lancer*. I don't want Finn leading me out of this harbor as though he's the one that's in command."

Smalley was finally rescued and carried to his bunk in the fo'c's'le where he collapsed in laughter, then passed out.

"He's asleep, sir," said Dougal, "and he's penniless. He must have popped into that tavern and gotten drunk. He forgot to mail your letters."

"Tell our steward to mark my dollar against Smalley's lay," said Dunston.

Dougal shook his head. "I warned you, Captain, not to trust that son-of-a-bitch."

Chapter 5

A week later, during *Lancer's* dogwatch off the coast of Labrador, the man in the crow's-nest shouted, "There blows. There blows!"

Out to the east where the black waters stretched to the horizon, Finn paused to watch twin gray plumes rise forcefully, then drift against the lemon-yellow sky. He saw a second humpback spouting. A small pod of those giants was homing in for the summer feeding.

"The old man won't bother with that kind of whale this far out to sea," Noah Anderson told Finn. "We ain't like those sperm whalers. We're what's called offshore whalers. We render down our blubber whilst ashore. The old man will try to keep on this tack until we're inside Cumberland Sound. He's got a little box packed full of four-leafed clovers from his daughter, Kate. I'm hoping they'll make it a good year."

They had one more day of clear sailing within sight of southern Baffinland. Then, in the northwest, Finn watched a low scudding bank of clouds moving across the barren mountain landscape. The whole coastline faded to the color of unpolished pewter. Not far ahead of them was *Sea Horse*, ghostly pale and rolling in a heavy swell.

"The barometer is falling," Acker told him. "Do you want to look at the chart?"

"I'll just follow the old man. He'll be looking for a safe haven to let this foul weather pass," Finn said.

A smoke bomb rose from *Sea Horse*, streaking white against the grayness of the sky. Seeing her signal flags, Finn, with Noah's help, called for the reset of *Lancer*'s sails.

"Get two lead-line men on the bow!" Finn called. "We've got no soundings for this stretch of coast."

"The old man's busy sniffing out the entrance to Butterfly Bay," Acker called.

"Stay in sight of *Sea Horse*," Finn replied. "This weather's turning into almshouse soup. How many fathoms on the lead line?"

The answer came back, "My dear sir, you've got towsens of waters."

Through the fog, following the now almost invisible ship, they traveled close along the steeply rising cliffs that promised deep water below. Finn and the crew watched nervously, then cheered as the narrow entrance to the bay appeared before them. Inside, remaining a safe distance apart, both vessels dropped their anchors.

Caleb had his starboard whaleboat lowered. Wearing oilskins, he was rowed through the driving sleet by his five-man crew. Tom Wiggins held the swaying rope ladder steady below as Caleb climbed and boarded *Lancer*, nodding to Tom Finn and Acker.

"Filthy day!" said Dunston, trying to perk up his soggy moustache points and shake out his dripping sideburns. "Sounds like the west wind's trying to roll the rocks off those blessed mountains."

"Thank God you found such shelter for us," said Finn. "It's going to storm."

"I was here three years ago," Caleb told him, "when we got one helluva surprise. A big bowhead rose so close to us that the green-hands panicked and she got away into the ice and we lost our chance to take her. A two-hundred-barrel cow if ever I laid my eyes on one. That was a tough season, bad winds, ice – and worse, damn few right whales."

"Hope we'll have better luck this season." Tom Finn waved his hand toward his cabin.

The old man hunched his shoulders and started aft, frowning down at the warped seams now opening on *Lancer*'s ancient, oil-soaked deck.

Inside, when they had taken off their oilskins, Pierre, the new ship's boy from the south coast, brought in the coffeepot, then ran out. The old man poured himself a half mug, then reached into a side pocket and drew out a large pewter flask, filling the remaining half of his cup with rum. "Want some?" he asked.

"Like a duck wants a pond to swim in!" Finn laughed as he added Caleb's rum to his coffee.

"Finn, you've visited Connecticut, our famous Nutmeg State. What did you think of it?"

"I was crazy about half the time," said Finn, "and seeing gulls and feeling iceberg chills."

"Well, you're lucky in one way . . ." Caleb snorted and poured more rum in his coffee. "You escaped those Women's Christian Temperance Union witches and their songs about the 'Evils of Drink.' They've got posters with paintings of the devil rum pasted up on all our tavern walls."

"Well, that's not so bad," Finn said. "Newfoundlanders love rum. Our trick is to find enough to go around."

"It makes me glad to be at sea again when I think of those black-rigged temperance sisters." Caleb offered Finn a Brazilian cigar. "They stand up ramrod straight outside the Cock and Spur, screaming hymns and praying aloud for sailors' souls, trying to thrust into the hands of decent sailing men those 'Fight the Demon Rum' pledges, then hand them a pencil stub to mark their X's. It's especially bad having my old Aunt Clarissa trying to press pledges onto me and my crew."

Finn laughed. "Well, let's forget the Temperance Union. We're both safe away at sea again. It's the natural home of man, as we Newfies say. The world is mostly covered in water, with just an island here and there to tie up to."

Dunston laughed and topped up their cups. "Have you had any rumpusing within your crew?" ask Caleb.

"No. Everything's going smooth as silk among us all. One of those French-Canadian dory men speaks damn little English, but he's a dancer and a fiddle player like you've never seen or heard before, and he sure keeps our spirits high."

Caleb unfolded a piece of paper from his inside pocket. "Here's a copy of *Lancer*'s new crew list, the names of the men and one ship's boy we signed on at St. John's. Can you read it? My handwriting is just awful on account of this boisterous weather."

Finn examined the crew list:

SHIP *LANCER* — CREW LIST & LAY
Departed St. John's, Newfoundland – Thursday, July 15, 1875

NAME	RATING	LAY
Thomas Finn	Master	1/12
Chris Acker	Mate	1/20
Otto Kraus	2nd Mate	1/50
Angelo Daluz	3rd Mate	1/55
Noah Anderson	Ship's Keeper	1/75
John James	Boat Steerer (Starboard Boat)	1/75
Samuel Douglas	Boat Steerer (Larboard Boat)	1/75
Rusty Tutter *	Boat Steerer (Waist Boat)	1/85
Lester Lewis	Cooper	1/50
Everett Roberts	Carpenter	1/95
Noel Wotten	Carpenter	1/95
Bob Norris	Ironsmith	1/140
Antoine Carpentier	Steward	1/175
Rafael Costa (*Sea Horse*)	Cook	1/115
François La Flèche *	Seaman	1/130
Luke Blais *	Seaman	1/130
Jean Duchamps *	Seaman	1/130
Franklin Town *	Seaman	1/130
Georges Oiseau *	Ordinary Seaman	1/175
Rory Decker *	Ordinary Seaman	1/175
Benoît St.-Onge *	Landsman	1/180
Kevin Shiffer *	Landsman	1/180
Jacques Moreau *	Landsman	1/180
'Ti Pierre *	Ship's Boy	Food & clothing only

"Is old *Lancer* holding up?" Caleb asked.

"She's leaking," said Finn, "enough to flood the rats' nests in her hold. But we got Moreau aboard. He's an ex-trapper from Trois-Rivières. He's got his trapline set and he's catching usually four or five most nights."

Caleb sat staring at the ghostly image of a woman hovering in his cigar smoke.

"The crew's quarters in the fo'c's'le are leaking bad. It makes me restless when I think of those good sailing men taking turns to pump themselves to death," Finn told him. "I've got a four-man relay working so we don't take on more water than we've got."

"Quit worrying," said Caleb, "we're hauling to our winter anchorage soon. We can heel *Lancer* over when we reach the Yankee slip and pull off her copper sheathing and re-coat her with tallow resin and sulphur. You help fill her up with oil and bone, then I'll guide you home." He sighed and poured coffee from the pot, then passed his flask.

"I'll pass this time," said Finn. "Coffee will do me fine."

"You're right to go easy on rum, lad, you're still young," the old man said. "Rum's the captain's curse. You drink it sparingly. God willing, you've got many oceans to cross. I brought you over three of these *Godey's Lady's Books* for trading," Caleb said as he carefully removed the flimsy fashion magazines that he had folded in his pocket. "There are some wonderful hand-colored pictures of elegant young women in this one. There's an article in here that says that they use only the best and springiest of whale baleen to go around the ladies' waists, and that they use the whalebone bustles to enlarge their dresses to give them a plumper, firmer-looking stern."

Finn laughed and traded him three pink-covered ladies' magazines he'd found in *Lancer's* cabin.

"I'll be going back now," Dunston told him. "You can row over and have a visit with me and Dougal tomorrow. It looks like this weather is planning to lay foul on us for a day or two."

Finn went out on deck to see the old man off and held the swaying ladder as Caleb climbed down among the rain-slick crew already in his boat.

Knickers and corset

"That was a dandy visit for us," said Antoine. "The old man brought over Tom Wiggins, you know, that short-chinned character they call Needles. He and I had the chance to finish off a half-done cribbage game I'd started in St. John's."

"Did you win?" asked Finn.

"No, no! He beat the hell out of me again. He's got a sly style that's hard to fathom, but I'm studying it. I'll beat him during these coming winter nights. You'll see."

Rain, sleet, then soggy snow each took their turn for two more nights and days. But on the third morning as the four-hour watch changed, the sun broke through racing clouds. The deck turned icy as *Lancer* once more followed *Sea Horse* out of their safe haven and onto the heaving ocean. The old man set sail on another northeast tack toward the eastern tip of Cumberland Sound, where he judged from other years that they might find an August passage westward through the drift ice to their anchorage near the Yankee station.

Several times during this voyage, Finn had watched Dunston use his Arctic knowledge with success. The heavy ice that had barred the entire entrance to Cumberland Sound had been so widely scattered by the storm that the two ships easily passed through it. Both crews sent up a cheer. A new tack carried them west-northwest, directly toward Blacklead Island.

"Blacklead Island's off our starboard bow!" the lookout in the crow's-nest shouted, "and we're just thirty-one days out of St. John's harbor!"

"There she is!" Old Noah pointed as he leaned against the starboard rail, with the new hands crowded around him. "See that red cliff shaped like a heart? That's given the Eskimo name for our Yankee island. They call it Umatjuak."

Both ships approached Blacklead Island, then drew into its lee. Baffinland, beyond their island, remained in the blue shadows, its mountains and sheer cliffs still sheltering those long white snakes of snow that never disappear.

"Some call them Huskies, others call them Esquimeaux or Eskimos, or Inuit, or Yacks. They live on this Yankee island," the ship's keeper told Finn as they stood at the rail, "but only when we're here. You can call them any name you want. They won't care, they don't understand you anyway. There'll be more of them living over at Niantelik harbor. Most seamen around here call them Yacks because we can't understand their language and they think their talking sounds like 'yack, yack, yack.' Or they call them Huskies because they're a lot stronger than any dog and willing to work.

"You'll get some wrong ideas about these people at first," Noah continued. "But I swear that after a year, or two, or three with them, you'll come away believing till your dying day that there's no folk alive as kind and sharing as these good family people. They're so decent they'll sometimes lend their wife to you, but that will only happen after you understand a little of their language and you act nice enough so the wife agrees. Now remember that, for it's important."

The mates on both ships started shouting orders and the seamen leapt up into the rigging to reef the sails as they glided smoothly into Caleb's choice of anchorages. The Baffin coastline curved around them to the north and west like an angel's white protective wings.

"Let go the starboard anchor," Caleb yelled.

"Let go the starboard anchor," echoed Finn.

Dunston smacked his palms together and shouted over to Finn. "You can thank your lucky stars that no other ships are here off Blacklead. That son-of-a-bitch from Dundee, he's usually here. I hope to God he'll whale off Greenland this year."

The whale ships were anchored half a mile offshore because of the big tides.

"Just look into that pretty little valley," Lester Lewis, the cooper, enjoying his veteran status, told the greenhands in the bow. "You can see our crews' quarters, the cookhouse, the mates' mess, and Captain Dunston's house, and over there our try-pots and the Dundee men's pots and bunkhouse. On either side of that valley, you can see our two separate haul-out places. They were blown out of that granite rock with barrels of gunpowder, then squared up with pry bars and pickaxes. That must have been one helluva lot of back-breaking work done by the Eskimos and the crews in the 1850s maybe, well before my time. See how those two slipways are separate? The near one is our Yankee slipway and the other belongs to the Dundee men. Oh, we get on with them well enough some years, but most years not. We usually share a few barrels of home brew over the winter, but we never, never mess around with each other's women or whales or boats. You remember that, all of you, if you want to keep your front teeth looking good!"

Sea Horse put out its starboard whaleboat with Caleb standing on his tiptoes to see all as he steered toward the island. As the bow touched shore, a cloud of snow geese rose honking into the air.

"Do you see that, boys?" The cooper laughed. "How peacefully that flock of geese was sitting there? That guarantees there's not a single human being on this island. If there were, those birds would not be resting near them. There's no Yacks, no kayaks or tents, no dogs, no umiaks, no women. Hear that? No women! What the hell are you going to do if they don't turn up? I'll tell you. When the moon grows full, you'll hear our crewmen out howling like a pack of wolves. It's no joke here on Blacklead if those strong hunters and their wives and daughters don't appear."

The old man's whaleboat bow was first to touch the gravel beach. Dunston was already wearing his Eskimo sealskin boots as he leapt ashore, as gleeful as a teenaged boy. He scrambled up the Yankee slipway and hurried straightaway to the island's best freshwater stream. There he bent and, scooping up a double handful of water, drank. Thomas Finn followed close in one of *Lancer*'s boats. He, too, looked keen as mustard, for this far north was a whole new, magical world to him. Eight boats went in. All together, like a horde of excited schoolboys, they rushed across the soft springy tundra toward the cluster of six buildings spread around the flagpole that made up the Yankee whaling station on Blacklead Island.

"Mate Gibson, I want you to keep a lookout man up on our hill at all times when it's light enough to see, in order to keep an eye for roving fish."

One group of greenhands separated from the others to stay near Lester Lewis, for they liked the cooper's stories and his friendly style. He led a dozen of them first to the crew's quarters. These were two long, boxlike, flimsy pine structures protected by the largest shoulder of the nearby mountain. These buildings were weathered gray and rested on foundations of huge, flat, uncut stones. Inside the crew's quarters, the floors were sagging. Each possessed a single door plus three small windows and many heavy layers of black tar paper tightly stripped and battened down on every roof. These materials had been shipped north aboard various vessels during the earlier years when the whales were so numerous along the Sound.

Fortunately, during the American Civil War from 1861 to 1865, rebel ships had stayed away from the eastern Arctic, choosing instead to destroy the whale ships off Alaska. Nevertheless, the New London Fisheries had sent in one old Navy cannon and several extra kegs of powder and ball to defend the Blacklead whaling station. The powder had long since been used to blow out paths through summer ice, while the balls stood rusting in two handsome pyramids beside the gun.

The most striking feature of the station was Caleb's house and the mates' quarters. Both places were greatly dignified by huge, bleached bowhead jawbones that stood like Gothic arches above both doors. The mates' house had eight bunks – one for each of the six mates, plus another for ship's keepers, if they chose to come ashore. Some recent Arctic windstorm had caused that house to suffer a nasty list to port. But, hell, the mates were used to having their bunks on a permanent tilt. They didn't complain, for they knew that they were there for whales and their fair share of the lay.

Captain Dunston's house

A newer, sturdier warehouse also served as a carpenter and iron-smith's shop where carefully stone-sharpened harpoon heads, whaling lances, cutting-in spades, and blubber knives were given gleaming razor edges. Dunston, an experienced captain, did not allow ship's boys to bunk in with the crews, knowing that that had caused problems in the past. He had the boys sleep in the cook-house with the cooks, which was hazard enough for them. Across the valley on the sidehill stood the Dundee whaling station. Unoccupied now, in the gathering mists it looked like a scattering of crypts in an unused graveyard.

Caleb hurried along the path to check his house. Lifting the copper ship's spike from the latch, he ceremoniously opened the door. It remained spotlessly clean inside. The valuable differ-ence between the men's wooden bunkhouse and this much smaller captain's house was its total sense of privacy. The inner walls had been completely wrapped and battened tight for warmth with old gray sailcloth. Beneath that lay a tight-packed layer of dried tundra moss that served as insulation, and a winter home for lemmings.

Caleb had ordered that the settee from his captain's cabin be unlashed and rowed in on the next boat, for he had decided to bring it ashore with a few other treasures to settle his house before the Eskimo families arrived. He placed it opposite his double bed.

Years before, a ship's carpenter had laid boards on top of his house rafters to form a storage space which could only be reached by standing on his homemade chair. In this loft, Dunston had placed all his personal items. It was a ritual with him to take them all down each season, admire them, then put them in their proper places. It felt good to Caleb to be in this little house again, far away from his wife and the much larger problems of Topsail House and Mystic.

First, Caleb affectionately lowered an old-fashioned brass and rosewood sextant and reread its London markings, then a Bible wrapped in oilskin that he used at burials, his waterproof sealskin parka, spare sealskin mitts and boots, then his winter caribou-skin pants and parka. All these garments had been neatly rolled and sewn by Nilak into tight, pillowlike sailcloth packages. He took down and examined a rolled pair of yellowing bearskins he used for winter traveling, a leather-covered writing box, a quire of unused Topsail stationery, and two unfinished whaling journals dated 1868 and 1870. He kept a large canvas bag of shot up there with an extra ramrod, a box of percussion caps, and his old-fashioned goose gun, a long-bladed snow knife, and a loose-headed hatchet. He also found his painted Chinese piss pot with its fancy lid which a whaling master from Bath in Maine had given him at a captain's smoker. Next came his worn Wellington boots, a dried, cracked oilskin coat, a tin of dried-out moustache wax, a shaving mirror, a straight razor and leather strap, a pair of pig-bristle hairbrushes, an extra toothbrush, tar soap, two towels, a washbasin, comb, large scissors, and smaller moustache trimmer. Yes, Caleb Dunston had his own special reasons for remaining neat and well-groomed, even on this far-flung Arctic island.

Where in the world was she, Caleb wondered. Oh, the whales would come again, no doubt. But without her here this house, this island would not mean a tinker's damn to him.

The most impressive object in Caleb's one-room house was the large, four-poster bed which occupied a good deal of the floor space. Its bottom was neatly gridded with ship's rope. Caleb's best local harpooner, Sagiak, who had rolled over in a kayak and drowned, had been clever at carving walrus ivory and whalebone, and had shaped four hand-sized sculptures of bowhead whales. Caleb had pegged one on top of each bedpost. Everett, the carpenter, had made his bedside chair, desk, bench, and work table. A small, upright cast-iron stove stood in the center of the room not far from the end of the bed. Its thin iron stovepipe rose up, then crossed the room to exit through a tinned hole in the south wall. Outside, the chimney's mouth was carefully covered with a rusted-wire cook's sieve to prevent flying sparks from setting other buildings ablaze.

Another unusual object in this room was a ship's model of *Sea Horse*, carved five winters earlier by Willie Kinney to entertain himself during that February's awful storms. He had cut the tail off his shirt to make cotton sails and had rigged it with linen thread. He had colored its hull with stove polish. He had lettered "Sea Horse" across her sternboard and had carved two small anchors for her bow. Four small whaleboats hung from their side davits, ready to take out after whales. Willie had presented it to Caleb on Christmas Day. The old man had nailed a block of wood on his north wall as a sort of shelf, and on this the model rested. Her paper flag with Stars and Stripes flew stiffly off the stern and her colorful Fisheries pennants jutted out from her fore- and mizzenmasts. Caleb's beloved sextant hung on its peg below.

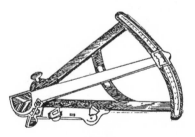

Sextant

"This house of mine is starting to look like old times again," Caleb said aloud as he hung his beloved sextant on its peg below the ship model. "But it does lack a woman." Peering out through the window, he went on. "Where the hell is she? Where the hell are all of them?" He then lit the stove that had been set a year earlier.

The next three days were filled with the coming and going of whaleboats as crewmen hauled ashore their own sea chests, then immense coils of new hemp rope and every kind of whaling gear. Caleb ordered that the Stars and Stripes be flown to reclaim the island and show the Yacks that the Yankee men, and not the Dundee men, had dropped anchor first this year. The old man had ordered the greenhands to go and raid the heap of Scottish hard coal – not to burn beneath the big iron try-pots for rendering oil, but first to fill the wooden bin behind his captain's quarters, and then the mates' mess stove and their own crew's quarters' stove, and finally the crew's quarters and the cook shack. Because not a stick of wood grew on any of these islands of the Arctic archipelago, Caleb was in a hurry to take possession of this dwindling treasure to use for the winter firing of all their stoves. The Highlander might arrive and start once more bellyaching about the stealing of their coal – even though the Scots would certainly bring many more tons as ballast, for in Britain good Welsh anthracite was plentiful and cheap.

On the third day after their arrival on Blacklead Island, Finn, who had continued to use his cabin aboard *Lancer* as quarters, came ashore to dinner. He joined Caleb in the small, rough-boarded mess hall that would be shared by both captains and their six mates. Caleb ordered the oil lamps lit and sat down at his end of the table. The mates could see that something was weighing on his mind.

"Captain Finn, I've been thinking that it would be a waste of time and Fisheries lumber for you to build another captain's house on Blacklead Island. There's a spare bunk you could use in the mates' quarters. What do you mates think of that idea? Could Captain Finn bunk in with all of you?"

The mates looked narrow-eyed at each other, then stared hard at the old man and Finn. The idea of having a captain lying around in one of their bunks listening all winter to every word they had to say did not sit well with them.

Chris Acker, who had come to know Finn best, spoke up, saying, "I guess it might be all right to have the captain living in with us so long as we could cuss him out sometimes and call him Tom. We wouldn't call him 'captain.'"

There was a long, uneasy silence from both Finn and the mates. "What do you others say on that?" Chris asked.

When no one answered, the old man said, "Well, Captain Finn and I will talk it over together . . . later. I'll let you know what I decide."

During that meal, all the mates started calling the ice master Tom and even made a Newfie joke or two. Finn laughed heartily with all of them, which made Caleb feel like a lone outsider. This new plan of his could blow right back in his face.

At the end of the meal, Caleb, who had been left entirely out of this ribald conversation, butted in, "Where the hell are the Eskimos? They've never been this late before. I had a boat steerer sail his whaleboat over to Niantelik harbor yesterday. He found only a few Eskimo families there. None of them were ours. Maybe the Highlander's going to winter in Iceland or hunt the coast of Greenland. I don't care where the bugger goes, so long as he stays well away from here. Maybe the Dundee partners have gone broke or maybe they've no need to oil their hemp rope any more in that godforsaken Scotch town. But all our Eskimos staying away, now that's serious."

"They're drifters, all right," said Shannon, "always wandering around, like those little bands of Indians clamming along the New England coast. If someone in one of our Yack families has a dream, it's bang! They're up and moving in the middle of the night – and who knows when another dream will bring them back."

Caleb felt a sense of uneasiness as he rose and left Finn and the mates laughing and joking together in the mess. He crossed over through the darkness to his house. There he lit the oil lamp and sat down by his desk, pondering over Finn's sleeping arrangements, which he himself had suggested but now decided would not work. Certainly, he would never dream of asking Finn to share his house, and ruin his fairest winter joys. He had only suggested that Finn should not build his own small house because he wanted it made clear to mates and crew and Inuit that he, Caleb Dunston, was definitely the one and only ruling captain on this whaling station. Caleb had always clung to his image of himself as father and pro-tector to the local Eskimos and his crews. But if that so-called ice master bunked in with the mates, Finn would soon become, in their eyes, one of them. Caleb being Arctic-wise knew that he could count on some sort of trouble during the long, dark months of winter from the mates and crews, who numbered more than fifty men. And if the Highlander did manage to appear, it would be hell. Then he would desperately need Finn to help support his judgments.

Next morning following their usual breakfast of weak coffee and lumpy oatmeal porridge and the last of the rancid bacon, with the green mold more or less trimmed off, Caleb broke the silence at the mess table. "Finn, follow me over to my house, I want to talk to you."

As soon as Caleb closed his door, he said, "I don't know whether I can trust you, Finn, to keep your authority over the mates this winter. I don't like them horsing around with you, calling you by your first name, and making you one of them. Live with them, but stay above them. Make them call you 'Captain.' Why don't you sleep aboard, keep check on that old hulk? There's no goddamned need for you to build another house."

"I don't agree with that," Finn answered coldly. "Your Fisheries provided the master of *Lancer* with the necessary lumber, nails, and roofing to put up a house, and I plan to build it. *Lancer's* carpenters will raise it following the plan I made whilst we were sailing north."

"Hold on, Finn. I'll decide what you will or will not do around here."

"That's not the way it reads in *Lancer's* master's papers." Finn stood firm, looking straight at Dunston. "They say I'm master of *Lancer*. You are in command of *Sea Horse*, a totally separate vessel. You and I, sir, hold exactly the same rank at sea, and on this station each of us is free to make his own decisions."

Caleb stared at Finn as a deadly silence widened between them. "I won't put up with this," the old man growled. "You're nothing but a goddamned ice hopper. I'm in full command here."

Finn glanced away outside the window, studying the small rise where he planned to build his house.

"What are you staring at out there?" the old man shouted as he jerked open his door. "Get outside and chill some sense into that codfish brain of yours."

72

Finn's face flushed deep red. He stomped out, slammed both doors, and strode straight down the embankment to the shore. He roughly pushed out *Lancer*'s whaleboat, rowing it hard with the help of two greenhands, trying to settle down his rage.

Climbing up to *Lancer*'s deck, Finn paused to catch his breath. "Noah, get ready," he nodded to his ship's keeper. "I'm going to order *Lancer*'s crew out here to row in every roll of tar paper, every stick of lumber, nails, tools, and stove. It's all there bundled in the aft hold. I'm going to build my house. I want you to help them load it in the boats, Noah. In the meantime, I'm out here sleeping aboard."

When Finn returned to shore next day, Chris told him, "Soon as the old man saw that house lumber you were sending in off *Lancer*, he went roaring around here in a helluva rage. He wouldn't speak one word to any of us mates. Just took five men and sailed off in his whaleboat. We watched him heading south along the coast, searching for Eskimos and whales."

"We'll all feel better when those roving Yacks come in to join us," said Shannon. "We mates were hoping that this could be a peaceful winter, but we see now that you're a scrapper. I'd say go ahead, build that new house of yours. You've got the right. The Highlander's not here, but you don't dare use his house."

"Oh, sure enough, I'm going to build that house," said Finn, "but I'm not looking for any bloody trouble."

Whaleboat with sail

Chapter 6

Johnny James and Angelo Daluz, two boat steerers off *Lancer*, were busy splicing rope outside the whaling shed. Angelo shook his head. "That ice man, Finn, is trying hard to outsmart Dunston. I hope to God they both settle down. The old man's in a rage and his mates are as nervous as teeter-ass birds. We're all nervous, I guess, because . . . well . . . where the hell's the Eskimos? They should be here by now. Believe me, this place won't be anything until the Yacks get back with their good-natured wives and daughters."

"Well, the Yack hunters . . ." Johnny looked at him, "don't forget them, if it's whales and corset bone we're after."

"Sure," said Angelo, "the Yacks are good, strong oarsmen and they know whales. They can get a little out of hand when they've been drinking home brew with our crews. But we've never had a man or woman killed on this island, not so far, not even one of those damned Dundee men."

"Oh, they're not all bad," said Johnny. "Once in a while we have a rough-up with the Scotch. But no knives or fids, mind you. A man can't do too much damage with his fists or these soft sealskin boots we wear up here. We've got real rules of decency on this island, considering there's usually three different tribes of people here."

"The old man's whaleboat's still down the coast," said Hammer Haden as he stepped away from the ironsmith's forge.

"I'll bet they've seen neither hide nor hair of right whales or Eskimos," said Bill Shelley. "When he gets back, we'll see him sniffing around those oldest rusty try-pots set ashore twenty years ago. He can't wait to see them cleaned up, fired up, and boiling away with rich-smelling whale oil perfuming the air again."

"You keep using fancy words like that," said *Lancer*'s sailmaker, "and they'll ask you to join the Mystic Poetry Society!"

Leaning against *Lancer*'s transom rail, Finn and his ship's keeper examined Blacklead Island.

"Captain Finn, do you enjoy being up here?" Noah asked him. Finn nodded, "I hope I will."

"You watch out for the old man," Noah advised him. "He can be hard as rocks. And if he comes back from this trip having found none of our Eskimos or whales, he'll roll in like a storm on you."

"I've been warned," said Finn. He leaned out and examined *Lancer*'s sternboard. The lettering was showing signs of wear.

"Lord knows, I'll be glad to see Inuit back here." Noah chuckled. "When they're around, this island comes to life. I like it here both summer and winter. There's really no seasons in between. I was nine years old when I first sailed into Cumberland Sound. My father was captain of a whaling bark and after my mother died, he brought me, their only child, north with him as a ship's boy. Lots of evenings, he'd try to teach me geography and navigation, then reading, writing, and calculations. I hated that last bit, but I was crazy about the free and easy Inuit way of living. I had lots of friends and often used to sneak away and eat and sleep with them in their skin tents or igloos.

"One night, I don't know why, I broke my slate, threw my chalk sticks overboard, and skipped out on my father's lessons. He came ashore and found me over in a tent where I was eating with a family – raw seal meat, the really good stuff – and right there in front of them he hauled down my britches and gave me one helluva beating with his belt. The Eskimos were horrified. Kumik, an Inuk boy who was my best companion, told me that his uncle had a camp up on an island and he'd help me escape. We borrowed his older brother's

75

kayak and I lay on its back deck. We took turns paddling north. I lived with that family for more than three months. None of the Eskimos told my father because they didn't like the way he'd hurt me. They couldn't understand any man doing anything like that to a son who would later care for him in his old age. My father must have thought that I was dead. They told me later that my being gone seemed to drive him nearly crazy. When I heard that, I came back to Blacklead. We never said one word together about my running away or the beating he gave me. Using an old logbook that same night, we started on my lessons again.

"But the really important thing was that living in that Inuit camp caused me to start speaking Inuktitut. That's their language. Now I'm old, I'm starting to lose it again, but I'm much richer 'cause I learned it."

"You're lucky you can speak it," Finn told him.

Noah nodded. "Later, I learned quite a bit about them and their religion. I found out how kind and decent they were to each other, and to me. Oh, I've heard what the mates and crews around here think. They say I only know how to speak Yack because I've had more nights to learn it while lying with their girls. But there's lots more to it than that."

He turned and pointed ashore. "When I stand aboard this ship, viewing Blacklead Island, I always imagine the place has the look of a big male walrus resting on its belly, with its head thrust in the air. I remember when the Dundee men first built that stone lookout up there on that highest hill. Today, I think of our Yankee station as resting on the saddle of the walrus's back. See where the island ends? Those are his hips sloping down to his hind flippers. You'll hear the gulls gather there on summer mornings to hold their laughing and screaming contests.

"Oh, by the way, have you peeked into the windows of the Highlander's house?"

"No," said Finn, "not yet."

"You better hurry," Noah said. "If you're going to build a house yourself, you might get a few ideas from his. Most years, it turns into a no-man's-land between our Yankee station and their Dundee

76

station. You can see the wide spacing with nothing in between. If Dunston sees you crossing there, he'll start yelling."

"Why don't you come in with me?" said Finn.

They lowered his No. 1 captain's whaleboat and both hopped in and set their oars. When they reached the Dundee haul-out beach, they tied up and climbed the bank.

Finn said, "I suppose the Highlander, whom everyone talks about, has got his house locked tighter than the Bank of Scotland."

He was wrong. The Highlander had fastened the storm door of his house with a French bayonet from the Napoleonic Wars brought over by him to trade, knowing that hard metal was what the hunters wanted. It rested loosely in the hasp, serving only to keep his door from blowing open.

Instead of drawing the bayonet they walked around the house and cupped their hands beside their eyes to peer through the three small windows. The interior of this Highland lair was brightly lighted at this hour by the long, low rays of Arctic evening light. Everything inside was swept and scrubbed as neatly as a Dutchman's kitchen. The most prominent item in the room was a narrow bachelor's bed that had been shipped over from Dundee. It had four chin-high, lathe-turned bedposts with a carved thistle blooming off the top of each, and a highly polished, heart-shaped mahogany headboard. Its inner support was a crisscrossed grid of hemp cordage of the type harpooners favor when hunting whales. A large, freestanding, Scottish-style armoire, a storage closet, had also been imported and stood in one corner.

Through the starboard window, Finn could see a fading photograph now sunstruck in its thick oak frame. "That's the widowed Queen Victoria," Noah said. "You'll recognize her. She's standing by a loch in a long black skirt and plaid shawl. Her Majesty is holding a salmon rod."

Beside her, wearing a kilt, tweed jacket, and stalker's cap, stood a beefy, bearded gillie, holding a pony with wicker hampers on its sides. Two huge flags were crisscrossed over the picture, one, the Saint Andrew's flag of Scotland, and the other, the British Union Jack.

77

"I wonder why that picture's there at all. Most Scots hate the bloody English," Finn observed, "and the Irish do as well."

"It's there because the Highlander claims that famous gillie as a first cousin of his. It could be true. When I was in their western town of Glasgow a few years ago," said Noah, "there were great rumors everywhere about Her Majesty and her same Scottish gillie, an expert in the ways of salmon. It's whispered along the Clyde that he protects the queen's own private waters. Her Majesty and that same gillie are seen fishing there side by side or sometimes slyly hidden in the shadows of her wooded glens. God knows, the respectable press would never dare to hint at what they might do in there together."

"Too bad about such gossip," answered Finn. "If that widowed queen is fond of both salmon fishing and her gillie, where's the harm?"

"No harm," said Noah. "Every man on this island loves fishing and all, but two I know of are . . . very fond of girls."

Finn turned away from the Highlander's window and stared out at the quiet sea. A dozen snow geese, wings half set, were coming in to land. "Kungo, kungo, kungo," they called, but sheered away when they saw that men had come again.

"I look forward to a good goose dinner." Finn sighed. "I'm tired of all that salt pork, salt cod, and oatmeal porridge."

That night, Finn stayed ashore and bunked in with the mates. He enjoyed their company, but he could sense a great unease amongst them. Instead of calling him "Captain" or "Thomas" or even "Finn," they simply called him "you" or nothing at all. Finn could see the problem.

After they were finished eating, Finn, having no better place to be, sat near the light of the small mess window and examined the back pages of his log where he had sketched out a crude drawing of the floor plan and the front view of the captain's house that he would build. He had drawn it hexagonal in honor of a religious uncle of his who built the same kind of house, he said, so the devil couldn't corner him. Finn thought that shape might help him and fool the wind outside and better circulate the heat inside.

Next morning, with the help of three greenhands, Finn searched the tundra until they found two huge bleached whale jaws. Collecting these was important to do early, for late September snows would soon cover them. These immense jawbones were larger than the ones that formed the arches over the entrance to Dunston's house or the Highlander's house.

On that same afternoon, *Lancer's* carpenters hammered into the ground six stakes with one in the center to check the measurements. Noah had told Finn that the site he had chosen on a low knoll was just high enough for good summer drainage from the spring snow runoff in mid-June. It also offered him a clear view of *Lancer* in her anchorage. No Inuit were there to do the heavy work, but his crewmen, urged on with promises of rum, slowly dragged in seven large, flat rocks to create a firm and level foundation for his curious, small house. Finn helped his carpenters, Noel Wotten and Everett Roberts, to set the sills. The house would be five paces wide.

By this time, *Lancer's* greenhands had rowed in all the lumber needed and many hands helped raise the wall studs, outer boards, and roof beams. Laughing and making jokes, they nailed on the six-sided, pointed roof. When the work was done, Finn broke out a two-gallon keg of trade rum and his helpers and the builders gave his new house a very noisy and irreverent blessing.

The island's lookout men, who had not yet seen a bowhead whale this season despite constant watch, interrupted the festivities. "Stunsail, stunsail south!"

Within two hours, Caleb's boats landed by the slipway. They had lost two whales. The harpoon iron had drawn out of the first one and the second had escaped them in the last of the drifting skeins of summer ice. This bad luck had set the old man in a violent mood. When he heard that the Yacks had failed to appear, that only made him worse.

He stopped and squinted at Finn's strangely shaped dwelling. "What kind of a piss pot-shaped house are you building when I warned you not to?" Caleb growled. "Do you plan to put a spire on top and hold church services?"

79

"I intend," said Finn, "to set a well-carved weather vane up there to point the wind."

"Better pray that it points to whales. There's damned few south of here," Dunston shouted. He turned his back on Finn and marched off into his own small house and slammed the door.

"You could ask Buffalo Munro," Noel Wotten whispered to Finn, "he might carve a fish for you. He's looking around to find a well-dried piece of pan bone to shape a special rifle butt this winter. But maybe you'd be better to wait until our hunters arrive. One of them, named Kiawak, is a clever carver. He could carve a handsome whale for you. And our ironsmith, Bob, will gladly hammer out a compass post."

Next day, Finn left the building of his storm porch to his carpenters and set out with young Sammy Douglas, a lively lad who was eager to climb the long path to the Dundee lookout. Finn carried his long glass in its leather shoulder case. It was a steep hike upwards, but the climb had warmed them by the time they reached the island's highest point.

Up there, the Dundee men had built a rugged lookout, a stone crow's-nest that was about chest high and oval in shape, just wide enough for two men. It was made up of the well-worn, pillow-shaped stones that lay scattered about the hilltop. These had been chinked with smaller stones and tundra moss. Across its narrow entrance hung a weathered sealskin. Onto the port side of the lookout was lashed a long steering oar with a split blade, but wood was scarce here on these treeless Arctic islands, so the oar now served as a flagpole with a pulley nailed at its top and a loop of rope fastened to a bottom cleat. Sammy unfurled and tied on the New London Fisheries flag. Inside, a long stone seat had been erected so the lookouts could stand or sit as they waited.

Finn adjusted his long glass and began to move its eye not far beyond the rocky shore, for it was during this season that the big right whales were fond of feeding around the edges of the islands, doing what the whalers called "rock nosing."

Because he could see no sign of whales, Finn passed the glass to Sammy, who stood up peering.

"Hold on!" said Sammy. "There's something down there, maybe a ship afire, or one of those damned steam whalers. Yes, two of them, both firing up their boilers."

Finn took the glass and steadied it on the stones.

"You're right, they're heading up the eastern shore, pushing through some summer slob ice."

"Probably Hull men out of England headed up to Pangnirtung or the Kekerton station," Sammy guessed.

As the two of them started down to spread the news, the sharp-eyed Sammy stopped and pointed. "There's also something moving north of us." He adjusted Finn's long glass as he sat down. "I'd say that's a woman's boat, a big skin umiak chock-full of Eskimo women rowing toward us. Look, there's half a dozen kayaks fanned out around them. Thank God those wandering Yacks are coming at last," said Sammy. He passed the glass to Finn and started yelling as he ran downhill.

Finn, like the old man and every other whaler, was down at the Yankee slipway to greet the Inuit when the big skin boat eased near the shore. It was a shock to the greenhands and to Finn to see the size of this first women's boat, for though much narrower, it was more than half the length of *Sea Horse* and ruggedly built. It held over forty people. A humped-over old man sat steering in the stern, and more than twenty Eskimo women and girls stood, facing forward, rowing. A dozen children played among the women or lay sleeping naked in someone's hood. The small, square-rigged sail made of split sealskins was kept soaking wet by one woman who regularly threw a skin bailerful of water on it to prevent the sail from sun-drying and splitting along its seams. Besides the humans in the boat, there were piles of folded tents, bedding, fifteen or twenty husky dogs, and numerous pups. The ones known to have uncertain tempers had their muzzles tied shut.

Finn watched Dunston as he spread his arms and gave a welcoming shout, then laughed with pleasure as he caught sight of

Nilak smiling and waving to him, heaving strongly on her oar. She was the first to hop nimbly from the skin boat before it touched the shore. Then all the girls, mothers, children, and dogs jumped or climbed into the shallow water to lighten and protect the skin boat from any contact with rocks. All of them were wearing knee-high, waterproof sealskin boots.

Then the hunters came in one by one, paddling their slender, one-man kayaks into the shallow water, easing themselves out carefully onto the kayak stepping stones that had been arranged there for that purpose who knows how long ago.

Caleb Dunston, like the others, walked down straight into the water, smiling, shaking hands with all their hunting companions.

"Pootavut, where the hell have you and your bunch been hiding?" Shannon shouted as he took a puff on his cigar and passed it down to his friend, still in the kayak.

Pootavut took three long draws, smiled, swallowed all the smoke, then coughed and handed it back to Jack, who shoved it in his mouth. In Pootavut's nomadic hunting camp, there had been not a shred of tobacco for the past six moons. Pootavut, no longer young, pried his short, thick, powerful body out of his kayak's cockpit, which had been made to fit him. He stepped onto the kayak stones and stretched, then offered Noah Anderson the freshly killed seal that he had tied onto the back deck of the kayak. Noah took it with pleasure.

The eyes of the Yankee greenhands widened when they saw a younger son of Pootavut's crawl out from beneath the kayak's front deck, followed by two half-grown pups that leapt out from under the back deck onto shore.

"Here comes Pudlat now." Angelo Daluz pointed to his friend's kayak. "He's for sure the best man that I'll ever know."

The women and girls squatted or sat comfortably on the sun-warmed tundra on the bank, resting their arms and smiling, breast-feeding their children, then began passing bundles of clothing, rolled-up bearskins, caribou sleeping skins, and bulky tents up the steep embankment. Both men and women helped carry the heavier seal-oil lamps of stone and driftwood tent poles, fish spears, coils of walrus line, and several new-killed and partly eaten seals. Most precious of all were two painted accordion cases. One read on its battered label "Kinderhook, New Jersey," and the other larger one read "New Haven, Connecticut, U.S.A."

The newly arrived women of all ages – grandmothers, mothers, young wives, daughters – were slyly eyeing each mate and crewman. They smiled and gladly shook hands with the crews, proudly exposing their sometimes frightened infants in their hoods, insisting that these Yankee men shake hands with every child, including the smallest, newest infants. When Caleb shook hands with Nilak, a handsome widow, every eye watched the pair of them, the Eskimos out of curiosity and the crews trying to guess if her arrival would help to ease the awful strain that was building between the old man and the younger ice master. None of these Inuit as yet knew or cared about Finn, and because he looked young, they took him for one of the raw greenhands.

Together, all these women and their daughters lifted up the now-empty umiak and carried it above the high-tide mark, then turned it upside down to rest it on four supports made of piled rocks placed there to keep the covering of their skin umiak safe above the teeth of hungry dogs. They carefully weighted the umiak down with a few flat, heavy stones and ran lines across to hold the boat in place, for Blacklead Island often suffered quick and violent winds. The girls and women did all this while talking animatedly, delighted to be once more among these strange *kallunaat*, smelly men with beards and bushy eyebrows. Some of these crewmen were well known to them, indeed had bedded down with them. But far more exciting were the nineteen new seamen they had counted, all fresh travelers from that other unknown world so filled with unbelievable treasures. These smiling women were short in stature and good-natured. Many of them had proven themselves a good deal stronger and more willing than most of these foreigners to work hard in the whaling trade.

"I'm going up to the house right now," Dunston told Dougal. "You take charge." He beckoned to Nilak. "I've got some sewing I want her to do for me."

A young Yack male, taller than most, ran across the stony beach, eager to shake hands with the old man. The sun had deeply tanned his face, for he had camped out with all the other families on the spring ice, hunting in the glare. "Remember me, Captain?" he asked as he trotted beside the old man. "I am Lukassi," he said in halting English. "I done the talking for you last time you were here."

"Oh, sure, Lukassi, I remember you. Now where are the other hunters?" Caleb asked him, climbing at a quickening pace toward his house, with Nilak moving close behind him.

"Oh, the other hunters are coming soon. These women, they all say their husbands glad to see you here again, Captain. All traveled a long way to get back here to you."

"Lukassi, I've ordered the two cooks to boil a couple of tubs of coffee," Caleb said, "so you tell everyone to take their mugs if they want some. The cook's got lots of brown sugar and a slice of plug tobacco to give away to each of you."

"Oh, thanks, I tell them," Lukassi nodded. "We all dying for tobacco, sugar, and coffee." He turned and hurried back to tell the others, for none of them spoke or understood more than a word or two of *Kallunatitut* English. They did, however, understand Yankee ways, and the important differences between their actions and those of the Dundee men more profoundly than most foreigners could believe.

"I wonder who Lukassi's father was," Finn asked Chris Acker.

"Who knows? Who cares?" Angelo Daluz chimed in. "It's my guess Lukassi's father might have been a Dundee man. He's got dark eyes like his mother and curly, reddish hair like plenty of Scots. He's fairly tall, and he's got the look of a goddamned seaman."

"Well, nothing new in that," said Needles Wiggins, "nothing unusual about having a horny sailor for a father."

Chris Acker looked out over the water and grabbed Dougal Gibson's arm as he pointed. "Here come two of their new whale-boats that the old man traded them a year or so ago. Those hunters are using their stunsails and rowing hard, but they're not getting anywhere. Lord, both those boats are near new and they look

84

twenty years old. Dunston's quick enough to trade them a whale-boat, then leave them nothing at all to keep the boats in good repair. These hunters are deadly harpooners, strong oarsmen, great dog-team drivers, and they take good care of their skin boats. But they don't yet understand wood or paint."

"Pass me that long glass, Finn," the old man grunted as he came back down from his house, now in a much more relaxed and gentler mood. He steadied the glass against a rock and studied the approaching whaleboats.

"Those two are moving slow as turtles because . . . because . . . those . . . Yacks have got a huge right whale in tow. Oh, my God! Just what I needed. Jesus, Dougal, take a look," shouted Dunston, his moustache points aquiver. "It's riding low in the water, but you can see it. Look at those black-backed gulls hovering just above it. Examine it with the glass, Dougal. You've got younger eyes than I have. Tell me, am I right?"

"You sure are, Captain. They've got one helluva whale in tow. She'll render down to a hundred eighty, maybe a hundred and ninety barrels of oil, I'd judge!"

Caleb laughed and clapped his hands together. "That's the second grandest thing that's happened to me today. Hell, in the long run, it's the best since we left home port. Thank God the Highlander's not here to try and dicker around and trade that prize away from me. Come on, Dougal. We'll go up and have a drink of rum to celebrate my first whale this season, then eat." He did not include Finn, and left Finn's long glass lying on a rock. "Let's go. With no wind and at the rate those Yacks are moving," he laughed, "it'll be a long time before they get here."

Hours later, a number of the crewmen were still watching the twelve Inuit manning the two whaleboats as they took long, back-breaking strokes toward the island.

"Will they bring that whale ashore?" one greenhand asked.

"No," said Noah. "The tide is running out on them just as they're coming in. They'll just beach that big fish, you'll see."

Lukassi, beside Noah, blew out his breath. "*Akvik angijuvingaluk!* Whale's a really big one."

"How much would it weigh?" the greenhand asked.

"We don't give a damn about weight or length," Noah explained. "We judge a whale by the barrels of oil its blubber will provide. Some young whales give only twenty or thirty barrels, but big cows like that one, always larger than the bulls, may yield more than two hundred barrels."

"Sky's clear. It's going to stay light almost all night," said Johnny James.

"Yup, light enough to work round the clock," said Sammy.

"After we've stripped the blubber off this fish," said Noah, "the dogs, the polar bears, and foxes will feed off that carcass until the next big tide floats it away. Then, the ravens, gulls and fishes will finish off the feast."

Finn judged by his head count that the male Eskimos old enough to row a boat now numbered thirty-one, including some elders and near-grown boys. He had noticed that all these nomadic wanderers, seated motionless among the rocks, became almost invisible, their tanned faces and animal-skin clothing blending perfectly with the rocks and tundra around them.

Kudlik, the boss from the north camp, was the first to climb out of his whaleboat. He came splashing up to Caleb, rolling as he walked like a bear. He was grinning widely, for this huge whale the hunters had towed behind them was Kudlik's treasure to trade, the results of which he would share with them. Kudlik shook hands with the now half-drunk Caleb and the mates, and nodded his head toward the enormous, pale-bellied beast that lay stranded behind them with the tide running out around her. "*Pijumaviuk?*" he asked Caleb.

Dunston understood those important words, meaning, "Do you want it?" "*Ahkaluna*," he answered, "certainly!"

The deal was struck.

Caleb turned, then sighed with pleasure as he watched Nilak come out his door and start talking joyfully with the other Inuit women as they consumed his gift of coffee brewed to the weak strength they enjoyed. Each had a hard, square, hand-sized pilot

86

biscuit which they carefully shared with their children. Soon they began to unroll their bulky skin tents and set them up, using the precious driftwood poles bound to form part circles. Inside, they spread their soft skin bedrolls, and arranged their drying racks and seal-oil lamps. Most intended to stay on the island until the whale ships' holds were filled, allowing the foreigners to depart.

Using ancient stone rings that had been placed there centuries ago, the women and older children rearranged these ancestral stones, setting them firmly back in place to hold down their own tents against the violent winds that they knew would come. These waterproof skin tents had the outer hair and front claws of the seals left on for ancient, shamanistic reasons undreamed of by the sailors.

Inuit summer tent

The tents, Jack Shannon told the greenhands, did not look like New England Indian tepees because these had a long entrance made from sealskins, split as thin as parchment paper to let in light; this entrance was a good place for a woman and her smaller children to sit while she sewed and they played during the milder days and nights when hordes of mosquitoes could drive animals and humans mad. The long skin tent entrances led to a warm, womb-like circle of darkness. It was an intimate place for living, loving, birthing, sleeping, and dying. The tent itself was a family's outer skin in the warm months of the year.

Lean, hungry huskies roved between the tents and along the shores, sniffing the ground for anything to eat, raising their muzzles to inhale the tantalizing odor of the giant whale that now lay stranded in a tidal pool beyond the beach. Several of the hungriest dogs had trotted out near the enormous carcass. They glanced furtively back at the hunters' tents, afraid to touch this prize.

Using whaler's hand signals, Caleb had ordered crewmen to the storage sheds. They returned loaded with the tools of the trade: large block and tackle, coils of rope, head spades, cutting-in spades, bone spades, blubber hooks, and various knives, each sharpened to a razor edge by the ironsmith on his grindstone. Their blades were carefully sheathed in sealskin cases.

Finn followed Caleb, Dougal, and the other mates as they went off to mess while the cooks and their apprentice boys carried from the cook shack large iron pots of stew and piles of freshly baked, pie-sized biscuits. Meanwhile, Inuit went to their newly erected tents and ate the raw red flesh of seal, ducks, or salmon that they had gathered on the way. Then they all sprawled out and rested, families sleeping together peacefully.

Evening came in utter silence and the sun, instead of sinking, crept sideways like a crab feeling its way along the mountaintops, reddening the hills, the ships, the toylike buildings of the Blacklead station, and the tidal waters around the whale.

By nine o'clock that evening, everyone was out along the beach. The tide had now receded so far beyond the whale that the hardest-thrown stone could never reach it. Caleb walked along the line of comfortably seated Eskimo hunters and gave out pairs of iron crampons to the most skillful men who had worked with him before. They smiled and nodded at him as they tested with their thumb the sharpness of the iron creepers before they unwound the leather ankle laces.

Caleb wandered out and in Inuit style stroked the whale he had been given, running his hand along the flexible black money bone in its mouth. These long, precious baleen sieves hung down like a giant's well-combed beard. There were about five hundred of the tapered strands, and the larger front ones were longer than a man with his arms upraised. This springy baleen corset bone was now so much in demand that those long, bending strands in this single fish's mouth would easily buy a good house, a champion trotting horse, or many, many acres of New England farmland.

"Have you seen other whales cut up on a beach before?" Finn asked Otto.

The German shook his head. "Sperm whalers stripped them in deep water, where the whole whale carcass can roll so easy."

The air was breathlessly still, and fortunately the whole local hatch of island mosquitoes had perished in the morning's cold. But others would soon fly off the ponds to plague them almost until the autumn snows.

"This is going to be quite a sight," said Finn. "Whaling's new to me."

Beached bowhead

The old man and the mates warned the greenhands back when Kudlik, the important man who had brought in the whale, approached carrying a long-handled, swordlike tool. Standing on his toes, he reached up and cut away a small portion of the enormous flipper that projected an arm's length behind its right eye. It was covered with the delicious black outer skin that the Yacks call *muktuk*.

With the help of his sons, Kudlik dragged back to his grandmother this most special of all gifts. The old woman, smiling widely, sliced off the first piece with her *ulu* knife shaped like a half-moon and took a bite, cutting with the blade held dangerously close to her lips. The other women gasped with pleasure as they watched this sacred ritual performed in honor of Kudlik's grandmother and the whale.

"There," Noah whispered to the ice master, "that first important part of the ceremony is done. Now watch. The hunters are about to perform their part. It's kind of like a dance."

Each hunter, as he approached the whale, spoke a word or two to her before reaching up and giving the huge creature several affectionate strokes and pats to show their gratitude and perhaps to show the amulets sewn on their parkas.

"Watch that man, Pudlat." Noah nudged Finn. "He's going to cut off that whole flipper. Like any Inuit hunter, he knows exactly where that giant knuckle joint is hidden and where to cut the tendons."

When the flipper fell, four of his relatives went forward and dragged the massive piece away among the rocks. Two of the older women went and sat on guard beside the flipper so that no dogs could eat it or defile it.

The Inuit with iron crampons hurried out beside the whale and bound them to their boots. Given a heave by their friends, these spike men clambered up the steep side of the huge fish, using their long gaff hooks like mountain climbers' axes. No sooner were these men on top of the whale than some, using their sharp spades, began digging for the smaller, spinal vertebrae, carefully cutting through the tendons, causing the huge, black tail flukes to fall. These wing-like, butterfly-shaped flukes were as wide as five men standing with arms outstretched, fingers touching.

"Don't we crewmen get to do anything here?" asked a Quebecois.

"Bide your time!" Caleb shouted. "All of you look sharply and learn how this is done. You may sometime have to cut up a whale and take the corset bones without these hardy Yacks to do it for you." The old man went on, "Stripping the blubber off a fish without thrashing its carcass around in the water, like those damned sperm whalers, is quite a trick to learn. Keep your eyes peeled, all of you."

When one Eskimo spike man struggled and finally gained the highest rise on the whale, a shout of congratulations went up from the greenhands, but there was not a sound from the Eskimo hunters or their families, who believed that the *inua*, or spirit, of this immense sea beast would be lingering close by, watching and listening to her own dismemberment through the eyes of her slowly departing soul. Silently, the hunters began their dissection with their sharpened iron spades. They all knew that the completion of this butchery would be impossible as long as the giant fish remained upon her back. When the tide floated the carcass a little, Caleb would have the challenge of turning her over with the capstans, peeling off the blubber as the whale was turned.

When Caleb and his mates walked down to make a close inspection of the whale, they found themselves already ankle-deep in a returning tide that was reddening around the fish.

"Have them grease that capstan with blubber, Mr. Gibson!" Caleb bellowed up at Dougal. "And you, Mario, see that those greenhands lay the oak planks neatly along the slipway. Two of our whaleboats are bringing in some extra rope, and chain, and tackle from *Sea Horse*."

The women and young hunters' sons had caught two dozen of the strongest dogs and had harnessed them into a fan hitch with long sealskin lines attached to a heavy Fisheries work sled. Strips of smooth whalebone had been screwed to its oak runners to make sliding easier.

The tide was almost to Caleb's knees when he paused to stare up at the whale's eye. It was the size of their cook's largest iron frying pan, dully reflecting now the low rays of the evening sun. The waters chilled his inner thighs as he watched Kudlik and Pootavut, the other Eskimo boss, wading ashore.

Lukassi, the interpreter, called, "Captain, Kudlik says that fish is floating just a little. What you want him to do?"

"Tell him, fasten the head chains," the old man called. "When that's done, cut the head off!" Caleb yelled. "Dougal, hail in all the strongest men and women round the capstan!"

The old man splashed up out of the rising tide, which had become waist-deep and numbed his crotch.

"*Atai! Manna, manna!*" yelled Kudlik.

"Get her going," Caleb roared. "Put your backs into it, gentle-men, and ladies, too. Let's roll this big mother of a fish."

A willing crowd of hunters, their women, and ship's crewmen began to heave around the iron-cored capstan, forcing their muscular weight against the thick, oak bars which turned slowly, grudgingly.

"Keep her going. She's starting. Heave!" the old man roared. "She's going over onto her side."

Two kayakmen set out toward the whale; their job was to cut free blanket-wide peels of blubber that would roll off the floating fish. As the fish rolled, they uncoiled the peels off her body.

"*Namuktuk!* Enooof!" Kudlik shouted so the foreigners would understand.

Now Finn watched the two men shearing the huge upper gum away from the fish's head, with its hundreds of dangling, quivering strainers of feather-edged black baleen. Before it fell into the water, the kayakmen stroked away out of danger. To allow its massive weight to be hauled in, the kayakmen returned and hooked on the tackle chain, attaching it to the immensely oil-rich tongue. Finn noticed that the tongue alone was larger than the mattresses from a dozen double beds all piled together.

"*Atai!*" Kudlik called, circling his hands, signaling to Dougal to start the windlass turning again, winching ashore this enormous weight.

"Go, go, *atai, atai!* Heave!" Caleb bellowed. "Heave!"

Buffalo Munro, Mario, Dougal, the greenhands, women, strong young girls, and eager lads grabbed the bars, helping to draw the precious whalebone load toward the shore.

"Now she's coming," Otto shouted, straining to guide the thick rope hawser so it would drag the tongue and rich baleen up the middle of the well-greased plankway.

Next came the first of the long, fat white blankets that had been unrolled from around the fish by the kayakmen. The old man signaled to the hunters who, with their sharp spades, cut the immense weight of blubber into four separate parts to reduce the weight. Then, reattaching hooks to the blubber, those who manned the capstan drew the thick blanket piece slowly up the ramp. The next three pieces slid more easily because the oak planking was now so slick with grease. The whale's huge rib cage, stripped and abandoned, stood more than the height of two tall men above the water.

For some reason that Finn could never understand, he turned his head and looked behind him. There, moving in the faint, white smoke drifting from the try-pot's fire, he saw several girls. He wondered if they were the ones his crew had told him they had bedded. The girls looked very young to him. They grinned and ducked back quickly out of sight. Finn's thoughts drifted to wild stories of the sailmaker's shed where some claimed they had nested two winters earlier with one or more of their chosen girls among yards and yards of yielding sailcloth. Thinking about it made Finn feel lonely.

Noah had told him that the old man had no objection to the mates or crewmen sleeping with the local girls, but he swore he'd put in irons any man of any rank who dared to strike a light inside any of the Fisheries sheds. It was well known that Dunston had once experienced a devastating fire and would become almost hysterical at the very mention of that word, for he knew how quickly wind-fanned flames could wipe away an Arctic whaling station.

Lukassi, the interpreter, came up to Acker, who was standing close to Finn. "Who is the captain of that other ship?" he asked, pointing at *Lancer*.

Acker smiled at Lukassi. "It is this man, Captain Finn. He is an ice master and captain of that bigger ship."

"You're joking me," said Lukassi. "He too young to captain."

"No," said Acker. "He's that ship's captain."

"You're lucky," gasped Lukassi. "Not much older than me and yet you're boss of a ship like that."

Try-pot and paddle

Chapter 7

"Finn, what the hell's gone wrong with you?" the old man shouted. "I see you standing around looking useless. That's my whale – totally. Maybe you can try to outsmart me later. Anyway, it's time for some coffee. I'm leaving the rest of the cutting to Kudlik and his people. Otto and Jack can boss the capstan. Dougal's coming and you can join us, Finn. Bring Acker with you."

Finn wondered about the old man's rudeness and anger. Was he weakening? Had he decided to set a different tack in his opposition to the new house?

Finn paused and looked back as the now-floating carcass of the whale rolled again. The enormous spiral of blubber continued to peel off the fish's flesh and bones. Moving just beneath the water, it looked like a shining white path slithering toward the slipway.

Finn followed Caleb cautiously into the old man's house. The colorful Fisheries pennant was now draped across the whole rear wall and the canvas curtains once more hung so they could be pulled against prying eyes.

"You'll notice I've put that settee over against the coolest wall so visitors are not likely to overstay their welcome," the old man said.

Finn felt relaxed enough to look at the three famous pictures, all in place. The largest, with its elaborate oval frame, was a sepia photograph of *Sea Horse* sailing off Block Island with her twenty-seven sails all set. The next photograph was of Topsail House in Mystic. The third was a limner's watercolor of Caleb and his high-stepping trotter, Dan. Driving the sulky was the old man himself, wearing racing silks and a jockey's cap, sitting grandly upright in the breeze, his moustache points bent back from the speed. Beside the picture, there was a carving made from a polished piece of corset bone shaped like a bowhead whale. This flat black cutout had a scratched, white oval at its center stating "239-barrel cow – Taken by C. Dunston, First Mate – No. 2 whaleboat off Blacklead Island, August 12, 1861." Finn noted that not a single picture of Dunston's wife or daughter hung inside this house.

In the window glass, Finn could see the reflection behind him of the handsome Nilak half filling four mugs of coffee, which the old man grandly topped off with raw trade rum. Noah had told Finn that Nilak was an important widow, sister to the camp boss, Pootavut. Now in her mid-thirties, she had been Caleb's Arctic mistress for the last six years. She was short, strong, quick-eyed, and as diligent as the best of good New England housewives.

Finn watched Nilak hurry outside and leap up to reach the new skin line she had strung between the house and an upright stunsail boom that held her work safe from the tearing teeth of sled dogs. Nilak was airing a quilt she had filled with Arctic eiderdown, two caribou sleeping skins, and two aging, red Hudson's Bay point blankets, as well as a long suit of Caleb's woolen underwear, and two pairs of his soft sealskin boots and thick, thigh-length, caribou-skin stockings. Using whalebone clothes-pegs, she had also hung four herring gull skins, which she planned to cut and sew into warm, waterproof slippers to go inside her lover's boots.

"Well, that's one helluva good start to a big season," the old man said to Dougal and Acker. "I mean, sailing in on the station and having Kudlik finally arrive to deliver me this first big fish, with her mouth loaded with more than a ton of money bone, which is to say a flowered carpetbag stacked full of money. With prices being as high as they are, a man can't really beat that, can he?"

95

Finn sat dead still and stared at Caleb. He quickly downed his rum and coffee as Nilak came in again. Finn saw the old man blink his eyes at her, a signal not to offer any more. Taking the message, Finn and the two mates rose and left. Was life here going to go on as mean-spirited as this?

Caleb took out his key and unlocked his sea chest and rummaged around inside until he found his pewter flask containing his own best rum. Unscrewing its top, he filled his cup halfway to the brim, then Nilak's with a quarter.

"*Coppilu*," he nodded to her, meaning, "coffee also." She poured a light skim of black coffee into both their mugs.

"Nilak, here's looking at you, dear!" Caleb smiled. "Drink hearty!"

"*Ayii!*" she answered softly and smiled at Caleb. Her dark eyes sparkled and her even teeth were white and worn slightly flat from chewing skins to chamois softness.

"Now this is worth drinking," said Caleb as they tipped back their heads and drank. "I've got a feeling that my goddamned ice master is going to be a millstone round my neck."

Nilak didn't understand a word that Dunston said. She and this captain of hers had been apart for more than a year while she had moved freely with her brother's camp, thinking only in her own language.

"Want another shot of rum?" he asked .

Knowing the word "rum," Nilak smiled and held out her cup.

"Oh, it's *piujupaluk*, very good, to be on this Yankee Island of ours," said Caleb, "thousands of miles away from those tit-headed Fisheries partners. Good to be back here alone with you, dear Nilak, and a good hunting season coming up, I hope."

Nilak nodded when she heard her name. She had appreciated the two Inuktitut words that her Caleboosi had injected. But neither of them really cared, for they had been friends and lovers for so long that they moved together into a bond of trust. The important fact about their life together, aside from little ups and downs, was a mutual feeling of comfort, yes, comfort, about everything. They both drank their rum.

"You want another *imialuk, rumlu, coppilu?*" Caleb asked her. "Just a nightcap before we take our nap?"

Nilak leaned tenderly against Caleb's side. "*Ahkaluna,* certainly," she said, and smiled at him.

Caleb poured a finger-and-a-half for her, then three fingers for himself. "I don't want to spoil this performance," he said. "It's been a helluva long morning. But who cares? That was one mothering huge whale Kudlik traded me to get things started this year."

Nilak was humming softly now and weaving like a dancer as she made her way to the inner door and took several tries to set the hook into the eye, then went and, bending, turned back the cover on the captain's double bed. Smiling, Nilak blew out the light, and, laughing, they rolled together beneath her homemade eiderdown.

No one rose on Blacklead until noon next day, for everyone was worn out from their previous eighteen hours of backbreaking work and whatever varied types of sail's loft play that had occurred. Caleb's main objective had been achieved. Not only had every pound of corset bone and whale blubber been dragged ashore, but some of the crewmen had even started to build their lemminglike winter love nests again.

Finn kept his eye on several good-looking girls as they helped the married women and younger boys stuff scraps of whale blubber for fuel under the four iron try-pots set up on stones above fire pits. These pots were big, so big that he had watched two women climb into a single pot and kneel to scrub out the rust. When the oil fire was started, it gave off thick, rolling clouds of smoke that smelled like bacon frying in his mother's kitchen.

The first load of blubber had been stored beside the try-pots in what Finn heard crewmen call the blubber parlor: simple wooden walls set up to keep the fat from slithering around. These yard-square pieces were first sliced thin with mincing knives into what most whalers called Bible leaves. These chunks of skin and blubber, like a big, open book, were then laid carefully inside the pots. When they began to melt, they quickly rendered into oil.

97

Looking across a try-pot, Finn noticed a girl he had not seen before. She could not have come ashore with all the others from the women's boat, for he would never have missed seeing a person whose looks appealed so much to him. She stood near the try-pots now, a step or two away from all the others, an overwhelming vision of a girl, with a smooth, tanned face, full lips, and wide cheekbones. Her hair was blue-black, shiny, and braided tight. It was her Asian-looking eyes that stopped him. They were beautifully upward curving.

When she saw that he was watching her, she quickly turned her back, then looked around and eyed him curiously. He smiled at her before she stepped away into the smoke. Although Finn moved quickly to port and then to starboard, trying to catch another glimpse of this unbelievable vision, she did not reappear.

"Do you know that new girl with the blue beads on her parka front?" Finn asked the interpreter.

"Not well," said Lukassi, carefully watching the young captain's eyes. "Her name is Pia."

Lukassi turned and hurried toward the small crowd of women who could still be seen through the drifting curtains of smoke and fog as they used long paddles to stir the slices of blubber, rendering them into oil.

Pia, that's a good name, thought Finn. It's short and easy to remember. He rested, leaning against a barrel top, turning to admire the many angles of his new, six-sided house. Looking back, he saw the girl again, bending double as she came out from one of the tents that stood upwind from the melting pots. This time she was holding a small child by the hand.

"Pia," Finn called to her. "Pia, is that your name?"

She stopped and raised her eyebrows, meaning yes.

"Is that small boy yours?" Finn pointed to him.

The girl used no words, but wrinkled her nose and shut her eyes, a woman's way of saying no. Finn did not understand.

"My name . . . is . . . Thomas, Tom . . . Finn."

"Ayii, Finnussi."

She corrected him, giving his name that smoother, rhythmic sound that Inuit prefer. "*Angiugkar umiakjuak ipunganai.* They say you're boss of that bigger *umiakjuak*, ship. Is . . . new house . . . they're building . . . for you?" She asked him in easy Inuktitut, hoping he might understand.

Finn could only smile at her, for he did not know the words.

She smiled back, then looked at her youngest brother. "He's got to – *annar usuktuk*," she said, pointing at his rear end. They both smiled again as she hurried the small boy away, for he was trying every step or two to squat down in the path.

"Your father's name, what is it?" Finn asked when Pia passed again.

Not understanding him, she smiled and, picking up the boy, ran toward the tent.

A feeling of desperation gripped Finn, for he felt certain that if he left this treasure of a girl to wander among experienced Arctic men, someone would surely grab her off before he had a chance. Hold on, he thought, get Lukassi or Noah to help you. Use your authority, but don't miss out on this.

That same evening, Finn invited Lukassi to view the inside of his newly finished house.

"Noel and Everett, with two Inuit and three Nova Scotians working together, built this house," Finn told Lukassi, "this wide bed, a table and small, slant-top desk, a bench, and two chairs, and now it's all but finished. I'm going to nail up *Lancer*'s red pennant over on that wall and hang a chart of Newfoundland over the bed to make me feel at home. We tested the new coal stove yesterday, it works fine. Isn't she a beauty?"

"Good house, good stove!" said Lukassi. "Need not you somebody to help here, keep clean? Camp bosses, ship bosses, every captain got some woman to help them. Our good hunters, some got two wives, three wives! You got not one. Got not . . . not got . . . how do I say that right? My English is still slow to come."

"You said it fine." Finn nodded. He studied his new pine floor. "Well, it's true," he said. "I'm going to need someone to keep this place shipshape, do mending, wash the clothes, and sweep up."

"Well, old Ikaluk, she knows houses, used to sweep up for the Highlander. He's not here yet, maybe not coming. So how about Ikaluk? She's a good widow woman, yes. She sews good. She could be kind of mother to you."

"I don't need any mother right now." Finn laughed. "I've had my mothering."

"An old woman is what Captain Dunston said to find you." Lukassi smiled. "Somebody who knows enough to sew your dick inside your trousers."

"That sounds like him," said Finn. "That old bastard could use some sewing up himself. Remember, Lukassi, the old man is very bullheaded. But I'm captain of my ship and she's bigger than his. Forget old women. He's not ruining my life."

"Then what you want me to do?" asked Lukassi.

"Don't ask any old widow. I'll decide who's going to work for me."

Lukassi leered at Finn, then wiggled his finger in an impish way.

Finn said, "Noah says that Supa's the father of that girl, Pia. Is Pia's family new here?"

"*Ayii*, Supa's never been here before," said Lukassi. "Ulayu's her mother. They just arrive yesterday. They sail over here from Kekerton in Supa's small skin boat. Supa ask me to help him with the talking so he can tell Captain Caleboosi that he want to hunt, to row boats, to work here with us."

"Is Supa a good man?" Finn asked.

"I don't know him," Lukassi said.

"Why did Supa leave Kekerton?"

Young Lukassi shrugged his shoulders. "I can ask him. Maybe he did something a captain not like up there. Or somebody did something bad to Supa or his family." Eager to change the subject, Lukassi smiled at Finn. "Most Inuit around here say you're not much older than me."

"I'm not that young," said Finn.

"You look young." Lukassi smiled. "Old Noah that sleeps out on your ship, he say he's too old to be your father. But you're his boss, his captain. It never happens that way around here."

Finn curled his finger against his upper lip and said, "If I grew a big walrus moustache, you'd see me as an older man. Find out for me about Pia's father. I want to know why Supa came from Kekerton."

"*Ayii, ayii,* Captain." Lukassi raised his eyebrows. "I'll ask for you." He hurried out the door.

Lukassi returned just as Finn was leaving.

"You still want to know what happened to Supa," Lukassi asked, "when they were up at Kekerton this spring?"

Finn nodded.

"The shipsmen up there are you know Scottiismen and Engliismen. Together they made some *imialuk* of their own, the strongest, baddest kind of drink. Like swallowing fire, Supa said. The big front stroke with a beard from their larboard boat was falling around drunk, making like he was a little boy just playing. That crazy man got hold of Supa's wife, Ulayu, and he started swinging her around until she was straight out like flying. Pia's mother started screaming. Supa stopped the man and made him put his wife down. The big man got mad at Supa and hit him so hard in the mouth that quite a few of Supa's teeth flew out. They say there's three ship's captains up there, but none of them see the trouble. When they hear about it, they all got mad at Supa. And the boss captain told Supa to take his family and to get far away from Kekerton, told him never come back. Told Supa he was never going to get any more gunpowder or shot, no fishhooks, no molasses, no biscuits, no tobacco, no rum ration – no nothing! After five days of getting nothing, Supa told the captain again that it was not his fault, that he only stopped the man because it looked like he was going to kill his wife. The captain didn't give a damn. He just told Supa to get out."

"My God," said Finn, "those bastards! Maybe it would help Supa's family if . . ."

"You want to hire Supa's wife, Ulayu?" Lukassi asked. "People here say she's a good woman. She say she washed and cleaned the mates' house up at Kekerton, and my aunt told me she's a real good sewer. You only got to look at Supa's boots to see how fine she sews."

The ice master stood in the middle of his house, staring up at the point in his new roof. "I don't need his wife, Ulayu," Finn admitted. "How . . . how about his daughter, Pia? Do you think that she can sew?"

"No, she is too young to sew," said Lukassi. "She couldn't sew boots that would keep out water, not unless her mother helped her. But she could sweep a bit, and maybe sew a button on your shirt or put a patch over that hole in your pants. *Ayii*, I guess she could do easy things like that."

"Yes, then." Finn coughed. "Her mother could help Pia sometimes, and I could give her spools of thread, and needles, and maybe some coffee and sugar and some tobacco twists," he suggested. "Why don't you go over and ask Supa and Ulayu if it would be all right for their daughter, Pia, to come over here and work for me?"

"*Ayii, ayii*." Lukassi smiled and rolled his eyes. "Don't go away, Captain. I'll be back damn quick."

An hour later, Lukassi arrived, this time pushing Supa ahead of him. "Captain, I asked this man about his daughter, Pia, working for you."

Supa shifted uneasily from one foot to the other, then leaned against the doorjamb. He began to speak to Lukassi in a deep, husky-sounding voice. The interpreter watched Supa's eyes intently, then turned his gaze to Finn's face.

"He say you can have her, but you got to be careful of her. He doesn't want you to hurt her. He say up at Kekerton, an oarsman nearly killed his wife, and when he tried to stop him, Supa lost four teeth and got to leave that place, forever."

Supa opened his mouth and showed the wide gap in his teeth. Finn shook his head in sympathy.

Lukassi went on, "Supa say he's nervous now about you foreigners. He don't want no trouble. He don't want to get sent away again by no captain."

"Oh, you tell him I would never hurt a young girl like his daughter," said Finn.

Supa started yacking fast and Lukassi translated. "He wants you to know that his daughter is not much good at anything yet. Her mother say Pia's sewing's bad and that she can't hardly even soften sinew in her mouth. And she's no good at scraping skins, she makes too many cuts. But if you want her, you can have her. Supa say if you're not bad to Pia, her mother will sew you sealskin boots and mittens that won't let water come inside."

Supa got excited and started yacking fast straight at Finn. "Is it true," Supa asked him, "that somebody as young as you is boss of that biggest *umiakjuak* out there?"

Without interpreting, Lukassi told Supa it was true.

"You must have lots of things to trade in the belly of that boat," Supa yacked back in Inuktitut. "My wife, Ulayu says her old button accordion has got some splits in it now. She's tried, but she can't sew it right to make the good noises it used to make. Maybe I go out in my kayak and harpoon a narwhal with a good, long tusk. Would you trade me a small accordion for that? My wife wants to know."

"Sure, I would," said Finn, "if you get me a really good, long unicorn tusk that isn't cracked or broken at the point."

Supa smiled, showing again where his four teeth were missing. "I'll get you a good one, Captain. I got good amulets from her." He pointed at a fresh bird's wing sewn to his parka and a bear tooth strung around his neck.

"Who's 'her'?" asked Finn, but Lukassi closed his eyes and wouldn't answer.

Button accordion

As the sun eased its way into an evening nest of clouds, Finn flung his pea jacket over his shoulders and hurried to mess. When he returned, he found Lukassi with Pia waiting just inside his darkened house. She didn't smile at Finn, but made her eyes go wide in recognition. She had four beautiful caribou skins rolled under one arm. The insides of each had been scraped pure white. When Finn lit his lamp, Pia let the skins drop to the floor.

"She wants to know if you want her to start working for you now," asked Lukassi.

"Yes, yes. I guess so." Finn nodded boyishly at Pia. "I don't know where she should start or exactly what she's going to do, but, yes, Lukassi, you tell her she's hired."

When Lukassi interpreted that, Pia told him she was binding the handle on a goose-wing brush so she could sweep his floor.

"And she says her mother's making you a pair of knee-high boots. And her father has been out in his kayak hunting all day for a narwhal, one with a good, long tusk for you. He has not seen the right one yet."

Pia seemed to enjoy talking fast in a high and pleasant singsong voice to Lukassi, but while speaking, she kept looking straight at Finn.

"She tells me she's not too good at sewing," Lukassi explained, "but she believes she's good enough to sew a sleeping bag for you out of those caribou skins. They will, she says, have the hair turned inside warm against your skin. She wants to know if she can sew it over here on your new, clean floor."

"Sounds good to me," said Finn. "There's lots of floor space here." He smiled nervously at Pia.

There was a long pause, then the girl pointed at Finn's bed and asked him in Inuktitut, "Bag single you want made by me?"

Lukassi continued to translate further, saying, "She says single bags are narrow, not too good."

Finn looked puzzled.

Pia continued.

"She asks if you want her to make a big double sleeping bag. You ever seen that kind, Captain?" Lukassi smiled. "Two people fit inside them just nice."

"I guess I've got to choose," said Finn, and he bit his lower lip. "Oh, well, you'd better tell her, Lukassi, to make a big one. Yes, a bag big enough for two."

Pia raised her eyebrows, then quickly turned around, leaving the soft caribou skins where they had fallen. Lukassi leered at Finn, then followed her out of the house.

Finn stood for a moment, his whole being caught in a silent uproar. Then, as he buttoned his old pea jacket, he performed a quick double pigeon wing, a dance step he had learned aboard a New Brunswick herring schooner. He had to get a grip on himself before he hurried outside. He could see Caleb standing near the try-pots, talking to his cooper, Ezra Morse, who was working with the help of the other cooper, Lester Lewis. They were knocking up the larger casks and hammering tight the iron hoops that bound them into form.

"I noticed, Ice Master, that there's been a lot of coming and going from that crazy-looking house of yours," the old man snapped. "And some of your crew are passing a rumor around that *Lancer* is leaking so badly she's going to spend her winter on the bottom of this sound. Are you going to let that happen? Is your whole mind set on nothing but bedding down with Supa's daughter?"

"Chris!" Finn yelled. "Otto! Both of you, come with me. We're going out to have a look at *Lancer*."

When Finn and his two mates got down into *Lancer*'s lower hold, the leakage was nothing like the rumor that the old man was spreading. Finn had assigned two greenhands to take turns on the pump, but when all the water had been pumped up and spilled out across the main deck into the scuppers and the pump had started sucking air, the pump men had settled down comfortably inside the empty cook shack, eaten their dinner, and gone to sleep. It scarcely mattered, there was so little water coming in that even one man on the Yankee pump could easily have handled Caleb's overblown crisis.

Finn cursed the old man for starting such a rumor, especially with *Lancer*'s hold jammed, at his suggestion, with airtight, empty oil casks that would float the ship if she did run into trouble. As he stood in the reeking, oil-soaked hold, he became steaming angry.

Hearing soft skin boots sneaking down the ladder, Finn turned and saw the old man coming toward him with Dougal and his carpenter behind. Dunston began to make a noisy show of kicking the bit of water and running his hands against the few small trickles that shimmered inside the tarred hull.

"What are you doing on my ship, Captain?" Finn yelled angrily. "She's dry as needs be." Finn's face was grim.

"Make damned sure you keep her that way," the old man growled.

Tom Finn gave Dunston a savage look. "She's pumped out all but dry and I'm having my ship's keeper check her hold every day."

Caleb stood and stared at him as Finn's temper flared again.

"I'll order you off my ship, if I have to," Finn warned him. "I'm not taking any more horseshit from you." Finn turned his back on the old man, bent, and pretended to fiddle with the pump.

"You shut your mouth, lad. I'm the senior captain of these two ships!" shouted Caleb.

The old man headed toward the ladder cursing. Dougal, following him, looked back at Finn and winced.

Three days later, _Lancer_ was fully caulked again and taking almost no water. Finn could hardly wait until she was safely locked in ice for the winter.

Noah leaned against _Lancer_'s rail near Finn and pointed into the water. "These Yack people believe there is a woman who lives down there beneath us. They've got a lot of names for her – Talulijuk, Sedna, or Tikanikamsilik. She's the one they say who controls the sea beasts. Whales, walrus, seals, fish. If the people get enough to eat in summer or winter, it's because she allowed the sea creatures to give themselves to the humans. It's got nothing to do with Inuit cleverness or whether they're good hunters. In their minds, it's got to do with sharing and a sense of respect for those other beings, the animals. Do you know how she got down there?"

Finn glanced curiously at Noah. "Have you been drinking by yourself out here, or are you serious? What's she supposed to look like?"

"Oh, I'm serious, but it's kind of a long story. Let me shorten it for you by starting in the middle. Sedna – most here call her Talulijuk – was a young girl who had recently become a woman and had given birth to a litter of half-human, half-doglike creatures out on a small island not far from here. Her father was bringing her back home with him when a violent storm struck them. The father's hunting companions had an abundance of walrus meat in their umiak and as the waves began to rise and splash into the boat, the hunters were forced to throw out whole sides of meat to lighten their load. But when all the meat was gone, the waves went on swamping the boat. 'Someone has to get out,' the men yelled, 'or all of us will drown.'

"Sedna, being the least needed among them, was then forced out of the boat. She screamed in desperation and tried to climb back in, but her father cut off her fingers and they became all the seals that swim. When Sedna tried to climb in again, he cut off her hands at the wrists, and they became all the walruses of the sea. Then, in a third and last, desperate attempt, Sedna hooked her arms over the side of the boat, but they were hacked off at the elbows and became all the whales of the world.

"Sedna sank beneath the waves and became the armless, half-seal, half-human goddess, forever angry at all mankind. Unless humans appease her and beg down through the ice for her to help them, she will hold back all the creatures of the sea. These northern sea hunters live where no food grows out of the land. They and their families would starve to death if even for one winter the animals failed them. That's how risky Inuit life can be," said Noah.

"Do you believe that?" Finn asked him.

"I don't know just what to believe," old Noah answered. "But these people here live by her rules."

Finn sent Acker and Kraus back to shore, but he lived aboard for the balance of the week, saying he wanted to check on the soundness of the new caulking and pine-pitch tarring on *Lancer*'s seams. But the more honest reason was that he wanted to keep away from the old man. He used this quiet period to let his outport Newfie sense of rage seep out of him and to think about his own life. What kind of money-grubbing fool had he turned out to be, abandoning the familiar life of ice master aboard *Huntress* to sail up here and find himself caught by this mean-spirited, cantankerous old Yankee bastard? He knew nothing about the Arctic whaling trade. He grimaced at his image in the small shaving mirror that hung on his cabin wall. God, was he only here because he had the luck to survive the horror of that dory, or would this be two years out of his life wasted on nothing? Finn lay down on the moldy gray settee and allowed his mind to wander leisurely over the women he had known, before it approached the exciting thought of Pia.

She seemed to grab Finn, causing him to heave up off the old ship's couch, wondering how she had filled him with so much yearning tonight. That thought caused Finn to draw in his breath. "I am not going to spend my life up here like some cloistered monk in a freezing monastery," Finn said aloud as he jerked on his pea jacket and hurried out onto *Lancer's* frosted deck.

Trying to peer through the gathering darkness, Finn could see three dim spots of light ashore. Was one of those his house? He wondered, would Pia be waiting inside for him, just finishing sewing their double sleeping bag? He had a second image of her standing straight-legged, bending with her animal gracefulness, tidying his floor with her clever goose-wing brush. Finn felt overwhelmed with excitement. Good God! he thought, it would take less than ten minutes to lower away and row ashore to find her. He had a clear vision of the soft brown fur inside their double sleeping bag. Would she really be waiting there? he wondered. He could see himself crawling naked into that wide sack with Pia waiting. He imagined them laughing, playing together, breathing excitedly, trying each other out for the first time in that ticklish, caribou-skin hideaway. "I'm going in this minute," Finn said aloud.

Noah Anderson came shuffling toward him, carrying the ship's lantern. "Bad habit, talking to yourself, Captain, when you're out here alone on deck."

"Noah, I'm leaving *Lancer* in your charge. I'm going ashore in the whaleboat. Untie that other rope and we'll let her down."

"Sure thing," said Noah, setting down his lantern. "I had the idea, Captain, that you were staying aboard for another day or so."

"Changed my mind," said Finn. "It's a calm night, and *Lancer*'s seams are holding fine. You keep those two greenhands ready to work the pump if she starts taking on water. There's something I need a lot tonight and it's ashore."

Noah coughed. "Captain, I heard you and the old man when you were having a shouting match down in the hold. You be careful of cursing out Dunston. You two could turn this winter into hell for everybody, Yacks and seamen alike."

The hemp ropes made a whirring sound as the boat went down. Finn scrambled over the side into the ship's fore channel, then hopped nimbly down into the center of the boat. He lashed two oars in place as Noah shone the bull's-eye lantern on them, then set out over the water toward Blacklead.

"Goodnight to you, Captain!" Noah called. "I hope you find whoever she is you're seeking."

"With luck, I'll settle this whole problem tonight," Finn answered as he rowed off into the starry darkness, taking long, strong strokes.

He tied the whaleboat to a heavy rock up on the beach, knowing that when the tide ran out, she would be let down onto a soft gravel bottom. Finn made a quick run up the steep bank beside the Yankee slipway, pausing when he reached the capstan to catch his breath and set his bearings in the dark. He walked swiftly along the narrow path worn in the tundra, heading toward the silhouette of his new house.

Suddenly, Finn stopped and stared in horror at the empty ring of stones where the Supa family's tent had stood. How could it be gone? He ran over and stood inside the circle where it once had been. There was absolutely nothing there at all!

He waited in the starlit darkness, trying to settle his mind. What in God's name had happened here? He walked quickly to his doorway and opened it. No one was there. He crossed the room and lit the lamp. There lay the wide, new sleeping bag, elegantly smoothed and spread across his rope-cord bed. A handsome pair of sealskin boots and mittens were perched atop his sea chest at its foot.

Only then did Finn see the note that lay on his desk, held in place by his pewter ink pot. Finn unfolded the paper and tilted it to catch the lamp's glow.

Friend:

Lukassi asked me to write to you saying Supa has gone with his family caribou hunting over on Baffinland. Supa told him it's a hard season to find caribou, but <u>THE Captain</u> sent him anyway. Lukassi says to tell you that Supa will be gone a month – or maybe more. I know you'll miss that family.

Chris

"Damn! Damn! Double damn!" Finn hammered his fist on top of the desk. "I wish that miserable son-of-a-bitch would mind his own bloody business and let me mind mine!"

Finn was too enraged to think of taking off his clothes, too mad to do anything but curse and fume in his frustration. Rolling himself in a pair of blankets, he flopped down on top of his soft, new sleeping bag. So overwhelmed with anger was Finn that light began to filter through his windows before he fell exhausted into a deep sleep.

Chapter 8

When the ice master awoke, he tried hard not to think of Pia or that awful bastard who mastered the Blacklead station. Instead, he concentrated on the springy comfort of his new wide, four-poster bed. Underneath, he could feel the thick warmth of the double bag. Everett had placed the small table he had made near the iron stove and his slant-top desk close beside the window's light. Tom eyed the new Fisheries lantern suspended by a long, thin chain from the central point of his house peak.

As Finn got out of bed, he swore aloud, "That's the last, damned, dirty trick that old bugger's ever going to pull off on me." He stamped his foot on his sturdy floor, releasing more of its pleasing smell of fresh-cut pine. It made him feel better. "Maybe I can wait one moon, but I pray to God, not two! Stay calm, Finn," he warned himself. "Winter's coming. Keep busy, get to know this country and the Yacks and crews. That dear girl, Pia, will be back here soon to warm your life. Make the waiting worthwhile, figure out a way to square up with that treacherous son-of-a-bitch."

Everett was whistling when he walked over to Finn's house, swinging his heavy toolbox like a boy. Whistling aboard ship was known to bring bad luck, but it was considered the exact reverse ashore. While the weather was good, Everett was eager to tight-caulk Finn's window frames.

"I heard the old man using Lukassi to interpret last week," Everett told Finn. "Heard him order that new hunter, Supa, to take his family and go look for caribou way over on the Baffin side. I heard him say, 'Don't come back for a moon or two.' I saw him fan out the fingers of both his hands four times, saying, '*Kuliitlu, kuliitlu, kuliitlu, kuliitlu, kuliitlu*,' then throw in another ten to make sure Lukassi and Supa understood he meant at least two months. When Supa agreed, the old man gave him a shot of rum and one of those little Eli Whitney kegs of New Haven gunpowder, a box of percussion caps, a sack of lead ball, and – let's see – some hardtack biscuits, sugar, coffee, a package of needles, and two plugs of Brazilian twist tobacco. The Supa family left, they say, with all of them rowing their small umiak over to the mainland. Supa had his sled and half a dozen dogs aboard because he knew they wouldn't be returning until the ice was solid. Supa said they'd wait over there for the river to freeze, then travel inland to hunt for caribou."

"That means," said Finn, "that the old man is totally against my hiring Supa's daughter to do my sewing and my housework."

"You've got that right," Everett nodded. "I told you he was hell bent on having you hire that old widow instead of that breasty little chicken."

"It's hard for me these days," said Finn, "to keep myself from killing that awful prick."

"Well, one thing I know for sure," said Everett. "I've been living up here with Caleb Dunston since he was second mate. That's years and years ago. And in all that time I've never known him to be what the minister in our Westerly church would call a proper, moral man. He's always been keen on the local women, especially this one, Nilak. He's never bothered any of his mates or crew about their choice of bedmates unless it starts a fight."

Finn sat and ground his teeth while Everett worked with his thumbs to soften the window putty. "What do the crews do with themselves when they're ashore all winter?" Finn asked Everett.

"I play cribbage most evenings, and in daytime help Chips rebuild that old four-holer behind the crew's quarters. Have you noticed that wrecked outhouse that got blown apart?"

"I've seen you working on it," Finn said. "What happened?"

"Last summer," Everett told him, "in the crew's quarters, they held the biggest poker game in living memory."

"I've never heard about that," Finn said.

"The third mate, Tim Cravenlow, was the biggest gambler this island ever saw and the stakes got so high between him and that crazy plunger, Lemuel Smalley, that the other players all tossed in their hands. Cravenlow seemed to be bluffing, as he sometimes did, and pushed all his chips out to the middle of the table. But Smalley's not a man to take an easy whipping, so he sent the ship's boy to haul out the three big unicorn tusks he'd traded from the Yacks, boarded up for safety and stashed beneath his bunk. Smalley laid all three of them gleaming yellow on the table to cover Cravenlow's bet. Cravenlow had to accept that and when it came time to show, Lemuel, bless him, laid down his five-card flush in hearts. Cravenlow had to push all his money across the table to Smalley. *Sea Horse's* crew started laughing, kidding him, and that made Cravenlow madder than a wet hen. He stomped out of our quarters and slammed the goddamned door so hard one hinge busted off. I haven't fixed that yet this year, but will before the snows fly.

"Three mornings later," Everett went on, "that old four-holer was jammed with Smalley , two harpooners, and a greenhand. All of a sudden, there was a familiar hissing sound and one of them yelled, 'Stand back, ice charge exploding!' Those four fellows, with the trapdoors of their longjohns flying , went scattering out just seconds before the charge went off. There was a mighty whoof of black-powder smoke. But fortunately they got away. It was a shitty trick, but thank God none of them got injured. It wouldn't take anybody long to figure out who it was that had pulled off a hare-brained stunt like that. It was Cravenlow, of course. I tell you that son-of-a-bitch was a crooked player and a soreheaded loser. The old man refused to let him north this year."

It was heavily overcast when Everett finished puttying the windows, drank down his cold coffee, and left. The day was waning and big, wet snowflakes were starting down when Finn saw Otto,

Mario, and Chris walking on the path toward the mates' mess, where they would join the old man and himself to eat their Sunday dinner after Dunston had thanked the Lord for the food. As Finn walked fast to catch up to them, he glanced westward at the bleary, sun-stained sky and judged that their first storm might come during the night.

Otto fell back to give Finn a warning. "The old man was snapping his fingers and humming yesterday. He's nervous as a trout in a stone trap. He let out the word to Dougal that he's going to corner you."

Finn found Caleb already in his place at the head of the table. Caleb nodded to the mates as they sat down, but did not even look at Finn.

The mates were game and took a few mouthfuls before they pushed away the cook's revolting sculpin and turnip stew and soggy dumplings made with ham fat. They yelled for bannock.

"I've sent for fresh meat," the old man said, and for the first time directed his cold gaze at Finn. "Did you get *Lancer*'s holes plugged up?" Dunston demanded.

Finn clamped his lips tight shut as he returned the old man's stare. None of the mates moved or showed any expression, for they knew that the old man was firing off another verbal cannonball in this captains' war.

Neither Finn nor Dunston moved or spoke, unwilling to give an inch, until finally both men rose, flung down their soup-stained napkins, and stamped out of the mess. Finn went first, slamming the door in the old man's face. The mates leapt up and watched them as they walked stiff as dogs with their hackles up before a fight that was far from settled.

The snow had ceased and the late autumn sun was only partly showing its upper edge across the mountains. A soccer game was just beginning with many of the ships' crewmen. Joining in were Eskimo hunters and their wives, young people, grandparents, including the smallest children who could walk, all laughing, shouting, and kicking, enjoying a noisy time together. But as he marched through the laughter, this was one of the few times in his life that Finn had truly felt depressed. He cursed himself for having taken this captain's job that would keep him locked in this Arctic world, perhaps for years.

Stepping inside his house, Finn closed the door as the last slanting patches of sunlight divided by his window mullions spread themselves across his floor. He felt disheartened after five lonely days aboard *Lancer*, followed by his rush ashore full of hope, only to find that the old man had sent Pia away. His feet were still blue from standing in *Lancer's* icy hold, and now he'd been insulted in front of all the mates. Finn folded his heaviest blanket into three, pulled off his boots, and tried to rub circulation back into his feet before he drew on a dry pair of hand-knit stockings.

Without undressing, he rolled his navy seaman's cap down over his eyes and ears to block out the light and sounds. As he lay there missing *Lancer's* comforting, cradlelike rocking, he could still hear the excited crewmates and Yacks laughing and shouting in the soccer game. Finn had been told that there would be no winners or losers. The noises drifted up the valley and were joined by the yapping of dozens of husky pups. He liked the blending of these sounds – shipmates, Eskimos, dogs, laughing girls – all mixing together, then echoing from the hill. These sounds soothed him as he drifted off to sleep. When he awoke, it was pitch black outside. He hurried out and wet the newly fallen snow. Inside once more, he ate a hardtack biscuit and slept fitfully till morning.

Finn was up and lighting his stove when Everett came in, searching for his box of tools. New snow covered the ground outside. "You sure let it get cold in here."

Finn could see his breath. "We'll put on the coffee. Get out the mugs from that new side cupboard you built," he said.

The October hunting moon hung pale outside his window as Everett told Finn about the old man's character. He said that Dunston was feeling mean and jumpy just because neither he nor any of the mates had been able to take a single fish.

"Let's forget the old bastard," said Finn. "A woman brought me a bucket of young seal meat yesterday. Let's fry some up. It tastes better than beef or pork or lamb."

That evening, Noah Anderson came in and ate with the ice master in his house. Seeing that Finn looked depressed, he said, "Come with me over into Kudlik's tent. You'll see why I liked living with them."

The two men were warmly welcomed inside and given the best seats in the middle of the bed. There they watched Kudlik cast out five small ivory birds made from walrus teeth. The sixth one was a more clever carving of the sea goddess, an amulet of the same size, but with subtle differences – breasts, a vulva, and long hair braids. The carefully thrown ivory figures landed every which way.

"I can't toss them right tonight," sighed Kudlik. "Let the grand-mother have a try."

She threw the six small carvings only once onto a flattened piece of sealskin. All six figures lay with their heads pointing east.

"That's exactly where me and my crew will go tomorrow morning," Kudlik nodded, "eastward. There should be a big one, or maybe two, waiting for us beneath the sunrise."

"Kudlik won't use the word 'whale,' of course," Noah whispered, "because those great fish are known by Inuit to hear and understand the words of men, no matter how far away."

"Shhh! Listen!" cried the grandmother. "It's that *oui-oui-miut* playing his fiddle."

"He's good," said Noah. "Inuit call Frenchmen *oui-oui-miut*, the people who say 'oui, oui' a lot. Oh, she says she'd give anything to play on a three-stringed box the way he does."

"Can you hear the stamping on that floor of his? That must be the fiddler and Captain Caleboosi dancing. Listen. Hear it? That's Caleboosi singing to the player on the box. I bet both of them are loaded up with rum. I wish I was dancing with them," the old woman sighed.

"Well," said Noah, "that fiddler won't last long at the speed he's going tonight."

Sure enough, the music stopped and Kudlik's wife bent to look through her peekhole in their tent. As she watched, the captain's door flew open and she saw the fiddler come reeling out, laughing as he fell on his back in the snow.

"You go help him up," Kudlik's wife told her husband. "Don't let that poor man freeze. He makes the best music I've ever heard."

After they had eaten and said goodnight to Kudlik and his family, Finn said to Noah, "I like their way of thinking."

"They'd have been glad to have you spend the night with them," said Noah. "Don't let yourself grow lonely in a friendly place like this."

The old man was out early in his whaleboat on that short autumn day as was Dougal with his oarsmen; for as Kudlik had predicted, two large bowheads had been sighted by the lookout, blowing some distance eastward off the island. Five boats, including Finn's, were in the chase.

Gibson was the first to spot a smooth hump of water forming on the surface of the sea, gliding forward halfway between the two whaleboats and the last of the drifting summer ice. Dunston stood up in the stern, watching little puffs of vapor appear, then a thick, foglike twin-jet of breath burst noisily into the air as one huge bowhead surfaced close to them. The sight of its shining black back breaking the surface caused the gulls to scream, then hover, crowding excitedly just above the whale. Finn was all eyes, searching for the second fish, which would be the first chance his boat had had of taking a whale.

With luck, these two bowheads might be easy fish to take, being inside the old slob ice and so close to the Blacklead station. Once killed, it would be a simple matter to have Inuit and crew from the two vessels join together with their boats to help tow their huge double catch ashore. This pair of mighty bowheads, unafraid of man, had separated and now rested, slowly filling their lungs with air. Judging by the near one's length and bulk, Dunston reckoned this would be a 180-, maybe 190-barrel cow. He trembled with excitement.

Finn watched as Dougal made a hand signal to his five-man crew and they laid into it, rowing quietly, using long, nearly silent strokes. It was an absolute rule that no oarsman turn his head to look forward at the whale. Dougal had drawn up just behind the old man's boat.

He was careful not to pull ahead. When Caleb judged that he was close enough, Dougal saw him give Kudlik a nod. The men in both boats gently stowed their oars and took up short paddles. Then, Pequot Indian-style, four of them turned and sat up on the cedar gunnels, stroking the boat through the mirror calmness behind the immense back of the whale, which seemed unconcerned about the danger now approaching her. Caleb turned his head excitedly. Dougal's crew was close behind him, also using paddles.

Rising cautiously in the stern, Dunston slung his bomb load across his back. Then, leaving his place by the steering oar, he ran forward and took Kudlik's place by the harpoon gun as Kudlik ran back past him, each of them stepping on the boat's thwarts between the four men paddling. Caleb reached the bow just as Kudlik grabbed the long stern oar. Caleb knelt and pushed the charge in the gun, then armed it with the harpoon lance and half-cocked the trigger. The fish was almost too close now. Caleb worried that a slip of some man's paddle striking the gunnel would alert this huge treasure, whose oil he desperately needed.

Finn watched this action just ahead of him, noticing that Dougal's boat had crept in directly behind the whale and very close to a small, blue-green iceberg, most of which lay hidden beneath the water. Dougal now ran forward from stern to bow. He armed his Norwich bomb gun, but instead of aiming, he waited for a signal from the old man, realizing that his boat, jammed between the iceberg and the whale's powerful tail, was in a dangerous position.

Bowhead tail

Caleb waved his left hand when he saw the whale's immense head rise very slightly, a sure sign that she was taking the last air she needed into her lungs as she prepared to dive. He fully cocked the gun's hammer and, before she could raise her tail flukes, fired. The harpoon and line went slithering out like a snake's head, carrying the hemp line just above the water. The iron harpoon head struck, burying itself deep inside the huge fish's body.

"Back off, Dougal, back off!" the old man yelled, too late, as he saw the bowhead's massive tail flukes rise too close to Dougal's chase boat and come smashing down. On the second blow, it struck the boat, breaking its bow, flipping up its stern, flinging out men and oars, tubs and canvas, while fathoms of loose hemp rope uncoiled from the tubs and spilled into the icy water. The huge bowhead, in her shock and pain, panicked. She high-humped her back and sounded, heading for the depths.

Finn, like the other harpooners and boat steerers, stood up to search the surface of the water round him, waiting for men's heads to reappear. Finn saw Dougal first, then the frantic face of Issy Steiner, as the heads and shoulders of the other four popped up.

The crew of Caleb's boat let out a yell as the diving beast spun out the line, uncoiling it from the old man's tub. The rope raced back around the loggerhead in the stern, then forward, smoking through the bow notch of Caleb's boat. When it snapped taut, the whale down near the bottom started to tow the boat away. Caleb had no choice but to snatch up the hand axe and cut the smoking harpoon line, freeing this huge treasure of oil and money bone. Hell and damnation, what else could he do? These men, in water this cold, would not remain alive for any longer than it would take to count to fifty.

Caleb and his hunters paddled hard to the rescue and Finn's boat followed, forcing its bow toward the two closest drowning men still struggling in the freezing water. Luke Blais lay face up near the berg. Charlie and one of the Eskimos grasped his arms and hauled him in. Luktak scrambled forward and leaned out to catch Dougal by the collar of his pea jacket. They dragged him into the boat. Finn, standing at the steering oar, caught hold of Rory Decker, while

Munro grabbed Tivi by the peak of his parka hood and dragged him over their boat's gunnel.

Caleb leaned far forward with the longboat hook, trying desperately to reach the last two men. Sammy, who was closest, managed to grasp the oak shaft, but as Caleb drew him in, they all watched helplessly as that powerful oarsman, Upingwak, sank slowly down through the pale green water and was lost forever.

The men who had been rescued sat gasping, coughing, trembling like sodden water spaniels. Finn pulled off his sealskin parka and wrapped it around the nearest man's shoulders, and others did the same. Using oars and paddles, with Caleb steering, those well enough from the remaining three crews rowed hard toward the island, encouraging the wet ones to try and work heat back into their bodies.

A crowd of men and Inuit women gathered on the shore as each boat approached. The women ran into the water, carrying skins and blankets. These they wrapped around the soaking men and, hugging them, they helped take them ashore.

"Take them up to their men's mess, throw coal on the stove, and have the steward break out the rum. I'll be coming right behind you soon as we've got everyone ashore," shouted Caleb.

All the crewmen, both soaking wet or dry, took long gulps from the two half-gallon rum bottles before Antoine and the cook began to choke them off and push them through the mess-hall door. Outside, Finn could see and hear Upingwak's widow wailing. It was awful losing a man, New Englander or Inuk. It was doubly bad to lose a friend when his wife and children wept in horror close by.

Next day, the west wind carried the double ringing of hammers. Two of the ship's carpenters, along with Kudlik and his sons, began in the boatwright's fashion to put together two new chase boats, one to replace Dougal's boat and the other to be used in trade for the 182-barrel cow that Kudlik had first towed in for Caleb. Both whaleboats were Arctic thirty-footers with strong, thin, oak ribs and a slightly heavier keel that had been carefully precut in Mystic and bundled together for just this purpose. The planking of light cedar had also been prepared in Mallory's boatyard. Six sweep oars went with each new chase boat and a short mast and stunsail, a stick boom, sternpost, coiling tubs, a boat steerer's long oar, two eight-foot hand harpoons, two long, iron-shafted lances, and several huge, new coils of the best hemp rope. These boats, with all their equipment, Caleb knew, had together cost 134 Yankee dollars. But it was worth the money. They were much lighter and faster than the Dundee boats, and here on Blacklead, Inuit thought it was good reward for a big right whale. All unknown to them, the oil and baleen would sell in New London for forty to fifty times that amount. After all, those great white houses with their grand Ionic columns, tall windows, and high widow's walks on top were what the whaling partners and the captains were having built in many towns along the New England coast, and they had to be paid for with a lot of oil and money bone. Kudlik had decided to keep one new whaleboat himself and give his old one to his own two sons. But, in fact, both whaleboats would remain under his wise command.

The gray autumn daylight was fading fast. The carpenters shuddered and pulled up their parka hoods. Turning their backs against the wind, they were forced to work with heavy mittens on. Next day, two of the boats each took a big whale. Crews enjoyed the smoke and smell of melting fat billowing across the island and hurried to help barrel the oil as winter pushed down harshly from the north.

Three days later, Finn watched as a dozen Eskimo hunters picked up the two finished boats and carried them carefully down the slope to the still unfrozen shoreline. They filled both with salt water to swell the cedar laps. The wind of the previous night had died and now they would wait for the air goddess, Sila, and the waters of the sea to do their work.

Next day, Kudlik's sons were eager to take their new whaleboat out and test it, and so was Dougal. They bailed then tipped them empty. In the distance, a dozen harp seals continued rising and diving to some rhythm of their own. Not far off the point, a pair of thousand-pound bearded seals seemed to enjoy the morning air before they, too, breathed deeply and dove down, hunting far beneath the surface for schools of fish.

Finn observed the other hunters as they left their tents, then went and ducked their heads inside the cockpits of their upturned sealskin kayaks, lifting them off their chest-high stone racks. They carried them down and laid them gently in the water, each man carefully washing his boots free of abrasive sand before easing himself inside. Tom Finn had read in some old Greenland explorer's journal that these slim kayaks were judged to be the most cleverly devised watercraft in the world, and the kayakmen showed him why that was true.

Kudlik's sons, with four more nephews as crew, pushed off, awed in their excitement. Every Inuit left on Blacklead Island stood along the low cliff's edge above the beach, for didn't this marvelous new vessel, in the deepest sense, belong to all of them? The whaleboats, like other trade items – knives, axes, muskets, canvas, sailor's caps, tobacco, molasses, flour, tea, coffee, accordions, bright calico, gunpowder, cheap perfume, and rum – were bringing welcome change.

Finn could see that some Inuit seemed as eager to leap out of their old way of life as any young ship's crewmen keen to experience any unknown, far-off world.

Noah Anderson, who stood near Finn, said, "It's easy to see that this light, fast, cedar whaleboat was by far the most important invention of the American whaling trade. Watch those Eskimos, so eager to own another of these miracles of white man's cleverness, which, with luck, can now be traded for another whale. Notice how much lighter and faster that craft is than one of those old, safer, heavier Dundee whaleboats." Noah asked, "Do you know the story of how these boats came to be invented?"

Finn confessed his ignorance.

Noah lit his pipe and began the story. "In the early days, on Nantucket, the white settlers were starving. They would go out fishing in their clumsy English lifeboats and fail time after time, since they lacked of any proper weapons or hunting skills to kill even the smallest dolphin. They had prayed – they were Quakers – and that had done no good, and they were searching the beaches trying to find a dead, decaying whale to keep them from starvation. When that, too, failed, they huddled around their beach fires, enviously observing a group of the pagan islanders, using their narrow hollowed-log canoes, paddling stealthily toward a huge fish not far off shore. The Quakers stared in wonder as half a dozen of these light vessels gathered around this enormous, air-breathing beast. Then, on signal, the Indians in the bows drove clamshell-pointed harpoon points into their prey and threw out man-sized sealskin floats blown full of air to mark wood drogues to slow the progress of the wounded whale. The Nantucket Indians, being a compassionate people, soon began to share some of the meat with their new neighbors and to take one or two of the braver, more likable, young Quakers out with them as paddlers on their offshore hunts so their families would have food that winter and whale oil for their cooking and to fuel their lamps.

"Finally, the Quakers were able to trade molasses, two old firelock muskets, and a small keg of gunpowder and shot for two of the dugout canoes, four harpoons with skin floats, and a dozen paddles. The Quakers quickly painted out the heathen Indian markings on the prows of these canoes, replacing them with paintings of two heavenly doves. Supplying sugar teats to keep one Indian as a lookout on a headland and inviting others in their canoes to guide them to the whales, the Quakers, who were at heart a truly enterprising people, slowly came to understand and then began to master this ancient hunting skill."

Noah was enjoying his own account of history. "It was only a question of time before the Quakers started building their own whale canoes. But instead of dugouts," he said, "they used thin cedar laps warped onto a stronger hardwood frame. With a six-man crew and a small stunsail, they were surprisingly fast. Soon the Quakers developed shipwrights on Nantucket and began to build new, improved whale ships with large blunt holds not at all for speed but to act like storage barns. They improved the rigging so they could go far beyond the sight of land to follow the more remote but more abundant toothed whales. At last, with their food problems solved at home, these Nantucket Quakers turned their thoughts to trade, setting out in earnest to hunt for oil and that great perfume binder, ambergris, in every ocean of the world. Out there they gathered the more peaceable savage islanders and sea hunters into their crews and trained them in their much more modern ways of hunting whales. It changed the way of life for Quakers, and Eskimos from Siberia to Greenland, and the South Sea Islanders as well."

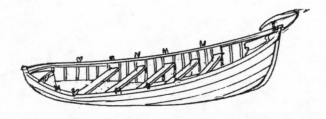

Whaleboat

Finn invited Noah into his house for rum and coffee after the ship's keeper had joined in supping ashore in the mess. During the visit, Noah saw the two ship's boys with Eskimo friends go and open Caleb's door to deliver a gift from Kudlik of one large Arctic hare and six white ptarmigan. After quietly hanging them inside Caleb's outer porch, Jose and Pierre ran away.

"Those two kids," said Noah, "will earn no share of the lay this voyage, of course. They get food from the cook shack and good winter clothing free from Inuit women. Jose's an orphan who grew up sleeping in the back alleys of New London, eating whatever some of the kitchen help threw away. And Pierre's a kid from south Newfoundland. The language they share together is Eskimo. Hell, being orphans is an awful way for kids to grow up. They're a lot better off with us. We'll make good sailors of the pair of them.

"I had a dream last night about Willie Kinney, *Sea Horse*'s old first mate," said Noah. "He was dancing around with that whore he tried to save. I wonder if his arm is better now. We had a mutiny with men killed because Willie wasn't mastering *Lancer*. It's a damn good thing you turned up with new crew, Finn."

"When we set sail from New London with our first crew, they were jumping up and down, eager to draw some pay in advance out of their share of the lay. Maybe six or seven dollars to tide their mother over while they were away, or have just enough to buy rye whisky and cigars to give a farewell party at the Cock and Spur. Now they're spending all their future money buying from the stewards' slops chests: oilskins, thick longjohns, stockings, mica glasses, mitts, gum boots, Dr. Feelgood liver oil, and poop pills. At slops-chest prices, those items do add up on an Arctic voyage. They can land a whaler home with very little money.

"Now on *Sea Horse* two years ago, there was only one way they got rid of that long, lean seaman, Randy Martin, who's aboard *Lancer* again this voyage. He's a good, hardworking hand, but after a year-and-a-half up north aboard *Sea Horse* when the agent added up his slops-chest bill, Randy's share of the lay worked out to just twenty cents. When our ship's agent handed him that little bit of silver, Randy got so mad he started swinging his fists and jumping up and down. He refused to sign off *Sea Horse*. He swore to God he was going to go and complain to his senator, his congressman and the New London and Hartford newspapers, telling them that Dunston and the robbing Fisheries partners had stole him blind. After three days of ranting, Fisheries decided to pay Randy off with four dollars – not because they owed it to him, mind you, but just to get him off the ship and shut him up. That's how they got his 'X' mark agreeing that he had no further claims on them. It's a miracle that Randy Martin came back north with us this year."

"Twenty cents!" Finn whistled. "That's less than a shilling! No wonder Martin gets Eskimo women to make his clothes for him!"

"Captain, you should know more about these Yack people. I'm going over to visit Pootavut," said Noah. "Would you like to come with me?"

"Sure," said Finn and they set off up the path toward the tents.

"See that?" Noah nodded. "The moment we turned in their direction, their tent flap eased open just a crack. These are hunting families. They miss nothing. They seem to have sensed beforehand that our minds had decided to go and visit them. Look. Pootavut's coming out of the tent. He's looking at his feet now, he's smiling, he's greeting us. Yes, his wife has come out of their entrance smiling, too. They're ready for us now."

"*Pudlarianiakpusi*," the husband called. "Visit, come on, you two."

As they bent themselves through the low entrance to the tent, the wife called in a high, unnatural voice, "*Taaktualuuvugut*."

"She's saying, 'It is dark in here,'" Noah explained to Finn. "That's to kind of belittle herself as a housewife, pretending her lamp's not burning bright enough to light and warm our visit."

Standing awkwardly inside, Finn whispered, "I wouldn't like to live inside this tent. It's too small, too shadowy, too crowded for me."

The hunter and his wife gestured toward the center of the sleeping bench, inviting their guests to sit.

"No need to whisper," said Noah in a normal voice. "This family doesn't understand a word we're saying. The tent roof is low for you, but you'd soon get used to a space as small as this. I did long ago. Their spaces need to be small to hold down the warmth. These *tupiks* of theirs are only heated by that seal-oil lamp and the heat that's generated by their bodies.

"See how quick the family moved to give us the best seats. They've placed us in the center of their sleeping bench, not because we're foreigners, but because we're their guests.

"Pootavut, his wife, and their children sleep in a line across this sleeping bench," said Noah, "that stretches right across to the other side, all of them with their heads toward the entrance so the hunters, so any of them, can get out fast. Aunts, cousins, and old folks sleep on the other side of the bench. That old woman, Kaupak, who is the grandmother here, tends a second lamp on her side of the sleeping bench during the cold days of winter. Look at her, Captain, smiling at you. See, her upper teeth are worn down almost to the gums. That's from chewing kids' mitts and sealskin boots soft in this household. When a woman dries untanned, waterproof sealskin boots over her lamp, they become hard. She will chew them until they're as soft as chamois gloves. Along with helping grandchildren grow wise, it's one of the last things that a good woman can do. In this household, everyone uses all their skills to make sure that they survive, like the children help their parents to load the boats and sleds.

"That old woman, Kaupak, has known a hard life sometimes," Noah told Finn. "Some years ago, I asked her how it was during the starving times. She told me that it wasn't too bad before they finished off the dog food and finally the dogs. She said a woman should give the food to her husband so he has the strength to go out and hunt for the family. Then the children should have enough to keep them from crying all the time. 'What did you do then?' I asked her. 'Oh, a woman can always lick her hands after cutting up the last of the meat for the others. There's always some delicious taste left there between your fingers.' But times like that are hard."

"I know what she means," said Finn. "I had a time of hunger in my life."

Pootavut drank a small amount of seal broth and passed the pot to Finn in recognition of his rank.

Noah smiled and explained to Finn, "Because he drank some broth first, he showed us that he's the head of this house. Now you, then I, will drink, as will all the others in order of rank. Now he invites you to fish for the best piece of meat that you can find inside the pot. Then you pass it to me to pick, then I'll pass it to his eldest son beside me. Being white men, they know we prefer boiled meat. They're very polite. And listen to the way they keep their conversation low because you and I are speaking together. They don't want to interrupt us."

"I've been meaning to ask you a question," said Finn, chewing with enjoyment. "What are those little leather bags, and bones, and bits of wings they've got sewn on their parkas, back and front?"

"They're charms," Noah answered, sipping, and then passing the bowl. "Amulets. *Pitukutit*, they call them. A shaman, *angakuk*, over at Niantelik traded those amulets to this family to help hold off sickness or bad spirits and to bring the animals to them." Noah smiled, "I know it probably sounds kind of unchristian to you, but in the south we do something like that, too. Think of it. Most of us go to church and listen to the minister or priest advising us and praying for our souls and singing. Our church people, too, give out charms. Little crucifixion crosses, for example, palms on Palm Sunday, and lots of Saint Christopher medals, which many of our sailors wear. And for those services, our priests want you to support them and their church by giving money.

"We think that animals were placed here on earth for the benefit of man. The Inuit don't agree with that. They think about animals as a kind of people like themselves, fellow survivors in a dangerous world.

"These Inuit people don't know money, so they have to invite an *angakuk*, that's a shaman, to come and live with them. Shamans are not hunters, they're priests without a church and they teach myths and taboos. While one of them – often with an apprentice in tow – is living with a family, that family feeds and clothes them. They're welcomed to sleep beside the wife or husband, or daughter or son, and enjoy the good hunter's life until the worth to that family is fully settled. Then the shaman will move on to another family and another healing. That's the way it's usually done."

"It's not so different in Newfoundland," said Finn. "Those priests who sail around to the outports will even settle sometimes for a bit of useful gossip, if you're short of potatoes to give them, or dried cod."

There was a pause in their conversation while they watched the old woman turn the boots on her drying frame above the lamp.

"I'll tell you something I've been thinking about," said Noah slowly. "These Inuit sitting here with us. You take a good look at them, Captain, for they and all their children are going to disappear. Yes, disappear, just like the big bowhead fish that we have almost hunted out. These people will have to utterly change their ways and become a lot more like us or they'll disappear."

"How do you figure that?" asked Finn. "They've done fine like this for centuries."

"Because we foreigners are so damned headstrong, so sure we're absolutely right. We've made big cities and big businesses like knitting mills. We've got huge ships and puffing locomotives, and a president and congressmen, bishops and cathedrals, all to prove our greatness. We wouldn't dream of trying to live life again in the straightforward, simple way they have here. I mean, truly sharing with each other, caring for each other – and giving up our ideas of personally owning damn near everything. Hell, no!" said Noah, sounding angry. "We've got a tight grip on the helm of North America and we're not going to change our course. They've got to skip to our tune or disappear, fade right out of sight. They must forget their old ways and learn to trade and think like us. Whales in trade for whaleboats. We've got them started running on our path now. There can be no turning back for them."

"You make damn sure you Yanks don't sideswipe Newfoundland," said Finn.

After a spell, with much politeness on all sides, they excused themselves and edged out of the tent.

"Captain, how's that other old widow working out for you?" asked Noah as they walked back along the snow path. "Does she clean your house, and soften your skin boots, and do your washing every now and then?"

"I'm holding off on the widow." Finn drew in his breath. "I've got a better plan in mind."

"I thought you had," said Noah, and he smiled at Finn.

Sealskin boots

Chapter 9

Darkness had fallen and the Arctic cold descended as the slim, bright curve of the new moon appeared. Blacklead Island dogs sent up a howling as they became aware of two excited teams racing across the new-formed ice and up the steep embankment toward the Yankee station. Finn blew out his oil lamp, pulled on his storm pants and parka, and jerked open his house door. He was enveloped in a cloud when the heat from his house turned to steam as it struck the outside cold. There was not a breath of wind. When the steam cleared away, he saw that hunters and crewmen were already busy breaking up a huge dog fight that had erupted between the island's dogs and these two new teams.

Finn went close to the sleds, peering carefully at these shadowy figures, then eagerly shook hands with Supa, his wife, two sons, and, finally, Pia, who was too shy to look at him. Dunston did not come out to greet them. One sled was piled high with caribou meat which Supa and his son were starting to unlash and pile inside a stone meat cache, safe from the teeth of hungry dogs. Other Inuit came out to welcome them and help them. Even grandmothers, eager to be sociable, joined in to unharness the dogs as the returning travelers were invited into the warmth of various winter tents to share in a feast of the meat they had provided and then to sleep in the center of the warm beds of their neighbors for the night.

Finn burned the oil in his reading lamp till late and wrote three weeks of October entries in his daily journal. He found it hard to concentrate and wrote badly. His hands trembled, for he felt far too excited to tackle such a routine task, feeling certain that Pia would come to him that night. He stripped himself naked and crawled into the sleeping bag to wait there, tensely listening for most of the night. She never came.

Next day, just before noon, he caught a glimpse of Pia outdoors working with her mother. They had unrolled some new caribou skins, had peg-stretched them taut upon the wind-hardened snow, and were diligently scraping them with their moon-shaped women's knives. As he stood watching out his small window, he saw Pia turn her head and look toward his window, then nod, half smile, and look away to answer some question of her mother. He watched while the two of them skillfully removed the membrane from the inside of the skins until they looked as smooth and yellow-white as rich farm cream.

Finn saw Pia's father, Supa, helping his two sons clear the snow from a patch of ground using their strange-looking handmade shovels. The winter tent they would erect was of ancient Eskimo design, but it now incorporated many whaler's materials, including a bundle of loose floorboards and a low frame made from the waste wood of ship's crates. Over this frame, Supa and his sons drew a piece of sail canvas. On top of that, they placed pieces of mosslike tundra the size of straw hats, then a second layer of old sailcloth all crisscrossed with sealskin lines to hold it down against the wind. A low, narrow wooden door facing the sea was leather-hinged onto the entrance frame, and above this door was a strong, pliable window made of pieces of walrus intestine sewn together. As the moon moved through the dimming sky of afternoon, Finn watched various members of the Supa family complete their building tasks.

When night came, through the pliable gut window Finn could see the soft yellow glow of their seal-oil lamp. Glancing at the other eight winter tents that had recently sprung up near the Yankee buildings, he wondered, Who are these people who can create a family dwelling in six hours, a home that will protect them throughout the Arctic winter, lighted and heated by a pair of small oil lamps?

Surely she'll come tonight, Finn told himself as he began excitedly restudying his three now-tattered copies of *Godey's Lady's Book* for March, April, and May, 1875. Finn was no great reader, but these copies had come aboard *Lancer* from a New London tobacco shop. This magazine was an item wildly revealing of female form and fashion. It was almost never seen in Newfoundland. The *Lady's Book* was famous for its heavily illustrated pages, sometimes with hand-colored steel engravings of beautiful women totally, yet suggestively, clothed. The back pages were best, bold advertising drawings of ladies in nothing but enticing undergarments, bathing suits, bloomers, knickers, bosom forms, corset stays, hoop skirts, and bustles, all fashioned with the springy black baleen which crewmen aboard *Lancer* and *Sea Horse* were so desperately trying to harvest. Finn liked to lie inside his covers gazing at the magazine and trying to imagine how many lovely, varied, naked female bodies *Lancer's* baleen bones would soon embrace worldwide.

Finn heard a sound and jumped up nervously. His outer door screeched open, and through the inner door stepped Pia. She was carrying half a dozen lean white frozen ptarmigan dangling by their thickly feathered feet. They reminded Finn of home in Newfoundland and of his mother's plump white flock of pullets. He smiled lovingly at Pia and grandly beckoned her toward the bed.

"*Akigik mamaktupaluk* – good to eat," she said, holding out the ptarmigan, then, smiling, dropped them on the porch floor.

"*Nakomik*, thank you," he said.

She widened her eyes, meaning, "Yes."

"*Sinikvikpiiujuk*," he said. "This bed is good." He pointed to her, and then to the new double sleeping bag that she had made.

She smiled again, then quickly left the house.

"Damn!" Finn leapt across to the window, then held his breath, fearing he would steam it. He watched the delectable Pia, surefooted as an Arctic fox, cross the hard-packed drifts. She pulled open her family's door and, gracefully bending double, disappeared inside their winter tent.

Tom threw on his parka and rushed outside, then stiffly wrote his yellow "T F" in the snow. Hurrying back inside, he slammed both doors. Who cared about the fact that he and Pia had so little language between them? As Noah said, good men learned to Yack in bed.

Turning off his lamp, he stripped naked, again looking forward to the soft, erotic feeling of the fur inside the double caribou bag. He lay awake, squirming, letting it stroke against his body, listening, quickly turning his head at the slightest squeal of snow. Was it Pia? No. Nothing but a damned dog trotting past his house. He rolled and hauled himself to Pia's side of the sleeping bag, trying to imagine what it would be like if she were there. That made him so excited, so heated up, that he had to throw back the upper part of the sleeping bag. He cooled slowly, then relaxed. Drawing the bag over himself again, he slept.

Next morning after mess, Finn and Chris Acker were able for the first time to set out on foot edging around the new-formed, rubbery, salt ice to *Lancer*. They told the mates at mess that it was to stretch their muscles, but in truth they wanted to see how much water the ship was taking after their recent caulking. *Lancer*, Finn hoped, would freeze in smoothly with no dangerous heaves of pressure ice against her hull.

They found almost no leaks now. They drank coffee and talked with Noah Anderson for a while.

Noah said, "I don't like just lazing around out here, Captain Finn, so I took the carpenter's spoke shave and I carved and spliced, then pegged, a new harpoon onto *Lancer*'s figurehead. I hate to see a good old ship like this one allowed to go to rack and ruin. It was really cheap of Fisheries to leave that harpoon broken."

The ice master and Chris started ashore, Finn probing before him with a chisel on a staff. Chris carried the heavy Sharps rifle because now, with so much darkness, male polar bears – which did not need to den like the females producing young – were difficult to see, and likely to be drawn in by the pungent smell of whale meat, or perhaps of living men. The layer of new-formed ice was being whitened with large flakes of falling snow.

When they climbed up beside the slipway to the island, the afternoon had faded into darkness. Jupiter hung low, its colors sparkling in the western sky. The bright half-moon had just appeared, causing the fresh snow that rimmed the island to glow like phosphorus.

"Better get a move on," Acker warned Finn, "or those hungry bastards in our mess will eat every bite of that caribou meat the Supa family brought back for us."

Finn broke into a run up the bank toward the station, hoping that Pia might be waiting in the house. His shoulders sagged when he saw that it was empty. Quickly washing his hands and face with warm water from the kettle, he stropped his straight razor and shaved carefully, before he tied on his red bandana neckerchief in the hope of seeing Pia later and ran to join the caribou feast. Finn did not bother to wear his parka as he trotted toward the mess, for the stinging night air made his body tingle in even its smaller parts.

The old man, perhaps having had a couple of rums and done heaven knows what else over at his house, came into the mess in his most outgoing mood. He called for a new bottle, uncorked it, and passed it around the table. The smell of caribou, Barbados rum, and simmering onions filled the room in wondrous ways.

"Here's greasy luck to Blacklead whalers," shouted Caleb, raising his pewter mug.

Finn and all six mates raised their mugs and drank, then gasped. The new sea ice and endless fields of pure white snow were having a wild effect on all of them.

"Is there anyplace you'd rather be tonight?" the old man bellowed.

"Nowhere on earth but right here," all of them yelled as they tipped back their heads and drank off the old man's gift of rum.

"I know a beautiful girl from Westerly that I sure wish were here tonight," said Otto Kraus. "I saw her wearing tight sailor pants in a pantomime. Thrown away her corsets, she had, honest to God. You should have seen her!"

Everybody laughed and begged for richer details until Rudi, the steward, appeared with a steaming double haunch of caribou. The old man again passed the rum around, then rose and started his ceremonial sharpening of the carving knife.

Shannon sang as he dealt out the plates. "There never was a piece of lamb or beef as tender or as tasty as this caribou," Jack hollered. "Pass the gravy and the fuckin' pickles, mate."

The coming of the vast white Arctic winter had excited them all and seemed to make each one of them feel clean and new again. The mates relaxed after dinner and used various mental finger counts and nicks on the edges of the table as they tried to calculate just how many barrels of whale oil their own whaleboats had taken or should have taken. But tonight, with all the rum and laughing and shoving, they settled for the general concept that they were just about to start doing a helluva lot better with the hunt.

Finn went back to his house and spent another restless night cat-napping or lying awake, listening and waiting.

Inuit hunters in the lookout next morning sighted high blows that turned steaming white – the jets from a pod of bowhead whales as they rested, then sounded in the open water not far east of the Blacklead station. All six boats broke ice as they put out with the old man, Finn, and four mates as boat steerers. Half of the oarsmen were strong, skilled Eskimo hunters, and half were New England greenhands on the learn. The hunters carefully showed the crewmen that they must not spit tobacco or knock pipe ashes into the water, which would disgust the sensitive whales. Their wisdom seemed to work, for between them they took three bowheads that averaged about one hundred and thirty barrels apiece on that first day, and two more near evening of the second day. They came home tired and cold. Finn's boat, with a different crew, struck the largest whale on the third day, but the harpoon iron got badly twisted and pulled out, and the big bull then fled so far out into the Sound that they dared not follow. It was long after midnight on the third day when their whaleboats came ashore between the Yankee and the Dundee slipways where two of the earlier whale carcasses lay waiting to be stripped. Gusts of wind were driving thick, new snow across the island, blanketing the roofs and tundra slopes of the whaling station. The oarsmen, their wrists red and swollen, climbed stiffly up the bank, stumbled into their mess, drank rum, ate groggily, then staggered dead sober to their bunks. Some fell asleep with their heads on the table, too tired to move.

When the late morning light grew strong enough for the islanders to see once more, the blubber was rendered into oil. Selected crewmen did the scraping, grading, and storing of the valuable money bone using long tables in a warehouse set aside to hold this treasure. The northwest wind was sharpening its knives, driving masses of freezing polar air to settle inside the bowl of hills west of their island. It would remain there, freezing the salt water into winter ice.

"I had a bad dream about *Lancer*," the old man said. "I'm going out to take a look at her hull again." He did not speak directly to Finn, but to the mates around the table. "I'll take Kudlik and go out there tomorrow midday."

Finn went out with Acker to be there before Dunston arrived.

Walking ahead of the others after their noon meal, Kudlik probed each step on the new ice carefully with the chisel end of his sealing harpoon, insisting that the old man and Dougal walk four paces apart directly behind him. Inuit were always extra cautious on these early days following freeze-up, knowing there would still be some dangerously thin weak spots in the ice. Kudlik and the old man and mate walked around both whale ships, agreeing that both were evenly and safely frozen in.

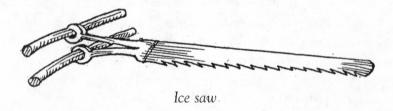

Ice saw

Sixteen men went out next day carrying long ice saws and chisels to cut man-length squares through which they drew up all four anchors and tied them in their bow positions. That day and the next, they took down all sails, unstepped the topmasts, and in every way prepared *Sea Horse* and *Lancer* to undergo the violence of a Baffin winter. The carpenters lashed up two cross beams between the foremast and midmast, then another to the mizzenmast astern. The crews drew two mainsails tentlike, covering the whole hull of each ship. This canvas roofing gave a festive feeling to all those who stepped beneath, as though they had just entered a circus tent. It would keep the decks drift-free when howling blizzards raged across the frozen sea. Finally, Caleb ordered his men to stretch a long hemp safety line between *Lancer* and *Sea Horse*, and a much longer lifeline from *Sea Horse* to the cathead off the Yankee slipway, thus enabling men to guide themselves, drunk or sober, from ship to ship and shore in blinding snowstorms. Beyond the whale ships, the salt ice continued to extend out toward the black open waters of the Sound. The wide channel between Blacklead and Niantelik Bay was narrowing every day.

Out on Cumberland Sound to the north and south, the salt water still refused to close, though all the bays and channels, protected by the islands, were now frozen solid. Pancake-sized chunks of salt ice were busy enlarging themselves, coming closer and closer together to join what looked like vast ponds of frosted lily pads.

When someone saw the lookout fire the signal bomb, the old man, Finn, and all the mates ran out of their mess hall at midday. The signal man had not raised the whale flag, and two young hunters' sons came running full tilt off the hill shouting, "*Umiakjuak! Umiakjuak! Makulu!*"

"Two ships sighted," Lukassi called out, "both coming this way!"

Finn ran inside his house and grabbed the telescope. Steadying it against his water barrel, he focused it south. Behind raised foresails, he saw two plumes of black smoke rising as the ships moved slowly toward them.

Dougal yelled to Caleb, "Those Dundee men are in one helluva hurry, using up their coal, with their boilers roaring, and all sails set, racing to get in here before the ice decides to block them out."

"That's got to be that desperate, goddamned Highlander," Caleb swore as he paced back and forth. "I had a terrible feeling in my gut that bugger would try to force his way in here. Just look out there! Every mothering drop of water between them and Niantelik Bay is covered over! Still, he's determined to ram his way in there, even if he has to rip his sails and bust his boilers."

"Thank God the ice around our anchorage is too thick for him to winter here," said Mario, "and if he dares to sit out where he is, that ice will crush them ships of his like a pair of eggs."

The old man shouted, "Lukassi tells me there's Yack hunters at Niantelik ready to dog-team him ashore."

When a bleary light came into the sky next day at noon, the old man could read *Blue Thistle* on one sternboard with his glass. She was followed by a second square-rigged whale ship called *North Star*. Both vessels were coughing up great clouds of black smoke. *Blue Thistle* was busy battering a path through the thickening ice as they worked their way around the headland that protected Niantelik Bay.

"Oh, the Highlander will go raving mad having to stay over there on Baffinland with all those wild Yack hunters and their families he doesn't know. They'll be coming and going any way they like, he and his crews of rectumites, or Jacobites, as the English like to call them. They'll go trotting in and out to the igloos with little kegs of that cheap apple brandy hidden beneath their parkas or tied around their necks like Swiss rescue dogs. I'll bet the Highlander will force both ships' crews to live aboard this winter, for it's now too cold to start building ashore." The old man laughed. "I wonder what caused that haggis-loving bastard to pull in here so late."

"We'll soon find out," said Dougal Gibson. "The minute that ice gets thick enough between us, you'll see him perched up on a dogsled rushing over here to pump us of all our whaling news – giving back none of theirs."

"Did you notice, Dougal, how *Blue Thistle* and *North Star* were riding high in the water?" Caleb asked him. "I'd say they've had piss-poor luck off Greenland." Caleb rubbed his purple nose to make sure it still had feeling.

"I hope Cargill thought to bring that distilling genius, Duncan Ross, back with him this year," said Gibson. "There's no man alive with more brewing skill when it comes to creating a barrel of powerful liquor out of withered, sprouted potatoes."

"And giving it a whisky color with molasses and tea," said Mario.

Pia came over every morning now and twice the old man came bursting through Finn's door soon after she arrived. Maybe Caleb's sudden visits were the reason Pia feared to come to Finn at night. Finn was becoming desperate. But what to do? He did not want Lukassi to have to translate to Pia or her father exactly what he had in mind, for he had heard that such news spread among the Yacks like wildfire. Oh, he had been in bed with a few semi-respectable young women in Newfoundland. But he had always kept away from dockside prostitutes, and living as he had on ships for almost half his adult life had left him shy and uncertain about the best approach. So Finn walked out across the ice to *Lancer* to ask Noah to help him string together the necessary words in Inuktitut that he would need to make his thoughts known to Pia.

Noah nodded and said, "Get out your pen and paper, Captain. You'll want to write this down."

When Pia arrived next afternoon, she smiled at Finn as she put the kettle on. Then, knees straight, while bending double in her graceful way, she began sweeping the already clean floor with her short, goose-wing brush. Everett had cut a biscuit tin and shaped it into a dustpan that she greatly admired. The cook had given her a proper broom, but Pia disdained that long-handled, foreign device and refused it.

Finn sighed as he watched the rhythmic swaying of her buttocks for a while, then, working up his nerve and studying his written notes, he cleared his throat and said, "Supa, *ataata*, your father . . . Ulayu, *anaana*, your mother . . . night, *unnuakut*, they not let come you house my . . . *uvattinut aikujau laungitutit?*"

Pia listened carefully, but when he was finished, she smiled and said, "*Kaujimangilanga*, I don't understand."

Finn tried again, this time nervously rearranging the words.

Pia closed her eyes and leaned forward, trying hard to understand him.

Finn sighed and Pia said, "Lukassi, *nau taima*? Where is Lukassi?"

He looked up Noah's word, "*quianak*, it doesn't matter." Finn looked frustrated.

Pia poured him a mug of coffee from the kettle and set it on his desk. Then, flinging her parka across her shoulders, she said, "Finnussi, gooo-byeee, you," and ran outside.

Finn felt utterly discouraged by his attempt at language as he pulled on his parka, blew out the lamp, and walked sadly through the overclouded noonday gloom.

Caleb sat stiff and straight at his end of the mess-room table. Finn noticed that his moustache had been unusually tightened into dangerous-looking points. When Finn spoke to Jack Shannon, the old man pinned him with a savage stare. The others began eating in expectant silence until Otto, trying to ease the tension, called out, "Mario, quit hoggin' them green dick pickles."

Nothing seemed to help. Finn's mood deepened. The minute the meal was over, Caleb rose and the mates followed him outside. When Finn failed to follow, the old man hollered in to him, "Ice Master, I've got the feeling that you're up to something bad."

Finn remained rooted to his chair.

"I hope you're not figuring to start something you'll regret."

Finn frowned and listened.

"I told you to hire old Ikaluk to keep your house and do the sewing." The old man held the mess door open for all the mates to hear.

Finn kicked the table leg and shouted, "That's my own private business, Dunston. Keep your fat snout out of it! I'm master of my whale ship, my crew, and my own house. I don't plan on doing anything around here that you haven't been doing yourself for years."

The old man slammed the mess-room door.

Finn waited a few moments before he jerked it open. Everyone was gone. He stamped across to his house. The stove was out and it was colder than a coffin inside. Finn reset it, poured in coal, then opened the draft and set the damper. Every single mate had heard that blowup, and now what would they think of him? He kicked the stove to encourage heat and to blow off some of his anger, then turned up the lamp above his desk and sat down, feeling a trembling in his legs as he restudied Noah's word list in Inuktitut, trying to wrap his tongue around each syllable and sound. Finally, he folded the paper and hid it back inside his journal, placed his inkwell closer to the stove, and turned out the lamp, perhaps hoping Pia had been waiting to come to him as soon as his house was dark.

Removing all his clothing, Finn slipped once more inside his wide, new sleeping bag. The thick fur tickled him, exciting him again. Its soft warmth cheered his heart. The anger slipped away from him as he stared at the oblong squares of moonlight let in by his frosted windowpanes. He waited. When Pia failed to come, he summoned up an image of her lying naked in her wide, family bed asleep, with her relatives resting close around her. That protective vision comforted him as he closed his eyes and slept.

Finn did not hear his door open or close again, nor did he hear the soft swish of skin boots moving toward his bed. Still, some inner sense caused him to wake. There before him, within easy reach, stood Pia. He did not move, and in the shadows she could not see his eyes.

Finn watched as she gracefully raised her arms and stripped off her parka, pulling it smoothly over her head. Then, folding it, she quietly placed it on his chair. He could see that she was naked to the waist. Slowly, she began to unbraid her hair, at the same time easing off one of her soft, knee-high boots with the toe of the other. Loosening her hip string, she wriggled out of her knee-length seal-skin trousers. The shadows of his window mullions wrapped around the contours of her marvelous body.

Finn began to tremble in the bed.

"*Sinikpiit*, asleep are you?" she whispered shyly.

"*Aggai*, no," he answered, and, reaching out, opened the sleeping bag to her.

Pia gasped as she slipped quietly in beside him. At first, they were both so overwhelmed they scarcely breathed as they lay facing one another. Finn reached out very cautiously and touched her with his hand. She twitched, then moved a little closer to him and their knees met. Pia drew in her breath, then, rolling over, turned her back to him. Their knees bent and folded together. Pia sighed, then giggled and hid her face in the pillow. Finn wrapped his other hand around her waist, then gently slid it down over her hips, using her weight to draw himself toward her. Then he flung back the top of the sleeping bag so he could admire the soft curves of her body. He wanted to cling to her, to keep forever these first wild, trembling moments. But neither of them had the will to wait for long.

Slowly, fumbling at first, then going faster, they began that overwhelming horizontal dance that is freshly and instinctively created by every living creature that succeeds on earth.

When Finn awoke next morning, she was gone. The mates had organized a roster of workers on the try-pots to render down the blubber. From his window, he caught glimpses of Pia through the smoke, working beside a group of other women. She was laughing.

When he was dressed and had his coffee boiling, the door opened and in came Lukassi, with Pia's father, Supa, close behind him.

"Good morning, Captain." The interpreter smiled. "Supa here wants to know if his daughter is working good and steady for you now."

"Why, yes," Finn answered cautiously. "Yes . . . I'd say so."

Supa spoke rapidly to Lukassi.

"Will she be doing it every day . . . or night . . . Supa asks me to ask you?"

"Both, I guess," said Finn. "Tell him I hope she keeps this house smart, makes the coffee, softens the boots, does the sewing. Yes, you can tell him Pia's working for me now . . . full time."

When Supa heard the answer, he and Lukassi smiled and nodded. "Supa says his wife will have to get old Ikaluk to help her with the sewing and the scraping of skins."

"That sounds like a good idea," said Finn.

"Well," Lukassi said, "Pia's family is gonna need maybe a cup of molasses every six days . . . and maybe a good handful of coffee . . .

and a packet of new needles, and an iron thimble. Her mother says the only thimble she's got is an old one made of walrus hide. Also she needs a piece of a worn-out saw blade so Supa can cut out of it a new *ulu* and a flensing knife blade. They both need one."

"I guess I can supply all that," said Finn. "Lukassi, you tell Supa I hope that's all he's got in mind."

"Yes, that's all his family wants," Lukassi answered. "His wife, Ulayu, told him to tell you that they don't mind Pia coming or going from your house day or night, as long as you have told them that she's working for you now."

"I understand," said Finn, studying the handsome new boots the wife had made and eager to change the subject. "Lukassi, ask Supa if he ever got that unicorn horn for me."

"No, not yet," Lukassi translated, "but he says he'll keep watching out along the floe edge for narwhals. He'll bring you the first good tusk he gets."

Supa and Lukassi smiled.

"That's good," Finn nodded, then turned away from both of them and pretended to busy himself by rearranging his ink pot and studying his journal lying open on the desk.

"He says good-bye, Captain," Lukassi called.

Finn nodded as he heard his inner door rasp open on its new iron hinges, then ease shut. The storm door opened, then slammed. Finn could hear snow squealing beneath his visitors' skin boots as the two men hurried away.

Finn did that quick, double pigeon-wing step, for everything was working out exactly as it should. He had completed the building of his own captain's house in spite of the old man's face-to-face attacks before the mates, and now he had settled with Pia's family and she was going to share his winter house with him. Finn smiled into the mirror. All he had to do was stand firm against the nosy bastard and make sure that both crews and Inuit on Blacklead Island knew that he was a captain of equal rank, but a far kinder human being. Finn welcomed the challenge. With Pia beside him each night, he felt that the coming of this gloomy winter's darkness would pass away too soon for him.

143

A few days later, to celebrate, Finn took Pia out with him for the first time to give her a private viewing of *Lancer*. On their way, they made a sport of chasing each other across the hard-packed snow that covered the thickening ice. Pia was, of course, much faster than Finn on snow, and he only caught her when she slowed her pace to be polite.

While they were on board *Lancer*, Finn had Noah drill two holes in a short oak plank and they suspended it on two unequal lengths of rope from the long bowsprit of the ship, thus forming a private swing for Pia. In this treeless country, she was absolutely thrilled at the new experience of swaying back and forth. As Finn pushed her, he sent her soaring high for the first time in her life. Pia gasped as she tried to touch the sky. This was a swing that Finn had not intended for use by teenagers or children. Noah had warned him that such a swinging motion might draw in and excite wandering sled dogs, causing them, perhaps, to try and grab the moving human on the swing. Inuit work dogs, like New England farmers' work-horses, were never treated as pets and had no close bonds with humans. They were never considered as helping human spirits. That distinction was reserved for the wild animals.

As the days passed, Pia became increasingly acrobatic on this swing and often begged Finn to take her out so that she might use it. He would go out with her and give her that first, second, and third long, running push to get her started before he went aboard where Noah would have lit the stove in the captain's cabin and put the kettle on. When Pia came in, she would make her favorite cocoa and Finn would add a splash of rum for both of them. Before long, they would be engaged in small, joyful wrestling matches on *Lancer*'s threadbare, green plush settee. But in the end, their play would turn to other kinds of excitement. Who minded that? Not Noah. He approved of the wild sounds of life and love.

Chapter 10

The new November moon brought violence with it. A four-day storm swept across the islands, packing in layers of hard, dry snow that would cling to rocks and tundra until long after the spring sun returned again. Now only a random pattern of gray, windswept granite ridges still showed on the mountains. All the ponds and lakes on Baffin Island were thickening with clear freshwater ice. But Cumberland Sound beyond its large saltwater bays looked black and sullen, refusing to freeze, except in slowly widening silver rims around island shores. The most enterprising Inuit families cut and formed snow walls around their double canvas winter tents.

Caleb kept one crewman and an Inuk hunter with a long glass watching from the higher lookout of the Dundee men, and Finn kept two men in the lookout above the Yankee station. The pod of right whales the lookouts had seen spouting during the mid-week were now far away, and no man of sense would take the chance of sailing out in a whaleboat and getting caught in new-formed, moving ice and being lost forever. These whales would not return until the Arctic spring.

As the winter's cold crept in and packed itself around the ships and the Yankee station buildings, slowly the weather changed and hung dead still. The ice between the Blacklead station and Niantelik Bay slowly, day by day, extended its smooth white armor across the black waters until one night the two huge bodies of ice clashed and ground together, sending out canvas-ripping sounds as their sharp edges coupled, then buckled upwards. Men woke when the ice began to give off deep booming sounds like cannons, feeling grateful that both whale ships were safely locked in their winter harbor, cradled properly in the ice to rest until summer came and set them free.

Three nights later, the Blacklead islanders yelled, "*Kamutik, kamutik!*" They saw a single sled with its big dogs fanned out wide, pulling hard, coming across the ice toward them in the pale light of the moon.

As they watched it, Jack Shannon told the greenhands, "It's a helluva lot safer traveling over unknown ice by dog team than to try it walking. Sleds have long runners that spread the weight. New ice covered with snow has different thicknesses. It can drop you through to glory mighty fast."

When Finn heard the mixture of voices calling, he leapt off his bed where he had been lying on top of the sleeping bag, his skin boots still on while he waited for Pia, dozing in the warmth of his glowing stove. He had had little sleep, but lots of exciting exercise the night before. He struggled into his new caribou-skin parka, tugging it clumsily over his head, then pulling up his hood as he rushed outside toward the cluster of humans who stood watching the oncoming dog team.

"That'll be the Highlander," the old man growled, "Andrew Cargill, with his man off *North Star* and a dog-team driver. Lukassi was over there two days ago. He told me the old brute has got something special to tell us. God knows what that would be. He'll be dying to root out every speck of whaling news we possess. Tell him not a word worth knowing. I'll offer the old bugger one of our cook's awful slices of leftover duff and no rum, nothing but dark American coffee. That's sure to cut his visit. I'll send Nilak over to her brother's tent and take him into my house. It's big enough for all you mates and them if you use the long bench and the settee, but stamp your feet and dust the snow off your goddamned butts. You there, Finn, you can come and join us to hear all the local

146

gossip firsthand, but keep your mouth shut. You can pass on what-ever suits you to your crew.

"But remember, Finn, you're way too green to even try to talk to this old fox. He lives secret as a skull-and-crossbones pirate, and he's up to his arse in cunning tricks. Don't let me hear you feeding him any truthful information, especially about whales or what's going on around this station. God knows, I, myself, wouldn't tell the Highlander what month it is. But, still, I guess I'll have to give him some wild estimate on how many barrels of oil we've taken, and probably admit to the mutiny, or he'll ride me about it later. We won't get much out of him as to why they hove in here so god-damned late with the ice all but cutting him off. He's always been so proud of that *Blue Thistle* and her big steam boiler that allows him to smash through autumn ice while we real American sailing men rely on seamanship and skill . . . well, with just a little help by pulling, you know, by our crews in whaleboats."

"Back-breaking tons of pulling!" the mates groaned.

"All of James Watt's fancy steam inventions didn't help those Dundee buggers this year, did it?" Shannon grinned at Dougal.

"I've never understood," said Mario Fayal, "why the Highlander, in all the years we've known him, has never taken a young Yack seamstress to heat his bed. Sweet Jesus, it's cold enough out here tonight to freeze the nuts off an iron bridge."

"I have no trouble understanding why the Highlander has denied himself," said Caleb as he spat hairs from the wolf-skin trim round his hood. "That man has always been too cheap to part with the trade goods that he'd have to give the father of some live-in girl." Caleb held his lantern high so all could see the ice master's face.

Finn gave the old man a withering look, but Caleb went on.

"I noticed that one Newfie greenhand could hardly wait to set his sails along that same damned course. These Yacks are generous, sharing folk, but it's deeply bedded in their tradition that whether captain or crewman, a foreigner has to trade something worthwhile to a girl's family if he wants their daughter."

"Here they come," called Dougal, eager to end that troublesome subject.

The dog team came lunging off the ice and up the island's steep embankment, ready to pitch into a violent fight with the Blacklead teams. Hunters ran in, kicking at the animals, while Cargill's driver jerked on his dog lines, yelling and swinging downward with his whip butt. Finn had learned that Inuit show great respect to the animals they must hunt for food, but little for the dogs that they must master.

The Highlander rose grandly from the sled and strode toward them smiling, ignoring the teams of fighting dogs around him. He had his right mitt pulled off and his big, blunt hand extended. "Aye, well, here ye are, Caleb! It does my old eyes good to see ye once again. And ye, Dougal, and Jack, and Mario. Good evening to ye all!"

They all shook hands with Andrew Cargill, then with Colin Culloden, his first mate traveling with him, whom they all knew and liked. The Highlander then began shaking hands with a dozen crewmen, and Inuit, their wives, and children in the lantern light, many of whom he remembered by name.

"You must be feeling the chill after that ride," said Caleb. "Come up to my house, Andrew. Bring Colin with you."

"I see ye're expanding yer wee colony, Caleb, erecting that strange, Chinese-style house. Have ye brought a Gypsy crystal-gazer up with ye to help you find the fish?"

All eight men followed Caleb and the Highlander in single file, as was the Arctic custom, dictated by the narrowness of the snow-trodden path.

Andrew Cargill had to duck low as he passed through Caleb's door, for he was a very tall, wide-shouldered man. When the house light struck his dark red, wind-burned face, Finn could see deep lines folded into his forehead and around his mouth, and noted that the gray eyes were hooded from years of squinting over glaring ice. He was older than Caleb by more than a dozen years and famous for keeping his logs and journals in a small, exquisite hand, carefully drawing each success or failure during *Blue Thistle*'s annual hunts for the big bowheaded fish. Later that same evening, Finn learned that little was known concerning the Highlander's private life back home, except that it was rumored by his crew that he had a small, shy wife and two equally shy, unmarried daughters living in a small but sturdy "crow's-step" house of stone in a village called Wormit across the Firth of Tay from their home port at Dundee on Scotland's eastern coast. Other whalemen gossiped that the Highlander lived like a hermit, hiding away from mankind during his brief visits on home shore.

"Ye keep it over warm in this wee house," said the Highlander as he pulled off his caribou parka. "Ye could only achieve such wasteful heat, Caleb, with the Dundee coal ye've stolen from us."

That's a hard way to begin a winter's conversation, thought Finn. It must be talk like this that has caused such bitter winters.

"Andrew, do your daily whaling journals look as neat as always?" Caleb asked as he settled in his desk chair and watched the mates array themselves against the walls. Dunston was trying to force the Highlander to discuss his recent journal entries concerning ice and whales – and why his Dundee vessels had appeared so late.

Cargill narrowed his eyes. Both he and Dunston were proud of the fact that they were among the captains who had held off going to sea until they had acquired a certain amount of proper schooling. Both of them could write.

"Remember when we met that strangest of all whale barks?" Cargill said. "Was she out of one of your northern New England seaports, or was she out of Nova Scotia? Anyway, they had two huge right fishes in tow."

Caleb laughed and tried to change the subject, but the Highlander would not be diverted.

"Ye mind, Caleb, ye asked that captain about his success during his voyage, and he brought out his journal with not one word written in it? Nothing but a series of wee drawings of suns rising, then suns setting, and the various phases of the moon, along with his code drawings of rough seas or calm seas, coastlines, islands, and whole whales portrayed for the fish they'd taken and only the down-going tails of those fish that they had struck, then lost."

Caleb nodded helplessly, seeing that he was being led astray.

The Highlander continued. "I mind saying to that ship's master, 'Strange way to keep a log. Do ye not keep a written journal, sir?' 'Naaw,' was that wild skipper's reply. 'There's not a man aboard this vessel as can read or write a word. But there's plenty of men aboard who know damn well how to take a whale!'"

The Highlander started chuckling to drag out his long, red herring of a tale.

"Tell me, Andrew, where have you come from just now?" asked Caleb, trying again to force open the annual question box.

"Home port of Dundee," the Highlander said evasively, looking along Caleb's visiting bench now sagging with his mates. He paused. Seeing that his explanation satisfied no one, he added, "Well, we arrived here in a bit of a roundabout way."

"Around about where?" Caleb demanded.

"Around the south, then the west coast of Greenland. Ye, Caleb Dunston, have yet to lay yer eyes on such ungodly glaciers and cliffs of calving ice!" The Highlander flung up his hands. "Och, well," he said. "It's all passed now, just part of the whaling game."

Caleb jumped up and went over to kick his stove. "*Marchons*," he shouted in memory of a wild French captain he had known.

"That smells like our sweet anthracite ye're burning, Caleb. I didn't haul that coal across the North Atlantic Ocean to heat yer bloody shacks. That Dundee coal is ours. Pray, tell me, Master Dunston, how many tons have ye robbed from us this year?"

"Oh, we've used very, very little, Andrew, and, as usual, you must have brought tons more of that cheap coal with you as ballast."

"Aye, we brought a bit," the Highlander admitted. "But we'll be needing much more coal to keep our two whale ships warm this winter, for I've ordered both our crews to live aboard this year. I'll have Colin come over to check and measure what coal is missing from our pile, then send ye a bill for all ye've nicked from me."

Caleb gave Cargill, then all the mates, a pained look. "Andrew, would you have some of our coffee and plum duff?"

"Och, no," said the Highlander, puckering his face. "But my

throat's dry. Tell me, Culloden, did ye bring along that wee jug of my brother's whisky as I instructed ye to do?"

Reaching into his leather ditty bag, Colin took out a bundled woolen shirt and unwrapped from it a half-gallon jug of the Highlander's pride and joy. It did not bear a proper label, but had instead a piece of paper glued to it with scrawly handwriting on it which proudly declared the maker and the year.

"As ye know, my brother, Duncan Cargill, runs the famous pot stills near Dundee. The European and English connoisseurs admit that Duncan makes the bonniest single malt whisky in the world," said Andrew. "My brother was generous enough to part with a barrel to me at almost wholesale price. I thought it might be helpful if we began this winter season in a spirit of trust and friendship by sharing a few drams of Scotland's most sacred brew. Caleb, I trust ye have some kind of drinking vessels kicking about this house. It would be a wretched thing to see us passing a jug of such glorious whisky from hand to hand among these mates of yours, forcing them to drink it from the blessed neck." He locked his teeth around the cork and grandly pulled it out. Then, striding to Caleb's doors, he jerked them open and spat the cork outside, losing it forever in the snow.

"That's not a bad first sign of peace," Dougal whispered to the mates.

Yankee men preferred any kind of rum, bourbon, rye whisky, hair-raising akvavit, or even Holland gin. They were not great fanciers of this ruined, peat-smoked whisky. But, of course, that wouldn't keep them from drinking every last drop that came their way as the bottle came round to the outstretched mugs.

"May yer harpoon irons hold fast!" the Highlander called out, and they drank and coughed and sighed. "Tell me, Caleb, how have ye fared so far this year?"

"We've taken eleven good-sized fish and a pair of half-grown calves," Caleb answered.

"Well, that's not so bad for a start," said Andrew, "before the winter closed ye down."

Everyone emptied their cup or mug or sealing jar, then held it out. Culloden poured another round.

"And you, Andrew?" Caleb asked.

"Och, well, we aboard *Blue Thistle* and *North Star* have not been quite so fortunate thus far."

Culloden refilled the Highlander's empty mug.

"What caused you to arrive so late?" asked Caleb.

"We dropped anchor off the Faeroes because a great number of those crazed pothead whales had flung themselves ashore. The Faeroe Islanders were busy grabbing all they could – and we joined in with them. They started yelling that the whales were theirs and raising the fires of hell. A bloody waste of time it was for us. Those damned black pilot fish carry but a half dozen barrels of oil and, being toothed whales, they've got no corset bone at all. Just as we set sail to leave the wretched lot to them, a wee bit of a storm arose and we were forced to run for shelter in the lee of one of their mountainous isles. Yon damned wind pinned us down for one whole week. All we got out of that first time-wasting delay was forty barrels of oil – and three dozen Faeroe sheep that our water gatherers managed to snatch and smuggle aboard *Blue Thistle* and *North Star* in the fog. And good eating, they were, at that."

The Highlander downed his second whisky, then poured himself another good-sized drink. Still holding the jug, he carefully gave the others less than half as much. "Now, Caleb, tell me about that other antique tub that ye have frozen in near *Sea Horse*. It was too dark for our barrel man in the crow's-nest to read her sternboard."

"*Lancer*," said Caleb. "She's one of our company's older and larger vessels chosen by me to transport out our oil and bone, in '76, I hope."

"Who's her master?" asked the Highlander, narrowing his eyes. "Do ye get on badly with him, Caleb? Does he prefer to stay aboard inside that frosty hulk rather than come in to socialize with a testy man like yerself?"

"No, no, wrong as usual," Caleb grunted. "He's an ice master who works for me by the name of Thomas Finn. He's sitting close beside you, Andrew. He's new to the whaling trade."

The Highlander shook hands with Finn and said, "Well, bless my soul, Master Finn. There's nothing of the Yankee twang in yer conversation. I can hear ye're a foreigner, perhaps a Newfoundlander. Or could it be ye're some other wilder breed from Upper Canada?"

"Newfoundland's my country, dear sir, St. John's my port, and Heart's Content's my home."

"Lord God, ye're a true colonial, a Newfoundlander!" The Highlander gasped. "How did ye ever find yer way amongst this crowd?"

The old man quickly interrupted, preferring to put his own twist on the tale. "I was the one who suggested to Fisheries that I take old *Lancer* mating north with me, believing I could fill her hold as well as mine," said Caleb. "I told them that my first mate, Willie Kinney – you remember him, Andrew – should be the man to master *Lancer*. But no, they threw out that idea and sent a new, young captain in Willie's stead, and that mere boy, who was the Fisheries president's nephew, failed to handle a mutiny and got himself and his first mate murdered. It was all I could do to quell the troubles, then return to St. John's, Newfoundland, to get rid of those mutinous bastards we'd left alive and take on new hands – Newfies mostly, including this so-called ice master, Thomas Finn. He may be an ice master," Caleb grunted, "but he'd never set foot in the Arctic or struck a proper fish before."

Finn looked grim, but said nothing in that small room now laden with the smell of sweat, layers of pipe smoke, and peaty whisky.

"Och, now, Caleb, yer fid is opening up the knotty puzzle for me," the Highlander roared. "Another of those foggy Yankee affairs, a mysterious mutiny, with the killings scarcely mentioned. Well, for yer sake, Caleb, and yers, too, Master Finn, I'll leave off my inquiry." He poured himself another drink and held out the bottle.

"No more for me," said Finn, giving Caleb a dirty look.

All the others took their dram and quickly drained their cups.

"I don't imagine you want to stay and share our mess? We're having seal kidney stew and the cook's duff," said Caleb.

"Sounds just right for ye over here." The Highlander made another face. "But no, I and Culloden must be heading back to Niantelik. But, Caleb, tell me, have ye a cork to spare that I might cover up the remainder of this jug of mine? If later we're caught freezing on our ships because of the coal ye've stolen, we'll need this whisky to warm our bones." He passed the bottle to his mate, as they started to get up.

"Hold on a moment," Caleb called, as he handed Colin a cork. "Our interpreter, Lukassi, brought back word from Niantelik that you have brought a missionary with you. For God's sake, Andrew, that can't be true!"

"Well, ye might say aye, or ye might say nay on that," the Highlander answered as he sat down again. "Yon painfully pious wife of the head of our Dundee Fisheries fleet forced her husband to agree that I would take a missionary north with me. As we were about to set sail, she and the other members of their Mission Society flanked my gangway to witness that their will be done. They sang hymns and prayed until they saw their Reverend McNab safely boarded, fearing that I might try to slip away or pitch him into the harbor."

"Then you mean yes, Andrew. You did bring a missionary with you to ruin this whaler's heaven?"

"Och, believe me, Caleb, there was naught else that I could do."

"Where is he now?" Caleb asked suspiciously. "Lukassi says that he's not seen hide nor hair of your missionary at Niantelik. Did you manage to toss him overboard?"

All of them watched the Highlander cast his gaze above their heads and purse his lips, loathing to give them any information that they might later use against him.

Finally, Cargill could hedge no longer. "I was forced to advise the Reverend McNab that there were vastly more Yacks gathered up at Kekerton. That yon poor souls were nightly set upon by those howling English hooligans from the Fisheries of Hull employed on that whaling station. I convinced him that all of ye Yankees and we Dundee men, although not perfect, were bonny men at heart and very few in number here and that it was our custom to hibernate peacefully throughout the winter, whereas there was constant hell's fire and brimstone burning up amongst those other rowdies who forced Yack girls to drink their awful brews with them. The

Reverend McNab rose to the bait like a trout eager to take the fly.

"And so to answer the pleadings of yon wee Bible thumper, I offered to have *North Star* wait for me in Abraham Bay whilst I diverted *Blue Thistle* north. In the early morning while everyone at the Kekerton station slept, I lowered a whaleboat and we rowed the reverend, with his cowhide trunk, to the strongest-looking shore ice I could find that might support him. I even waved farewell to the wee missionary as he disappeared in the ice fog."

"Now that was decent of you," said Caleb.

"Aye, I'd done my very best for him. I piled on the coal to get up a head of steam in *Thistle*'s boiler, then mated over here with *North Star*. Ye must have been watching us, Caleb, forced by ice to keep away from our own Blacklead Dundee station while we battered our way into that godforsaken ships' shelter across the way. I'm having the Yacks and crewmen build high, strong snow-block walls around both vessels to protect us from yon nasty winter drafts that come roaring off the Baffin cliffs."

"Where's the master of *North Star* tonight?" asked Caleb.

"Ye don't know Duncan Sinclair? He's captain of *North Star* this year. A man most fond of 'lit-trature.' Sinclair says he'll just be well content to sit and read this winter away. He's brought a whole trunkful of books with him. But, mind ye, he's no great scholar. Sinclair admitted to me that he brought not a single copy of the poems by Robert Burns. He's reading that book, *A Tour of the Hebrides*. Can any of ye imagine any man with a mind so iron-bound as that? Och, well . . ." The Highlander sighed. "We two must be off before our cook padlocks the food away for the night and lays his drunken head to rest."

Colin winked his eye at Dougal and at Shannon, then drove the borrowed cork in hard and rewrapped the bottle in his woolen undershirt, packing it safely in his ditty bag.

"Come over to visit whenever ye've a mind to, Caleb, and bring this new master, Finn, with ye."

"I'll be much too busy this winter for anything like that," Caleb snorted.

The Highlander pulled on his parka and hauled his woolen bonnet down about his ears, jerked up his hood, pulled on his hairy double mitts, and waving, ducked out Caleb's door.

Watching through the window in the moonlight, they could see Culloden and the driver running hard on the snow beside the Highlander, who was seated sideways on the long sled. When it thundered out onto the ice, the dogs fanned out, each running hard to keep the heavy runners from catching up and killing them. Colin and the driver jumped aboard.

Caleb turned away from the window and looked at the others. "Did you notice how long I made the old goat wait before telling him about our mutiny?" He laughed. "Hold hands as you go to your bunkhouse, boys. It's chilly outside and I wouldn't want you falling down drunk and freezing off your most active parts."

Highlander's bonnet

Less than a week later, when Caleb and Dougal were returning from the warehouse in the gloomy darkness of the afternoon, their island sled dogs sent up an excited howling.

"A big dog team is coming in," warned Mario Fayal. "Coming from Niantelik."

"Their sled is heading over there beyond Captain Finn's house. There's three men and one big woman." Dougal pointed. "See her wearing a long-tailed sealskin *amautik*? The men are unloading the sled, so they haven't just come over to deliver a message to you, Captain. No – see, they're busy cutting and building an igloo in that snowdrift. Looks like they've come to stay."

Caleb went into his house with Dougal and slammed the door.

"*Kapiasukpunga,*" Nilak said as she ran out of the house.

"Why's she scared?" growled Caleb. "They're not staying on my island. But what I don't understand is why our Yacks aren't out greeting them. You can see narrow cracks of light opening around the doors of their winter tents, but not a soul is stepping outside to help or invite them in. Why are they just peeking? Dougal, will you bring Lukassi to me?"

Dougal went and came back right away. "Lukassi says he's afraid to do the talking for you. He says that big woman's got her own interpreter with her. Nilak says, and I say, too, be damned careful of her, Captain. She's . . . dangerous."

"Big woman? Careful? Dangerous?" Caleb grunted. "What the hell's all this?"

"If you don't mind, Captain," Dougal said, "I'll go and tell the mates what's happening."

Caleb shook his stove and poured in half a bucket of borrowed coal. He certainly wasn't going to give any strange, off-island Yacks the chance to strip their heavy parkas off in his house, and he knew how much they hated any place that was too hot.

His outer storm door squealed, then his inner door pushed open as a powerfully built woman thrust her way inside his house. A small man scampered after her. He closed both doors, then took a strangely crooked stance, careful not to glance at Caleb. He remained behind the woman, staring at the floor.

The big woman stood glaring at Caleb. Her dark eyes opened for a moment, then narrowed again as she drove her thoughts hard into Caleb's being, focusing her entire attention on the sharp points of his moustache, wondering how she would handle this dog child from the other side of the world. She mumbled something to the twisted man in a brusque tone that made Caleb nervous. He watched her carefully for some moments before he began that twitching of his hands that signaled he was angry.

"This big woman here," the interpreter said, "she wants to ask, are you giving a frolic this winter?"

"That's none of her business. Is that what brought her over to this island of mine?"

"Yes, she wants to come over to that frolic."

While the interpreter repeated her words to Caleb, the big woman carefully watched his eyes.

"Who are you?" Caleb demanded of the big woman. "I've never seen you before. Where have you come from?"

She pointed west, answering him in rapid Inuktitut, causing her interpreter to look up for the first time. He had a cast in one eye which caused it to slip sideways as though he were quickly examining Caleb, then every other object in the room.

"Her name is Kowlee. She says she didn't think your memory would be strong enough, but she remembers you from years ago."

"What are you people doing over on this island?" Caleb asked again, nodding toward the new igloo going up in sight of his window.

"Building her house," the interpreter answered.

"You're planning to stay overnight?" asked Caleb.

The dwarfed man repeated the question, then answered, "No, she's going to stay here all winter. She says that's because she's very mad at Andrewsikotak."

Caleb had heard the Highlander called Andrewsikotak before. It meant "Long Andrew."

"Why is she mad at him?" Caleb queried.

"She don't want to answer you right now because she's still too mad to let that red hair man go back inside her mind."

Caleb looked at this woman with her fancy, appliquéd skin parka drawn tight across her massive breasts. Her face had the widest cheekbones he had ever seen. Her hair was braided and coiled round her ears in a Yack style years out of fashion. Her eyes, forced into narrow slits against his strong lamplight, had jet-black pupils giving off two glistening points of light. Her lips were heavy and sensuous beneath a short, tight nose. Small rivulets of sweat were starting to trickle down her face, for the room was sweltering hot, as Caleb had planned. He could not help but stand in awe of this strange woman who seemed as wide in the shoulders as Otto Kraus.

Caleb's moustache twitched and his hands turned into fists. "You tell her," he rasped, "that not a one of you can stay here. This is my island and I've got my own crews and my own Yacks here with me.

I don't need any more. You can leave tomorrow morning . . . early, very early! Understand?"

When the twisted man interpreted Caleb's words to her, she nodded and said, "*Itsivaut*," and the twisted man brought her one of Caleb's chairs and she sat squarely on it near his door.

Lord God, thought Caleb, what's happening? Am I losing control here?

The interpreter said, "She tells you, turn your lamp down, Caleboosi. It's bothering her eyes."

Caleb stared at this woman and the hunched man. His face, like the two of theirs, was now shining with sweat.

She spoke one word to her interpreter. Caleb was amazed how fast he hobbled over, pulled out Caleb's desk chair, climbed onto it, and turned out the lamp.

"What the hell's going on here?" Caleb yelled at them in anger, then, stepping to his stove, he began stirring the coals to raise the heat. "Just wait!" he shouted. "I'll thaw your frozen arses for you."

Suddenly, the darkened room began to crackle and fill with smoke and the pungent smell of dried wood burning. Caleb looked up from jerking the lid of his iron stove and to his amazement saw Willie Kinney's model of *Sea Horse*, perched on the east wall of the room, burst into flames. As Caleb leapt toward it, fire engulfed the hull and masts and spars and the flag, then the thin cord rigging glowed before it shriveled, curled, and fell. With his bare hand Caleb knocked the burning model off its wall block. The dry canvas above his sextant was burning, too. "Fire! Fire!" he yelled as he beat out the circle of flames with his one free hand, then stomped on the model that lay smoking on the floor. Fire terrified him and he found himself trembling from head to foot.

To rid himself of the lifter and the hot stove top, he slammed them back on the stove. When he turned around, the smashed model lay in darkness and the wall fire had gone completely out. There was only a small half-moon of red fire glowing on the wall, and when Caleb properly replaced the stove lid, that, too, disappeared.

"To the devil with the pair of you!" yelled Caleb, and, striking a blue sulphur match, he relit his lamp, then turned its wick up high.

The big woman leaned sideways in Caleb's chair and jerked wide the porch door. The dwarf went out and kicked open the old man's outer door. A blast of heat rushed out and turned to steam in the frigid air. He stood crouched in the open doorway.

She spoke rapidly to the interpreter, never taking her eyes from Caleb's face.

"She say maybe Andrewsikotak is right. You are a badder man than him."

"That's a pile of crap," yelled Caleb. "The Highlander's a helluva lot badder man than I'll ever be!"

"Inuit over here say you *Amerikamiut* trade bigger, better presents than the *Dundeekut*."

"Damn right, we do," gasped Caleb, relieved to find his house was not on fire.

What can I give this man-eating woman, he thought. The minute you give an Eskimo a present, it's their custom to leave your house. He looked around. There was really nothing Caleb felt that he could spare – none of his clothes, or flags, or the pictures on his wall. I've got it, he thought, and, standing on his desk chair, he reached up into his storage loft, pushed aside his old oilskins, and drew down as though it were pure gold the gallon jug of malt whisky which the Highlander had given him as a New Year's gift in a year when they had more or less got on together.

The big woman pulled out the cork, sniffed it, then tasted this treasure, carefully holding it in both hands.

"*Kujannamik, aksualuk!* Thank you oh so much, so very much!" she cried, and began talking rapidly to Caleb.

Her interpreter translated. "She says you are a gooder man than Andrewsikotak. He never give her any good *imialuk*, you know, good, strong drink he brings with him from across the sea, only that awful stuff the Scottismen make over there in greasy oil barrels."

The open doors were swiftly chilling off the room.

The woman rose and, clutching the big bottle to her huge chest, she smiled like a delighted child. "Goo-night, Caleboosi, tankyoo," she said as she and her interpreter strode out, and she happily slammed both doors.

Less than a minute passed before Dougal rushed inside. "What did she have to say?" he asked, then looked at Willie Kinney's model lying broken on the floor. "We saw your lamp go out and a fire start glowing in your house, and we raced over. But then your lamp went on again and the flames were gone, we could see and hear you three arguing, waving your hands, so we stayed outside."

"First things first." Caleb shuddered. "This house of mine was burning. Sweet Jesus, it was bright with fire!"

"We saw it," Dougal said.

"You're damned right you saw it," Caleb gasped. "It started with Willie's model. I don't know how or why, but that model of *Sea Horse* burst into flames. I had to go and knock it off the wall and pound out the burning canvas behind it, though I don't seem to have any blisters raising on my hands. God, that big woman took it hard when I told her she and those Yacks she brought had to get off my island tomorrow morning early. That was after her interpreter told me she was planning to hang around here for the rest of the goddamned winter."

"We just saw them. They're getting ready to go, leaving their half-built snowhouse," said Dougal. "They're on their way back to Niantelik."

"How I managed that," Caleb said, "was to haul down that big bottle of peat-colored whisky that the Highlander forced off on me. I've never liked it, so I gave the whole damned gallon to her. The big woman admitted that I was a helluva lot better present-giver than Andrewsikotak." Caleb smiled. "Oh, she'll probably go straight back and show that jug to Cargill. That old bastard will have a fit when he sees her clutching his brother's precious malt whisky!"

"I'll bet he will," said Dougal, "but I can't see for the life of me where you've had any fire in here!"

"Well, look at that ship's model, it's burned. And look at the wall where it sat, it's scorched black."

Dougal bent and picked up Willie's model and sniffed it. "Stamped on, yes, but not a sign of fire!"

"How about the wall over there?"

"It's not burned," said Dougal, feeling the wall. "That woman must have unnerved you, Captain. She had you seeing things. Hold on. You take it easy. Your stove needs some coal."

As Dougal lifted the round iron lid, Caleb saw a red and fiery moon reflected against the wall above *Sea Horse*'s bracket.

"See, that's how she tricked you," Dougal said. "I'll take this ship's model with me. Everett and Needles Wiggins will be glad to step its masts and rerig it all for you. It's a damned shame to see poor Willie's model busted up. I wonder how Willie's making out these days."

Next morning, Caleb shouted for Lukassi. "Hop to it, lad. I need some help. Me and Nilak mostly understand each other, but this time I'm not getting my thoughts through to her. I've asked her to make something special, but she just doesn't seem to get it."

"What do you want her to do?" asked Lukassi.

"I want Nilak to sew the end of this white fox tail inside the top of my pants so it will hang down in between my legs. When I try to tell this to her, she only starts to laugh. See her giggling now? It's because she doesn't understand what a goddamned good idea I've got."

Lukassi smiled, but managed not to laugh. "What is the idea, Captain? I don't understand it either."

"Oh, Lord, what I have to put up with trying to explain things to you people! The idea is that the real cold and wind is coming soon and I want to hang this fox tail down my pants Indian-style to keep my dick from freezing. Got it, Lukassi? Tell her it's an old Indian trick."

When Lukassi tried to explain that, both he and Nilak went into gasping, wet-eyed laughter.

"Cut that out," Caleb yelled. "I'm serious. This is a helluva good idea used by Naskapi and Micmac and it really works in the cold. Keeps the crown jewels warm and frees your legs to snowshoe fast."

"Wait, wait, Captain." Lukassi held up his hand. "What's Nas-ka-pi mean?"

"It's a kind of Indian."

"What's an Indian, Nilak asks. She's never seen one."

"Sure, she has. Jesse Big Man's a Pequot Indian. And Orval Windtree, he's a Mohawk. They probably both wear them."

"Not Jesse Big Man. Her cousin would have told her if he wore anything like that. Her cousin, Tiviak, she knows him all over."

"Well, women are built different and don't have a man's problem. Ask her if she can sew in this damned tail for me, or do I have to get her pretty little cousin, Tiviak, to do the job?"

"Oh, Nilak says she'll do it," Lukassi said.

Nilak had turned away, pretending to look out the window, but anyone could see that she was laughing still.

"Remember this, Lukassi, women north or south can be kind or cruel to a decent man sometimes."

Compass rose

Chapter 11

"Now those are my overall plans for our New Year's Centennial frolic," the old man said as the mates and Finn sat round the mess-room table smoking the last of their best Brazilian cigars and finishing off their regular, large-sized bottle of Saturday night rum. "Who's going to work on the little details? I don't want to see the beginning of this special American centennial celebration turn into the usual brawl. Have you all got that?" Caleb demanded.

"This is to be an important, serious occasion. I'm going to prepare a speech about our beating all those Scottish troops, and English Navy and redcoat English bastards out of the thirteen colonies, and about General Washington, Abe Lincoln, Ulysses S. Grant, and the rising power of the United States . . . unless there's been some kind of war or local uprising down there since we sailed. I want my every word interpreted by Lukassi to these local Yacks who will all be aboard. It'll do them good to hear more about our true American history instead of having those Dundee men start singing about the Battle of Culloden. Hell, that was way back in 1745! We're going to celebrate our country's second century starting January 1876."

"Captain, how about I translate your speech into Portuguese," said Mario, "then Lukassi can yack it up for the locals and Dougal can translate it for the Dundee men 'cause most of them can't understand our American lingo anyway."

"Go ahead," Caleb agreed, giving Finn a dirty look. "If we don't have any other speeches but mine, that's fine."

"One thing's sure," Jack Shannon said, "the Dundees will come charging over here as soon as they spot the ship's covering glow and see our flags and pennants flying. They'll know damned well we're having a frolic."

"At least one full mug of hot rum for everybody before the speech," Otto Kraus demanded in his stern German accent. "And another half mug of rum right after, or all the crews will start throwing punches just to get the party going again."

"And don't forget," said Dougal, "we want to keep a sharp lookout for that extra barrel or two of home brew that the Dundee men may sled over here just in case they make us roaring mad at them and we cut off their rum supply. I've heard they brought that gin-distilling genius, Duncan Ross, with them this year. They say he smuggled two sacks of juniper berries right across the waters."

"We need an expert to organize the beauty pageant," said Caleb, "some half-decent mate who gets on well with all the hunters and their wives, and especially the daughters."

"How about Mario? The Yacks all like him and he even tries to yack a bit himself."

"Fine," the old man said. "Mario, you organize the beauty pageant. Now, who will be the contest judges, and what are we giving for first prize?"

"Well, Captain, you gotta be one of the judges," Mario said. "And of course, the crewman who wins the draw, he'll get the beauty queen herself. She's always been first prize."

"Yeah, that's how we've always done it," Shannon said. "It's only fair to the girl."

"But what will *she* get for a prize for being the best beauty?" asked Finn, who Caleb had naturally left out of all these earlier American decisions.

"Hell, she'll get the winner of the draw," roared Otto Kraus, "*und Gott in Himmel*, I hope it's me!"

"Yeah, well, you might think you'd be the greatest treasure," said Mario. "But what if, God help her, Rusty Tutter wins the draw? Have you seen him lately? His ratty-looking face is almost hidden by those bushy sideburns and his beard."

"Well, that's the chance these Yack girls got to take," said Angelo, "if they want to be our beauty queen."

"If the pageant queen doesn't like whoever wins her, she can always jump over the side," said Chris. "These young Yack girls can outrun any of our crewmen. They know how to zigzag faster than a rabbit."

"Her first prize can be a piece from that bolt of awful purple calico," said Caleb.

"Are we going to let the Dundee men in on this draw?" asked Finn.

"Hell, no!"

"Hell, yes!"

"Why not?"

"Hell, then, let them draw."

"Sure, be generous. We only have an American centennial once every hundred years. We should let the Highlander be one of the two judges," Caleb said, "so if the fun gets out of hand, I can lay half the blame on him. We're going to hold the frolic aboard old *Lancer* because she's got a bigger, wider deck."

"I'm not so keen on that," said Finn. "Her decks are cracked and leaking already."

"You heard me," growled Caleb. "The frolic's going to be on *Lancer*."

"She can take it, friend," the mates shouted. "She's a century old herself."

Caleb added, "You'll be in charge of decorations under the canvas, Angelo."

"The first thing I'll do," said Angelo, "is hang our storm lanterns high above the reach of those leapin', fuckin' Scots. We'll decorate *Lancer* from stem to stern. It'll be the grandest of any goddamned frolic we've ever had. We'll fly every signal flag we've got, to make her look like a circus tent."

"Good, this centennial is going to be some Yankee fling," said Caleb. "It'll overwhelm the Yacks as well as the Dundee men!

"So, we've picked our mates in charge of the local beauties and the decorations," said the old man. "Angelo, be damned sure you nail high the red, white, and blue bunting so no playful horse's ass can pull it down and wrap it around himself like last time. Get Rudi to help you with the food. It's always a lot better giving a frolic on board ship instead of ashore. Aboard, we can double *Lancer*'s watch and order them to boot off unruly frolickers. God knows how those Newfoundlanders and Canadian hands will act. I'm determined that this is going to be our grandest, most dignified American celebration ever!"

"We agree with that, sir," shouted Jack, "if you'll have Rudi bring us another pitcher of rum."

The old man laughed and shouted, "Rudi!"

Finn called out to the mates, "Don't let the frolickers, especially those Dundee men, dance too damned hard on my ship's deck!"

"Aw, Finn," the old man snorted, "you're a born damned worrier."

"Let's show the Dundee men that old skit of ours about Bonnie Prince Charlie. I saw some English crewmen do it in Boston," said Jack. "There's a lot of funny pushing and shoving in that one. We tried it out on some Scottish fishermen in Cape Breton, Nova Scotia."

"Did they like it?" Dougal asked.

"Not so well as we did," Shannon admitted. "You've noticed that I've had a kind of gimpy leg since then, and the top of my right ear flops. It's never going to right itself again. Well, I guess they were trying to tell us that they weren't so fond of that joke as we Connecticut men. So maybe we should skip that one."

"Captain, captain!" Lukassi called as Finn stepped out of his house with the intention of having a leak. "Every Inuit is happy about this big feast and dancing frolic that your ship is giving for them. Our hunters are ready to go and get the meat."

"Oh, are they? Good," Finn answered.

"These hunters will be glad to take you and some mates with them. You ready to come? I'm going."

"Sure I'd like to go," said Finn.

"When?" asked Lukassi. "How many days we got before this winter feast?"

Finn counted. "I figure sixteen days from now."

"Not much. We gotta hurry. Hardly any light these days. And the winds can come down hard on us. Make sure you bring your best caribou-skin parkas, pants, mitts, boots, sleeping bag . . . everything warm you got."

Two mornings later, having borrowed a narrower caribou-skin bag from one of the mates, Finn said good-bye to Pia and departed with five dog teams carrying six of the island's best hunters, plus Dougal, Buffalo Munro, and Lukassi. By midday, a storm had swollen, hitting them with the worst weather during this coldest quarter of the year. Traveling against the icy wind caused white frost patches to form on the whalers' faces if they tried to look into the wind for half a minute. Blizzards had left the snow so solidly packed that even when a man drove his skin boot down hard, his heel left no impression.

With almost no weight on the sleds, the dogs straightened out their tails and ran hard through the moonlight with steam swirling off their backs.

"What kind of meat do we want for this feast?" Finn asked Lukassi, who was sitting close beside him.

"Well, caribou, that's everybody's favorite. And seal meat. That's good, especially for the cook making sausages. I hope these hunters with us see some flocks of ptarmigan. Everyone likes them."

"I know," said Finn. "They're as good as my mother's chickens."

"We could try for some foxes," said Lukassi. "Do the kallunaat guys like the fox meat?"

"I'd say no," said Finn. "But we sure enjoy those big Arctic hares."

"You making a big mistake there," said Lukassi. "The asses of white foxes are mumuktoaluk, very tasty!"

"Forget them," said Finn. "If we can get about twenty to twenty-five caribou, and maybe ten or fifteen seals, and a hundred red char salmon, and all the hare and ptarmigan we can get, well, that should be enough."

"Good," said Lukassi. "If we see a bear, we take that, too. Bear meat is kinda sweet like sugar. We eat everything from the bear except the liver. If you shoot one, make a hole and drop the liver through the ice. Bear liver is so strong it will kill the dogs, but the meat is good. A white bearskin we give our wives or mothers to lay beneath the bedding. Some of your mates are glad to trade a bearskin to take south with them."

"Lukassi, you've heard a lot about living down south. Would you like to go there with me?" asked Finn.

"No, thanks, Captain." Lukassi shook his head. "I heard about that war you had in your country between north men and south men, lots of them cousins, even brothers. Make piles on piles of dead men. It sounds just crazy to me. Inuit never hate each other that much."

"Hell, I didn't mean that far south," said Finn. "I mean my country, Newfoundland. It's a good place. War is kind of hard to explain."

"I guess it is," said Lukassi. "Do you like being up here, does it make you feel different?"

"No, not so different," Finn told him. "I really like it here. I like the people."

"I know now that my father was a whaler," Lukassi said, "could have been a Yankee man or a Dundee man. I don't know his *kalluna* name. People here called him 'Aupuktok,' red hair. I grew up thinking I was Inuk like all my people, but a young whaler told me I was half Yack, half whaler. I crept into Captain Caleboosi's house when he was away and I looked in his mirror. I could see he was right, I didn't look just the same as all my friends. I got curly hair, brown, like a lot of whalers."

"Do you care much about that?" Finn asked.

"Yes, I care," said Lukassi. "It meant I would not grow up as clever as my friends. That I'd always be kind of clumsy and not understand things just like you, like all the whalers from away."

"You should try to think half the way a whaler thinks if you're half whaler," said Finn. "Whalers here, both Yankees and Dundee men, believe that just because they're sailors, that makes them ten times smarter than the Yacks."

"Well, they're crazy if they think that!" Lukassi laughed.

"Maybe, Lukassi, you're the best of all. I mean, being half one and half the other."

"Well, I'll try to think that way, Captain. Maybe you're right." He pointed. "At the end of this long bay, two hunters and their dog team are going to stop and stay. It's a good sealing place, they're going to do their hunting there. Another sled and two men will go over to the fish lakes for the salmon. The rest of us on three sleds will go inland looking for the caribou. Too bad there's no *umingmuk*, musk oxen, left around here. You Yankees and Scottismen loved to eat them, so you sent us out to kill them for you, and you ate them all. My mother says nobody's seen a musk ox around here since she was a girl."

When they reached the end of the bay, they halted. Finn, Dougal, and Munro waited, shivering, kicking their feet against the sleds, hoping to feel pain which would give a welcome sign of life. The sailors watched in respectful wonder as the hunters worked calmly together in the murderous cold, skillfully cutting and fitting each wind-hardened snow block into the low spiral of an igloo dome. They made their igloos exactly to size, depending on the number of persons who would sleep there for the night. It took less than an hour to build one. This igloo, with seven men helping to build it, was just big enough to sleep ten men.

While the hunters worked to finish the igloo, the three others fed the forty-six dogs. They had brought with them old hemp sacks filled with pre-chopped, fist-sized chunks of frozen whale meat. To Finn, it looked like feeding packs of ravenous wolves.

When that was done, the hunters and the mates crowded eagerly inside and blocked the low snow entrance with another chunk of snow. After the day-long battering of the numbing winds, it was like entering heaven to be inside this glittering snowhouse, glowing and warm from its seal-oil lamps. It felt comfortable as spring inside, though never warm enough to melt the snow blocks.

Each man ate all his belly would hold of a rich mixture of seal meat, which was known to warm a traveling man, and chunks of unleavened bannock slathered with plum jam, then two mugs of weak, Inuit-style coffee, this time laced with rum and black molasses.

Finn was glad to have a single caribou sleeping bag. The men arranged their bags and lay down, the Yankee men wearing all their woolen underclothes and their knit hats pulled down well over their ears. They all sighed and snored or slept like babies, not hearing the dogs that lay outside the snowhouse howling at the moon, or welcoming the snow that drifted over them and kept them warm.

The first two Inuit hunters rose early when their bladders threatened to burst and with their snow knives cut a huge hole in the windward wall of the igloo. The whalers and the hunters roared in protest at their joke, but it did get everyone moving fast. While still in their warm sleeping bags, they struggled into their boots, pants, and parkas. The Inuit, disdaining morning food, rolled up their bags and sleeping skins and tied them, then hurried out the wide, new exit. As some lashed their weapons and their few possessions on the sleds, others busied themselves catching, then quickly hitching, all the dogs.

"This is one helluva fast, rough way to start a day," groaned Buffalo Munro. "Even on the prairies with the Sioux, we took out time to gnaw some buffalo jerky while we brewed a pot of coffee in the mornings."

"Not these folks," said Dougal. "They're nomads. When they start moving in the cold, they move fast. Our most famous Arctic explorers have taken a whole month to travel over country that these Yack hunters can cover easily in what they call six sleeps."

Dougal was right. Less than fifteen minutes after Finn awoke, all five teams were harnessed, the sleds loaded, lashed, and moving, with the hunters running beside them, yelling, pushing, urging their dogs to greater speed.

When they reached the end of the long bay, the weak twilight of the overcast midday was fading into night. Pudlo and Tunu, the driver, and another hunter with Finn stopped their team. The others rested.

Lukassi said, "They're going to try around this place for seals. They've seen some *aglos*."

"What do you mean *aglos*?" Finn asked him quickly, then pulled back half his hood to hear the answer.

"Holes that seals start making in autumn when new ice comes. Seals keep holes open using their front claws. They make maybe four holes so they can breathe, then hunt in water below, use these holes to breathe different air all winter. Tunu and Pudlo, on your sled, are going to build an igloo here and hunt," Lukassi told Finn. "You want to stay with them?"

"Sure," said Finn. "What about the rest of you?"

"We're going on to the fish lakes, sleep there. Then two men stay fishing through the ice, the rest of us go inland. Maybe some caribou will share their meat and hides with us. That's the way Inuit think about it. Look close, Captain. All our hunters, they got lucky amulets, shamans' charms, sewn on their parkas. See, I got three of them." Lukassi pointed.

"I'll stay here," said Finn, "with these two seal hunters."

"Good," Lukassi answered. "They're glad to have you. The rest of us should be back after five sleeps, maybe six," Lukassi told him, "if the weather stays good like this. When you've got all the seals you can carry on that long sled, you three go back to Blacklead Island. If we have good hunting first, we all meet here, then travel home together."

"Good luck," Finn yelled, waving at Lukassi, Dougal, Buffalo, and the others, as the four teams moved off into the hissing, blowing ground drift that whipped up the snow.

It was not much past three o'clock when Tunu and the younger hunter, with Finn's help, finished their much smaller igloo, fed the dogs, and crawled inside together. They lit their seal-oil lamp, but not without a lot of trouble.

"Difficult living here, no women," Pudlo said slowly in Inuktitut, and Finn, understanding the words *arnak* for woman, and *kudlik* for stone lamp, nodded in agreement. It was a woman's art to keep the long flame fueled by melting seal fat burning evenly, giving off both light and heat to flow around the low snow dome without allowing the temperature to rise above freezing. For that would thaw the igloo and make it drip, forming a dreary ice fog inside.

"*Okuujuk*, warm," said Finn. He meant relatively warm, once they were free of the endless blasts of wind and driving snow.

"*Kaakpiit?* Are you hungry?" Pudlo asked him.

"*Ahalee!* Certainly," Finn answered, proudly using the new words that he was learning from Pia. "*Kaakpunga.* Hungry am I."

Pudlo and Tunu squatted inside the new house entrance and ate a large amount of thawing meat. Finn heated his portion as best he could, awkwardly dangling it from his knifepoint over the lamp flame. Then, like the other two, he crawled into his sleeping bag and slept. They were awakened by the excited howling of the dogs.

Tunu and Pudlo sat up naked, then swiftly pulled on their long boots, pants, and parkas. Cutting open the entrance, they ducked their way outside. The dogs were in a great uproar by then. Finn, still clearing his head of sleep, heard a heavy musket blast. The dogs began to yap. He waited, then heard a second shot. The dogs fell silent. He could hear Pudlo's voice, for the wind was down. Still struggling into his clothes, Finn saw a long snow-knife blade come through the wall, to start enlarging their low snow entrance. Pudlo, bending, thrust his head inside, a solemn look upon his face.

"*Nanualuk*, bear, big. Shot now. We're going to toss the meat and hide inside so the dogs won't get it. *Atai*, Finnussi, be ready."

"*Ayii*," Finn responded, though he had only vaguely understood what Pudlo meant.

Rising, he waited, then one whole red bear ham was flung inside. Finn pushed back their three sleeping bags as the rest of the meat landed on the igloo floor and finally the large, rolled white bearskin was thrust inside. Finn worked hard piling the heavy meat against the curved snow wall near the entrance.

"Seal hunting we are going," Pudlo said.

Finn hurried outside to see them off.

"You stay, guard meat."

"*Atsuuk*," said Finn doubtfully. "I don't know."

"*Ayii, sinilirit*. Yes, you sleep," said Pudlo, smiling at him.

Finn refitted the snow door and they chinked it tight against the wind. He could hear the hunters moving off with their eager dogs. He crawled halfway into his bag again. The light from the seal-oil lamp was still burning, but with a low, ragged flame. He tried to brighten it without success. Staring at the large pile of red meat, he drew comfort knowing that at least he wouldn't starve. He remembered his mother, after a hard day's work at the cod racks, listening to his and his sister's prayers, then tucking them in bed and kissing them goodnight. Pia, like other Eskimo girls, was horrified at the foreign practice of kissing, real mouth kissing. They preferred a kind of gentle rubbing together of their noses and sniffing, each enjoying the pleasing, sometimes exciting smell of another human of the opposite sex. Pia certainly excited Finn and he was starting to understand instinctively her different wishes, her different ways. Finn wished to God that Pia could be with him now. She would certainly know how to keep the damned lamp from going out, and how to brighten his life in other ways.

As he lay down again in the warmth of the sleeping bag, Finn closed his eyes and saw the image of Kate, yes, Katherine Dunston. Tall and lean, standing so erect on the deck of *Lancer*, dark eyes smiling at him from beneath a jaunty bonnet that just suited her. So different in character and appearance from her goddamned stepfather. It would have been impossible to imagine how that brute and Kate could be related. Why had Kate not appeared more often in his mind, he wondered. Probably because of Titus Kildeer. But now that poor man was murdered, and poor Kate did not yet know his fate. Finn hoped that he, himself, would live to see her sometime, yes, sometime again.

Finn had not brought his uncle's pocket watch with him for fear of breaking it during rough sled travel. He had no idea what time it was when he awoke, and only went outside again because he had to. It was pitch dark and overcast with the wind rising again, drifting like a sandstorm on a dry beach. Hurrying inside, he replaced the door. The lamp was almost totally out and the igloo was now deadly cold. The once-warm, red pile of bear meat had frozen and taken on a grapelike, bluish hue.

Finn sat up and ate two of the large sea biscuits, covering each with a layer of stiff plum jam. It tasted delicious. Sitting still inside his bag, he dressed awkwardly, then rose. This smaller dome was too low to allow him to stand upright. He took the double-edged meat knife that had been left inside the house and cut the snow door open again by slicing all around it, careful not to let it fall and break. Once outside, he quickly replaced the block, and tried to snow-pack the cracks around it.

Rising from his knees, Finn noticed that the wind had dropped again and that there was a faint gray dawning light at the eastern end of the bay. He jumped back in alarm when he saw, on top of the igloo, the dead bear's skull staring at him. It had a piece of thin red cloth fluttering from between its teeth. What bloody pagan sign was this, Finn wondered.

Lying beside this weirdly decorated head lay his rifle in its canvas case that Pia's mother had made for him. In the Arctic, all firearms were left outside in their protective cases, the reason being that if the guns were taken inside the igloo, the rapid change of temperature would cause the metal to sweat. Once outside again, that dampness would freeze, their hammers would not cock, nor would the trigger work. Of course, Tunu's and Pudlo's old-fashioned muskets were gone.

Finn hung his modern Sharps carbine rifle in its case across his shoulder and peered carefully around him to see if there was another bear. There, far down in the bleary whiteness at the eastern end of the bay, were two small, dark figures standing motionless some distance apart. Their dogs were lying near the sled. Something caused Finn to lurch around, staring behind him. But nothing was there. Starting out, he judged that it would take him about fifteen minutes to reach the men. The hard snow cover on the flat, sea ice seemed made for perfect walking. When he was halfway to the men, he could feel his body, then his hands and feet, begin to warm again.

When he drew nearer, Tunu thrust out his mitted hand, silently signaling Finn to stop. Pudlo was standing on half a caribou skin which he had bundled around his feet. He was bent forward, staring at the snow, and had already taken up his short harpoon. Finn waited without moving. Even in the poor light, he could see a small, dark feather fluttering above the ice hole at Pudlo's feet.

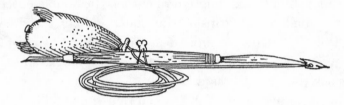

Inuit harpoon

Suddenly, the feather rose and Pudlo struck downward through the ice with his harpoon. When he felt the harpoon head imbedded, Pudlo flung aside the shaft, struggling to keep a grip on the skin line. He was hauled to his knees by an unseen force beneath the ice.

"*Kaigiit!* Come!" he called to Finn, who ran to him and grabbed the sealskin line.

The seal, invisible to them, fought back. But soon they could feel its strength weaken. It was dead. Finn kept a hold on the line, while Pudlo took up the butt end of his harpoon shaft, which had an iron chisel. He started chopping around the thumb-sized breathing hole until it was large enough. Then, carefully, the two men drew the seal up through its ice hole and onto the snow.

Finn stared at the animal in awe, for he had never seen a seal taken from beneath the ice in this way.

"*Piujuk,*" he said to Pudlo, who made a quick sign by covering his own mouth, warning Finn to silence.

It was not the custom among Inuit to show pleasure at the death of a fellow creature who had given its life for those who live above the ice. After all, this seal had been thoughtful enough to come to the breathing hole and offer its flesh to Pudlo, but not, of course, its *inua*, its soul. Finn knew almost nothing of Inuit ideas of life or death, but he wished now that Noah had told him more.

Pudlo moved off to another hole and Finn followed, staying away from Tunu, who had already taken a seal. Finn tiptoed a stone's throw away to wait over another seal hole that one of the dogs had sniffed out for Tunu.

There was no moon that night, but through the endless fields of stars, northern lights came shifting down, their greenish fingers glowing like the restless hands of ghosts. The three hunters went on waiting, eager for the smallest sign that would tell them that a seal had risen into its breathing hole. Finn could not imagine in this increasing wind and numbing cold how the other two could remain stock-still. He hobbled quietly to the dogsled and crouched on top of it, trying to make himself smaller, anything to get his feet up off the biting cold of the snow.

When he saw Tunu struggling, he ran toward him. Tunu had another plump hair seal. They enlarged the hole and drew it out. Finn this time looked respectfully sad and silent.

"*Kaakpunga*, I'm hungry," Pudlo said when he came up to them. "Cold it's going to get out here."

"*Uvangalu*," said Tunu, smiling and pretending to shiver as a joke.

They rolled the three pig-sized seals onto the sled and yelled at the dogs, then all three ran beside the team to warm themselves.

Inuit igloo with cache

The lamp Finn had tried to tend had gone out and the once-warm igloo now reminded him of a frozen meat larder. Tunu, with some difficulty, trimmed the long wick, then relit the stone lamp, using one of Finn's waxed matches. He sliced snow into their battered kettle and it began to melt. Pudlo had stayed outside to cut blocks to build a meat cache attached to their house. He left the top open on the cache so they could heave in the frozen quarters of bear meat, and the three seals. Only then did they complete the cache's dome and feed their dogs with the whale meat they had protected by burying in the snow beneath the place where they slept.

The three ate all the fresh seal meat their stomachs would hold, and drank many cups of molasses-sweetened coffee. Crawling into their bags, the hunters immediately slept. Finn had to wait for the shivers to drain away from him before he, too, was lost in dreams. There was Kate again, and now Pia. Yes, he wanted Pia. She knew all about this other way of life.

When Finn awoke, both men were gone. He felt somewhat ashamed that he had not awakened and gone with them. The lamp was burning nicely. He tamped the wick and tipped it slightly to increase the flow of oil. Enjoying his small sense of accomplishment, he watched the long flame burning evenly. On this morning – if it was morning – he used the knife to shave snow off the inside igloo wall and filled his tin cup, then held it over the flame, his skin mitt protecting him from the heat until the water simmered. He then crushed some coffee beans with the knife butt, put them in the hot water and mixed in a thin trickle of molasses so sugary it could not freeze. He ate two sea biscuits with plum jam and felt a sense of contentment rising through his body as he stared up at the millions of small snow crystals that made up their igloo dome shimmering in his newly brightened lamplight.

If only Pia were here, he thought, then wondered why he hadn't wished that the girl he knew from Portugal Cove were here. "Oh, my God!" he said aloud. "She and Dunston's daughter would probably hate it here. Even if I had the double bag with me, what would they have said when they saw that pile of raw purple bear meat lying right beside them!"

Finn lay down and allowed his mind to wander back to Pia. She was exactly right for a house like this. Yes, Pia, taught by her mother, knew almost everything she needed to know, not just how to survive, but how to enjoy the delights of this free and open winter country, with its towering, blue-shadowed mountains and deep, ice-covered fiords. There was no earth here. No plants or crops would grow. There were only the animals who could graze on the tundra plains or hunt each other and those beneath the sea. Only nomad hunters and their families could survive here at the top of this miraculous world.

Finn slept again and awoke with a start. Had he heard the hunters returning? He listened and slowly it dawned on him that these sounds were different – no dogs yelping, no human voices. Finn turned his head cautiously, following the alarming sound of heavy padding, sniffing, then a low moaning, groaning, and rough scraping against the outside of the igloo.

"Tunu! Pudlo!" Finn called their names, then knew he'd made a mistake.

The rubbing stopped and there was a long silence. Then the heavy sniffing and clawing began again.

Please, God! Don't let that be a bear. Finn scarcely dared to breathe. My rifle . . . where's that fuckin' rifle? It's lying in its case up on top of this igloo. Oh, sweet Jesus! What am I going to do? Where's the meat knife? Here it is. What good will this hand-length blade do against an animal that size? Noah had told him of a bear that had caught a woman in her igloo, and her young daughters said that the bear had taken a long time feeding on her before it finally killed her.

Finn quietly drew on his caribou parka. Then, bending double, he eased into his skin boots and over them his knee-length pants. The lamp was burning low. He was grateful for the light, although if he had considered the strong, delicious smell the hot oil exuded for the bear, he would have snuffed it out.

He saw the snow blocks bending inward under a tremendous weight, watched the snow mortar between them crumbling, trickling in like frozen sand. There was a long silence, then the grunting and sniffing intensified. Finn stared at the bending wall in awe. It could be nothing but a bear, nothing else could sound or force the wall like this.

He drew away from the place where their outside cache wall adjoined the igloo wall, where the blocks had started to break open. Now his back was pressed against the opposite wall. Crouched and trying to make himself invisible in a fetal ball, Finn heard several powerful blows, then the terrifying sound of frozen skin tearing, and bones being crunched and broken. An awful blowing and grunting confirmed that the huge beast had broken through their meat cache wall and was now feeding ravenously on their seal kill.

Oh, God, let that damned brute fill its belly until it explodes, Finn prayed. He rolled down his woolen hat and jerked up his hood, then held his hands over his ears, trying to block out the monstrous sounds no more than a man's length from him, with nothing in between except a trembling wall of snow. Where are those two hunters? And where are all the dogs that warn people against bears?

The unseen animal must have been starving, for it was choking down the seal meat, grunting like the huge pig that Finn had helped his father raise on their small farm at Heart's Content. He had always been terrified of that ill-tempered boar, but he was a thousand times more frightened of this unseen bear, knowing that he would probably have to face it alone without a weapon, without any kind of help.

Finally, he could hear its stomach rumbling as it backed out of the meat cache and padded slowly, sniffing around the igloo, stopping right beside him. Finn remained dead silent, crouching on one knee. Then, slowly, he experienced the greatest relief that he had ever known. The sound of the bear's paws faded as it moved away. Finn crawled trembling into the furry, womblike safety of the sleeping bag, which he then pulled over his head. It was utterly dark in there, but his eyes remained wide open and his hearing sharp.

Finn would never know how long he stayed like that, but finally he thrust his head outside the bag and lay there gasping. All around the igloo there was only blessed silence.

He jumped when he heard a heavy musket boom down near the end of the bay. Then silence again. No wind, nothing, just a deadly quiet hanging all around him. Finn rose and cut away the door with the short meat knife and listened.

Not long after, he heard the distant thumping of the heavily loaded sled as the team hauled it across hard, wave-shaped drifts. He stepped outside again and heard the sharp crack of the whip and the "Ouk, ouk, ouk!" of the driver as the big dogs suddenly came crowding around him.

"*Nanualuk!* Big bear!" Tunu's head nodded in the dark. "Finnussi, you lucky. A whole seal he took into his belly. Now he give it back to us."

As Finn's eyes grew accustomed to the dark, he looked again at the wreckage of their snow-block cache, torn wide open, with meat scattered everywhere. Pudlo, whip in hand, was yelling at the hungry team, keeping them at bay until the men could reclaim the meat, rebuild the cache, then properly feed the dogs.

"*Nanuk?*" Tunu said, and pointed.

There on the sled, lying on its back, already skinned and looking exactly like an enormous, naked man, lay the second bear, with his white pelt rolled and tied like a pillow beneath its head. Behind it lay four seals.

"*Nanuk, tanasana.* Bear, same one," said Tunu. "We followed his tracks back to you."

Finn helped Pudlo dig up and feed their frozen whale meat to the team while the dogs were still harnessed. Tunu was busy with Finn's sharp pocket knife, cleverly disjointing the bear into manageable quarters. When finished, they worked together building a whole new cache that was much larger than the first, then piled in all the meat and repaired their greatly weakened igloo.

This time Finn was the last to crawl back inside the snowhouse and replace the block. He refilled their trade kettle from the snow wall and finally got the coffee heating over the lamp. Tunu and Pudlo had sat down on their sleeping bags. They ate their fill of the rich bear meat, then lay back, sniffing at the wonderful smell of molasses, jam, and coffee. Finn had to wake them when the coffee boiled.

After the hunters fell asleep again, Finn tried not to think of the bear ordeal. He felt glad to be alive, but certain that he would never be the same again.

A storm wailed over them next day and they did nothing but eat and sleep and eat again. On the following morning, the wind had died. Finn went out and, looking to the east, he watched the full moon rising like a frozen face. Neither daylight, nor darkness, Finn discovered, had anything to do with the hunting of unseen seals in the warmer waters beneath the ice.

They departed next day. First lashing their grub box on the front of the sled, they next tied on their sleeping skins and extra outer pants and parkas, leaving the remainder of their long sled to fit the lamp, the abundance of bear meat, hides, and seven frozen seals laid neatly side by side, everything bound firmly in its place. It was an immense load, so heavy that the three men had to walk and push hard on the sled to help the dogs over even the slightest hard-packed rise. There was no thought of riding.

They had traveled perhaps five hours from their abandoned igloo when Pudlo looked back and pointed. Turning, Finn could see all four other teams, a dark string in the distance, following their trail. They slowed, allowing the others to draw closer. Finn could see that they, too, were walking, their sleds piled shoulder high with meat.

Two hours passed before Finn's team reached that first big igloo they had built. Finn felt small beads of sweat making their slow tracks down his back. They stopped and repaired the side of the snowhouse. Night cold had seeped down on them, and Finn was so tired from their relentless work that he could scarcely put one foot in front of the other. Pudlo and Tunu busied themselves talking amiably together, rapidly cutting new snow blocks for the three large new caches they were building against the old igloo. They piled all their meat inside of one, and the others they left open for their friends who followed.

Dougal's team was first to arrive. He and Finn helped the fishermen unload nearly a hundred plump, red-fleshed salmon, many of them as long as a boy's arm, all of them frozen hard as stone. Then Lukassi arrived with Buffalo Munro, both walking and pushing beside the other three teams. The hunters with them built a fourth igloo-shaped cache until the snowhouse was entirely ringed with caches into which they stuffed all of the remaining meat.

"How many caribou?" Finn asked when they were all inside the igloo.

"Twenty-three," said Lukassi. "We could have taken more, but we didn't need more. I'm tired and . . ."

Lukassi fell asleep while still talking. The other hunters laughed and shook him awake.

"Did you get some of the caribou?" Finn asked Buffalo Munro.

"Yeah," Buffalo answered, "maybe one or two."

"He's fooling you," said Lukassi. "These other hunters say they wish they knew how to shoot a gun his way."

"My Sharps rifle didn't do me any good when that bear came," Finn admitted. "It was outside on the roof."

"Didn't you have a knife with you?" asked Lukassi.

"Yes, but what could I have done with that against a bear?"

"Everything." Lukassi laughed. "You cut a hole in the snow roof, reach up, pull your rifle inside, then listen carefully to where the bear is, and shoot a bullet or two through the wall into him. That's the Inuit way. It almost always works." He laughed again. There was a pause. "Good night, friends," sighed Lukassi as he fell back deep asleep.

They rose at noon next day, and only reached the Blacklead station sometime during the night. The hour didn't matter at this darkest time of year. Finn saw the lamplight glowing in the frosted window of his house and then Pia running with others toward him. God, it felt wonderful to be alive, to feel the joy of being back, so close to the warmth of her again!

Chapter 12

"This is going to be the greatest fuckin' frolic any of us has ever seen," said Mario Fayal. "We're going to have more than a hundred and forty jumpers out on *Lancer's* deck eating like husky dogs, drinking like camels, and kicking up their heels, trying Jesus only knows what kind of dancing."

"Never you worry about the drinking part," said Rudi Haas. "Leave that to the brewmasters. Our job is to do the cooking. We've got all kinds of meat now after that hunt."

"Yeah, we know," said Rafael Costa. "But how the hell you want us to cook it? I say make sausages, good Portuguese sausages."

"Forget them," said Angelo, "they're too big. The crews will throw those at each other."

"A stew would be the easiest kind of food to satisfy this crowd," Domingo Pulvur called from his stove. "I knew a cook from Fayal who made a stew out on the Azores that would keep folks dancing, and singing, and galloping to the outhouse all week long. I know any kinda meat or fish makes good stew. Chop it into chunks – necks, brains, lungs, livers, hearts, heads, feet – everything. Start by melting the bear's lard and the caribou back fat, then add the last of those sprouting onions, bruised turnips, and a lot of garlic mixed in seal oil. Next, melt snow water and add any other vegetables from that old root pile in *Lancer*'s hold. It will smell so damned good that when the strongest oarsmen come aboard, they'll faint!"

"What are we going to use to hold this stew?" asked Mario.

"*Lancer*'s still got a pair of old iron try-pots on her deck for rendering whale oil out at sea," said Rudi. "They're rusty inside, but we'll put Jose and Pierre in one pot with rough sharkskin pads and whale oil mixed with sea salt. We'll make sure they scrub it good. We light the fire in the brickworks under that try-pot. When the ice melts, we start shovelling in the chunks of whatever's lying around. The ptarmigan have been skinned local-style, and that old bunch of eider ducks and geese we tried to smoke are tough as shoe leather, but they'll melt right into this brew."

"How many gallons does one of those try-pots hold?" asked Antoine.

"Two hundred and fifty gallons," Mario answered.

"Hell, a hundred gallons should be enough to feed this crowd."

Rudi shouted, "Yeah, well, remember those goddamned Dundee men always try to sneak a barrelful back with them."

"We've got damned few plates," said Mario. "How are they going to eat it?"

"Out of their drinking mugs," said Rudi. "All of them bring mugs as big as piss pots to be sure they get their share. They'll use them."

"Then we've got a hundred good-sized salmon," Antoine pointed out.

"Leave most of them raw, you know, half frozen," said Mario. "That's the way the Yacks eat them – and probably the Dundee men, too."

"We're going to need some kind of baking to go along with all of this," suggested Antoine.

"True," said Rudi. "You could make a big batch of those baker's balls you're famous for that need whacking against the table before you eat them or you'll break your teeth. We'll stack them navy-style on the deck to remind folks of our Revolution in 1776."

"What about a frolic cake?" asked Mario. "A real big Azores *bolo rei meunto delicioso* with rum and raisins. We've got lots of sacks of old flour and we oughta use it up before the weevils walk away with it. The minister's wife in Mystic sent us some red and blue coloring and a pound of those little silver Sen Sens, the kind the church choir singers use to wipe the smell of gin off their breath. The old man and Finn can toss a snow knife to see who gets to cut the cake."

"We can brew a lot of weak coffee in the other try-pot and lace it heavy with molasses. Then we'll make a couple dozen sheets of toffee for the little kids and their parents," said Mario. "The Yacks love toffee."

Everyone agreed: it was going to be one helluva party.

It was nearly ten o'clock on Friday night, December 31, 1875, when the old man checked his timepiece. About then a spectacular show of northern lights appeared over Blacklead Island, probing down toward the glowing, canvas-covered *Lancer*. Out from the whaling station came a wavering parade of Union Yankee freemen and Newfoundlanders mixed together with every single island Yack. They were running, dancing, and skipping over the snow-covered ice. Greenhands mixed with young Inuit were kicking a soccer ball ahead of them. Two seamen were doing cartwheels and somersaults, while others took turns banging on a pair of Civil War drums and trying to play on fifes. This grand parade was happening as the merrymakers rushed toward this enormous Arctic celebration that would not happen again for another hundred years.

Two sleds were being dragged out to *Lancer* by Yack hunters and seamen, each proudly fitted by the women into their dogs' harnesses. On top of these sleds were lashed two new thirty-one-and-a-half-gallon barrels normally intended to measure whale oil. Rudi, the brewmaster, had made some Dusseldorf brandy that he swore was stronger than gunpowder. He had had one greenhand he trusted stand on guard over this treasure, allowing it to age for nearly a week.

The old man, Finn, and Noah had sledded out early so that they would be aboard to greet the guests, who arrived wearing outlandish costumes of their own devising. Some crewmen had wrapped themselves in split flour sacks that they had painted with moons and stars and fanciful designs. Behind them, for the moment at the back of the parade, a group of young Yacks was gaining on the crewmen, literally by leaps and bounds. Rushing out ahead of them all was a squealing host of girls and younger wives. This was going to be one helluva frolic!

Frolic bunting

Lancer, fully lighted and ringed by her protective snow-block walls, was aglow with ship's lanterns gleaming through her sail cover. It was like a vast circus tent on top of which fluttered dozens of colored signal flags all bathed in Arctic starlight and the aurora borealis. What a sight! A low entrance across the gangway had been hung with doubled sailcloth to capture all the body heat.

The two barrels of Rudi's home brew were noisily rolled up *Lancer*'s gangplank. The top of these barrels had scarcely been knocked open before the Yankee freestyle music began – a wild mixture of drumming, accordion playing, banjo strumming, fife blowing, and harmonica trilling, not to mention human voices singing in various keys in at least four different languages. Every sailor and Yack, both male and female, wore around their neck the very largest mug that they could find. One of the greenhands was busy pumping the try-pot bellows furiously, causing the stew to simmer and four ironsmith's pokers to glow cherry-red. These were thrust sizzling into the tea-based rum punch that filled an enormous, battered pewter bowl. Caleb had generously supplied two kegs of cheap trade rum to lace the punch.

The old man was openly sociable toward everyone, even Finn.

"I figure since we are both captains we should join in giving this centennial bash," the old man said to Finn as they shook hands. "Let's call it a truce just for tonight."

"Fine with me," said Finn.

"Then remember to come up and shake hands and congratulate me heartily as soon as I finish my speech. Everyone aboard will think that I've forgiven you for building that crazy-looking house of yours. That way, Finn, you won't have to make a speech and our guests can get on with the party."

Finn nodded suspiciously.

"By the way," said Caleb, "is that girl, Pia, coming?"

"No, not tonight," Finn answered. "I had Lukassi advise her to stay home with her mother. Now they're both mad at me for causing them to miss this party."

"Nevertheless," said Caleb, "I think you made a wise decision. I don't want any rumors drifting back to the partners or Mystic or New London about any wild shenanigans involving a ship's captain or even an ice master and the girls who keep house, do I?"

Finn was about to give a disastrous answer, but was interrupted by a thunderous roll on the drums. The old man leapt into the line that snaked across *Lancer*'s deck toward the barrel where each person received his or her first mugful of centennial punch.

The Yacks were the first to display that loose-kneed, elbow-waving walk that had made this Yankee punch so justly famous. It set off all of them hooting, howling, and skipping in their soft skin boots, the local hunters and seamen trying to dance each other down. Meanwhile Nilak and the other married women joyfully yack-yack-yacked, with their sharp eyes observing every move.

After the third round of Blacklead punch had noisily been served, Noah Anderson gave a warning shout through the gamming horn. A hush fell over the crowd. In the freezing distance far across the ice, they could hear the skirling of bagpipes coming from Niantelik. The children ran and squatted down, peering beneath the gangplank cover, then turned and shouted, "*Scottiismen!*"

Not more than three stone throws away, and well ahead of his horde of Dundee men, marched the Highlander himself, swathed

188

in a chieftain's plaid with waggling kilt and sporran beneath his heavy parka. He was flanked on either side by two kilted pipers, and beside them four more clansmen, carrying tall, flaring, oil-soaked torches. What a sight these Scotsmen made, all of them wearing some bits of Highland dress costume over their warm, caribou clothing.

Captain Andrew Cargill was, of course, the first to place his foot aboard the Yankee ship. Pulled down over his ears, he wore his bonnet with a red turrie on its top. He looked up in mock amazement at the lights, the multi-colored pennants, and the patriotic bunting festooned everywhere. He called out in Gaelic, "*Mo bheannachd ort Fhir Chinn Iochalainn! Dunston and Finn a muigh.*"

"*Gott in Himmel!*" whispered Otto Kraus. "What kind of yacking is that?"

The first Scotsman to board after Cargill and the pipers laid a pair of Highland backswords crossed on *Lancer's* deck. Taking only one long drink of whisky offered by his first mate, Colin, the Highlander began to leap with clever, tiptoe steps between the blades, in a lively sword dance that sent his kilt awhirl. From the tops of his sealskin boots, it was clear that he had slyly bound his thighs with a heavy, pinkish woolen cloth to protect his knees and his nether parts from freezing. For their bold march across the ice, his two pipers had done the same.

When the Highlander's traditional dance was ended, the Dundee men pushed forward their cook, a huge, heavyset man with russet-colored sideburns and bright red jowls that trembled when he sang. This cook raised an oaken staff above his head and all could see suspended from it a good-sized walrus gut filled with ripe haggis. Inside this ballooning bag was a heavy mixture of oatmeal porridge together with heavily peppered walrus heart and liver, and onions that had been carefully aged since their arrival.

"Haggis!" he shouted proudly. "The royal feast of Scotland's kings."

The Blacklead crewmen winced, held their bellies, and made awful retching sounds. Others clutched their throats and ran to the monkey rail, some only pretending to throw up. Then all of them turned and staggered back to their cook's table, holding out their mugs for rum. But already a pack of rugged, thirsty Scots had formed a solid ring around the punch bowl.

Both accordion players joined in playing a Virginia reel that had surely come across the seas from Scotland. Seamen with Eskimos of all ages formed two lines of fourteen persons each. Fiinn could see Kudlik and Pootavut dancing with abandon. Caleb grabbed Nilak's hand and joined them. They whirled together in two great circles, weaving, ducking under hands until sweating and dizzy, then collapsed, exhausted. Immediately, a second group took over as the music took on an even wilder cadence. The soft skin boots of the women skipped in rhythm with the men. The long tails of their parkas swung waist high through the air, giving the frolic a feeling that everyone aboard had lost control.

Then *Lancer's* French-Canadian fiddler struck up another tune that set the New England farmhands gobbling like turkeys then leaping like spring lambs.

The Highlander and his crewmen had brought with them their largest mugs. But, thank God, they had not come empty-handed. Their local hero, Duncan Ross, had saved the day. Four Scottish oarsmen rolled two barrels of his homemade whisky noisily across *Lancer's* deck.

"Where's Captain Sinclair tonight?" Caleb asked the Highlander.

"Och! Sinclair's back aboard *North Star* doing his usual," Andrew snorted. "Leaning back in his wee rocking chair with yon half spectacles perched upon his nose, reading poetry and making unreadable little notes along the margins. I swear to ye, Caleb, that man will read himself to death."

"Where's that big woman, Kowlee, who lives with you over there?"

"Och, that bitch!" said the Highlander. "She's too mad at both of us to come to this year's frolic."

A thick walrus-hide line had been stretched at twice the height of a man across *Lancer's* deck and fastened to opposite whaleboat davits. A pair of strong young Inuit hunters pulled off their parkas, then, bare-chested, leapt up, grabbing the line. They began to skin the cat and whirl like high-wire acrobats in dizzying ways accompanied by female screams of delight.

The drums rolled and the stunsails that had hidden *Lancer's* stage were hauled back by two sailors. The fiddler and a banjo player, standing on one side, began playing faster and faster. Suddenly, six Yankee oarsmen attired in makeshift kilts leapt out on the stage. These men of great husky shapes and sizes were heavily rouged and made up with burnt-cork mascara, their lips painted ruby red. They drew loud shouting and applause from their audience. Those who dared to imitate their wild, bungling dance steps fell backwards on the deck.

Outside, at exactly twelve o'clock, one, two, three, four, five, six small wooden kegs of gunpowder were chain-exploded at a safe distance from *Lancer's* hull. Eighteen seventy-six was here. America's second century had begun!

The Dundee men were so excited by the warlike rumble of explosions that they knocked off the tops of both their barrels of homemade hooch.

"Fuck the British," sang the Yankees.

"Fuck the English," sang the Scots.

Some crewmen collapsed onto the deck, laughing at the sheer cleverness of their political wit. The volume of all their voices overwhelmed the squalling of the bagpipes and thundering of the drums.

Sea Horse's tallest crewman, Jesse Big Man, disguised as Liberty, wrapped in a costume of painted sailcloth, stepped to mid-stage and ran up the Stars and Stripes on a short, makeshift flagpole. Lester had carefully rigged this flag with a wire cross stay that held it outstretched as in a powerful breeze.

"Hip, hip, hurray!" yelled all the Yankees.

"Hip, hip, hurray!" the Scots joined in.

"Hippa, hippa, ray!" shouted all the Yacks.

What a feeling of togetherness! What a celebration!

Now, with some over-jubilant pushing and shoving from the audience, the long-awaited beauty pageant began. Seven shy but handsome Eskimo girls were already coming out on stage as the stunsails were drawn back. Some of the girls had to be pushed a little by their mothers or older sisters.

"Where's Pia? She's good-looking," Otto shouted to Finn. "Why isn't she entering this beauty pageant?"

Others looked around. "Where is she? Why isn't she at this frolic?"

"Pia and her mother have stayed home to guard my house," yelled Finn.

"Guard your house! From what?" Mario laughed. "There's not a soul on Blacklead."

"Well, the dogs might break in, so Pia and her mother stayed behind."

Of course, Finn knew that Pia was in tears at the thought of missing this frolic, and especially the beauty contest. But her mother, a woman of experience, remembered other beauty pageants she had entered and won, and agreed it might be just as well that Pia remain at home.

Caleb and the Highlander, who had always been the judges of such important events as curling matches, major soccer games, and beauty pageants, walked to the foot of the stage and expertly eyed each contestant. They whispered together for a moment before stepping forward. They placed the gilt-painted crown on the head of a lovely, red-cheeked teenage girl, Nilak's sister. It was the right moment to hold the lucky draw. Caleb reached into a small keg and drew out the ticket with the number twenty-two.

Lukassi shouted, "Twenty-two! *Avvatiilu makulu!*"

Mario yelled, "*Vinte-dois!*"

"That's me," whispered a young Scot, a greenhand from *Blue Thistle*, and he showed his ticket.

"Scots wha hae!" bellowed *Blue Thistle*'s crew. "She'll make a man of ye!"

"Good luck, dear lad!" called the Highlander.

"It's all the tail you'll ever need, me son," yelled the Newfoundlanders.

"*Tusunamik!*" the Inuit mothers called to the girl. "You're lucky you caught a young one."

"That boy's got a lovely smile," Nilak told her sister.

The new beauty queen was rushed off stage by her female cousins and to the entrance of the fo'c's'le with the lucky winner of the draw. The shy boy was probably about her age. There was much shouting, laughing, and applause as an eager crowd of young Yacks closed the hatch above their heads.

Now the Scots and Yacks and Yankee men were engaged in sports-like wrestling, rooster crowing, and weird face-pulling games while weaving and jumping in two long lines toward the quickly emptying barrels.

"Cut the jumping," Finn yelled, "or you'll break through old *Lancer*'s deck!"

"*Achtung, achtung!*" Kraus bellowed. "Stop *der* leaping, *Fräuleins und liebchens*. Food wraps is now coming off."

As the cook whipped the sailcloth away, Charlie Flender reached across the table and picked up a wedge of cheese. Examining it in the light of the whale-oil lamp, he began to sing: "There are skippers in the cheese / They're as big as bumblebees . . ."

He pulled one out and held it up and half the crews sang, "There are skippers in the cheese . . ." while the other half began wolfing down this rare luxury that, like the green dick pickles, had disappeared from their chow line months ago. The Inuit made awful faces and held their noses, for they could scarcely believe the revolting and savage habit of eating cheese, with or without the bugs.

Otto's booming voice may have saved old *Lancer*, for the snake-like lines of frolickers stopped their stamping and crowded hungrily around the long plank tables where the food was piled in the style of a Rhode Island clambake. Two harpooners stood giggling and swaying by the steaming try-pot, trying to ladle out the stew. Each guest ate a huge amount. Some of the crew tried to break the cannonball bread by bowling it hard against the mainmast.

Otto shouted for order as the cake was ceremoniously cut by Caleb and snapped up as if by a pack of wolves.

When the feasting was over, the stage curtains were jerked open and the main skit began. There in the middle sat a broad-shouldered Rhode Island oarsman dressed as a farmer's daughter. "She" was sitting on a three-legged milking stool. A Holstein cow approached her. It was easily seen by half the audience that this was no real cow, and the other half of the audience had never seen a cow. This one had been cleverly constructed by the sailmaker and the carpenter. Everett had made a realistic head of pine, with leather ears and a pair of powder horns. The sailmaker had stitched the front half and a back half together out of old sailcloth, then painted on its Holstein markings with hot black pitch. The front half had bovine eyes and red, smiling lips. All one could say of the back of the cow was that it swayed, had a tail, and was very drunk. Even by genuine milkmaid's standards, this cow was going to be very hard to milk!

The unknown farmer entered, his face hidden by a large straw hat and oakum beard. He gestured to his daughter to get on with the job.

Now, the revellers were spread all over *Lancer*'s deck, some watching, others lying, relaxing on their elbows or resting on their backs, Scots, Yacks and Yankeemen lying peacefully together.

The farmer's daughter began to milk in earnest, carefully aiming each teat at her wooden bucket. She started counting each imaginary squirt aloud as she aimed from each of the four teats, "One, two, three, four . . . five!" When she reached that impossible number, there was a terrible yell from the back of the cow as it kicked the milkmaid's stool from under her. What followed was the ripping sound of stitches as the cow parted and both halves went galloping off stage. This skit caused laughter, jeers, and many unanswered questions from the Yacks.

Next came the other side of the coin. As tradition had it, Eskimos would have their turn. This made the old man, the Highlander, and most mates nervous, for it was always the annual favorite. First came a Yack playing an Azorian tune on his button accordion while wearing a chef's hat and singing in a perfect wordless imitation of Rafael Costa, called by the crew "the wailing cook."

Suddenly, a character came roaring out on stage wearing a skin mask with bushy eyebrows, sideburns, and a dagger-pointed moustache, instantly recognized as the old man. This figure did a frantic, whirling dance, dragging a long, skinny boy doll dressed to match the ice master in one hand, and a stuffed right whale doll in the other. This caricature of the ice master and Caleb and his longing for whales seemed about to cause a fight when suddenly two other figures in long-tailed female parkas came rushing out, each one clutching her captain to her breast. Roars, whistles, and laughter greeted the Yack actors as one by one the female figures split and ran off, dragging the old man and grabbing the ice master doll. The audience roared and applauded for more.

"The Yacks are carrying those damned skits of theirs too fuckin' far," the old man grumbled to the Highlander.

"Och, nooo! Their skits are getting finer every year." The Highlander thumped Caleb on the back. "That was a perfect imitation, especially of ye and that expensive seamstress of yers!"

"Forget all that," said Caleb. "Remember two years ago when they did that skit of you in that bushy sideburn mask and bonnet, when you kissed your piper hard right on the mouth and did a leapfrog over his back? Remember? You were mad as hell at that."

"Och, well, the Yacks were going miles too far. But this skit," said Andrew, "I've just been assured by yer own mates and crew that yon skit is true to life. The Yacks had ye and Finn down to a T!" said the Highlander as he turned away and secretly filled his mug with his brother's whisky.

"I must admit," said Caleb, "your Dundee men have behaved themselves quite well this frolic. Do you remember that big Guy Fawkes brawl you gave several years ago when you burned his effigy in straw?"

"Well, now, I don't remember any of the details," said the Highlander. "As ye can see, our men and yers are now well beyond the brawling stage. It's love or sleep that's firmly in their minds. Look how many are lying sprawled about this deck, out cold, or just catnapping – Dundee men, Yacks, Yanks, Canadians, Azorians, Newfies – all alike. It must be like viewing the awful carnage on

Lord Nelson's deck after the Battle of Trafalgar. Let's go back to Finn's cabin and rest ourselves a wee bit."

Slowly, some of the dancers and the singers were beginning to revive, dizzily staggering to their feet, holding onto mast or rail as they tried to catch their second wind.

Andrew Cargill was at heart a competitive old Scot, whether it was for whales, winter harbors, or songs. When they came out of *Lancer*'s cabin, Caleb saw the Highlander seize his chance. When Andrew made a secret signal, his only piper left standing put the chanter to his lips. Blowing out his cheeks, the piper started pumping up the bag, using his arms like the wings of a dunghill rooster about to crow. A moaning, groaning blast arose, causing many collapsed revellers to raise their heads, also to moan and groan.

To the slow shrilling of the pipes, the Highlander began to sing:

Oooh, ye take the high road
  and I'll take the low road
  and I'll be in Scotland
  afore ye.
  For me and my true love
  shall never meet again
  on the bonny, bonny banks
  of Loch Lomond.

"It goes straight to the heart," said Dougal Gibson as he listened with tears welling in his eyes. "His song and that piper of his remind me of the hills of home."

"Yeah, kinda," Buffalo Munro consoled him as they leaned against the booby hatch. "I knew a young Scotch sodbuster out in the badlands of Dakota. Every Saturday night, he'd get lonely for some lass back home. He'd take out a squeeze bag and start blowing and marching back and forth at sundown. You could hear that pitiful wailing all across the prairie. We didn't know how to stop him. But some nearby Sioux, they did. One of their horsemen put on paint, rode out to his cabin, and shot that piper dead. Of course, we had to send one of our buffalo hunters over to shoot the horseman. Locally," said Munro, "they still call that the 1869 Piper-Indian War. We sent two of our skinners over to his patch of land to bury him, along with his bagpipes and his dog. I tell you, wars, even little wars, are no damned good."

It was the hour when morning would have been showing in Mystic or Dundee, but there was not going to be any proper show of dawn at Blacklead during this darkest season of the year, only a graying of the overcast sky at midday. On that special night of the frolic, a few sailors and their newfound loves remained on *Lancer* for private reasons. Most of the Dundee men, under orders from the Highlander, followed him back to the ships at Niantelik. They could be heard piping and singing heroic marches far across the ice. Some had to help the others to navigate, but all got back alive. Famous Arctic frolics such as this were all too rare.

Finn and the old man left the ship and started back to the island. Many near them clung fiercely to the blizzard safety line, though the air hung dead still. Finn and Caleb saw two old women ahead of them walking slowly, leaning together, supporting each other, tired after eating, drinking, and singing during the frolic. One of the old women staggered a little, then sat down on the ice, and her friend squatted close beside her. Finn hurried forward, with Lukassi not far behind him. This grandmother from Kudlik's family smiled at Finn and spoke to him.

Lukassi interpreted. "She tells you she's only got tired and had to rest. But she'll be up and walking soon."

"I'm not going to leave her out here on the ice," Finn said. "Lukassi, you help her up on my back. There . . . she hardly weighs anything. I'll carry her back to her bed. Ask that other lady if she can walk along beside us."

The other old woman smiled and nodded. "I've seen you carrying lots of babies on your back," she said to her friend, "but I never thought I'd see you riding in a captain's hood."

"Oh, hell!" said Caleb as he walked beside Finn. "I forgot to give my speech about the true meaning of our centennial celebration.

197

Probably these Yacks, and half the Portuguese and Scots, have no idea why we gave that costly frolic."

"It's probably just as well," said Finn. "I don't think Mario Fayal was in any state to make a good translation of your speech in Portuguese, do you?"

"Well, no," said Caleb. "I saw him lying on the deck while two of the pageant beauties tried to help him to his feet."

"And how about Lukassi? Didn't I see him lying not so far away from Mario?"

"I guess you did," said Caleb. "He was right beneath my feet when Noah and I were round-dancing with the boat steerers."

"Too bad for you not giving your speech," said Finn. "But you can always record it in your log."

"I guess that's what I'll have to do," said Caleb. "But even without my speech, which is somewhere in my pockets, we did give one helluva slam-bam New Year's frolic."

Chapter 13

"It's one of the perils of wintering up here," said Noah. "We've never had a doctor. Everett takes care of all the dentistry in the carpentry shed. Have you watched him clamping his patient's head tight in that big wood vise, then twisting and turning with his pliers until he can snatch the bad tooth out? He doesn't charge a penny and young crewmen take advantage of his generosity. Some want to wear home a walrus ivory earring to show the girls they've been in the Arctic whaling trade. Well, Everett drills them an ear hole with his smallest brace and bit. But I guess you couldn't call that practicing serious medicine.

"A few years ago," Noah grumbled to Finn, "one of the Fisheries sent up a young apprentice doctor to live on the whaling station at Bon Accord. He got into trouble for chasing young local boys, but he never had a single case of injury and not a one of us got sick that year. So neither the Fisheries in New London nor in Dundee has ever wasted another penny by sending in a doctor." He sighed and put a hand to his chest. "Right now, I'm sorry to tell you, Captain, I need one."

Finn went over and told Dunston.

When Caleb spoke to Dougal, he looked worried. "Angelo and I saw old Noah yesterday. He's sick, and I'm afraid there's nothing we can do for him. If he's going to die, he'll die."

"When I took breakfast over to him," young Pierre, the ship's boy, told Everett, "Mr. Anderson told me he was too tired to eat. He says he doesn't mind dying here one bit."

"Remember, lad, if you've got the luck," said Everett, "you just might manage to get old yourself – that is, if you don't catch a real bad flu or let a right whale kill you in the ice."

Old Noah knew that he was going. He asked to say good-bye to Finn. After doing that, his breathing took a sorry turn, and near midnight, on Sunday morning, the 5th of March, 1876, Noah Anderson died. Finn, Chris Acker, Angelo, and Otto Kraus sat by him to the end. When his breath would no longer fog the lens of a long glass held to his lips and beneath his nose, and the pulse in his neck was gone, Finn laid two pennies on his eyelids to hold them closed. Chris tied his best clean kerchief round Noah's head to keep his jaw from sagging and crossed his arms and legs. They all three helped to tie them neatly with white cotton strips. Then, wrapping Noah's body tightly in his blanket, they carried him over to the warehouse, and laid him out on the baleen-scraping table.

Finn duly recorded in *Lancer*'s journal that their ship's keeper had died natural, having given up on breathing. "God rest his soul," Finn wrote as well. Later, he got Dunston to date and undersign his entry.

When young Pierre heard the news in the morning, he wailed like a baby, for he, being closest to Noah, felt most affected by his death. They had spent a lot of time together aboard *Lancer* and had become best friends. Pierre, being orphaned early, had known no other father except Noah.

The wind that week continued to blow so hard that they could not hold a burial service on Monday, Tuesday, or Wednesday. Lester Lewis, the cooper, asked Finn if he wished to have Noah's body placed in a new oil cask.

"I could knock up a really special one for him with a dozen iron hoops," said Lester, "one as big as our crow's-nest atop the main-mast. Of course, he can't be really buried because this island's just a hump of rock with a thin layer of tundra underneath the snow."

"Putting Noah Anderson in a barrel just doesn't seem right to me," said Finn, "especially after us seeing those barreled-up mutineers sent off to the Royal Navy."

"Well," said Lester, "we had a big Maine stroke called Jumbo who froze to death up here two winters ago. I hooped him into an oil cask. Of course, a bear got hold of that barrel and rolled it halfway round this island. You could see the trail and the claw marks on the barrel, but that bear just wasn't strong enough to get inside at Jumbo. When I put hoops on my barrels, Captain, they are there to stay."

The carpenter, Everett Roberts, joined in the conversation. "Lester and I would be proud to build that friend a proper coffin. I know you can't dig graves on this island, but we can pile the rocks right on top of that box and pour hot water in between them Inuit-style. Their women know how to make an icy mortar no damned bear is going to claw apart till summer."

Both men agreed with that, knowing it was Inuit custom to heavily weigh down the dead with stones to keep the body from wandering.

"Go ahead and build him a real good coffin," Finn told him. "I'd like to record in *Lancer*'s journal that we all did our best for Noah."

Everett found a short sled and Lester and he staggered out through the driving storm, holding tight to the long line of hemp rope set up to guide them to the ships in just this kind of weather. Everett picked out the best chestnut boards and special copper nails he needed, and together they hauled everything back to Blacklead, along with two cases of Jamaica rum that the ice master said he had saved for a wedding or a wake.

With his oil cask gauge, Lester carefully measured the ship's keeper for length, depth, and width, then Everett built a beautiful, tapered coffin that fitted Noah's body like a glove. Young Pierre spit and polished every one of the round-headed copper nails until they gleamed like cherubs' eyes.

This March blizzard seemed determined to roar on forever. Finally, they were forced to hold a short graveside service anyway.

On Friday, in spite of the weather, they rousted out the crews. That was none too soon, for Inuit had an overwhelming fear of any human body that was left loose.

The wind was whipping fine ground snow around like beach sand, making it impossible for Finn to read the burial service, so the old man took over, saying that he could quote it from memory. At the last moment, he admitted that he only halfway remembered the shorter service, but that he would make up any parts he didn't know. The local hunters and their wives, elders, and children, who seemed little inconvenienced by icy, boisterous weather, came out in full force, for they were always interested in learning how foreign shamanism worked.

The pine headboard that Chips Bell had so carefully carved read:

R.I.P.
N ANDIRSEN
Born Neewport, R Is – 1807
Died Blackled Is
Mar 5 – 1876

Finn thanked Bell for carving the marker. "You did a perfect job," he told him. "I didn't know that you could spell."

After the headboard had been roped and rigged upright between four heavy stones, Captain Dunston conducted the service for those gathered, using his gamming horn. But even then his words were snatched from his lips by tearing winds, and scattered into a terrible jumble of nouns, verbs, and adjectives that flew across the frozen Sound.

The old man nudged Pierre, who was standing near him with long tear streaks frozen white upon his cheeks. It had been the ship's boy's duty each morning to run the Stars and Stripes up the flagpole that stood near the cannon between the captains' houses. Pierre had done this so often in the wind that the flag had already become frayed and shortened by one-third.

"Pierre, you should lower that flag of ours to half-staff. That's the custom when someone's being buried," Dougal whispered.

Pierre ran to the flagpole and, holding his fur mitts under his arm, he lowered the flag halfway down, then retied its halyard, careful not to freeze his fingers onto the iron cleat.

Instantly, there was excited shuffling and yacking among the Inuit, who suddenly shouted as in one voice, "*Hippa, hippa, ray! Hippa, hippa, ray!*"

The whalers, hearing this, decided to protect their lady loves and hunting companions from any feeling that Inuit did not have a proper understanding of American customs, and also bellowed out a second "*Hip, hip, hurray*, tiger!" That final parting salute ended Noah's burial.

"He must have heard that," said Lukassi. "It would make him glad."

The double crew of seamen struggled back across the uneven, hard-packed drifts, then made a run for the dark, womblike comfort of their mess hall, flinging themselves inside the entrance. Stamping, coughing, wheezing, they beat the fine snow from the fur of their outer parkas, boots, and wind pants before they stripped them off and hand-warmed their cheeks and nether parts. In the mates' mess, Rudi Haas had mixed a wicked hot rum punch laced with that famous scurvy fighter, sugared lime juice, plus a slug of molasses from Barbados.

"Thank God for the Yacks," sighed Mario as he stared through the patch he had cleared on the frosted window. "Look at them, still working away at the graveside, piling heavy rocks on that coffin."

Inside the winter tents, their women had the kettles boiling. Each brought out her own and poured water over Noah's grave so it would freeze and lock each stone in place.

The old man, with his steaming mug in hand, stared out the clear spot in the window at the Inuit figures who were almost hidden in the blizzard as they completed the burial task.

Caleb nodded his head outside and turned to stare at Dougal. "They're not going to put the stones on me. I'll be long gone from here before that time."

Hearing the fiddlers' music, they rolled a barrel of rum over to the crews' quarters where they joined in singing for Noah "Drink to Me Only With Thine Eyes." But, soon enough, the Canadians and the Newfies got going and the spirit of the gathering turned into a dockside hoedown, with the addition of the banjo, three mouth organs, and Noel's cheerful twanging on his Jew's harp. Then Johnny James played the spoons against his knees. Finn thought they had given Noah the finest wake that any good ship's keeper could conceive.

The stinging cold of winter clung to Blacklead Island through the month of March and Nilak grew more beautiful in Caleb's eyes. Finn could see the light expanding every day, and his life with Pia continued to be grand. But those mates and crewmen less fortunate in love who had suffered lovers' quarrels and fisticuffs with other suitors began to curse the weather and swear that spring would never come. Both crews, as usual, turned edgy during this return of the light. Many of the men began seriously grumbling and were eager to pick a fight. They were anxious to see the spring ice floes open, for that would allow them to set out in the whaleboats to pursue the bowhead fish once more, to jam their ships' holds with oil, and to leave this isolated island and return to that other life – well, for at least a little while.

Inside the crew's quarters, Jack Shannon and Otto Kraus suspiciously sniffed the odorous bunkhouse air as they carried out their monthly building inspection. At the end of the room, Otto snatched back a hanging blanket to see what these men were hiding.

"What the hell is this?" Shannon shouted. "Are you guys making your own spring brew just because you're bored? What the devil's made you bored, you bastards?" He spread his arms. "I'm not bored. Otto's not bored. He loves it here on Blacklead any time of year. Buck up, men, the big right fishes will be back here soon. They'll be nosing along these ice floes before you can say Beelzebub."

"That *gottverdammt* brew smells awful." Otto grimaced. "How does it taste?"

Robin Crooks, always a bold and fearless soul, was first to break their silence. "That brew's going to be all right, but we're not. We're starting to feel marooned up here." He was an imposingly large and heavyset man with enormous shoulders, arms, and hands developed from years of rowing.

"What do you mean marooned?" Jack asked him. "You're surrounded by beautiful Yack girls, fine fellow seamen, and, God knows, we've got lots of lovely spring weather . . . coming . . . later, probably."

"Yeah, well, we know we've got Yacks . . . and blizzards," Crooks grunted. "I'm speaking about real New England, or maybe Canadian, women. We were talking about them yesterday in this bunkhouse. I asked for a show of hands and found out that not a one of us knows how to waltz a goddamned step. Oh, a few of these guys can do some kind of sailor's hornpipe or Eskimo jig, but when it comes to waltzing around with real Connecticut or Rhode Island girls, none of us has even had the chance to try it."

"It was voted last year, for the first time in the history of the world," Noel Wotten told the mates, "that the New London Seamen's Mission would let women inside. The plan is to hold proper dances in that hall four times a year. And we're sure as hell all going if we get home this year."

"Yes, and no minister's wife or priest is going to do the choosing of which girls and women they allow to come in dancing," said Angelo Daluz. "I mean, every girl is welcome who's willing to take the chance."

Otto gasped, "Do you mean to tell me none of you can waltz? Gott in Himmel, that's an awful shame. Here's the bunch of you standing around this bunkhouse, looking at the greatest German waltzer that ever sailed out of the port of Bremerhaven. Don't drink too much of that awful pissy brew you're making, or I'll dizzy all you bastards when I give you my first waltzing lessons!"

"Me, too, I'll teach you waltzing," Jack Shannon volunteered. "My older sister taught me everything she knew."

"I'll bet she did!" called a deep voice from behind the blanket.

"Just watch me," said Jack, and he lightly raised his arms and went whirling around the bunkhouse as though he embraced a beautiful woman. "This floor is going to give out!" he shouted. "And

205

this place looks and smells like a walrus shed. Fix the fuckin' floor tomorrow, open the doors, and air out this wank pit of yours. Hang up a few more lanterns, but don't set the place afire. Your first waltzing lessons will begin on Monday during the dogwatch."

Next day, Jack hurried over to Rudi Haas, the steward, whose job it was to make out charges for stuff sold from the slops chest. "We need a roll of that widest pink trade ribbon and another of the baby blue," Jack said. "No, I'm not going to buy it. I'm only borrowing it. You'll get it back. Trust me!"

Otto went to the sailmaker and borrowed two small cakes of yellow marking chalk. Then he and Jack got together with Jacques Moreau from Trois-Rivières, who could make his homemade fiddle sound like a fancy violin.

When Otto and Jack arrived, the bunkhouse had been aired and swept. Noel and Everett had patched up the worst weak spots in the floor. Half a dozen whale-oil lamps gleamed through the musty air. Every man stood nervous and alert. A few of them had trimmed their sideburns. Others had shaved.

"Now," said Jack, "watch this." Raising his arms, he made a signal to the fiddler who played slowly as Shannon began the first steps of the waltz. "Did you get that?" he asked them. "Come on, some of you get out here on this fuckin' floor and try it."

Three or four of the usual exhibitionists, who could be counted on to act up in the fo'c's'le, immediately clumped out.

"Stop the music!" shouted Otto. "*Sehr gut*. I'm going to do it for you right, and with the chalk, young Pierre is going to mark my footprints for you."

The pattern of each footstep was outlined on the floor in sets of six.

"Now watch. Jack and I, we are going to do this waltz together."

They held out their arms to begin. There was a lot of rude snorting and elbow-digging.

"Hold on," yelled Orval Windtree. "We can't tell which of you's the sailor and which the dame. You're both so goddamned pretty!"

"We guessed you'd have that trouble," said Otto. "So hold out your arms, boys. Half of you get the gentlemen's blue ribbons tied in a nice big bow, and the rest of you get the ladies' pinks."

Slowly, the dignified sound of the fiddle filled the bunkhouse.

The waltz was accompanied by Wotten on his harmonica. Pierre and Jose continued to dart about, marking each proper footstep that Jack and Otto took. Finally, a snakelike line of dancers followed them, stomping so firmly in the chalk marks that Jesse Big Man managed to kick his right foot through the floor.

These lessons proved truly popular. For dozens of evenings, both crews practiced waltzing. The learning process was slow at first, but as winter lost its grip, these thick-wristed oarsmen and their harpooners, so clearly separated by the ribbons they wore, were waltzing gracefully together around the bunkhouse floor. Yack girls and women crowded around the windows to study the whalers' movements, quiet but open-mouthed with sheer amazement and delight. Not, of course, because these men were dancing with other men, for their own hunters had always danced in contests with other men. And Inuit women, too, had always danced facing one another. That was the custom. But at no time did they touch each other. What astonished these nomadic women was seeing foreign men whom they had come to know so very, very well, each locked in a strange embrace, whirling round and round to the fiddle during these first bright nights of spring.

When Caleb heard that these waltzing lessons were under way, he approved of the whole idea. "It's a dandy way to break the winter doldrums instead of brawling with those Dundee men. Nobody's thrown a real punch or suffered a broken nose since that last visit from *Blue Thistle*'s crew."

One Sunday morning, Caleb woke in the darkness during a roaring snowstorm, hearing the faint sound of male voices singing in one of the farthest storage sheds: "Lead kindly light / Mid the encircling gloom."

Yes, he was hearing a hymn sung as part of a small service usually led by Ezra Morse, a minister's son. Caleb knew Ezra would be holding a Bible reading for twelve to eighteen of the crew members. Yes, there were some real churchgoers up here, he thought as he rolled over close to Nilak. I guess I should be down there with them in that freezing shed to lead the service, but it's so much easier just to lie back here and enjoy this bed.

After the blizzard, Lukassi hurried into Finn's house, brushing the new snow from his boots and parka. "Did you hear, Captain, what happened to the old widow last night?"

"No," said Finn.

"That old woman, Kudlik's mother, took a walk last night."

"Where did she go?" asked Finn.

"Nobody knows – somewhere out in the wind and snow. They couldn't find her tracks."

"Why did she do that?"

"Well," said Lukassi, "she just decided she had grown too old to go on living good."

"Did she tell people that? How do you know?"

"She left us all the signs, the way most old people do. She waited until that big storm was blowing when she knew we couldn't find her. Then she folded her outer pants and parka very neatly on her place in the bed, went outside, and started walking. By the morning, she'd be covered over somewhere. She was a wonderful old woman. Don't worry, Kudlik's family will find his mother and bury her the right way when summer comes again."

"The grim reaper has struck twice," said Finn.

"Supa's here to see you," Lukassi called next day as he opened the ice master's door.

The two of them came in, and without asking, Pia poured three cups of coffee, tipping two spoonsful of brown sugar into her father's, one into Lukassi's, and none at all into Finn's, for she knew he had a tender back tooth and didn't look forward to having the carpenter pluck it out for him. Supa glanced at his daughter and she, without bothering to put on her parka on such a bright spring day, eased out the door and ran over to her family's winter tent to visit.

Supa reached around the door of the storm-porch entrance and revealed his ivory narwhal tusk. It was long and straight as a spear, beautifully spiraled, with deep curves. Finn, with his arm extended high above his head, could just touch the shining tip.

"This is the good unicorn horn Pia's father has been promising you," said Lukassi. "Supa's got a lot of other ideas this morning. He asked me to talk for him."

"What does he want in trade for this?" asked Finn as he stroked the treasured tusk.

Lukassi translated that and Supa replied, "'Pitaat. Tunituiinakpara, it's a gift only.' He says he wants nothing for it. Take it. He gives it to you."

"Nakuumiralungaasit," said Finn. "Thanks a lot."

Supa smiled.

The three of them drank their coffee as Finn admired the long, honey-colored ivory with its left-hand twist. He couldn't help but think of what a tusk like this would sell for in St. John's or, better, in London or Canton.

"It's a bit hard for me and my family living around here," said Supa, through Lukassi.

"Why?" asked Finn. "What's so hard about it?"

"He says he feels like he's a poor man," said Lukassi. "He says he's got nothing but an old skin umiak, a woman's boat, that leaks. His kayak's not too bad for hunting seals or narwhal. But if Supa had a new whaleboat – with his two sons, and his two brothers, and his brother-in-law to row as crew – he could go out this spring and get an *akvik*, a big right whale, that he could trade you for that boat. Then he'd never feel like a poor man again. He'd think himself as fine as Pootavut or Kudlik. He says they're both camp bosses because they've each got proper whaleboats. He wants to be like them."

Supa studied Finn's face carefully before he spoke again. "Now Caleboosi, the old captain, he's a very generous man. I heard he gave Pootavut, the brother of that young widow, Nilak, a whale-boat and everything that's needed with it – harpoons, lances, rope, tubs, oars, mast, and sail. Yes, everything. Then he took a whale which he gave in trade to Caleboosi for that same boat."

"What's that got to do with me?" Finn asked sharply.

"You've got Supa's daughter, Pia. And you also got that narwhal tusk," Lukassi told him. "Supa's family's got nearly nothing from you."

Finn stared steadily at Supa, but did not answer.

Supa decided to take the chance. "Maybe I'm going to take my whole family over to live at Niantelik. Their interpreter over there says that the younger captain at Niantelik needs someone to dust the books and papers in his ship's cabin. Maybe he wishes my daughter, Pia, would go there and help him. Maybe we'll all move over . . . soon. Maybe tomorrow. I think that captain will give me a whaleboat even if they're not so light and fast as your Yankee boats."

Finn bit his lower lip, imagining the pain it would cause him to lose Pia, especially in a way so obvious to everyone on Blacklead and at Niantelik. He had to think fast.

"Lukassi, you tell Supa I could give him the precut wood for a new whaleboat, then Supa and his sons, with my carpenter's help, could build it up and Supa could pay me back with the first right fish he takes. But only if he stays here on Blacklead with Pia can we start the trade. Lukassi, you tell him that for me."

Lukassi carefully interpreted every word.

Supa made his eyes go wide and nodded his agreement. "*Atau,* grand. I and my sons will gladly stay and help your woodman put my new whaleboat together." Supa smiled, showing the wide gap in his teeth. "I'll trade you our first right fish and all its *sukkak,* mouth sifters, for that."

"Lukassi, you go find Everett or Noel and send one of them over here to see me," said Finn. "Tell Supa I'll let him know when one of them is ready."

"I'll bet they'll build it on the south side of their shop," said Lukassi, "now that the spring sun is starting to bare the rocks and warm up this whole country."

The killing winds had blown away with the strengthening of the sun. The crews could enjoy its warmth, but had to be careful, for a day out in the spring's glare would make anyone see everything bright pink at night. That was the trouble with Arctic sunlight bouncing up off the snow along the floe edge where they could now hunt. The first right whale of this new season had been spotted from the lookout. Two whaleboats had crossed the ice and put out. Caleb's whaleboat had struck one, but he had been forced to cut the line before the whale broke up their boat in the moving ice. Three days later, the man in the lookout spied what he believed to be a large, dead whale, though it carried no waif flag to indicate that it had met its fate at the hands of a whaler. He watched it carefully, fearing it might be a sleeping right fish that would soon dive. He was eager to gain the sighting bonus given to the man who first calls out a whale that is taken by one of their crews.

Slowly, this black form drifted on the tide into a place between the islands where it started bobbing like a heavy piece of driftwood, in a way that no living whale would ever do. The lookout man trained his long glass on two Dundee whaleboats still far away, but heading for the whale. Immediately, he fired the smoke bomb in the air and hauled up the flag. Then, cupping his hands around his mouth, he shouted to a man below, "Dead whale, south sou'west! Dead whale!"

Lookout signal

The Dundee men had their stunsails up and the breeze was favoring them, but they were still a long way off.

The mates and men from *Lancer* and *Sea Horse* came galloping out of their quarters. The lookout could see the ice master and the old man, each shading their eyes and peering up at him before each extended his long glass out toward the whale.

"Those Dundee buggers are after it already!" Caleb bellowed.

Three Blacklead boats were being skidded across the shore ice upright on their keels, three men running, pushing hard on both sides of each boat. They did this until the boats began to break through the thin ice near the edge of the open water. Only then did the six men leap into their boat. The old man ran down, threw his weight into the effort and hopped in, setting his long steering oar in place. Finn did the same, leaping into his whaleboat. Dougal with his crew and boat rushed out after them. The crews pushed off, pulling mightily on their oars, while others set up the stunsails. Taking a hard tack, they quickly gathered such speed that the crews unshipped their oars in favor of sail.

"It's the bull I struck three days ago that must have later died," yelled Caleb when his whaleboat cut close to Finn's. "I stuck a long lance in him and that fish went berserk. We had to cut away or he'd have drawn this boat into heavy ice. Did you hear that, Ice Master?"

Finn refused to acknowledge the old man's claim that this was his dead whale lying out before them. It had no waif flag in it. So far as he could see, it was anybody's whale. A large carcass such as this could be worth six or seven thousand dollars.

Caleb swung the boom and changed his tack, trying to gain an advantage over the two Dundee whaleboats that were closing in on the whale. Caleb was ready with his harpoon in the bow, mad to secure this floating treasure for himself.

The winds were now favoring the Highlander in his Dundee boat. The boats seemed destined to arrive at almost the same moment.

Finn hauled his sail closer to the wind.

Caleb had moved to the bow of his boat. "I'm going to harpoon this bloodied fish again, then drive in my own waif flag just to show that Dundee poacher that this floater's mine."

The Highlander was standing in the bow of his lead boat almost in striking distance of the whale. Finn, too, was standing in the bow.

"Hold back, Finn!" roared Caleb. "I'll do the sticking for my Blacklead station!"

Ignoring him, Finn drove his harpoon into the whale's flank a moment before the Highlander flung his iron.

"That's my floater!" bellowed the Highlander. "My harpoon struck him first, three days past!"

"Never!" the old man yelled as he pierced his blue waif flag deep into the back of the dead fish.

"What in God's name are you trying to pull off here?" roared the red-faced Highlander.

All three whaleboats had their prows thrust tight against the carcass of the whale. The oarsmen, when they got the chance, rubbed their hands possessively along the bowhead's soft, rubbery outer skin.

"Damned bad luck," the Highlander growled. "My Dundee waif, which I stuck in him three days ago, has come loose." Cargill stood on his tiptoes in the bow, searching for the original wound.

"Hogwash! This is my whale," Caleb shouted at him. "See my waif? I harpooned him a couple of days ago. I got the chance to lance him not far from the heart, but he got going again and I had to cut our line away or this fish would have killed us. I knew damned well I gave this whale its death stroke. Back off, Cargill. Honor my waif! It's my fish, mine!"

"That's a load of Yankee sheep shit, Dunston, and ye damned well know it! I saw ye plant that waif just now. Any decent man would tell ye this is my whale! Admit it," the Highlander roared, "it's my fish!"

"I was the first iron in today," called Finn. "It's my whale, unless one of you can prove it's not."

Caleb turned and gave Finn a withering look. "We're much closer to Blacklead than Niantelik," he shouted across at Cargill. "All five whaleboats here should join together and help haul this floater into our nearest slipway. There, when the tide is right, we can dig out my first harpoon for proof and after that, we'll give a medium cask of rum for your crew's help. Do you hear me, Cargill?"

213

"We'll settle this matter ashore," bellowed the Highlander, and anyone could see his sideburns bristle, for he was working himself into a nasty rage.

It was a long, hard row, with the wind against them, but with twenty-seven strong men on the oars and a favorable running of the tide, they managed to beach the great fish by midday.

"This bull of mine will go a hundred and thirty-five or forty barrels," the Highlander proclaimed as he tied on his climbing spikes. Then, helped by the harpoon line and several of his crewmen, he was heaved up onto the whale, where he pulled out and cast down Caleb's waif flag. "There, just as I told ye, Master Dunston, here's my Dundee hemp line trailing my harpoon head into its carcass after I was forced to chop it away."

"I cut that Russian hemp myself," Caleb shouted up to him. Then, taking the hemp line in his hands, he jerked it violently, hoping that the shivering effect on the whale's outer skin and quivering blubber might bring the Highlander crashing down.

But no, old Cargill remained up there scowling down at Dunston, his legs spread wide, one fist cocked on his hip, the other gripping Dunston's waif like Moses with his staff. "What's to be done?" the Highlander bellowed. "The fairest thing, Dunston, would be for the two of us to share this prize."

"To hell with that!" shouted Finn. "My harpoon first pierced this floater and unless one of you can prove your claim, this whale is mine!"

"I'll not be cheated by ye two in this matter," roared the Highlander as he ran clumping down the back slope of the whale toward its huge tail flukes, then leapt into the shallows beside Caleb, who raised his arms, but not fast enough to ward off a powerful blow to the face.

Caleb's nose spouted blood that spread dripping off the points of his moustache. "Damn you, man!" he roared, and stepping close, he swung a heavy punch that struck the Highlander across the ear. A score of crewmen formed a loose ring around them, the Dundee men and Yankee men urging their captains on, while laughing, cursing, kicking water, then fighting among themselves.

The Yack hunters, a peaceful, sharing people, were wise enough to stay away from this act of sober savagery between the foreigners. They did not laugh, cry out, or protest in any way. Men, women, and children stood motionless along the tundra bank above the fray and watched.

The Highlander swung another rounder that caught Caleb just below the eye. Then Caleb struck again, this time splitting the Highlander's lip and loosening a tooth. The pain caused Andrew to reel back, his eyes closed. Caleb could easily have struck him another blow, but he held back.

Finn and the big Dundee mate rushed out and stood between them as the rest of the crewmen stopped yelling and fighting. The Highlander pulled off his tam and used it to wipe his eyes and stanch the flow of blood. Then Caleb took a blue bandana from around his neck and wiped his nose and swelling eye. The fight was over.

Nilak ran down the slipway with Pia. Both carried the best medicine they knew, scraped patches of lemming skin which they dipped in cold salt water. After they had gently cleaned both captains' faces, they applied these bandages, which would dry and shrink, drawing the wounded flesh together.

Lukassi ran up to them with news. "Pootavut and Kudlik say they know how to force through that harpoon head and you captains can see it. Do you want Kudlik to do that?"

The Highlander remained silent, afraid to disturb the cool skin Pia had applied to his bleeding lip. Caleb did not answer either, the two men being careful not to look at one another. Finally, Finn said, "Yeah, why not have Kudlik show us that iron."

Kudlik's son went running to the slipway for a long iron rod which Kudlik forced into the old wound following the rope's path, while Pootavut cut an arm-sized hole in the whale's opposite side. It was not long before the three captains saw the cut hemp rope disappearing as Kudlik forced it through the carcass.

Then Pootavut came around from the other side of the fish, holding up the harpoon head that had struck the whale.

"Now," growled the Highlander, sounding a little less sure, "we'll observe the Dundee mark stamped on that iron."

Every crewman crowded close to see it.

"It's not your Dundee mark," Caleb yelled triumphantly.

"It's not yer Yankee fishery either!" bellowed the Highlander in glee.

Many of the crewmen, Yanks and Scots, started laughing, shouting, and kicking icy water at each other.

"That's a strange iron, that one," the Highlander said, examining it with care. "That 'TL' mark will be from that whale bark, *True Love*, out of Hull on England's east coast. I saw her up off Greenland last year. She'll be working out of Kekerton this season."

"Well, screw them Limey bastards," yelled both crews.

"Imagine letting a big fish like this one get away from them!" Caleb said. "Especially it being what I'd judge to be a one-hundred-and forty-barrel bull."

One of the Dundee greenhands was bending, helping the Highlander remove his climbing spikes.

"Well, it's settled now," said Caleb. "This bull is here on Blacklead and it's ours."

"The hell it is!" the Highlander roared. "We Dundee men helped ye haul it here and ye'll bloody well help us render down and haul exactly half of this oil and corset bone back to Niantelik."

"Never!" shouted Caleb. "Never!"

"Splitting that whale oil three ways is the only way to do it fair," Finn shouted. "But since my iron was the first between us three, it's only right that I alone should claim the corset bone."

All eyes turned to Finn and then to the old man, who stiffened and roared at him, "You goddamned traitor!"

Nilak hurried in and gently tried to rearrange the skin patch below Caleb's eye. He warded her off.

"I'm for peace," Finn said. "Let's all go up to my house and we'll have some rum. You two bare-knuckle fighters and you mates come on with me. I have a half keg of Jamaican rum that I've been saving to celebrate just such a fair and decent three-way split as this."

It was the first time that any of them had seen the ice master act with such utter and independent authority. The two older men were shocked, and followed him without another word.

"Lukassi," Finn bellowed, "tell Pootavut and Kudlik to muster their men and start the cutting."

"Great balls of fire!" Shannon whispered to Dougal. "Did you see that young Newf turn into a hard-nosed whaling captain right before our eyes?"

"He'd better stay tough," said Dougal, "because the old man's going to kill him when he thinks again of Finn jumping in like that and claiming his third, and all the corset bone, and insisting they give the Highlander his one-third share."

Next day, Caleb watched the Dundee crewmen slicing their third of the whale into Bible leaves and packing them in barrels. Instead of cooking them, the Scots preferred to let the spring sun and time melt them into oil before and during their long voyage home.

When the old man got Finn alone, he cursed him. "You're a bitter fuckin' disappointment to me, Finn. You tricked me into choosing you to help me master *Lancer*."

"Well, what's done is done," said Finn. "At least we all three got our fair share of *True Love*'s whale."

"There was no need at all for us to share that fish with that grasping Dundee poacher. It was your fault, Finn. Who do you think you are, some goddamned Supreme Court judge? Christ, imagine you siding with that Highlander, encouraging him to snatch all that oil away from me! Then you, you greedy bastard, claiming a third of that oil and the money bone as well! To hell with you!"

Chapter 14

When Caleb awoke early, the most bitter part of his anger with Finn had drifted away. The overflow of bright spring sunlight filled his house with hope. Caleb, still lying in his bed, felt he could sense the coming of the whales. He stretched luxuriously and drew Nilak to him.

Something caused him to turn his head. He saw the youngest greenhand craning his neck to get a peek through the old man's curtain. The boy ran around the house and tapped on the door.

"Cook wants to know, sir," the boy called through to Caleb, "should he trade flour for three half-frozen seals? He says there's no meat left on this station, not even whale meat."

"Tell the cook I'll come over to talk to him. And you, goddamn you, lad, quit peeking in my window! Hear me?"

He nudged Nilak, then wrinkled his nose. "Seal meat, you go smell it, tell if it's good or bad."

Not long after Nilak left, Dougal came in and Caleb waved him toward a chair.

Caleb began, "The big bowheads should be arriving on this full-moon tide. In the meantime, the snow's still hard, just right for dog-team traveling and good igloo building. Nilak would be glad to go out on a hunt and so would Lukassi. Supa was born an inlander and is said to be the best at tracking caribou. We could take off for maybe ten or twelve days."

"That's a fair idea," said Dougal.

Caleb sniffed. "My only problem is that bastard, Finn. If I leave him here in charge, I could come back and find him ruling the fuckin' roost, with the mates, crews, and Yacks all dead against me and firmly on Finn's side. I hate the idea, but the only safe thing for me to do is to take Finn with me and leave you, Dougal, here in charge. Nilak will be coming and it won't hurt if Finn brings Pia. Supa will want to take his wife and their two sons to use as drivers. That's seven, eight, nine with Lukassi. If the weather doesn't turn on us, the whole damned thing could be sort of like the old days. I could use a break like that. We'll take three long sleds with about ten dogs in each team. That will give us enough carrying space to bring back lots of caribou. God knows this station needs fresh meat, and once the bowheads start migrating along these floe edges, we'll all be busy hunting them."

"Right," Dougal nodded.

"I'll tell Nilak to get our boots ready. She'll be glad we're all going hunting, glad to change the scenery."

She looked surprised when he made a face but said he would take Finn and Pia. She smiled and nodded in agreement.

"Yes, we'll go with you," said Finn when Caleb told him. "Pia's eager to travel, see new places, and so am I."

"We won't be gone much longer than twelve days if the weather holds," the old man said. "I'll leave Dougal in charge. If it's not storming hard, we can make an early start tomorrow. Tell Pia's mother to make sure your extra skin boots, mitts, clothing, everything is ready. I'll tell the cooks to make us fifty bannocks and make sure he goes easy on that fuckin' baking powder. I don't want to die of heartburn out there. It's about time we got off this whaling station for a while. There's nothing to do here until the whales come nosing along the ice floes again."

Finn nodded, pleased to see that the old man had decided to act more or less like a human being.

"Remember one thing, Finn," Caleb pointed at him. "As far as Mystic and New London are concerned, this is an all-male hunting expedition. Do you get my meaning? When the two ships arrive in New London, there will be no talk of women traveling with us, and not even women living on my Yankee island! Have you got that, Finn?"

"Queen Victoria would be royally mad as a wet hen," Finn answered, "if she heard you claiming this island as your own in the middle of Her Majesty's northern realm!"

All nine of them left Blacklead in the long, cold light of early morning with many Inuit, mates, and even a few crewmen out to see them off. The three teams howled and yapped, eager to start the competition with each other. They had been fed walrus meat the night before, and were quick to start blowing their rich morning farts back to those unfortunates who rode the sleds.

"I swear those dogs do that to us on purpose," Caleb raved.

Running beside the sled, Lukassi told them, "Supa says he's going to travel straight west across the sea ice, then head inland using that widest river that flows down through the mountains."

Finn was up and running now beside Pia. She was sitting expertly on the moving sled, smiling and holding her hood against the still cold wind.

Later, when they reached the frozen river, Lukassi whispered to both captains, "You should speak softly out here. We are coming into the country of the animals. They can hear you and understand your words even when they are way off."

Finn thought of this as Inuit superstition. Still, in this vast and unknown country, he seemed to feel another presence. It caused him to remember Lukassi's warning and, like Inuit, he began to whisper his words.

"We're being carried like a pair of greenhands up into this un-marked snow desert," Caleb told Finn, "by some of the best natural navigators in the world. They've got no maps or compasses, no charts, no sextants. They're not even counting on the stars to guide them. They use their instincts and the carefully stored directions given to them by their fathers and their grandfathers describing ancient journeys and their exact memories of the coastline and the inland. Look ahead. See those two stone markers piled to look like men? Nobody knows how old they are."

Caleb admitted how much he enjoyed traveling with these people who had, perhaps like the animals, retained their navigational instincts. "Often when I'm sitting around in the Captains' Rest, our talk turns to the Yacks. A few scorn them as Gypsy wanderers. But being out here on the trail with them beside you always wipes away that kind of ignorance. These people live life in a way that's hard to understand, but perhaps it's the way life should be lived."

Inuit stone cairns

When the three sleds reached the high, flat inland plain, their drivers halted the dogs. Finn marveled at the sight before him, for few foreigners had ever seen this almost endless sweep of treeless plain bordered by distant mountain ranges made beautiful by the elegantly shaped snowdrifts that cast azure shadows curving westward like ocean waves.

This hard-packed spring snow was perfect for igloo building. They erected two domes each night – one just large enough to accommodate four persons, while the other took five. Both these houses were built by Supa and his eldest son, Kovik, in less than an hour's time. Lukassi and the other son fed the dogs, while Caleb and Finn marched back and forth to keep warm, though rarely speaking to one another.

To pass the time, Caleb tried hard to crack the whip Inuit-style, wishing to imitate that hard, loud crack used not to strike the dogs, but to scare them to go right or left. Caleb had no success. He offered Supa's whip to Finn, who tried to crack it a dozen times before he, too, gave up. Supa laid down his snow knife and, smiling, approached them. Taking the short wooden handle with its twenty-foot lash, he ran several paces forward, then with one smooth motion made its tip fly out and crack louder than a rifle. He handed Finn the whip and went back to building the igloo.

The women skillfully chinked snow between the blocks. Finn finally tried to help Pia in this endeavor to hurry forward the whole cold process, but there was a special trick to chinking because the snow in Finn's hands would powder like sand and refuse to stick. He never truly mastered this builder's art.

Inside the back half of each igloo, the women used their *ulus* to slice the snow until it became soft and yielding under sealskins and bearskins spread hair side down, while caribou skins spread hair side up formed mattresses under their sleeping bags. The women lit a seal-oil lamp in each snowhouse and they all ate. Crawling into their wide bags, they made love almost motionlessly, then sighed and fell asleep.

Late on their third day of travel, they had seen no game, and Caleb, like Finn, was becoming restless when the dogs swerved and hauled their sleds across sharp hoof tracks and small, brown scattered droppings on the snow. On the fourth day, Supa sighted caribou. He jumped off, halting all three sleds. These were quickly overturned to act as anchors against the pulling of the overeager dogs.

"See them . . . up ahead?" asked Lukassi, pointing. "*Kuliitlu makulu.* Supa sees twelve. I see only nine. They are lying on that low rise."

The women had seen them, too. But these caribou remained invisible to Caleb and to Finn for an embarrassing length of time even though they, too, were experienced hunting men used to sighting distant seals or whales. Both captains drew their long glasses from their grub boxes and opened the brass eye-caps. Bringing their telescopes into focus, they studied the hill with care, but saw absolutely nothing but snow. Caribou are brown in color, thought Finn. How could he and Caleb fail to see them against this sea of Arctic whiteness? They both had modern Sharps carbine rifles that had seen recent service in the Civil War. And with the women watching, each captain was keen to be the one to make the first kill.

Long glass

The caribou lay calmly, studying this array of dogs and humans, a sight that they had never seen before. Because it was extremely cold and the caribou were lying with their heads upwind, their breathing had laid a coat of white hoarfrost over every animal's back and flanks, rendering them all but invisible, except to watchful Inuit eyes. Only when two of the caribou stood up did Finn and Caleb see them.

Supa beckoned the captains and his elder son, Kovik, to march straight forward in close single file, to appear less threatening to their watchful quarry. Finally, Supa stopped and cautiously beckoned Kovik to come up beside him. The lad knelt, holding his grandfather's short, strong antler bow parallel to the snow. He drew back hard and sent his arrow winging silently toward the caribou. It landed harmlessly among them. He tried again, and once more missed. The caribou remained undisturbed.

Supa stood his musket upright in the snow. Then, taking his son's bow, he knelt and let fly an arrow, which this time drove deep into the chest of the closest animal. The caribou jumped, then twitched its shoulder muscle like a pony flicking away a horsefly. It began to dig with its sharp front hooves beneath the snow. Then, as they watched, it knelt down quietly and died. Since there had been no sound, none of the other animals showed alarm.

Supa gently turned and offered the bow to Caleb, who shook his head, certain that he would miss. Finn smiled, but also refused.

Then Supa pointed at both captains' rifles as he slid his own old muzzle loader from its sealskin carrying case.

All three men knelt and cocked their weapons.

"*Mana!*" whispered Supa. "Now!"

Each muzzle lurched back as it blew out acrid smoke, roaring so loudly in that vast silence that it made both the animals and the women jump.

The caribou turned in panic, running first one way, then another in the gunfire, before two more of them staggered and fell. Each captain believed in his heart that he had been the one who had struck down the first and largest of those beasts, that certainly Supa, with his old musket, had missed.

All three quickly reloaded. But now the caribou had gathered into a tight herd and were running fast. Caleb and Finn both fired long shots and missed.

Supa waved. Lukassi, his other son, and the three women now drove forward on the three sleds, digging in their heels, trying to slow the excited dogs. Supa's wife and Nilak expertly skinned the three still-warm caribou, while Pia held the carcass legs and studied the methods of the older women.

Leaving his two sons to build the igloos, Supa and Lukassi once more set out with Caleb and Finn and in the evening brought in five more caribou.

"We figure we each got three caribou today," said Caleb. "Lukassi, tell that to the women, will you?"

"It's not the custom," Lukassi replied, "but I'll tell them if you say I should."

The two older women looked uneasy when they heard this boast, then, helped by Pia, they quickly skinned these last five caribou while they were still warm. Supa borrowed Caleb's sharp pocket knife, using it to divide all the carcasses into manageable sections.

The hunters built their two igloos early that night and Lukassi asked Caleb if he could sleep in theirs instead of sleeping in Supa's family igloo. Caleb could not guess why Lukassi suggested this new arrangement, but they had enjoyed a fine day and, in the spirit of companionship, the old man agreed.

Nilak, once inside the igloo, hung their meat pot over the flame of their seal-oil lamp, knowing that these captains preferred cooked meat. They rapidly spread the sleeping bags, talking and laughing softly as they waited, sometimes shaving more snow to melt inside the pot. It was beginning to steam as they filled it with the most tender parts of caribou, which soon simmered in the broth, filling the snow dome with a mouth-watering smell. Finn lay back on his double sleeping bag spread over the polar bear sleeping skins. The women stripped away the caribou flesh close to the bone and fed it to their captains, who agreed that this meat was far better than the best prime beef they had ever tasted. Lukassi said he didn't mind whether his meat was cooked or raw, which was taken as a sign of his mixed parentage.

"Don't let that girl, Pia, turn you into a savage," Caleb warned as they relaxed beneath the glistening dome.

Pia stopped and listened when she heard her name, then smiled and went on eating.

"Savagery is one of the terrible dangers facing civilized whaling men," said Caleb, and he nodded toward Lukassi. "We treat you more or less like one of us," he said. "Lukassi, we're allowing you to hear many secrets we whites hold among ourselves. But don't you ever translate this to these women. Understand?"

"Ayii," answered Lukassi. "I understand. Except, what does that word, 'savage,' mean?"

"Well, I'll explain it to you some other time," said Caleb. "Tell Nilak to fish around inside the pot with her hand and pick me out a good-sized chunk of meat."

As for Supa's family in their adjacent snowhouse, they believed that the cooking of such fresh meat was a disgusting habit, very destructive to the taste, and probably painful to the souls of the animals killed. The family took the raw meat in their teeth and with sharp knives sliced it off incredibly close to their lips.

When their feast was over, both men went outside and made their yellow stains against the snowhouse before they struggled awkwardly inside. Then, crawling into their wide sleeping bags, they pulled off all their clothing. Nilak had placed her stone lamp near her head to enable her to tend it at least once during the night. Beyond Pia and Finn, beside the snow wall, lay Lukassi in his narrow bachelor's bag, already fast asleep.

"Most folks living down in Mystic and New London find this good life up here impossible to understand," said Caleb. "I mean, a wide snow bed neatly filled with five contented people." He wiggled closer to Nilak.

"They'll never understand it," Finn agreed, "especially not in St. John's. They don't know the Labrador Inuit the way we do."

Having nothing more to say, each captain rolled sideways to concentrate on his smiling bedmate. What better place could any traveler dream of being?

"This fur tickles, but I like it," Finn admitted.

"Tikools," Pia giggled, trying to repeat that pleasant-sounding foreign word.

They had perfect weather next day, and toward evening the men took five more caribou. The following morning, Caleb and Finn took two out of a good-sized herd, and Lukassi, with Supa, took four more. They could have taken many others, but they knew that no matter how cleverly they piled the frozen haunches, ribs, and shoulders, they would not have space to lash them onto the sleds.

"That's enough," Caleb called to Lukassi. "You've got to save at least one seat on the sled for me. It's one helluva long trek back to Blacklead Island."

"I know how hard that is," said Finn. "I had to do it coming back from our hunt before the frolic."

When Caleb was riding on one high-piled sled, he said to Lukassi, who walked beside him, "I was wondering . . . if you would. . . ." He paused. "Like to sail south with me this year. My wife and I don't have a son. I thought maybe you'd like the *Amerikamiut nunanga*." He smiled as he used the Inuktitut words for the United States. "I was hoping you might come to live with us down there."

Lukassi looked at him in surprise, his gray eyes widening. "I've got my mother to take care of here, and my younger brother, and my two sisters. They're like me, they got no father."

"Well, that's too bad, son. Maybe I could be a kind of father to you, and you could have my name. You'd be Luke Dunston down there – that name would fit you fine. You'd have a new mother in Mystic. She's kind of a pain in the ass, but you'd probably get used to her. And you'd have a sister, that's my stepdaughter, Kate. She'd make a dandy sister for you. Would you like that?"

Lukassi kept on walking, looking out at the horizon. "The *Scottismen* say the whaling has gone bad for them. They've got almost no oil, no bone in their holds. Maybe the whales have gone off to some other place to get away from the killing, or they're all dead from the bomb guns. Did the whales swim down into your waters?"

"No," said Caleb, "but our hunt should do better this season."

There was another long, uneasy pause.

"Well, son, what do you think about the idea of coming south with me?"

"No, I can't do that, Captain. Like I said, I got to help my mother and the others. I got to stay to hear captains' words, then change them into Inuktitut or nobody's going to know what anybody's talking about. I don't want to go, Captain. I got too many things that needs doing around here."

"Lukassi, you say the Dundee men took almost no whales this year?"

"That's so," answered Lukassi. "They got almost nothing except that dead fish you split with them. Inuit believe it's because that big woman living at Niantelik is mad at Andrewsikotak. He's mad, too. He says they're going next year looking for whales in Hudson Bay. They heard there's maybe a few big whales left over there."

"I guess we Americans will soon be leaving here for good," said Caleb. "With us gone, and those Dundee men leaving, I guess your people will have to go back to living like wild animals again. Wandering around. Searching for food, probably some of you starving to death."

"Our people say it didn't used to be like that, Captain." Lukassi nodded. "Inuit here likes living free. Sure, hungry maybe sometimes.

But I think it's worse when Inuit families are gathering around the whalers, just like gulls and ravens hanging around the ships and stations, seeing what new strange stuff your ships will bring in to trade or throw away. But other Inuit still live far along the coast. You've never seen them, Captain. They live the way they want to live – hunting, moving with the animals, sleeping anytime they want, doing anything they like to do. Nobody's their boss. It's a good way to live, Captain. I did it lots of winters when I was young. I'll be glad to do it again."

"If you come south with me, Lukassi, you could maybe someday learn to be a captain. If you go to school first, then learn some worthwhile sailing tricks from me, you might become a sea captain."

"I don't want to be a captain," Lukassi admitted. "I know an Inuk boy from Niantelik that a Dundee captain took home with him to *Scotiilann*. They tried to keep him there even when he begged them to let him come back here. But they wouldn't let him go. That boy knew a third mate off the *Alice Daggett* that was sailing back here. That man helped the boy to sneak aboard ship and hide down in the hold on the night before they hauled anchor. Lots of Dundee crewmen gave the boy water and shared their food with him. Soon they were too far away from *Scotiilann* to turn the ship around. Then the boy came up on deck and showed himself. The captain gave the boy a few hard smacks for hiding away, but then gave him work as cook's helper, and the boy got back safe to his family."

Caleb shook his head. "That boy probably missed a wonderful education."

"I asked him," Lukassi continued, "what it was like to live in a big *kallunaat* place across the ocean with horses, and trees, and pigs, and little dogs, and girls with red and yellow hair, and cats that scratch. The boy said mostly being there was terrible. It scared him. He kept feeling more and more ashamed of himself. He said some people tried to be good and smiled at him. But he couldn't understand their words, and there was nothing at all for him to say or do but go with them to church or sit at a long desk in a big stone school. He said he sat and watched it rain against the window glass all winter long, and only wished that he were living here with Inuit in clean, white snowhouses. Sorry, Captain, I gotta stay here with my family, my own people."

"You're making a big mistake, Lukassi." Caleb sighed. "I'm sure you could learn to be just like us."

On the following morning, they started their long trek back to Blacklead. At midday, they crossed two dog-team tracks. Both Supa and Lukassi examined them carefully, saying they did not believe these teams had come from Blacklead or Niantelik. They followed the tracks, for these strangers, too, were heading east toward the coastline. In the evening, they saw blood splashes on the snow where these nomad hunters had made two caribou kills.

After dusk on the following day, a small glow appeared in the distance. They halted. Supa and Lukassi climbed a small rise. When they returned, Lukassi said, "Two igloos."

Supa was wary of this unknown country, as were all the other Inuit, for they greatly feared that those snowhouses might be used by terrifying inland spirits. Supa turned the sleds and moved back, saying that only in full daylight should they run the risk of going near them. They built their two igloos behind a snow rise and slept, but not too soundly, trusting that their dogs would warn them if danger approached.

In the morning, Supa and Lukassi crept forward and observed the igloos carefully with the ice master's long glass. "They look like Inuit to us," Lukassi said when they returned.

Supa halted their sleds more than a musket's shot away from the igloos and waited. A dozen adults and children hurried out of the two snowhouses and stood motionless, staring at them. Supa, Caleb, Finn, and Lukassi walked forward and four men from the igloos came cautiously toward them. No one carried weapons.

"*Kanuiipisiit?*" called Supa. "How are you?"

Thus the conversation began and these strangers gained confidence and drew closer.

"We're from farther north, the place whalers call Bon Accord," said the spokesman for the strangers. "We're hunting down this way."

Supa answered and Lukassi translated. "I told them that we're from Blacklead Island and that you two are *Amerikamiut* whaling captains from the south."

Now the two groups were standing close together, all nodding, smiling at each other. These were rough, long-haired, shaggy men, tanned dark as coffee from the sun's glare off the snow. They must have been handling a lot of meat, thought Finn, living off the land all winter, for their parka fronts had a dark, shiny, greasy look.

"This old man, Kayak, he's the boss with them. He says the whales have gone away from Bon Accord, and the captains up there said that they are leaving when the ice breaks and not coming back. Nothing left to trade there. These three families moved away. The other two men are his brothers, and that one's his brother-in-law, and the others are their families. They have never hunted caribou down here before. Kayak says that they hoped they could find work with these whalers. This man, Kayak," Lukassi told them, "he asks you two captains what they should do. You hear that, Captain Dunston? These men are used to taking orders from whaling masters now."

"You tell him, Lukassi, that they should go to Niantelik," Caleb said. "The Dundee men might have some work for them. The spring whaling's about to start again." Caleb leaned toward Finn, saying, "They're a scruffy-looking lot. Not the kind I'd want hanging around my island."

"They ask us to come and visit their camp," said Lukassi. "They say they have lots of caribou meat and they'd be glad to share it with us."

"No," said Caleb. "You tell that man we have too many dogs with us and so have they. We don't need meat and we don't want a big fight starting here that might cripple some of our animals so they can't pull our loaded sleds."

Lukassi interpreted. "We can easily stop the dogs fighting, Captain."

Supa and Kayak agreed.

Lukassi added, "It makes us all look rude and bad if we don't visit them at all."

The half-grown boy who stood not far behind Kayak shifted from one foot to the other, not listening to what was being said.

Lukassi spoke rapidly, not as interpreter, but directly to Kayak.

There was a long pause with nothing said. Then Caleb nudged Finn's arm and, turning, said, "Let's go."

"Wait, wait," said Lukassi. "Don't you recognize that boy standing back there behind these people?"

"No," said Caleb. "Why should I?"

"Because," said Lukassi, "he's your son. His name is Caleboosi. He's your own son."

"What's that you're telling me? What do you mean, 'my son'?"

"He's your son. Don't you remember, Captain? You used to have his mother do the sewing for you. She died a few years after. Remember her, Captain? She was called Okalik, Rabbit."

"Well, yes, I guess . . ."

Caleb and Finn took a dozen paces forward and looked more closely at the boy. He did appear to be only half Eskimo, although his face was tanned almost as dark as all the others. Finn thought, That boy does look a helluva lot like Dunston.

"*Ayii*, he used to be your son," said Kayak, looking shy. "He was adopted by me and the wife from a family who came from down this way years ago. We heard that their daughter, Okalik, had been sleeping with you over one winter into summer before you sailed away, and this one, Caleboosi," he nodded toward the boy, "was born to her maybe six or seven moons after you had gone."

"Tell the boy to come over here," Caleb said nervously.

When Lukassi interpreted those words, young Caleboosi stepped several paces backward and crouched, ready to run. The boy was dressed in ragged, torn skin clothing, and his hood was tattered, but no worse than any of the adults.

"Maybe we should be polite and go in and visit this camp," said Caleb. "What did you say this boy's name is?"

"Caleboosi," Lukassi answered. "That's the way we say your name, too. They put 'oosi' on the end to make it sound better to our ears. Like that third mate, Phillip, over on *North Star*, Inuit call him Pillipoosi, and me, not Luke, but Lukassi."

Kayak invited the two captains, their women, and Lukassi down into his large family igloo through its long snow porch. A pile of hunting weapons and tangled coils of skin line were flung carelessly just inside the entrance. Its tunnel was almost filled with quarters of caribou meat and the dome of its interior was badly smoked from some ill-kept oil lamps. The whole interior, especially their wide bed, had an unkempt, scrambled look.

Kayak made space for them on the bed, but only Lukassi and the three women sat there. The two captains remained standing.

"Where's the boy, Caleb-oosi?" Caleb used the word awkwardly. "Does he sleep here?"

Kayak nodded, and another child standing by the entrance ran out to get him, then returned, saying to Lukassi, "Caleboosi, he won't come in. He's scared of *kallunaat*."

"He seems like a nice boy to me," said Caleb, and when Nilak and Pia heard that, they both widened their eyes in agreement.

"*Ayii, surusiapik*, a good boy!" answered Kayak's wife.

"Perhaps," said Caleb, "he might like to come to Blacklead Island and live with his real father for a while."

"I'm his father now," answered Kayak. "He's my only son. My wife and I have fed him, brought him up ever since he came off his mother's teat. Caleboosi is going to live with us and be a hunter. He'll take care of me and his mother when we grow old." Kayak pointed to the shy-looking woman sitting next to him. "We've picked a good wife for him, and when they have children, all our family can live together." Kayak smiled at the two captains. "That's the way it's going to be."

Caleb said to Lukassi, "Tell them they won't need Caleboosi much when they get down to Niantelik and find work there."

Kayak didn't answer, he just looked at his hands and his wife blinked as though she were about to cry.

"Lukassi, you go outside and tell that boy, Caleboosi, that I've got a present for him, a good one."

Lukassi went out and came in again, herding Caleboosi before him.

232

The boy stood shyly, but expectantly, before this unbelievable new father. Caleb pulled up his parka and, reaching into his pocket, took out his brass-mounted, staghorn knife and unfolded it, showing the boy its beautiful, shining blade. Caleb extended the knife toward his newfound son, handle first.

Caleboosi took the knife and gasped, then shyly he showed it to his adoptive father, Kayak.

"*Tusunamik!* You're fortunate!" said Kayak.

The boy handed the knife to Kayak, who felt the sharp edge of the blade, then passed it to his wife, who nodded, closed it, and gave it back to her beloved son.

Staghorn knife

"Niantelik is not far from our island," Caleb said through Lukassi. "I would like Caleboosi to come with me to visit in my house at Blacklead." He paused. "All the rest of you folks go to Niantelik. You'll find work. I'll speak to that tall, mean-looking captain over there. Then, later, we can meet together and see what we are going to do to make this right for everybody."

"I've got no whaleboat," Kayak said, taking a different tack. "All I got is my family. And this one son, Caleboosi, he'll soon get stronger. Then I got two brothers and a brother-in-law. We're enough for a boat crew. Me and the brothers have done a lot of rowing for one captain at Bon Accord. Even though I got no whale-boat, you're talking about borrowing, maybe taking Caleboosi away. He's the only son my wife and I got. How will we stay alive when I get too old to hunt and we got no son?"

Caleb did not answer for some time and the igloo seemed to fill with gloom.

"Lukassi, you tell Kayak that if this boy, Caleboosi, can come and live with me as my son, then I might be willing to give him a new whaleboat. Kayak and his brothers can help my carpenter build it, if they all work hard together. I've got the wood for a whaleboat down inside the belly of my ship. Of course, Kayak must give me – and only me," Caleb looked hard at Finn, "the first big fish he takes. When I have it, then that boat will belong to him."

Kayak's eyebrows raised, "Yes, that would be good, for a while."

Lukassi nodded. "A whaleboat would be something that could help support them all. He says if you are really going to give him a new boat and everything that goes inside, then he'll let you take Caleboosi to your island with you, at least for now, and he'll give you the first *akvik*, bowhead, when they get one. Yes, he agrees to that."

Finn saw that Kayak's wife was crying, with her head down and her shoulders heaving.

"Lukassi, you tell Kayak that I agree," said Caleb. Then he asked Caleboosi, "Are you willing to come with me . . . with us?"

Lukassi repeated that question and there was a long pause while Caleboosi looked at his feet, then his father touched his back, and finally the boy raised his eyebrows in a sad way meaning yes.

"Tell Nilak to get the boy's things together, ready to travel with us," Caleb ordered. "We're going now."

Caleboosi's mother sat crying, trying to help Nilak roll up Caleboosi's sleeping skin. She handed him his caribou-skin mittens she had been drying for him over her lamp. Kayak herded the boy out, smiling bravely, speaking rapid Inuktitut to Caleboosi in his most friendly and encouraging voice.

Nilak and Pia smiled and made much of Caleboosi as they walked to their sleds, one on either side, holding him. Caleboosi kept turning, staring back at his foster parents. His father, Kayak, looked at the snow beneath his feet and his mother began weeping so hard that she turned her back and drew her large hood forward until it covered her whole face.

As they moved off, Caleboosi remained shy and nervous of the two foreign captains and refused to walk near them. He broke away and ran back to help Supa's two sons to push and struggle with the other two sleds.

Well before noon, the powerful spring sun caused the snow crust to soften and collapse under the weight of the sleds. They stopped and built their two igloos and slept, planning to rise only when the chill of evening came again, then travel on the hardened crust throughout the paleness of the night.

They saw Caleboosi whispering something to Lukassi, who then came over to Caleb and Finn. "Caleboosi wants to sleep with the Supa family," Lukassi said, "because he likes Supa's sons and they understand his language."

"Yes. Tell him, Lukassi, that his father says it's all right for him to sleep over there."

"You tell him we're all glad to have him with us," Nilak told Lukassi. "We'll make new boots, new clothing for him when we get home."

"Finnussi," said Pia, "you can help teach him to speak *Amerikatitut*."

"Jesus, doesn't she realize he's a Newf?" Caleb whispered to Lukassi. "Finn can't speak real American at all."

"I didn't notice that," said Lukassi.

"Well, forget it. A good scrubbing and new clothes will make all the difference to this son of mine. I've always wanted a son."

"He seems to be a fine boy. Have you got any other sons?" Nilak asked Caleb through Lukassi.

Caleb looked at her. "No," he answered. "He's the only one – as far as I know."

"Oh, then," said Nilak, "it will be good for you to trade a boat for this son of yours. He's half *kalluna*. We think he looks a lot like you. And he can take care of you and your other wife in your old age."

When the travelers came up off the snow-covered ice back onto Blacklead Island, those flesh-eating nomad Inuit who hunted with them should have had eyes for nothing but the glorious piles of frozen red meat hauled back to be shared. But the truth was the islanders, their wives, the mates, and crews scarcely glanced at the meat, so shocked were they to see that this mixed hunting party of nine had traveled across to that vast Baffin inland beyond the mountains where no humans dwelled and had returned with a tenth human, one whom none of them had ever seen before.

235

Chapter 15

Young Caleboosi's arrival had come as a complete surprise to everyone on Blacklead Island, but now it was clearly understood that he was Captain Dunston's native son. That fact interested all the Yacks, and the Connecticut men even more.

After Nilak and Ulayu got Caleboosi scrubbed and his hair washed and cut to Caleb's standards, both the old man and the women were eager to dress him in fashionable, totally new, cut-down sailor's clothing supplied by Caleb. These clothes carefully followed the Arctic whaler's style, that is to say, outwardly Inuit, inside foreign. The women cut off long, new Union underwear, shortened and tucked woolen trousers, made a handsome flannel shirt and, for the cooler days, a little, hooded duffle pullover with sail-canvas cover, and rebuilt a small captain's hat. Of course, these motherly women made Caleboosi all new Yack-style clothing as well: water-proof, knee-length sealskin boots especially softened, and long caribou stockings with gull-skin slippers, and double mittens with thick wool on the inside and handsome sealskin outside, and, natu-rally, a full-hooded sealskin parka designed with a tall point of pride, and wide, knee-length outer pants for easy running.

The young girls on Blacklead were excited by this new boy who now wandered among them in such splendid array. But being only ten or eleven, young Caleboosi was as yet unable to respond in any way but childlike games. He had not found it easy to recover from the sudden separation from his parents, yet at the same time he was experiencing the pleasure of having many new children around him. Some had entirely Inuit faces. A few, like himself, looked half like whalers.

"Caleboosi seems a shy but thoughtful boy," Dougal told the old man. "I never saw his mother, but that boy certainly looks a lot like you."

"Pour yourself some coffee and spike it, Dougal. I've been sitting here planning what I should do with Caleboosi now that I've reclaimed him. I intend to take him south with me and treat him as my son."

"Has he learned any English?" Dougal asked.

"Scarcely a word," the old man answered. "That's part of the trouble. I can't teach him anything except through Lukassi."

"Well," said Dougal, "are you planning to take him into this house to eat and sleep? That might be too much for everybody – you, Nilak, and the boy."

"You're right," said Caleb. "What I plan to do is to have him live over with Lukassi's family. Lukassi's mother is a wise, warm-hearted woman, and her brother, Sagiak, is one of our best harpooners. Of course, neither of them can talk American or that thistly Dundee way of speaking, but Lukassi could help him learn to talk like me."

"That sounds good," said Dougal.

Caleb stood up. "When you see Lukassi, send him over here to me."

Dougal quickly drained his mug and hurried out the door.

"Mate Gibson told me to come see you," said Lukassi as he opened Caleb's door.

"Come in, lad, and rest your bones. I've got some questions for you. First, would you and your family be willing to take my son, Caleboosi, to live with you until we fill our holds with oil and both ships are ready to depart?"

"Sure, Captain. My mother and my grandmother have been talking to Caleboosi. All my family likes him. We'd be glad to have him stay with us."

"Good." Caleb nodded. "I'll see that the cook makes up a generous box of family food each week while Caleboosi's staying with your folks. You just tell Caleboosi I said he's living with you. Oh, and Lukassi, for God's sake, try hard to teach that boy as much of the American language and our ways of thinking as you can. I swear I'll make you a gift of my best Sharps rifle if you do that for me. I'll give it to you before we sail."

"Honest, will you?" gasped Lukassi. "Your new Sharps rifle? No hunter around here's got a gun half as good as that!"

"Well, I'll give it to you," Caleb promised, "with all of my ammunition. Now remember, I don't want my son arriving in Mystic with me and him saying nothing but 'Sunikiak? What that?' or 'Kimmikjuat kapiagijaka, of horses, I'm afraid.' I'm going to change my son's name to Master Caleb Dunston, Junior, on the day he leaves this island. I want him to get used to a decent name before he goes to school."

"I'll teach him best I can," said Lukassi. "You're not just fooling me about that new Sharps rifle, are you? Will you really give it to me?"

"I guarantee that. You take good care, help Caleboosi, and that Sharps rifle will be yours. Talk to him, Lukassi. Encourage him to play soccer with our younger greenhands. Give him a chance to get used to as much of our language as he can."

Spring's long light was rising, strengthening, reaching farther across the ice each day. Dunston ordered the crews to pour long lines of Dundee coal dust reaching from the ships to a weakness in the floe ice where they expected in a month or so to break free. This black dust would attract the sun and burn the dark line slowly down through the snow and ice. The joyful winter frolics and bitter arguments and fights that Caleb, the Highlander, Finn, and sometimes the mates and crews had had over women, whisky, whales, coal, and housing were now fading fast from memory. The trip inland had helped Caleb and Finn to mask the worst of their differences and to let the old ones lie quietly smoldering in their minds. In this new spirit, Caleb actually asked Finn, in front of all the mates at mess, if he would like to go out with him to hunt at the widening floe edge. Finn readily accepted. Such was what a good dose of spring sunshine could do for Arctic men.

Caleb, Finn, and Caleboosi took off by sled toward the open water that lay beyond the floe edge. Pudlat followed them with his whaleboat mounted on a second, stronger sled pulled by sixteen dogs. In the boat with Pudlat were four of his strongest oarsmen. A Yack driver ran alongside, guiding the sled. Finn and Caleb sat together sideways, with Caleboosi in between them. All three were wearing small, dark, round mica glasses against the glaring sun off the snow. Their driver now climbed up and stood up on the moving sled, searching the calm sea beyond the ice. All four were dressed in native clothing – everything, that is, except for the three short-brimmed officers' hats. They wore these not just to show their authority, but also because the hats had built-in woolen ear coverings that could be pulled down from the inside. Young Caleboosi was very proud of his small captain's hat with its New London Fisheries badge protruding from his hood. Finn, while in St. John's, had bought himself a Newfoundland colonial officer's cap with its insignia of the Royal Maritime Crown. He never failed to wear it, although he knew that the very sight of this British badge rubbed the old man the wrong way.

The white sun's glare behind them had produced a huge silver sun dog ring, much larger than a rainbow, with another half-round ray mirrored off its top. The whole sky was a deep azure blue, reflecting the sea, a perfect day with not a breath of wind. They could see some distance away along the ice shelf. When they arrived at the water's edge, they stopped. Pudlat's whaleboat remained perched upon its sled, its crew waiting, watching for the right fish that they hoped would appear.

Young Caleboosi took sly, sidelong glances at the captains sitting on either side of him. He regretted the fact that he was much smaller than they were, but now that he had his new captain's hat and clean clothing just like theirs, it made all three of them seem equal in his eyes. He had become different from other Inuit boys. Certainly, he was the only Inuk privileged to sit here with these two important men. Yes, he readily admitted to himself, in some outer ways he was becoming one of them, a *kalluna*, a person who would grow bushy eyebrows, a small captain who had risen high above the family that had raised him.

In Caleboosi's eyes, these two strange men beside him could never be as skilled as Inuit hunters. Still, they were new and interesting human beings. He especially liked the younger captain called Finnussi who was almost as tanned and handsome as some Inuit hunters of that age. Lukassi had carefully explained to him that this younger captain was only a few years older than Lukassi himself. Caleboosi spread his fingers inside his right mitten and started counting, *atausik, muko, pingasuut* . . . yes, his five fingers spread three times. Caleboosi thought, he's lived maybe only fifteen winters more than me. Was that possible?

What kind of life had Finnussi lived before he came into this country? Caleboosi wondered. What had made him special? How had he become the boss of so big a ship, so many men? Inuit hunters had befriended Finnussi, and Caleboosi had heard that lots of Inuit girls and older women liked him even more. Caleboosi wished that Finnussi could be his father. He admired the red outside pocket that Pia had sewn on Finnussi's fur parka breast to hold his mica glasses. Caleboosi wished he had one, too, for it looked grand.

Caleboosi's thoughts turned to this older captain on the other side, the one Lukassi had told him he must call *ataata*, father. Could he ever feel right doing that? If he did go sailing far away with these two men and learned to live and speak like them, would he become a handsome captain, boss of a huge ship with more *kallunaat* sailors than he had fingers and toes? Would white sailors build a fine, all-wooden house for him? Would clever old widows sew his boots? Best of all, would someone's beautiful, smiling daughter like Pia sleep beside him? Why not, thought Caleboosi, why not go south if that old man wants to make you a captain? He stole another glance at him. Dunston's sharply pointed moustache frightened him. I wish this younger captain would ask me to be his son, thought Caleboosi, then Pia could be my new mother and we'd all stay here together.

Caleb interrupted his son's daydream by saying to Finn, "We're going to teach this boy of mine to hunt. I mean, with a proper gun. Lukassi says my son told him he'd only been allowed to fire a musket once." Caleb smiled at Caleboosi. "I brought out that little ptarmigan rifle for him to use."

"You stay here, Finn, with the boy, and teach him how to hunt seals. You're supposed to be good at that. Since sealing used to be your game, you can help young Caleboosi learn the tricks. I'm going to mosey along to Pudlat's whaleboat."

Finn looked longingly at Pudlat's hunting crew some distance from him along the ice shelf. Goddamn it, thought Finn, I'm out here after whales. Why the hell should I sit here teaching his child to shoot?

Finn took up the little .25-caliber rifle and waited until a seal's head appeared in the water, then fired. He purposely missed it by a hand's breadth. He quickly reloaded and handed the rifle to the boy, who sat down on their sled with his elbow propped on his knee to steady his aim. He looked to Finn as though he knew what he was doing. When a second seal's head appeared, Caleboosi fired and hit it. Luckily, it floated, buoyed up by its winter fat.

Finn took up their triple seal hook and whirled it around, then threw it out beyond the seal, drawing it carefully back so the hook caught the seal. Caleboosi excitedly drew in the line. It was his first seal. He was delighted.

Finn looked again toward Pudlat's boat. The old man, with his bomb gun over his shoulder, was still walking toward the Inuit hunters. Finn looked around and thought, I've never seen a better day in any country. It's just right, windless, with those ice mirages rising and distorting like magic along the whole horizon of the sea.

Suddenly, Finn shaded his eyes. There she blows, his mind screamed to him. There's a right fish surfacing before my eyes. Finn looked again along the edge of the ice. Pudlat and his crew crouched motionless, watching, waiting while the bowhead breathed, then sounded.

The old man started running toward Pudlat's boat with his bandolier of bombs bumping wildly against his hip. Finn snatched up his bombs and whale gun and set out in a rush to try and overtake the old man, beat him to Pudlat's boat where he could demand the right to act as boat steerer. If Finn could outrun Dunston and take command of Pudlat's boat, he could claim that whale as his own fish, providing he harpooned it. It's a rotten trick, Finn thought, but hell, who cares when a huge fish like that is a prize to be taken by me or Dunston, or the Yacks?

Caleb was gasping hard when Finn passed him. Caleb sensed he could not outrun those long, lean legs of Finn's. The ice master nodded as he dashed past. He saw the big bowhead rise and blow, then rest again, filling its huge lungs with air, calmly preparing for another dive. Finn kept on running, taking a chance of frightening the whale. The huge black giant arched its back upward and began to dive. Its enormous tail flukes lifted gracefully into the air, then lingered like the outspread wings of a butterfly before it plunged down into the icy stillness of the sea.

Pudlat and his crew had seen the big fish. They had whispered magic words and rattled the small Scottish farthings placed inside a whale's fist-sized ear bone, confident that this fish would heed the exciting sound and swim toward them.

When Pudlat and his hunters saw Finn and the old man racing along the floe edge toward them, they understood their purpose and quickly unlashed the whaleboat and skidded it straight off its strong oak sled until its bow was hanging over the water. They lost precious moments trying to straighten the harpoon line that was badly coiled inside the tubs.

"*Tuavvi*, hurry!" Pudlat whispered as he watched the old Caleboosi slow, then stop, and the young Finnussi run even harder toward them. They left the harpoon line in a mess, desperate to launch their whaleboat before Finn could reach them. The boat started to slide into the water.

"*Uvattiaruk pinnak* – wait, don't!" Finn bellowed, his voice loaded with authority, though he knew he should be silent when confronted by a whale that would certainly be listening.

At that moment, like the whoosh from a giant kettle, twin white spouts of steam once more exploded into the icy air close to them. Pudlat's crew froze in various positions, afraid they would alarm this enormous relative that had so willingly come to the shaman's rattle. Even Finn stopped dead and remained like a runner on the mark, holding the harpoon gun, his bombs still swaying against his hip. Then, sensing that the fish would dive, he took the chance and made the last dash that carried him to the side of Pudlat's boat. The whale raised its head, its large eye now above the surface watching the action around the whaleboat. The startled bowhead dove beneath the surface before it had properly taken in its huge breath of air. That meant the fish would have to surface again, and soon.

Pudlat was far too polite a man to try and keep this foreign captain at bay, so Finn leapt uninvited into his whaleboat and scrambled forward to mount his harpoon gun in the swivel hole at the bow, then turned and ran back across the thwarts to grab the steersman's oar. Now Finn applied his captain's privilege and took full command of Pudlat's boat. He knew that Inuit preferred to use paddles instead of oars when near a whale to make less noise as they approached the wary giant. So Finn signaled them to do just that.

Pudlat stood in the bow and Finn stood on tiptoe in the stern, watching, his arm clamped over the long steering oar. These two very different kinds of hunting men searched, looking for any sign of movement on the water's surface. Pudlat's face was invisible to Finn, hidden by his upturned parka hood, but ahead of them two Arctic terns paused in flight, then hovered, heads down, watching something in the water.

Pudlat hand-motioned to the left and Finn responded with the steering oar. Not one of the four oarsmen turned his head, but all of them stared stone-faced at Finn, trying to read what was about to happen by the movement of his lips, his eyes. Pudlat rose gracefully, wedging his shin in the kneehole, as his eyes searched the glassy water. Suddenly, he held up both arms, his mittens wriggling, a sure sign that he was watching a rising line of bubbles. His left hand waved to port and Finn corrected their course.

Suddenly, Pudlat looked back at Finn, this time his eyes and mouth wide open with excitement. He beckoned violently to Finn, then, turning, raced back between the oarsmen toward the stern.

Finn let go of the steering oar and leapt forward from thwart to thwart, passing Pudlat exactly halfway between bow and stern.

Finn slipped and Pudlat's cousin on the stroke oar caught him round the waist, saving him from going over the side. Finn took that last, long step that landed him in place beside his mounted harpoon gun. Pudlat had everything just right. Finn armed the gun with one of his bomb charges and remained there steady, gasping with excitement, waiting for his chance.

The bubbles began to rise in a straight line, then burst on the surface into little puffs of vapor, each one increasing in size. The gulls were gathering screaming overhead. Finn leaned forward, astonished at the whale's enormous bulk as, blue and shimmering, it rose beneath the boat, looking as big as the rain-slick roof of a hay barn. Now he could see its tail flukes fanned out like a black butterfly's wings moving just beneath their bow. Finn snatched off his mittens and, without taking his eyes off the hump of water caused by the rising fish, made a quick hand motion and the boat swung away from the fish's tail. Finn was making sure that their boat would not be lined up with this huge beast's flukes when it felt the shock of his harpoon.

This shiny, black-skinned giant broke through the surface. Its twin blowholes opened as it blew, sending up a double spray of thick white mist which soaked the crew. Finn's hands were shaking as he knelt in the bow, trying to steady, then aim, the harpoon gun. Using both thumbs, he hauled back the stiff iron hammer and curled his forefinger around the trigger. His whole body was trembling as the mountainous whale's back rose to dive. He took aim and fired. Through the acrid smoke, he could see the harpoon line slithering just above the water's surface like a brown snake as its black iron head plunged into the body of the whale.

The enormous tail flukes rose, casting a shadow over the boat, then smashed down, narrowly missing the bow, causing a wave of water to tip, then all but sink the whaleboat. Again the tail flukes rose and crashed down as the panicking giant reacted to the pain. Finn could hear the oarsmen working the wooden bailers, sloshing out the water, struggling desperately to save themselves as the wounded animal sounded. Finn could feel hot blood running down his chin where his teeth had bitten into his lower lip. The long hemp was uncoiling, running back straight as a ruler from the tub, then smoking around the lion's tongue post in the stern before it rushed forward with deadly force between the oarsmen, back through the iron bow notch, and downward into the water. The harpoon head was holding fast, buried somewhere deep inside the diving whale.

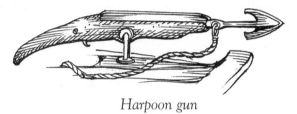

Harpoon gun

Finn, still shaking, let go of the gunnel. Turning like a drunken man, he once more began the dangerous race from fore to aft, leaping from thwart to thwart to regain his boat steerer's position, careful to avoid the deadly rush of rope. As Pudlat came past him, he clasped his hand on Finn's shoulder. Was it a sign of friendship or just to steady both of them? Finn would never know.

Just as he reached the steering oar, the boat lunged sideways with the hemp line running out too fast. Finn grabbed the stroke man by the hair to regain his balance, then snubbed the rope around the tongue post to try and slow it. He could smell the hemp line scorching, see it smoking. The bow lurched downward and the boat's stern rose high in the air. Pudlat let out more line as the huge fish continued its run.

"Jesus, help us!" Finn cried. "Make that toggle iron hold fast and, please God, keep this fish from heading in toward that fuckin' ice!"

The Inuit had unshipped their oars and the stroke man reached back and poked Finn in the chest and grimaced, signaling him to shut his mouth. The boatmen had not understood the words that Finn had shouted, but it was against every Inuit tradition to call out or show emotion during the hunt, especially after a whale had been harpooned and still might, or might not, decide to give itself to the humans.

Why did I forget that? Finn cursed himself, then thought, Aw, to hell with them. My Christian prayers are being answered. This fish is keeping away from the ice and my iron is in there deep and holding fast.

The importance of being quiet and respectful to a harpooned whale was absolutely contrary to the habits of the Yankee or Dundee men. They liked to whoop and holler out in triumph and delight, fill their hats with rushing air, and stomp their feet to warm them during those long, gut-trembling tows behind a whale, as they thrilled to what they liked to call a New England sleigh ride.

When this 170-barrel bull surfaced again, the Yacks began the business of hauling in fathom after fathom of line and recoiling it quickly, and this time neatly, into the tubs. Finn signaled Pudlat, who armed, then fired, a second harpoon into the fish, just at the waterline, to make doubly sure they held him fast. This panicked the whale. It veered north with newfound strength, swimming straight toward the long white floe, then dove. If this fish chose to go beneath the ice, they would have no choice but to cut away the line or be smashed to pieces against the unbreakable mass that stood before them.

Pudlat felt around beneath his bow cover and came up with an old vinegar bottle, as the crew hauled desperately, bringing in more and more line, trying to close the gap between the boat and the whale. Now Finn watched a trick that he had heard of, but had never seen before.

When Pudlat saw the bubbles rising and the water swell again, he crouched down, cupped his hand around a thick sulphur match, struck it, and held it to the wick that he had carefully prerubbed with seal grease and gunpowder. That wick, plugged into the neck of the bottle, was short, and he had to fling it hard and fast. It landed a boat's length starboard of the fish as it towed them toward the deadly field of ice.

There was a brief moment as the ice rushed toward him that seemed to Finn to take a hundred years, then the sinking bottle of gunpowder exploded with a dull thump, forcing a geyser of white water into the air. The huge fish swerved away in panic and then, thank God, began to tow them out to sea again.

After three more surfacings following almost half-hour soundings, the fish rose to take a desperately needed breath and rested, slow to dive again, for its immense strength was running out. The oarsmen carefully hauled in and coiled the line inside the pair of tubs. Pudlat glanced back at Finn with a solemn face, but made no offer to change places with him.

The four Inuit crewmen put their oars back in their locks, then, on Pudlat's signal, took a dozen long, strong strokes, positioning him a man's length behind the left eye of this enormous creature. Pudlat drew back his long, iron-shafted killing lance with its razor-sharp head, called the ace of spades by Yankee whalers. Then, with his right hand cupped around the hickory butt, he drove the lance deep inside the whale and churned it back and forth, trying to find and sever the main arteries to its heart.

When he found them, all hell broke loose as the mortally wounded whale went into a flurry, rolling over and over in its death throes, thrashing much too close to the boat. Dark red spumes of blood gushed out of its wounds and breathing holes. The artery flow sprayed into the air. It covered them, transforming the men in the boat into creatures painted solid red.

These blood-red Inuit oarsmen backstroked off as quickly as they could, then, like Finn and Pudlat, wiped their faces and sat watching as quietly composed as any row of Sunday parishioners in a church pew. Some fingered their shaman's amulets in gratitude to the goddess. The ice master, silent now as all the others, remembered the line from a prayer: "Bless those at peril upon the sea."

One religion or the other was slowly taking its effect. The great fish of fishes, in its final flurry, had bound itself in the long hemp line. Pudlat took up his second lance and waited, but he had no need to use it. The bowhead, which was almost twice as long as

247

the boat and immensely wide in girth, lay peacefully dead. The Inuit crewmen stroked forward and caressed the animal, thanking it respectfully. Then Pudlat made the necessary knife slits in its lips and the oarsman stitched closed its enormous mouth with sealskin line.

After cutting and attaching a third safety line, Finn and all five others took up oars and turned the whaleboat. With long, hard strokes, they started back toward the jagged white line of shore ice. Tom Finn had just experienced the greatest thrill of his life, for had he not for the first time mastered a whaleboat that took a big whale fair and square? He would hold the joys and fears, the wild excitement of this chase, inside him forever. Finn put his back into the heavy work. Dozens of gulls and Arctic terns now reeled and screamed, and often landed on the whale in tow. The spring sun moved slowly westward just above the distant mountains, spinning golden paths along their valleys.

Caleb sat on the wide oak sled examining his scars and broken fingernails and cursing Finn's good fortunes. His son, Caleboosi, seemed restless and unhappy as he stood kicking the snow with his skin boot, wishing he had been in on the whale kill. What a damned shame, thought Caleb, to have a real son who, for the time being, could not understand the many wisdoms his father had to pass on to him. How could this son know that Caleb intended one day to leave him Topsail House and who knows what fortune in the Union Bank?

It took more than three hours of slow, back-breaking work before the bow of Pudlat's boat touched, then slid along the edge of the main ice. When Finn turned his head, he could see Caleb, Caleboosi, and Pudlat's nephew hurrying toward them, driving Pudlat's sixteen dogs, which pulled the empty work sled. The man on lookout also had been watching them. From Blacklead Island, Finn could see three other teams hauling sturdy blubber sleds across the ice toward the kill.

Finn unshipped his oar and eased himself out of the boat onto the ice, dead tired.

The old man nodded to him. "Finn, you made out not too badly for a Newfie ice master who's trying to learn the whaling trade. That big bull should corset up one helluva lot of pretty girls! Look at the Yacks rushing out here to help Pudlat." Caleb snorted. "I'm glad it's *Lancer's* whale, not theirs, so we won't have to trade it away from them. Oh, you should give Pudlat a little something for his help – maybe a new mate's hat with a gilded Fisheries badge like mine on front. His boat crew should be satisfied with a new mouth organ each, and maybe enough worn-out sailcloth for their summer tents, bright head scarves for their women, and a two-gallon keg of that raw Newfie rum for them to celebrate their luck."

"The rum will clinch it," Tom Finn agreed. "But I'd say those few gifts aren't half enough."

Finn had been roughly calculating his profits during the long row, exulting over the ton of valuable corset bone that bull would have packed in its mouth. It alone would be worth more than three thousand U.S. dollars. This fish's oil should fetch the Fisheries maybe three or four thousand dollars, even with oil prices down the way they were in late June, because of the recent depression that had swept the country.

"Yes, I'd say we wouldn't be losing too much profit if we paid back these Yacks with even twice as much stuff as you suggest."

"Finn, you're absolutely counting on us getting all that oil and bone safely home, aren't you? Well, let me warn you, it's a helluva risk." Caleb grunted. "I don't want you giving away too much to these people. You'll spoil it for the rest of us while you try to impress them with your colonial generosity. Forget that, Finn. You can throw in six more red bandana neckerchiefs and one of those big, fourteen-dollar, Brooklyn button accordions. God knows, Pudlat and his crew love rum and dancing. Don't you get too fuckin' fancy on us."

A strong, iron tripod was unlashed from a sled and quickly set up on the ice. It was half as tall as a man. The northern whaling men used this device to gain leverage, the same way the southern whalers used a ship's mainmast to haul up, then roll and peel the blanket of blubber off a sperm whale's crang. As they worked to strip the huge skeleton, a flock of screaming gulls gathered in a feeding frenzy, lunging at the bright white fat.

"Oh, my God, it's awful!" Jack Shannon told Dunston, then Finn, when he arrived with the extra teams. "We just got word of what that missionary has been doing to those poor, benighted English whaling bastards up in Kekerton."

"What?" demanded Caleb.

"One of their whaleboats got caught in ice and blown across the Sound and landed not far north of here. They were Hull men off the whaleship *True Love* who got stranded on the ice with their boat sprung full of leaks. They had eaten so many raw gulls and eider ducks, they swore they were starting to scream and sprout feathers when our Yacks saved them and sledded them to Niantelik."

"What did the Hull men have to say?" asked Finn.

"After the Highlander had dosed them up with enough hot rum, seal stew, and oatmeal porridge, they napped, then had a torrent of news to tell about that missionary. His name's McNab, and he's been spoiling all the fairest joys up there, they say."

Nilak smiled as she stepped into Caleb's porch and closed the outer door. Then, pulling off her parka smoothly over her head, she entered.

"*Ukuujualuk*, it's hot," said Nilak, leaving open the inner door as she drew both sailcloth draperies across the captain's windows. She blinked at *Lancer*'s ship's boy, Pierre, who was peeking in.

Caleb rose from his desk where he'd been trying to calculate the additional oil and bone that he must take before they could start the voyage south. He opened his sea chest and took out the gallon jug of good Barbados rum protected by its woven basket of reeds.

Nilak held out their two pewter cups while he poured.

"Want some, do you?" Caleb smiled. "Well, I don't blame you. You probably want a drink as much as I do. Remember in the old days when you used to hate the taste of rum? Here's to you, dear girl!" Caleb raised his cup to her.

Nilak raised hers and smiled as they drank together.

Caleb shook the grate in his coal stove. "I'm going to have another," he said, and, lifting the green glass jug, he poured two drinks. "But let's not get dizzy-headed," he said as he set on the candle table his turnip timepiece with its chain and golden whale and eased off his gull-skin slippers.

Nilak laughed and pulled off a blue-striped shirt that Caleb had given her. Then, blowing out the candle, she drew back the canvas curtain so they could see the night sky. It was filled with stars. The moonlight reflecting off the snow caused the whole room to glow.

The captain was ready for her when his love slipped in beside him.

Kudlik's grandfather, Kiasuk, who had twinkling black eyes in an ancient-looking face, was visiting his son's family on Blacklead. He was said to be their keeper of stories, old and new. Lukassi introduced young Caleboosi, who liked him very much. They soon became fast friends. The old man taught Caleboosi more about Inuit ways and culture than he might normally have learned during his whole life. In fact, Lukassi admitted to Caleb that old Kiasuk had utterly changed Caleboosi's way of thinking.

Caleb often stood and proudly watched his newfound son from inside the house as Caleboosi kicked the Scottish soccer ball with the younger greenhands and Inuit boys. He could hear Caleboosi calling out to the running, dodging crewmen in pure American expressions such as "Boot it over here . . . buster!"

It's working well, thought Caleb. The young share languages so quickly when they play together.

Two weeks later, Caleboosi's adoptive parents came over from Niantelik to visit him on Blacklead Island. His former father, Kayak, told him they had moved in with some cousins there. They had rowed as part of a boat crew for the Highlander, but they had had no luck whaling. Kayak and his brothers were ready to start working with Everett on their promised whaleboat. They began the day they arrived. Caleb was anxious to have them finish the new boat and start hunting so they could quickly take a whale for him, then get the hell off his island, for Kayak made him nervous. He certainly didn't want this family hanging around, disturbing Caleb Dunston, Jr.'s first steps toward the civilized world.

Caleboosi's former father, Kayak, and especially his mother, complained to Pia's parents that their son seemed only partly glad to see them and overeager to run back with the young *kallunaat* to kick the ball. During the days of boatbuilding, his family said Caleboosi ate only once with them and spent the whole meal telling them about the grandfather's tales of earlier times before foreign whalers arrived, when there was no iron, only bits of driftwood, and not a single *kallunaat* thing to trade.

A few days later, Kayak and his family departed in their new whaleboat and Caleboosi came for the first time on his own to visit Caleb in his house. He spoke some Inuktitut to Nilak, but mostly he seemed eager to try his new American language on his father. "Cap-in Doon-stoon. You lookin' purdy good, fa-terrr," the boy said haltingly to open the conversation.

"I'm feeling good because of you," Caleb answered, smiling broadly.

"You sees whalesss any swimmin' tooo-daay?" his son asked him.

"No," said Caleb, careful to pronounce his words. "I hope I see whales tomorrow."

"Ohhh, thaaa's goood." Caleboosi smiled. "Lukassi say myyy Amlican woords growingg gooder."

"He's right," said Caleb. "Don't worry, son, a Mystic or Stonington schoolmaster will soon get hold of you and shape you up."

"*Uuai!*" Nilak exclaimed. "*Kallunaatitut kaujimalirktuk!* He's learned a lot of your language. Young Caleboosi's words are starting to sound just as awful on my ears as the speech of you men with bushy eyebrows!"

Chapter 16

"The *angakuk*, that big woman," Lukassi told Finn and Caleb when they came into the mess hall, "she's going to do some flying tonight over at Niantelik. She asks, do you want to come and see her, maybe go flying with her?"

"Flying? What the hell do you mean flying?" Caleb asked suspiciously.

"Well, I don't know," said Lukassi. "Nobody knows. She says she don't even know how she does it herself. But that whale woman's going somewhere tonight. She says she's going to travel where no Inuit or *kallunaat* are allowed to go before they're dead."

"Why can't they go where she's going?" Finn asked him.

"Because there's no path to that place. You can't walk, drive dogs, paddle, or sail there. And," said Lukassi, "you probably wouldn't want to go there even if you could because you'd never find your way back, unless she had ahold of some part of your body."

"Sounds like a lot of hogwash to me," the old man snorted. "What do you think we'll see, Finn, if we go over to Niantelik?"

"He doesn't know, Captain," Lukassi answered. "Nobody knows. I'm afraid of that big woman. But you two bosses might want to ask her to go traveling for you, see what she can see. I'll try to interpret what she tells when she gets back."

"Could be interesting," Finn nodded. "We haven't visited Niantelik for a long time."

"I hate that place," said Caleb, "with those cheeky Yacks and Dundee crewmen stumbling around."

"Well, I'll go over," said Finn, "There's nothing doing here on Blacklead tonight."

"Oh, I'll go, too." The old man kicked the stove. "Go ahead, Lukassi, arrange for a dog team. We can set up a sail on the sled if the wind holds right. It won't take us but an hour or so to get over there with this hard snow crust over the ice. When does all her fake flying start?"

"Soon after you get there," Lukassi answered. "She knows that you're coming, so she'll start readying herself while you're eating and drinking with Andrewsikotak."

"How could she know we're coming to Niantelik?" Finn asked. "We didn't even know ourselves until right now."

"That's the way that woman is," said Lukassi. "She knows everything before it happens."

"Should we let the Highlander know we're coming?" asked Caleb.

"He'll know you're coming by now," said Lukassi. "She lets him know what's going on sometimes."

"Will he come to this Gypsy's palm-reading?" The old man tightened his moustache points. "Does she use a crystal ball of ice?"

"Oh, nooo!" said Lukassi. "She'd never invite Andrewsikotak, and he wouldn't go if she begged him."

"Why not?" asked Finn.

"Because she says both those captains over there are getting meaner and meaner with the trading," Lukassi answered. "She told me never is she going to help them again."

"She sounds like one of those crazy cootie hunters," Caleb snorted, "crazy as a loon."

"Loons not crazy, they wise," said Lukassi. "Everyone here knows that. Both you captains, remember, take that big woman some presents, good ones, or she could go against you."

Caleb looked at his turnip watch. "We'll be ready to leave at four o'clock. You, Lukassi, pick a driver with a good dog team and come

254

for us in front of my house." The old man went out to read the wind off Finn's weathervane, hoping it would hold steady to the west.

For their cold sled journey across the bay, they were able to rig a sail. Caleb wore his earflaps jammed down. He smoked two cigars and scarcely spoke a word to Finn until they halted the team beside *Blue Thistle*.

"You must be goddamned crazy," said the old man, turning and leering at Finn, "urging me to come over here in this murderous fuckin' cold to watch this big bitch try to kid us with some of her Gypsy tricks."

Dog team with sail

The two of them climbed stiffly off the sled and stood at the bottom of *Blue Thistle*'s gangway. The Highlander waved them up the ramp. He was hunched over with a wretched cold, his face blue, his eyes rimmed, his nose flaming red.

"I heard ye were coming earlier today. I hope ye've brought along that kind of powerful rum medicine ye Yanks drink." Andrew wheezed. "Colin and I have already had a drop or two of my brother's best whisky."

The old man grunted and pursed his lips, which made the hoarfrost on his moustache glisten. "Christ, man, we're cold," roared Dunston. "Are you going to have us talk out here?"

"Och, nooo," the Highlander said, and led them to his cabin. He and his first mate were in the middle of a domino game. Colin also seemed quite drunk.

The Highlander poured himself and Colin another whisky, but did not offer Caleb or the ice master a single drop. Instead, he pushed across to them a tin of Edinburgh shortbread and a pot of lukewarm tea. "Colin saw ye sailing over here this evening on yer sledge."

"We were going so fast," Finn said, "we had to unharness the dogs and let them run beside us."

"Young Lukassi urged us to make the trip," said Caleb. "He told us there's something special going on tonight."

"Och, that two-tongued lad of yers is wrong, dead wrong again," the Highlander wheezed. "Everything here is nice and quiet and it damned well better stay that way! We observe Yuletide, Hogmanay, and St. Andrew's Day. That's all."

"Well," said Finn, "Lukassi told us to bring our best harpoon irons. He's going to take us to visit your big woman to see what the spring whaling might be like."

The Highlander rose unsteadily and opened his cabin door. "Well, if ye're finished yer shortbread and tea, Caleb, Lukassi must be waiting for the pair of ye to lead ye to that yon igloo of hers." He coughed again and sneezed.

"Would you and Colin like to come with us?" asked Finn.

"Never!" rasped the Highlander. "I wouldn't go near yon slippery slut for all the bowheads in the world."

Caleb stared at Finn. The first two parts of Lukassi's prediction had proved true – first, the Highlander had known that they were coming, and second, he had refused to join them.

Lukassi was carrying three of Caleb's harpoon irons and three of Finn's when they saw him duck into the round entrance porch of the largest igloo. Caleb and the ice master nervously followed him inside, stepping cautiously down a blood-spattered, curving snow tunnel built to hold meat and keep out wind. Pushing open a hanging seal-skin, they could see that inside was a large, domed room.

At first, both captains had difficulty seeing anything. The light from two half-moon-shaped stone lamps was dim, their long flames ragged, smoking, and neglected. The snow dome was badly sooted from these untended lamps, and the sight of it, Finn knew, would have distressed Nilak, Pia, her mother, or most other Inuit women.

There were more than a dozen strange Inuit inside this igloo. Caleb recognized only two of them.

In the very center of the wide, snow sleeping bench that was covered with a tossed jumble of bearskins, a worn ship's blanket, and caribou hides sat the big woman, Kowlee. Caleb easily recognized her, but there was something different about her now. Her inner parka, with the hair turned in against her flesh, was covered in front with grease wiped from her hands. Her hair was a tangle, except for two thin rat-tail braids that now hung down beside her face, and there was a fatty puffiness around her narrow, glistening eyes.

She peered first at the ice master. This younger captain was new to her, though she had heard numerous tales of his house and the swing he had suspended from *Lancer*'s bowsprit for his bedmate, Pia, and she knew the other women's views of him as a good-natured, lively dancer who liked children. Now, with her powerful, tattooed wrists and arms, she pushed aside the Yacks who sat near her, then beckoned to the captains. "*Itsivaalauritsi*," she commanded.

"You sit there, Caleboosi," Lukassi interpreted for her. "And, Finnussi, you sit close there, on the other side of her."

Lukassi remained standing before her, for the big woman had offered him no place on the long bed.

"God," Caleb sniffed, "I hate everything about this place. It's gray and soggy and disgusting! There's not a single Yack household on Blacklead Island as miserably run down as this frozen pit. No wonder the Highlander refused to come with us."

The big woman frowned as she leaned forward and spoke in rapid Inuktitut to Lukassi, who looked surprised.

"What did she tell you?" the old man asked.

"She said, 'The Highlander knows she might have killed him this time if he'd dared to come with you.'" Lukassi translated hesitantly. "Be careful of your answers. She seems to understand the words you say." Lukassi hunched his narrow shoulders nervously. "I don't know how many languages she understands or speaks. You two say only good things in this house."

Caleb and Finn became tight-lipped and disdainful, glancing sideways at what they considered an incredible female freak.

"Do you bushy-eyebrowed men know why you've come here?" she asked them in Inuktitut.

"*Aggai* . . . no," Lukassi answered for them.

"You tell me what she asks," Caleb ordered, "and I'll tell you how to answer, lad. We want no smart-ass tricks going on here." The old man scowled at Lukassi and the big woman.

She spoke again and Lukassi translated. "She says you're here to learn, and she's going to teach you something – maybe good and maybe bad. She warns you both to listen hard. Keep all your body holes wide open. She may or may not find what you are hoping for."

The big woman made a hand signal to her oddly twisted apprentice, the one who had been with her in Caleb's house. He rose from his place by the entrance and held a large, flat, tambourine-shaped drum over her lamp flame. He heated it until the caribou parchment skin tightened. Then he struck the drum's round wooden edge with his short, stout stick. It gave off an ominous, booming sound.

The drummer shuffled until he found the correct place beneath the smoke-darkened igloo dome. Crouching, he began to dance, rotating, flipping the drum's face. He turned it, striking one edge, then the other. Slowly, rhythmically, he began to circle, hunching his shoulders, showing his teeth until he seemed to shrivel inside himself. Sometimes, he tapped the drum so softly that the captains could scarcely catch the sound, then he would suddenly shock them with a frenzied barrage of frantic beats.

The big woman shook herself and straightened as though she had been asleep. Strangely, she began to mumble weird, repetitive words in rhythm with her apprentice's drumming. "*Ayii, ayii . . . ayii ayii.*"

"What's she muttering about?" the old man grumbled to Lukassi.

"I don't understand most of it," Lukassi whispered, "but the words she's singing, they're getting stronger. Goes like this:

That woman down there beneath the sea,
She wants to hide the whales from us.
These hunters in the dance house,

They cannot right matters.
They cannot mend matters.
Ayii, ayii.

"See her gasping, breathing harder? I think she's pumping up to dive or maybe fly. Listen, she's singing:

Into the spirit world
Will go I,
Where no humans dwell.
Set matters right will I.
Set matters right will I."

Hearing her words, Inuit in the house began to cry out and stiffen their bodies.

Seeing this set Caleb's nerves on edge, made him feel as though something strange had crawled inside of him. Caleb leaned across in front of the big woman and said to Finn, "I've got to stop her. This is goddamned madness. She's making fools of us. I'm leaving." But, like Finn, he felt powerless to move. It was as though an uncontrollable numbness had wrapped itself around their guts, binding them to the sleeping bench, making them helpless beside this awesome, swaying, sweating woman.

Faintly at first, then stronger, they heard animal sounds emerging from her throat. The moaning notes that came from deep inside her were like a giant church organ playing low chords in some abandoned cathedral. Her throat utterances seemed to crawl over Caleb's body like hermit crabs. They were utterances so unworldly that no human voice could have formed them. This cacophony of sounds became so deafening that it shook the igloo dome until bits of snow mortar showered down from between its blocks.

The drummer now leapt close to the big woman. Jerking down her parka front, he reached between her heaving breasts and drew out two winter weasel skins yellow with age. Blue trade beads had been sewn into their eye sockets. The big woman held the weasels in her hands, moving them, aiming them like a pair of pistols first at Caleb, then at Finn. Yacks in the igloo cried out and shrank away from them. A young wife in the igloo became hysterical as the whale woman caught hold of her own two hair braids and clamped them hard between her teeth, then started swaying. Finn noticed in the lamplight that the tattoos on her sweating wrists and hands as well as the blue lines on her face seemed to have turned dark indigo blue.

The dwarf began to beat the drum again, this time faster, louder. Suddenly, the big woman extended her arms and smashed the weasel skins together in her fists. When Caleb looked into her face, her eyes were half rolled back and crossed, a sight that sickened him. Trembling, she arched her back like a drawn hunter's bow, remaining bent, face upward, until her skin lost all its color. Was she frozen? Was she dead?

Lukassi shook both captains' arms and smiled. "You can say any bad words you want to now," he told the captains. "She's gone. She can't hear you now."

The others in the house began to hack and cough and wipe their noses, then to gossip freely.

"Why do you say she can't hear us?" Finn asked as he stared in alarm at the stiffened posture of the woman.

"Because she's gone," said Lukassi. "She's left this igloo."

Caleb made a sour face. "This is nothing but some hypnotist's dream we're having. Just look at that goddamned woman with her greasy hair braids jammed in her mouth."

"You wait," said Lukassi. "She'll be back. I'm glad she wasn't here when you said that about her hair."

"If she's not here, where is she?" Finn demanded.

"She's gone into the *inua* world, you know, the other spirit world," said Lukassi, "where animals and humans can talk together, dance together if they want to. Big snowy owls can marry little lemmings. That is known. It's that other world she's visiting right now. She looks frozen stiff, but see how the sweat is running down her face?" said Lukassi. "Feel the heat that woman is giving off, just like a hot stove. There, did you see her twitch? Maybe she's still on her way there, maybe she's flying back."

"It was damned cold in here," said Caleb. "At first, I didn't want to take my mitts off. And now . . ."

"It's hot as hell in here," said Finn. "Look, this igloo's dripping and there's gray fog forming in the dome. She's starting to tremble like . . ."

"Be careful what you sa —" At that moment, Lukassi was struck violently on the back. The blow flung him forward against the ice master's chest.

"Look, for Christ's sake! What's that?" Caleb gasped as a huge, dark shadow began to pass around the inner igloo wall. "The damned thing's being followed by another. You can see it in the lamplight."

"*Akviit*, whales!" whispered Lukassi. "Big bowhead whales. Here comes another."

The dark, dreamlike shadows of the huge beasts began to circle the igloo walls and became distorted as they disappeared out through the entrance passage. Strange, unworldly, high-pitched squeals, then grunts and long groans had followed them around the snow dome. The sound seemed to come up from far below them, through the snow and ice that covered the sea beneath their feet.

The big woman collapsed, her hair braids falling from her mouth. The sweat upon her face turned into hoarfrost. Her eyes were so far rolled back that Finn could only see their whites.

"*Pingasuut*." Lukassi's voice was shaking. "Three of them. That's how many big whales she's called in for you. She brought them up to show you. I guess she's asked them to give their bodies to you captains."

"What should we do now?" Finn asked, trying to keep his voice level.

"She's probably waiting for the harpoons," said Lukassi. He held them out like a baby in his arms.

"*Mitik. Mitiapik.*" The big woman slowly straightened, then whined in a small girl's voice. Her drummer wiped her sweaty face. A child climbed down from her mother's lap and made her way across the igloo's soot-blackened, icy floor. The child held out a loon-skin bag to her.

"*Nakuumiralungaasitu.*" The big woman very gently thanked the child.

Leaning across Caleb's lap, she grunted as she strained to reach some of the white whale blubber that was melting into oil at the edge of her lamp. When she had enough fat on her fingers, she heaved herself back into an upright position. One by one, Lukassi handed her the harpoon irons. She carefully greased each cutting edge. Then, reaching into the loon-skin bag, she drew out a handful of soft gray eiderdown. This fluff she shaped like a protective pillow along the head of each razor-sharp blade.

Speaking rapidly through Lukassi, she said, "Tell these captains those killing heads will not bother the whales. They will seem to them like the soft stroke of a feather. Those whales will not fear them when they come to the boats and see these amulets."

The dwarf handed each of them a blood-red sea-pigeon's foot. Both of the captains stared at them, then quickly hid them in their ditty bags.

"Have your women sew these webbed feet onto your parka fronts," said Lukassi, "before you next go on the hunt. Finnussi, she says she's going to give you something else."

She spoke more words to him, and many in the igloo smiled and started coughing. For the first time, the two foreigners heard the big woman chuckling as she rummaged through the loon-skin bag beside her. Finally, she found what she was looking for – a finger-length baculum, a seal's penis bone. It took her somewhat longer to find what Lukassi explained was the sinew drawn from the thigh of a snowy owl. This she carefully wound around the slender shank of the penis, then tied a knot and bit off the unwanted end. She tenderly put this amulet in her mouth to warm it, then slowly drew it out and, leering at Finn, handed it to him.

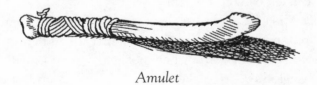

Amulet

262

"The main part's over," Lukassi called as he pushed his way out of the igloo into the snow porch and returned with the good-sized crate of gifts, the selection of which the captains had left to Lukassi and Dougal. They had taken food and knickknacks from the slops chests of *Lancer* and *Sea Horse*, and both captains' private food lockers. The crate contained some heavily sugared jam and plum preserves, two pounds of tea, four pounds of coffee, a stone jug of molasses, a large comb, a cheap red-gold Chinese mirror, several packages of colorful Italian seed beads, twenty-four brass thimbles, a dozen packages of various-sized needles, and Caleb's centennial gift from the Highlander, another large jug of his brother's best malt whisky. The big woman sat regally waiting as Lukassi laid out the contents of the box before her.

She did not look at the foreign captains as they ducked out through the entrance passage and hurried with Lukassi and their dog-team driver toward their sled.

When they were seated, Caleb grabbed Finn's arm. "I never in all my life saw anything like those whales' shadows moving and moaning around that igloo. Did you?"

"Christ, no." Finn shuddered. "I still can't believe my eyes or ears. That drum beating seemed to freeze my guts and go pounding up and down my spine. Let's get out of this place."

When they were halfway home to Blacklead, Finn jumped off the sled and ran for a while, then seated himself closer to Lukassi. "What about these red sea-pigeons' feet?" he asked.

"They're *pitukutit*, amulets," Lukassi answered. "She says they're going to help you captains with the whaling."

"But that little seal bone with the sinew tied around it, what's that for?" asked Finn.

Lukassi slyly smiled at him. "That was Pia's idea. She asked me to tell the whale woman that when you're in bed with her, you get, you know, just too damn excited. She says you're way too fast, always getting far ahead of her."

"Lord, Jesus, did you tell the big woman that in front of all those Yacks?" Finn asked.

"I had to," Lukassi said. "If you're too fast, well, you can't help it. Pia asked the whale woman for some kind of amulet to slow you down."

"Who knows? Maybe it might work," the ice master said. "I'll try not to lose it."

"Oh, it won't matter if you lose it. You could drop it right here in the snow or anywhere while you're traveling in this country. That amulet will go on working for you."

The sled ride back to Yankee Island was slow and without the help of a sail, for they were facing a stubborn headwind that was paralyzing all of them.

"Cold enough to freeze the nuts off an iron bridge," Caleb quipped, but Lukassi and Finn made no reply.

When they reached the Blacklead station, while the driver took care of the dogs, the three of them stumbled into the mates' mess, trying to stamp life back into their feet. Caleb poured rum into their thick broth bowls.

"Do you want to hear what that woman once told me?" Lukassi asked.

"Go ahead," said Finn, flinging his frosted fur hood back to uncover his ears.

"Tell your story fast, lad." Caleb shuddered. "I'm dying to crawl inside a good, hot bed."

"That big woman told me that when she goes off flying, it's not at all like dreaming or like dying. Dreaming can sometimes tell a sleeper about the past and sometimes, maybe, about what's lying ahead. Flying, she says, can make a woman on wings see life more clearly. It is like peering through a piece of new lake ice."

"What did she mean by that?" asked Finn.

"During one flying she made last spring," said Lukassi, "she soared over a sun-melted hill showing fresh green patches of caribou moss."

"Hold on!" Caleb yawned. "You can tell that story of hers to this ice master. She's nothing but a goddamned fake. I'm going to bed."

"She'll be mad as hell if she hears you saying that, Captain, and she probably does."

"Go ahead, tell me," said Finn as he and Lukassi hurried toward his house.

"Well, she wanted both of you to know that dying is just like blinking your eye. Just one step and you're through that narrow entrance hole that's edged with eider feathers. It leads to the other country."

"Do you believe that, Lukassi?"

"Sure, I believe it," Lukassi said. "Where do you think the older people and the dying children go? Where do you think all the bowhead whales and musk oxen went, and the seals and walrus, caribou, fish, and birds? All of us go there. Some change, some don't. But she says we all go through that same outgoing hole."

Finn said good night and hurried inside his house. Pia was naked in their sleeping bag, smiling shyly as she waited for him.

"*Pitukutit*, did get . . . it, you?" Pia asked. "Did give it . . . she, to you?"

Trembling cold but excited, Finn nodded as he stripped off all his clothes and rolled half frozen into bed. His feet still felt like ice blocks as he unwrapped the amulet to show it to her. It took no time at all for Pia to thaw him out. Then slowly they got started. Pia sighed.

"*Piujupaluk!*" said Finn. Then he gasped in English, "This is really good. It's taking me forever. I think I can go on and on forever!"

"Strong amulet," said Pia. "I think . . . maybe . . . she fix . . . youuu. Yes, oh, yes, youuu fixed."

"I'm never going to quit," the ice master groaned. "I'm in full command back here."

"*Tuavilaurit*, hurry, please," said Pia. "I ready, ready. *Tuavilaurit*, hurry, please."

"Oh, sure," Finn laughed. "God, this is how life . . . ought . . . to beee . . ."

The icy wind went howling round the six sides of his Newfie house. The windows rattled, and the weather vane went spinning atop the pointed roof. But neither Finn nor Pia cared. Slowly, they relaxed, gasping, sighing, regaining their breath. Pia turned herself around. They placed their noses side by side and sniffed, enjoying the blended human scent of man and woman.

Then they tried it all over again to make certain that the amulet really worked.

"Perfect," sighed Finn as they peacefully moved off together into that other closer world of rest and sleep and sometimes wondrous dreams.

"Finn, do you want to go out this morning and try it?" Caleb called down the mess-room table after breakfast.

"I sure do," said Finn. "The wind's down and this spring fog is drifting off. It's going to be a beautiful day."

"The lookout signaled that he saw a pair of whales out east of here," said Dougal. "They were in heavy ice, but that should clear soon."

"The whales are late this year," Shannon remarked as they all got up to leave. As they pulled on their parkas to leave, he said, "Say, what the hell's that bright red foot you've both got sewn on your chests?"

"Oh, Finn and I are just going to harness up two teams and put our whaleboats on the sleds and go out with our crews and see what we can see along the floe edge. Have the lookout keep the long glass on us, and if we have some luck and take a whale today, you send out a mate with four Yacks and four big dog teams and we'll strip the blubber off it right there at the floe edge."

Finn and Caleb, their eyes bright with expectation, looked down at their web-footed amulets and sledded their whaleboats along the edge of the glaring spring ice, stopping, watching, and going again throughout the entire day and well into the white night. But they saw not a single whale.

"I told you she was nothing but a fuckin' Gypsy faker," Caleb yelled across to Finn.

They traveled dejectedly back toward the station, each riding in his boat lashed atop a long sled. Finn as well as Caleb and their drivers fell asleep. Fortunately, the dogs hauling the sleds knew their own way home.

Lukassi was out to meet them when the teams arrived. "There was something the whale woman told me that I maybe forgot to say." Lukassi looked down shamefacedly at his boots, then up at both of them.

"What did she tell you?" Caleb demanded.

"She told me to warn Finnussi that after the first night he tries out his amulet, the one to slow him down, no whales would come, knowing he would be too worn out to handle his feathered harpoon."

Caleb stared at the ice master in wide-eyed disbelief. "Finn, did you try out that damned *pitukutik* she gave you when you got home last night? Is that why you were tuckered out and nodding off all day?"

The ice master glanced down at his web-footed guillemot fetish.

"You must have," Lukassi volunteered. "If you didn't use it, one of you would have got fast to a whale today."

"Damn you, Finn, and your overeager Newfie ways," roared Caleb.

"Well," Finn mumbled, "I just wanted to see if it would work or not, that's all."

"You contain yourself tonight, you hear me, Finn?" Caleb ground his teeth. "Your cockiness has probably cost us one big bowhead fish worth thousands and thousands of dollars."

"Hold on there," said Finn. "I thought you told me you didn't believe a word that old bitch told us."

"Well, I'm going out again tomorrow morning," shouted Caleb. "Heed me, Ice Master! You've been warned! I knew I should never have allowed you to build that weird-looking house of yours. Your nightly jumping up and down beneath that pointed roof may have cost me a giant fish! You cut that out, you hear?"

Whale harpoon

Next morning at 6:00 a.m. they went out together, and before noon Caleb's eiderdown-covered harpoon point was buried deep inside the body of an enormous bowhead whale. Finn struck it, too, just for security's sake. The huge creature seemed to take both harpoons as easily as a pair of feathers, and because they quietly obeyed the Inuit rules, the huge fish's soul departed quickly and almost without a struggle. Certainly, that peaceful giant had not suffered any triumphant Yankee shouts or laughter or pipe ashes or had tobacco spat into its waters from the crews of either of those now humbled and respectful captains.

Later, Caleb and Finn stood at the floe edge, admiring what the old man judged to be a 185-barrel cow. While they discussed this huge success and guessed at the worth of this fish's baleen sieves of money bone, the big dog teams and equipment arrived.

"I wonder where the Highlander's been hunting," Finn asked.

"Down along the western Baffin coast," the old man told him. "As you know, *Blue Thistle* and *North Star* suffered rotten luck last autumn and word is, they've had not a single whale this season." Dunston stroked his red-footed amulet. "I guess Cargill would have fared a good deal better if he had handled that whale woman as we did, in a more respectful style."

At the end of the April moon, the Highlander arrived over the ice from Niantelik, starting in a fair breeze that later failed him. His journey, aided by a square-rigged sail, had been slow and, to everyone's surprise, Andrew Cargill had his driver halt their sled on the sea ice out in front of the Yankee slipway. There he sat quietly waiting. Behind his team were scattered dozens of shallow azure blue ponds, formed by snow melting in the spring sun on top of the still-solid ice.

Caleb, Finn, and Dougal started down the island's embankment, shading their eyes from the glare.

"That's not like old Cargill," Caleb said to Dougal. "What the hell's wrong with him? Why isn't he coming up to visit? Isn't he even going to try to get a drink off me?"

"Good day to ye, Caleb, and ye also, Finn and Gibson," the Highlander said, not rising from his sled. "I've come to take back some barrels of gunpowder from our shed, and if ye've already stolen all of mine, I'll borrow some from ye."

"Gunpowder?" said Caleb. "What the hell are you planning to do with gunpowder at this time of year?"

"I need it to blow a channel in the ice because, well, I'm planning to leave early."

"What in God's name would cause you to leave early, Andrew? The best of the whaling's about to begin!"

"I'm taking *Blue Thistle* home," Andrew answered. "The ice is not so thick over at Niantelik this season. I've had coal-dust lines laid down to help and I'll soon be able to blow and saw-cut an early passage."

"Well, you can't go anywhere this month nor next," Caleb snorted.

"I know ice as well as ye do," the Highlander coughed. "Dunston, I calculate that our two crews, helped by all those Yacks, can blow the ice and hack a channel wide enough for *Blue Thistle* to slip free of Niantelik in June."

"I'll be watching," said Caleb. "It would seem a miracle to me."

"I'll surprise ye all," the Highlander said. "My crew and the Eskimos over there have volunteered to cut the ice where the river flow has weakened it beneath. 'Tis no more than six feet thick. We'll make a half-mile passage just wide enough for *Thistle* to ease through and reach the open waters of the Sound."

"It's never been done so early," said Caleb.

"Aye, well, my lads are game to try it."

"Tell me," Caleb asked, "why in the devil are you in such a rush to go now?"

"Och," said the Highlander, "it's been a miserable failure with the fishing, both last autumn and this spring. We've taken but one small whale. That makes a disastrous pair of seasons for us. We've not gathered enough oil and bone between our two ships even to partly fill *Blue Thistle*'s hold. I may hunt a wee while off south

Greenland, Caleb, then I'll be finished with the whaling game. I'm taking *Blue Thistle* and my crew home to Dundee."

"It doesn't sound like you, Andrew, to do a thing like that. Is there something wrong with you?"

"Aye, that there is," the Highlander grunted. "I've got a weird feeling deep down inside my gut that even the best malt whisky does not seem to cure. I've come over here today to say good-bye to all of ye. And if ye'll be kind enough, Caleb, I'll borrow six of those grand, long-bladed Swedish ice saws from ye, and I'll take all the powder and any fuses ye can spare. I ordered Captain Sinclair to remain behind with *North Star* and winter over at Niantelik for another year, then take home as much oil and bone as they can manage. The hunting's been so bad for us, I'm coming to believe I'm jinxed. Or can it be, Caleb, that we've killed off all but the last of these grand bowhead fishes? There's not much left here with grease except the little white beluga whales, narwhals, and walruses."

"Well," said Caleb, "that's hard news for all of us, Andrew, that you're feeling poorly."

"It's the way life goes," the Highlander grimaced. "Have ye any mail ye'd like me to try to deliver for ye? I'll be sailing home by way of Godthaab, and Reykjavik, Iceland, and may meet some Yankee vessel that's New England-bound. They'd be glad to pass your mail on to Connecticut."

"Don't worry about our mail, Andrew. Take good care of yourself." Caleb looked away. "That sun will be softening the crust and you'll have a slow, wet journey back. I'll send Dougal over tomorrow with a sled or two, delivering you gunpowder, fuses, ice saws, and any letters we may have. If you need more men for cutting ice, you let me know. We here wish you all the luck, Andrew. God protect you."

"Come, shake hands with me, ye three," the Highlander said. "I'll probably not be seeing ye again. Good hunting, men, and a good, long life to ye and Finn and Dougal, and both yer ships' crews."

They shook hands wordlessly.

"Usk, usk!" his driver called, turning the sled. The team and driver were eager to go.

The Highlander waved his arm, but for reasons of his own, he did not look back at them. Caleb turned away and Finn saw him wipe his eyes.

The snowhouse walls began to soften and collapse. Early in June, Inuit picked high, dry gravel patches and erected their summer tents. Many times in the weeks that followed the visit from the Highlander, they heard the dull boom as small kegs of gunpowder shattered the spring ice at Niantelik. Word came across that the Dundee men, and Inuit hunters, and their wives and sons were helping cut the long path that would free *Blue Thistle*.

On the big moon tide of June, a shout went up from the Blacklead lookout as the first black smoke appeared above the hill and *Blue Thistle* eased her way round Niantelik's headland, following the newly made path in the ice. The Highlander fired a smoke bomb and sent it streaking high above her masts, sending Caleb and the others his final farewell.

"Dougal, be quick!" yelled Caleb. "Clear the touchhole and ram a bag of powder into that old Fisheries cannon and we'll give Andrew an answering salute. No cannonball, mind you, Dougal. There's no further need to try and put that dear old bugger under. What will I ever do without that old goat to hound me for stealing his coal?"

Chapter 17

"This has been one of the best fishing seasons I've known in my whole life," said Caleb. "It's like the good old days. It's as though those big bowheads were being drawn to us. I need just one more good-sized fish to fill *Sea Horse*. I'll admit to you, Dougal, it's a damned shame the Highlander got sick. Lukassi says the Dundee men are still not having too much luck, but, by God, we are! And you, Finn, I'll bet you could scarcely cram another cask of oil into *Lancer*'s giant hold."

"That's near the truth," said Finn. "I'm starting to wonder if old *Lancer* will bear up under that weight of oil and bone. I'm throwing all her bricks and try-pots overboard. Maybe we should leave part of the load here to take out next year."

Caleb frowned and the needlepoints on his moustache twitched. "Forget that bird-brained idea, Finn. The bone will mildew and the oil will sour. The casks dry out in summer and start to seep. I'll tell you right now, Ice Master Finn, we're taking out every fuckin' drop of oil and length of corset bone with us this time. A chicken heart never won a whaler his full lay. *Sea Horse* and *Lancer* will set out together mating home. And, Finn, I'm doubly anxious to get going this year.

"Nilak and Ulayu have almost finished that new small captain's

272

suit I'm having made for Caleboosi. Can't you hardly wait to see him in that rig? I don't want him arriving in New London, then in Mystic, with soggy skin boots a-sagging down, wearing ragged seal-skin pants, and a tattered, chewed-up parka. I want those partners at the Whale Fisheries and our neighbors near Topsail House to first see Caleb Dunston, Jr. dressed to the nines so they'll have a first-rate opinion of my newfound son. Don't you think he's looking more civilized every day? I wonder what my wife and my daughter will think of him."

"And I wonder what he'll think of them and going to school and living in a town," said Finn. "God knows the Labrador Eskimos say they hate St. John's, and the St. John's townsfolk ain't too crazy about the Eskimos either . . . well, at least at first. They didn't like their Beothuk Indians either."

"Look!" Caleb pointed. "There's Nilak with Pootavut, her brother, and his wife all folding up their tent. They're leaving. Nilak told me she'd be going to camp up north with them. She cried last night because she says she dares not wait behind to see me off. She has to help the other women row their umiak. They won't stay here after we leave. There are better hunting places for the food they want, and the walrus herds are gathered up north. She says Pootavut and his sons have to cache enough meat for the winter."

Caleb stood alone on the island's embankment as he watched Nilak with the others rowing hard. She could hardly bring herself to look at him. Caleb wiped his eyes.

Finn had *Lancer* already jammed to the gunnels with oil and bone. Caleb thought, What's gone wrong with me? How is it that Finn's had so much luck?

That very day, Finn's whaleboat struck and killed a 117-barrel cow. "This one's a gift for you, sir," the ice master announced proudly. "Her oil is more than *Lancer* can carry, but I'll manage to take the bone myself."

Caleb snatched off his hat and flung it in the air. "That's good enough for me, lad. That will fill up *Sea Horse*. She's my last whale this year. I've got to admit, lad, you sure have learned a lot about the whaling trade from me."

"And the Inuit," said Finn.

The weather had been mist-hung and cold during the end of July. Then, with the change of the moon in early August, Blacklead Island was beset with veering winds and rain. This was followed by a brief warm spell, and a late hatch of mosquitoes rose off the island's ponds in stinging hordes. The sun created blue-gray sheets of water that spread out over the rotting sea ice on the bay. Large black holes appeared in many places until the bay looked like a huge Swiss cheese. The idle crewmen sighed as they stared out restlessly from the bunkhouse door or bleary window, forgetting now their faithful local girls. They began once more to idolize the American and Canadian beauties shown so handsomely corseted in the engravings of the now-tattered ladies' magazines. They could envision waltzing with them in Connecticut, that warm, dreamlike land of plenty with decent liquors, sweet corn, pumpkin pies, fresh-caught salmon, juicy beefsteaks, lamb chops, fresh hens' eggs, lobsters, and beer.

Both ships' stewards formed a pool to bet on the day and hour when the captains would order them to start to cut and blow along the coal-dust lines that had sun-cut a path down through the weakening ice to once more free their ships to sail. The winners of each pool would collect their winnings on the day they all signed off ship at the New London Fisheries dock and received their fair share of the lay in cash. With the holds crammed full of oil and bone, each crewman knew that his share of this lay would be immense.

The crewmen stared out at the rotting ice. "Come on, sun, get fuckin' hot!" they shouted. "Come on, sun, let's go!"

Lukassi warned them that the ice out near the ships had been sun-licked with so many holes that he'd be afraid to walk on most of it and that they should ride the long sleds.

Mario told the old man during mess, "Every crewman on this island says he's willing to do double duty on the ice saws whenever you've a mind to cut those vessels free. We've reset their masts and rigged their cross stays, sir. We're dying to go."

The old man stared down the mess table at Finn. "Have you got that old wreck of ours tight-caulked enough for you to try and ease her south?"

"She's as shipshape now as she's ever going to be," said Finn. "My carpenter's got so much tar hemp hammered into her that the inside of her hold looks and smells like a mud hen's nest."

"Dougal, go tell the ironsmiths to start sharpening our ice chisels, saws, and axe blades. Tomorrow, we'll sled out those little barrels of gunpowder and start the work. We've got to get both vessels cleared and ready for this next moon tide."

They used four dog teams hauling long sleds for transporting the explosives, men, and tools. The Yack drivers, knowing they would be crossing many open cracks, edged around the dangerous places, avoiding the porous ice. As soon as they arrived at the ships, Caleb ordered both sawing tripods set up close to *Sea Horse*.

"Go ahead," the old man shouted. "Start by cutting a line an arm's length out from around *Sea Horse*'s hull."

When the men opened the first hole, Caleb probed down with his ice measure. "The mark on this long rule shows that the ice here is only half a fathom thick and we know it's soft and honey-combed. It should be easy enough to cut it using the tripod and the six-man saw. We'll drill and plug in some gunpowder charges. That should help to open the coal-dust channels."

Pia winced when she heard the first explosion, then sat thinking before she sighed and continued to soften Finnussi's new sealskin boots. But the greenhands around the ships kicked up their heels and shouted after each explosion, then once more resumed their singing and their sawing:

Home, boys, home!
It's where we want to be.
Green grow the grasses
In North Amer-ikee!

It was hard, slow work to free a ship set in Arctic ice, but no captain had ever figured out a surer, faster method. These crewmen were eager and more than willing, helped by lots of strong, friendly Inuit, eight at a time, to grab the wide handles of the saws the moment the crew tired.

"We are going to sally *Sea Horse* out of this motherin' ice right now," yelled Caleb. "Come ahead, men, scramble aboard! Finn, send your crew over, too. I want every man from both ships and every Yack who's within shouting distance, captains, mates, crew, cooks, any girls who are hiding inside that fo'c's'le, and the ships' boys, too. Let's go!"

When everyone was in place, Caleb shouted, "Now all together, gang, start sallying her back and forth, back and forth." He began making quick, long strides. "Greenhands, watch me do it! Starboard to larboard, and back again. All together, here we go!"

The men and women all started gleefully moving in unison, many holding hands for friendship and for sport.

"That's it!" Caleb shouted. "We'll get *Sea Horse* a-rolling like your granny in her rocking chair. Listen to her knocking the small ice off her hull. Keep on sallying, boys, sallying . . . again! Come on, again!"

Both crews were now running crossways on the deck and singing:

Sally her over hard, dear girls,
Then sally her back with me.
Move your arses fast, my boys,
We'll bust her out to sea.

"You're doing it, friends!" Caleb yelled. "Keep her rolling, rolling, rolling."

"There, she's free! She's free!" Dougal shouted, and he, like all the others, fell down gasping on the deck.

The stewards went around and poured everyone a tot of rum, then filled their mugs with hot plum duff, and the feeling aboard *Sea Horse* became as joyous as a frolic. By the end of the day, the men were so exhausted that many were too tired to eat. They stumbled down into the fo'c's'le, fell into their long-unused bunks, and slept like hibernating bears.

A gigantic breakfast of rich seal stew and bannock, accompanied by another belt of rum in their coffee, got the crew going strong again next morning. Soon a channel to the sea lay open.

Now *Lancer*'s larger channel had to be sawed, mined, and blown free to give her passage out to open water. Both crews, with their Inuit helpers, trotted over to help. As they worked the saws, the crews tried not to think of the cruel gap their leaving would create among these nomadic people. It meant parting with so many warm-hearted women.

"Tomorrow night," said Caleb as he stood with Dougal and Finn leaning on *Lancer*'s port rail, "that moon will be rising full. We'll haul anchor, reset our rudders, and set sail on the flood tide. Just think, I might be home with Caleboosi in a couple of months, if our luck holds out."

They fastened two ships' hawsers and long hemp hauling lines to *Lancer*'s bulging sides and coiled them neatly on the decks, prepared for their exit next day, when the men would haul the ships out beyond the shore ice into open water. Some crewmen slept aboard that night, too tired to move. But the more devoted lovers made their way back across the rotting ice, most of them on long sleds, for this would be one of their last nights in the sail loft.

"Ice Master," Caleb called as he limped toward his now-empty house. "Don't you lie abed tomorrow morning. I'll be hammering on your door at five. I've ordered Supa and his sled to be ready to take us out. We'll eat aboard and be ready when the hauling starts. Only when both ships have been anchored safely out beyond the ice will we go back into Blacklead and start the farewell frolic."

Lord, Jesus, five o'clock is early, thought Finn. The old man probably prowls around all night now that Nilak's left him.

It seemed only a moment before Dunston was hammering on Finn's door. He flung it open, hoping to find the pair of them naked and in some impossibly erotic position. He was disappointed

277

when he found Finn half dressed and Pia's body hidden by the bag.

When they arrived on *Sea Horse*, the two ships' crews, with the help of twenty hunters, took up the tow ropes and hawsers spaced evenly on both sides, then towed her into the Y-shaped channel they had first cut. Two great cheers went up as the heavily loaded vessel gained momentum and floated into the open waters of the bay. Next, the two crews and all the Yacks took hold of *Lancer's* hawsers. She was much heavier, but with the help of several dog teams, they finally hauled her free. A shout went up as both ships dropped anchor, riding free in open water. They were ready to go.

When Finn and the others sledded back, he found Pia sitting at the corner of his desk, peering out the window. He looked over his shoulder at the lively pencil drawing she was making of *Lancer*. She had saved a piece of good paper from inside a fancy Scottish shortbread tin. Pia was proud of Finnussi and his huge ship.

"*Piiujuvingaluk!* Very good," said Finn, admiring her uninhibited, natural skill at drawing.

"This is for me," said Pia in Inuktitut, "to keep so I can look at it when you and your ship have gone. I've made this other *titirktugak*, drawing, for you." She showed him. "This is our house. So you won't forget it. These are the two big jawbones at the door and the whale that marks the wind above our roof. And that's us, standing close together near the door."

Finn understood only a few of Pia's words, but he could easily understand both her drawings, and he absorbed their meanings perfectly. To hide his feelings of sadness, he said, "*Kaakpiit*, are you hungry?" Then, turning, he shook the stove and poured in almost the last of the Highlander's coal.

Pia took her small sealskin bucket out to the storm porch and returned with fourteen smallish, pale-green murre eggs. They were Pia's share of her cousin's earlier gathering from the Baffin nesting cliffs. She rubbed some fresh seal fat inside the iron skillet over the heat and cracked all the eggs into it. Finnussi, she knew, loved his eggs cooked and she had grown used to them that way. They both sniffed the air as the delicious odor filled the small, six-sided room.

Together, they ate all the eggs with the last slices of the pan bread the cook had given Pia when he had come to say good-bye to her.

When they finished drinking their half-strength coffee, Finn opened his uncle's watch case and pointed to the time. "It's early, but I'm tired from working on the ship," he said. "Bed into go I. *Sinigiaktulirkpunga.*"

"I'm coming, too," said Pia. "I'm not tired. But I want to lie close to you."

After an hour's sleep, Finn felt Pia's hot breath in his ear. That started the very best, the longest, and most satisfying of all their couplings, thanks to the amazing power of the amulet. The feelings between them seemed so strong that they could never break apart. Yet, he knew that he was leaving tomorrow, and that was final.

When Finn fell into his second, most luxurious sleep, Pia rose and slowly dressed herself. Slipping out the door, she crossed over to her family's summer tent. There she sat, talking softly with her mother until her shoulders began to tremble and she wept, making not a sound, hoping that her mother might not notice. But, of course, she did, and tried to console her daughter.

"I came to like most of this lot of *kallunaat* well enough," Ulayu said, "but aren't you glad you don't have to go away with them to their other family places?"

"Yes . . . I'd rather die than go there." Pia sobbed. "Finnussi showed me one of those shadow pictures of a tall woman. He said it was his *anaana*. She was wearing a black parka, very fat and rounded in the rear end, no hood. It was as long as a sleeping bag. How could a woman dressed like that ever run beside a sled or help launch a whaleboat into the water? I could never dress in such a way. Oh, well, I hate it that he's going . . . tomorrow, I think. But Sila, who controls the weather, she'll decide that."

"These damned Yacks, they never change," Caleb grumbled. "We're the ones who are giving them this farewell frolic. We're going to supply most of the food and all the drink. We're decent enough to give them the last of our old trade goods instead of just throwing the stuff away. All our food stores that are weevily or moldy, we're leaving all of that for them because we've got no room aboard for all that. Yet, I hear, Lukassi, that a few of these cheeky bastards won't even wait to come to dance and say good-bye to us. They say they've got to get on with their own hunting. Well, to hell with that after all we've done for them!"

"They don't mean it like that, Captain!" Lukassi said with a pained expression on his face. "Kudlik and the *angakuk*, the big woman who called so many whales to Finnussi and even some to you, she and other elders say feasting with you out under the open sky, dancing and singing, and laughing at the animals you and they together killed is just too bad, too dangerous. They can't do it."

"Why?" Caleb snorted. "What's their fuckin' problem?"

"They're worried, Captain, about who will be watching us," Lukassi replied, "strange *inua*, souls . . . *turngait*, spirits, huge birds may be hovering above. We can't see them, staring down at us, or evil little lemmings peeking around the rocks, narwhal and bowhead whales peering up at us through those rotting holes in the ice. They believe the animals are losing all their trust in us. They're starting to mistrust Inuit for helping you foreigners. They fear all the sea spirits now because you people laugh and sing at the death of the good sea mammals and spit tobacco in the water. That's insulting to the whales that we've helped you kill. The big woman says we got to hide ourselves when doing any kind of feasting with you because the whales are nearby, watching. I mean, they watched you people throw away their meat that they came so far to give you. She only asked from Talulijuk for you to take those same three big whales she showed you in her igloo. You and Finnussi killed many, many more. Now you got both ships packed full of their oil fat, and their *sukkak*, the shrimp sifters, you tore out of their mouths. I mean, how are those whales ever going to feed themselves without their sifters in that other place where all of us are going to live again?

"The big woman says those deep-thinking ones, the *akviit*, whales, are like ourselves, but built with bigger lungs and bones," said Lukassi. "They have souls like us, you know. They never did you any harm. We call ourselves Inuit, the people. You call us Yacks or Eskimos. We don't care. I'm not a *nanuk*, bear, or a *netsik*, seal. We use our name Inuit to show we are different from those other creatures, not from you. We know you're just one kind of human, and we another."

"That's a lot of hogwash," Caleb growled. "What are we going to do about this, Finn? Let's call off this fuckin' frolic."

"Well, no," said Finn as he looked around him, "this island, which really belongs to Queen Victoria, isn't near as civilized as Heart's Content or New London, but maybe we should hold this feast the way these local Inuit would like it. If we stand up four stunsail masts and stretch a sail over their tops and rig it, we could make a kind of flattop tent on shore. Lukassi, do you think these folk would feel safer if they were feasting with us under some such cover?"

"Sure, they would," said Lukassi, "that's all they want. If you leave the side canvas that faces the sea hanging down so that the older folk can stay out of sight from sky and water, that would make it right with them."

"Well," Caleb sighed, "I suppose Angelo and Jack could help arrange that."

"When the big woman comes," said Lukassi, "she'll want to see the flap hanging right to the tundra to protect everyone from the eyes of Talulijuk, that underwater woman. She's the most dangerous spirit of them all." Lukassi nodded toward Caleb and Finn. "Right now that sea woman under the water must be ripping mad at both of you."

"More fuckin' mumbo jumbo!" Caleb groaned. "But what the hell, if doing it under a piece of canvas is going to make these people happy, let's do it. Lukassi, go ahead, tell the Yacks we'll rig some kind of cover for this frolic. Let it dangle down to hide their view of the sea." Caleb looked up at the sky. "I don't think we'll have a drop of rain tonight, but who knows?" He turned again to Finn. "These people never thought to invent a hat for their heads, nor any pockets in their coats or britches. They don't know what money is. They've never even dreamed of inventing a wheel! Well, I've tried my level best for years to civilize them but, believe me, Finn, as you can see, it hasn't worked too well."

By five o'clock that evening, the cooks had all the food prepared and the Blacklead Islanders could see Niantelik's two skin umiaks and two Dundee whaleboats approaching along a narrow opening channel in the ice, carrying about fifty people in all. As the umiaks landed at the far end of the island, they could see the big whale woman leaning like a figurehead above her vessel's prow. She didn't bother to look up at the Blacklead folk, but continued to stare down into the still waters as though waiting for some strange creature to come swimming beneath her.

The Blacklead Islanders had no choice now but to welcome the Niantelik Inuit and the Dundee men ashore. Kudlik ordered two of his brothers to pound hard on their drums, while their wives pumped desperately on their accordions, causing many to scream, then moan. The Yacks from Niantelik leapt ashore, then, crouching, hands atop their heads, rushed forward and crowded beneath the canvas, trying desperately to protect themselves from the sight of terrifying eyes. Caleb stood in front of the tent with young Caleboosi beside him, handsomely attired as a young boy captain.

When the big woman came ashore with her walleyed apprentice, she climbed calmly along the spit and stepped beneath the canvas. She nodded and smiled at Lukassi, Kudlik, and Supa, then frowned at Caleb and at Finn. She waited, impatiently staring at Dunston until he asked a shipman to bring a seat for her. The big woman dreaded squatting on these wretched foreigners' chairs, for she knew how dangerous they could be. But, keeping her feet well spread beneath her and her strong thighs tightly gripped on either side of the wobbly seat, she managed to stay upright. She seemed plumper now, perhaps from eating all the Yankee delicacies from the box and drinking the Highlander's outsized jug of malt whisky that had been Caleb's gift to her.

Among the braver Niantelik folk, Caleb recognized his son Caleboosi's adoptive parents. Caleboosi left his side, ran to greet them, and stayed close to his family throughout the evening. They kept smiling at him, admiring their son's new captain's suit.

"Having him back makes us really happy," they told Lukassi.

"He'll soon be big enough to row the new boat with his father and brothers."

Caleboosi waited until his parents had joined the others before he said to Lukassi, "Feels good, me with my family all together again. I wanted . . . to be a captain, but . . ."

By the end of the feasting and the singing, the Yankees, Dundee men, and Inuit had finished off the last barrel of the awful-smelling Blacklead brew. It had grown a gray-green scum of mildew on top, but that didn't deter the guests, for it still had a punch. To impress this whale woman, Caleb had secretly shared mug after mug of his best private rum with her.

Finn stood for a while near Caleb outside the makeshift tent as they watched the full moon rising, and prayed that the next day's weather would allow them to set sail on their long journey south. Together, they stepped back beneath the covering of the tent and tried to catch the spirit of this frolic. But this event fell a hundred times short of their great centennial bash, and many crewmen and Yacks who had managed to stomach the brew were tipping over and falling asleep.

All had grown silent beneath the canvas cover. Then, slowly, the whale woman's crooked man began turning and thumping the rim of his drum, releasing its deep, booming sound. The big woman began to tremble as though gripped by some ferocious force. Using both hands, she flung herself upward from the chair. Placing her hair braids in her mouth, she spread her powerful arms and thighs and began slowly stomping, moaning, turning.

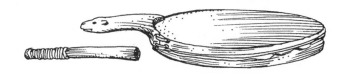

Skin drum and stick

"Stop!" shouted Caleb, trying to head her off. "Stop! Wait! Lukassi," he shouted. "Where are you? Come and speak to this damned woman for me. Tell her I don't want any more goddamned mumbo jumbo around here. Tell her that we're pulling out tomorrow. Lukassi, you tell her thanks for everything." He winked at Finn. "If she wants me to give her one of those long harmonicas or even that last button accordion with the slight tear in its squeeze box, I'll give it to her . . . free . . . if she promises to get the hell off this island of mine tonight. I'm going to bed now, Lukassi, and so are you and all our mates and crews. You tell her that it's been a dandy farewell frolic, but now the brew barrel's empty. Have you got that, Luka –?"

The old man's words were was cut off sharply, for at that moment the tent began to tremble violently. What was happening? Was this a sudden storm or an earthquake? There was no sign of wind, and the ground seemed steady. But the tent was shaking furiously. Then the whole canvas above them began bellying and booming like thunder, luffing like a topsail buffeted by typhoon winds. Women and children began to scream. Even the hunters and the crewmen shouted in terror as the whole canvas structure ripped apart and collapsed on top of them.

"How did that goddamned woman do that?" Caleb yelled as he struggled, like the others, beneath the stench of burning mildewed sailcloth. It took some time before the choking crewmen and Yacks could free themselves from the smothering tent and douse the blackened holes where the fallen lanterns had caused smoke, then fire, to spread beneath the canvas.

"She didn't do it, Captain," shouted Otto Kraus. "I was watching her. It was dat little son-of-a-bitching drummer. I saw him *mit* mine eyes."

"The hell he did!" Jack Shannon yelled through his fit of coughing. "That little bugger was drumming right between me and Mario. We three helped each other out from under all that smoking mess."

"The drummer didn't do it!" Mario called to Caleb. "I swear to Jesus on that!"

"Well, what the hell did shake the tent?" yelled Dougal. "The damned thing fell on us!"

"There's not one breath of wind out here," said Chris Acker.

"Don't ask me," Lukassi cried. "If I knew about that, I'd know everything." He secretly jerked his thumb toward the whale woman who was standing at the front edge of the collapsed tent, braids still between her teeth, staring wide-eyed at the pockmarked ice.

"Ask her how it happened," Caleb demanded, "even though I'll never believe a fuckin' word she says."

The big woman refused to look at Lukassi when he approached. Instead, she began moaning, then flung her head back and her arms wide as she marched straight down to the water where her umiak was waiting. Every Niantelik Inuit and the dozen Dundee men from *North Star* ran after her.

"It'll be one helluva relief to clear off this whaling station." Caleb's brow was deeply furrowed. "I didn't mind it when Otto accused that drummer of pulling a rope or kicking a pole to bring our tent down. But when Jack and Mario swore the drummer didn't do it . . . it all stopped making any sense to me. Well, I'm just going to forget it. To hell with all of them!" he yelled. "We're leaving on tomorrow's tide. Lukassi, you make sure my son, Caleboosi, sleeps in your family's tent near you tonight, and that he goes straight aboard with you tomorrow morning. Hold his hand, you hear me? Quiet, everybody, quiet! I'm heading off to my house to sleep. I need sleep!"

Finn was so exhausted that he did not wake when the first morning rain turned to icy gusts of sleet that rattled like birdshot against his house. Pia ran her warm hand across his chest, then placed her nose gently beside his nose and sniffed, and he returned the sniff. He had come to enjoy that elegant signal of affection far better than the coarser foreign act of kissing. Mornings had always been their favorite time together, and this was an even greater union than the day before.

With feelings of love mixed with intense excitement at the prospect of leaving, he rose. Before pulling on his finest clothing, he hung a towel around his neck, brushed his teeth with salt and just a touch of gunpowder for stronger cleansing power, then shaved cautiously with his straight razor. He glanced in the mirror, then neatly brushed his hair, wishing that he had asked Pia to cut it for him one last time. It was too late now.

Pia lay in their double bag sadly watching him, remembering the innumerable number of times they had made love with one another, but never conceived a child. Oh well, she thought, maybe one will start inside me after he is gone. She wanted someone to remind her of Finn, to bring back the memory of all the pleasures they had shared. Finn had told her that he hoped to arrive again next summer and would spend another winter or two with her. But would he? She thought not.

There was a hard pounding and both doors were immediately kicked open. Caleb thrust his head inside.

"Hurry, man! It's blowing up to be a terror out there! My son Caleboosi's already on my sled with Lukassi. He's dressed up to look exactly like me in his new hat and slick oilskins. He's just rearing like a pony to be off and see the wonders of the outside world." Caleb was flushed with excitement. "Good morning, Pia, my dear. Glad you're awake and sorry that I've got to drag away your sailor. We're heading out to the ships right now. Come on, Finn, wiggle your ass. I've got a sled with a boat tied on it waiting for us. Get Pia to give you a hand jamming things into your sea chest. Hell, man, I don't care if she's buck naked."

"Pia, don't get up," said Finn. "I'll pack the sea chest."

"You look mighty perfect lying in that furry bed. That's how I'll always remember you. Good-bye, my dear." Caleb twitched his moustache points and blew Pia a foreign type of kiss.

Pia smiled and called to them, "Goo-baay, oold Caleboosi. Goo-baay, Finnussi."

Finn wiggled into his sealskin parka, noticing a small new amulet that Pia had sewn onto it. He shouldered his bring-near glass, rolled tightly in *Lancer*'s pennant flag, and pulled on the beautifully soft waterproof boots that Pia and her mother had made as his going-away present. He put on his best captain's peaked hat with its bright gold colonial officer's badge, then snatched up his rifle in its new sealskin case.

There were tears in Pia's eyes when he turned back toward the bed. "Take good care of yourself, dear. I'll try to come back . . . maybe . . . if I can."

"Come on, Ice Master," the old man roared. "When it's over, it's over. We're late and that fuckin' southeast wind is rising. Grab the other end of your sea chest, man. I've got a ship out there for you to sail!"

Finn reached out and touched Pia's shoulder. "*Tavvauvutit.* Good-bye," he said.

"*Puigurktailigit,* don't forget this," Pia said and handed him the small penis-bone amulet.

"Without you I won't need this," he said, placing his nose beside hers for one last sniff.

Both doors slammed as Caleb and Finn pushed out of the house, and Pia collapsed back on the bed.

Later, when Pia had composed herself, she wandered over to her family's tent. "Do you think Finnussi will be lonely for me?" she asked her mother.

"*Kitaapik,* maybe for a little while," Ulayu answered, "when he's on the ship. But when they reach the place where they keep their other women, he'll be all right. Kayak's wife says she saw one of those other women aboard a ship at Kekerton four summers ago. That *kalluna* woman was dead white in the face, with round gray eyes and a long thin nose. She was tall, with a skinny waist. She stood very straight. Her gray parka was so long it brushed the deck and the strange part was she had a huge ass." Ulayu shaped her hands to show her daughter. "Most think she was the captain's woman. She wore a gray headcover tied beneath her chin, stiffer and deeper than a parka hood. Probably she was bald, like a lot of their older men. She had thin, stern lips and seemed to fear the sun. That captain didn't allow a single one of our young women down into the fo'c's'le with his crew while that woman was aboard. No drinking, no dancing, no accordion or Jew's harp playing, which caused lots of that captain's crew to make awful sour faces at her when she turned away from them. Before that ship sailed away, they unloaded some supplies of boxes, new oars, tubs with line, pickles, rum, and other food the whalers needed for the winter. Then they loaded all the casks of oil and bone to give their ships room enough to hold another kill of whales."

"Was she a Yankee or a Dundee woman?" Pia asked.

"Who knows?" her mother answered. "That ship flew no flag and none who saw that woman could even make a guess."

"What am I going to do," Pia sighed, "now that Finnussi and his ship are leaving?"

"I guess you'll do what your father and I have always planned for you. You'll marry Tiriganniak, that good young hunter from a family that is with us. He is the son of your father's best friend and his wife, who's my best friend. They're now living up near the walrus rock. We did what is the custom, Pia. We gladly promised them that their son, Tiriganniak, could marry you when the time was right. He was only two years old and you had not yet been born."

"Oh, Tiriganniak," Pia said. "Yes, I've known him all my life."

"You'll like living with him," Ulayu said.

Pia hunched her shoulder. "Yes, maybe I will."

"Remember," her mother said. "I didn't like your father at first, but my parents had arranged my marriage to him. When we started to have children, he was good to me and I got to like him, love him best of any man I ever knew. You'll probably learn to love Tiriganniak, too."

"Maybe," Pia said.

"Your sewing is better. You are a bit older and wiser, so now when we go in your father's new whaleboat to make winter camp along the coast, Tiriganniak will come and ask your father for you. And this time, we'll let him sleep in our igloo for the winter. After that, if you two get on well together, then you'll be married. You'll go and live with his family."

"What if I don't like him?" Pia asked.

"Well, you can marry someone else, if you can find a better man. But they can be hard to find. There aren't many young hunters who have not been spoken for. Stop thinking about that shipman. He's sailed away now and that usually means forever. Tiriganniak is a man you can stay with and have children with, and you can share a life with all of us together."

18

"Sou'easter's freshening," Caleb called out as the crew rope-hauled Finn's sea chest up from his whaleboat onto *Lancer*'s deck.

"Lord, God," said Dougal, who had climbed the rigging, "look! The wind and tide are forcing in the ice. We're going to be beset by heavy floes. It's going to block our way out to the Sound! We'll be lucky if we don't get nipped."

Before they could sail, the eastern exit between Blacklead Island and Niantelik Bay had piled up with groaning pressure ice. So strongly had the wind and tide affected the pressure ice that in some places the huge, blue-white barrier was being heaved up higher than *Sea Horse*'s bowsprit. As the crews watched this heart-sickening sight, each man kept his mouth clamped shut, afraid to curse, for they knew all too well that this ice could easily trap both ships and hold them for another year.

"There you are, goddamnit! We're caught. If only you hadn't begged me to wait and give that useless farewell frolic," Caleb shouted on his gamming horn.

Finn had left his ship and was feeling with his soft skin boots the quality of the snow-covered ice. Then, edging up a towering bergie bit, he stood focusing his long glass, searching for cracks and other signs of weakness in the glaring pack ice.

"We should have been out of here beyond that fuckin' ice you're staring at!" Caleb shouted.

For eleven long, sickening days of violent winds, the two ships waited, locked behind this fortress wall of groaning ice. It was bound on one end to their island, and at the other to the rocky coast of Baffinland, cutting off all passage. Both ships moved to anchor in a position much closer to Niantelik, where Finn and the old man judged the jam of ice showed the best signs of opening first. Young Caleboosi seemed the only person unmoved by this disastrous event. The boy wore his new costume and found himself a place to sleep on the replaced settee in *Sea Horse*'s cabin.

But soon young Caleboosi began to pace the deck at night. He seemed downcast and scarcely ate his food. Another odd thing about young Caleboosi was that he had totally given up the American language.

Anxieties among both restless crews grew so that insult-yelling incidents and countless fistfights broke out, until suddenly the wind shifted and blew off Baffin Island. The sky cleared as the heavy clouds went flaring out in mares' tails and disappeared.

Mario took to praying aloud, "*Pater noster, qui est in caelis, sanctificetur nomen tuum . . .*" He prayed that this new wind would open the barrier of ice.

Just before noon on the twelfth day of their captivity, the man in *Lancer*'s crow's-nest called down to the deck. He had spotted a large umiak sailing toward the Blacklead station.

Caleb climbed into the rigging and checked this native vessel with his long glass before he ordered his own No. 1 whaleboat lowered off the starboard side. Caleb weighed the thought of taking Caleboosi with him, but decided against it, not knowing who these newcomers might be. Caleb, Jack Shannon, and four oarsmen set out to meet the strangers, leaving Dougal and Finn in charge of the ships, and Lukassi to care for Caleboosi. The horrendous barrier of ice to the south showed no signs of opening.

"Look behind that big skin boat," the lookout called to Caleb. "I can see black slivers spread around it on the water – hunters in kayaks, maybe."

A light breeze ruffled the waters. Caleb ordered the whaleboat's stunsail raised, then stood on his tiptoes, holding the steering oar. "Those are a different gang of Yacks, I'd judge, all heading for my island," Caleb called to Shannon in the bow. "I wonder who the devil they are."

"If this breeze keeps blowing in our favor, we'll soon see," answered Shannon. "Whoever they are, they're welcome to our place – unless we're jammed in here for another winter."

The four oarsmen grimaced as Shannon voiced their greatest fear, then ducked as Caleb quickly put about, recklessly swinging the stunsail boom just above their heads. Caleb leaned on his steering oar, resetting their course toward the umiak.

It was late afternoon when the two very different vessels drew close enough for Caleb and his crew to hear the sounds of singing and see more than a dozen women standing, facing forward, rowing hard. A withered old camp boss sat steering in the stern. Big sled dogs with their mouths tied shut were whining and pups were howling with the singers as children scampered playfully among their working mothers and piles of tight-rolled sleeping skins, sealskin tents, stone lamps, coils of line, and battered, blackened kettles. The volume of the women's singing increased and Caleb could see the kayak hunters hold their double-bladed paddles still, cautiously keeping a separation between themselves and the women's boat.

Caleb gasped with surprise and pleasure when he saw that the lead woman rowing was his beloved Nilak. She had been gone for almost a month. Nilak smiled and waved at him without pausing in her singing or her rowing. Caleb signaled back to her with true delight, for had they not enjoyed the very best of lives together?

The words used in their song were just the usual "Yack, yack, yack," but now Caleb could hear a familiar cadence. Could they be singing . . . "What a Friend We Have in Jesus" . . . in Yack? Oh, my God, yes, that was it, in Yack!

Caleb changed positions with Shannon, moving into the whaleboat's bow, where he stood watching the strange figure that crouched in the square prow of the umiak. This shrouded human was struggling desperately, flinging his arms outward, then curving them above his head like a netted crab. Then it became clear that it was a short, hungry-looking man shaking and wriggling to force himself into a clean white missionary's surplice. Slowly, theatrically, he rose before Caleb and stood, awkwardly balancing himself on the shifting hides and sleeping skins. He adjusted his small, thick-lensed glasses and ran his hand through his bowl-cut shock of auburn hair. Craning his neck, he stared suspiciously at Caleb, then at each man in the whaleboat before he spread his arms and called out in a Dundee burr.

"Let it be known to all ye sinners, these bonny Eskimo lasses along with their wee childer are now safe in my new Presbyterian mission. They have all been baptized by me. Many more, when I can find them, will be similarly blessed. Would ye sailors care to hear another hymn from my new converts?"

Not waiting for an answer, he turned, imitating a church choir master, and waved his arm. The rowing singers raised their voices in another chorus as they, in their own language, sang:

Bring me my bow of burning gold,
Bring me my arrows of desire.
Yack, yack, yack, yack,
Yack, yack, yack, yack.

"Oh, dear God," gasped Caleb, and he flopped down in the bow like a man struck by lightning. "How did you trap all those women so quickly, Parson? Have you baptized all their husbands as well, those hunters who are hanging back?"

"Och, no," replied the missionary, catching a grip on the bow of Caleb's whaleboat. "That's always a wee bit more difficult, ye see. It almost invariably takes many years longer with the men. But since ye're interested, Captain, I've been told by the Scottish Mission Society that difficulties in baptizing pagan men have proved similar in almost every corner of the heathen world. Those male sinners sneaking along behind us," he waved his arm toward the kayakmen, "they're a predictably stubborn lot. But their wives were open-minded women, quick enough to seize upon my holy Christian message. Oh, there's no doubt their men will soon follow. You see, I've carefully instructed these women through my interpreter, Siawak, a convert come with us from Kekerton, and all these women have promised both Jesus and me to have no intimate form of intercourse with their husbands or his friends until those men have fully embraced the Christian faith. On my advice, through Siawak, these devout women have sworn that they'll carry a needle into bed to make blessed sure their husbands get my pointed message continuously, and exactly where it hurts the most. In China, Africa, and Malaya, Christian missionaries doing the Lord's work have discovered that a woman's needle can make their heathen husbands pay much sharper attention to our Christian message. Yes, it invariably hastens the whole baptismal process."

Caleb grunted as he rose and, shaking his head, wordlessly broke the missionary's clutch on the bow of his whaleboat.

"But wait, tell me," called the missionary as the two boats floated apart, "what is yer name?"

Caleb remained glowering, speechless, in the bow.

Shannon called out from the stern, "He is Captain Caleb Dunston, master of our ship, *Sea Horse*, loaded at anchor near that ice – and eager to get away from the Bible-thumping likes of you!"

Caleb's coughing interrupted Shannon.

"All our men who have wintered on that Blacklead station are now aboard our two vessels. We're homeward bound. And you?" snapped Caleb. "You must be McNab, the missionary. We are sailing from our Blacklead Island now . . . but only for the coming winter. We'll be back!"

"Well, that island's never been yer private property, Captain," called McNab as the distance between the boats increased. "And, believe me, I shall stay and erase all yer sinful antics here."

"Well, it's a blessed fortune for us," Caleb called back, "that your arrival was delayed until we were fully loaded to depart. Take care of the graves this autumn, Pastor. Good, honest whaling men are resting there. Mate Shannon," Caleb snapped, "make ready to put about!"

The crewmen ducked as Shannon swung the stunsail boom above their heads.

When they had drawn apart, Caleb told Jack that he had decided to spend the night on Blacklead. "Take me to the beach, then come in for me at the first sign of loosening in the ice." Then he called out to Nilak, "*Uvaatsiaruapik*," "A little later." But she and the other women had started rowing and singing another hymn and did not hear him.

With the shifting wind, the ice was changing. As Caleb's boat drew near the Yankee slipway, Shannon asked him, "Are you sure you wouldn't like some company up there, Captain?"

"No, no, Nilak will be visiting soon. You tell Dougal and Finn to stand the watch themselves tonight and keep a close eye on the ice. If this wind strengthens, the lot of it could start to open on the tide. Have Lukassi tell young Caleboosi not to worry. I'll be returning soon."

Caleb grasped his ditty bag and eased himself out over the bow and into knee-deep water. He splashed ashore. The crew backed off through the ice with Shannon pushing with the steering oar.

When Caleb reached the top of the steep embankment, he stopped to regain his breath and look along the valley at the Blacklead buildings. All except Finn's crazy, bright wooden house were old and gray, now falling into disrepair. The violent winds that had blocked their passage to the south had struck the Yankee station hard. The door of the cook shack hung at a drunken angle, supported only by its lower hinge. The whole entrance porch and roofing to the mates' mess had been blown away and lay scattered across the landscape. The large crew's four-holer outhouse had been flung down and destroyed again. The black tarred roofing of the warehouse had been torn to dangling tatters, and the whalebone weather vane that had stood so boldly on the peak of Finn's house had been blown off and now lay in the gravel path, its iron directions twisted.

Stepping over it, Caleb noticed as he approached his own house that the storm seemed to have done little damage there, but the winds had toppled and rolled the neat line of empty oil casks everywhere. The storm and the coming of the missionary had somehow changed the old man's comfortable sense of owning this island. It now seemed a desolate no-man's-land to him as he sadly envisioned the coming of winter storms.

Caleb cupped his hands around his mouth and shouted, "Anybody here?"

The last few Inuit families who had remained a little longer looked out of their tents, waved halfheartedly, then closed their doors. Yes, his life here, like the whales, was finished.

As Caleb drew the large copper spike from his door latch, he could hear the arriving women singing faintly down at the water's edge. They were no doubt landing their big umiak at the Dundee slipway. A great feeling of sadness swept over Caleb as he stepped inside his house. It was still more or less the same tidy, orderly room that had been kept by Nilak with her cheerful energy and short goose-wing brush, but it could never be the same without her.

He lit the stove, pausing only for a moment to stare at the sadly vacant space where his settee had rested. Then he sat by his desk and read an article on President Ulysses S. Grant on the now-yellowing front page of the three-year-old edition of the *Mystic Press*. Caleb crumpled it into the stove and on top laid some boxwood he had split. As it flared up, he shook in the last of the Dundee coal.

Walking to the stream, he filled his kettle with fresh water and, returning, put it on the stove. When the water began to boil, he threw in a handful of coffee and waited to fill his mug. He took down a small pot of brown sugar and a wooden box from which he removed the last two stale hardtack biscuits and three slightly mildewed prunes. The memory of the polished mahogany dining-room table at Topsail House, set with blue Canton china and heavy silverware, with his morning mail beside the daily paper, and Nellie serving him rich, fresh-ground coffee, a platter of hot johnnycakes with maple syrup and butter, fresh eggs, and plump farm sausages – the sight and the smell of all that went gently drifting through his mind.

Looking out his window toward far-off Baffinland, Caleb saw the sun's rays beaming just behind the western mountains, faintly sugared now by last night's fall of snow. He unrolled his huge, untanned bearskin that each year had turned increasingly yellow and opened his old spare chest to take out a faded Hudson's Bay blanket. Covering the skin, he sat, staring at nothing, waiting for the stove's new warmth to spread throughout his house. When it had done so, he pulled off his hat, sealskin parka, pants, and boots. He unrolled his soft eiderdown sleeping bag, remembering Nilak years ago smiling, working diligently beside him, filling the large flannel bag with gray down retrieved from the nests that hundreds of female eiders had used, then left behind. He lay down in his woolen shirt, long gray underwear, and woolen stockings. Slowly, his lonely feelings began to relax and change into passionate new reveries of what he planned to do this night. Caleb realized that he wasn't young any more. He remembered that he'd had a birthday back in May, but, hell, being forty-eight wasn't all that old.

His thoughts were interrupted by the women singing in Yack again: "Jesus loves me, this I know / For the Bible tells me so." The unexpected coming of the umiak had unsettled Caleb. Just when he had totally reset his mind toward the all-encompassing task of sailing south, seeing Nilak again had both excited and disturbed him.

Perhaps I should have stayed aboard *Sea Horse*, he thought. When a love affair is over, it's over. Still, Nilak and I never said good-bye in bed the way we should have, because she had had to leave so quickly with her brother. Well, certainly, thought Caleb, tonight's going to be the night to fix all that. It's only right. We'll do the right thing by each other.

The singing in Yack turned to:

Onward, Christian soldiers
Marching as to war,
With the cross of Jesus
Going on before!

It was stronger now, causing the island's sled dogs to join the women in the chorus. Caleb drew back his window curtain. Yes, the new arrivals were setting up their tents on both sides of his freshwater stream. He had always demanded that the Yacks camp well away from there, remembering the sight of dog turds floating in that same water he used for drinking.

Caleb fell asleep, and when he awoke, it was to the high-pitched wail of women singing hymns. They were terrifyingly close to his house this time, accompanied by a badly played accordion. These women's voices seemed to quaver with anticipation.

Caleb rose from his bed, pulled on his inner gull-skin slippers, and slipped over to the window. The ice master's house was ablaze with half a dozen whale-oil lamps and the last of Finn's candles.

These female voices sang in their own language, which Caleb only partly understood. But he could hear new words mingled and repeated: "*Godee, Jesusee, Sataanasi.*"

Finally, the accordion and the singing stopped, and through Finn's window, Caleb could see and hear the red-headed missionary reading cautiously selected biblical passages from the New Testament that he had asked to be translated last winter into Inuktitut with the help of the interpreter's wife at the Kekerton station. Like missionaries everywhere, McNab had skipped the Old Testament entirely, for it contained far too much violence to risk any explanation.

Caleb watched the Reverend McNab, now decked out in his clerical white collar. His costume below the neck consisted entirely of native sealskin clothing that these women had so eagerly sewn for him.

Caleb shut his eyes and took a long drink from his pewter flask. Opening them, he saw moving along the path, in the squares of light cast from the ice master's windows, the withered old man who had steered the women's boat followed by eight younger kayakmen – undoubtedly the singers' husbands. The old man stopped when he saw the weather vane lying on the ground. Slowly, he bent and picked it up to study the whale carving before he laid it down again and continued on to the very farthest tent. There, each kayakman ducked down and disappeared through its low entrance where he judged they could scarcely hear the singing. Caleb took another drink and laid down on the bed.

Weather vane

When Caleb awoke again, the world was silent as dawn crept around his house. He felt the other side of the bed. It was empty. Caleb remembered that he had stored his Chinese piss pot in the loft above his head. He rose, jammed on his gull-skin slippers, and hurried outside. There, not far away, standing in the hovering mists of morning, Caleb saw, faintly at first against a newly fallen frisk of snow, the tall figure of a man. "Oh, dear God!" he said aloud, then closed his eyes and blinked. "That can't be you! Andrew?"

He pinched himself and thought, I'm not drunk, I'm wide awake. This is impossible! Caleb closed his eyes, then opened them. The Highlander was still there. Caleb took two paces sideways to change the angle of the light. "No, that's no trick," Caleb whispered. "It's you, Andrew Cargill. I'd know you anywhere."

Andrew was holding out his trembling hands, trying to warm them from the heat that rose in shimmering waves off the boiling try-pot.

"Andrew!" Caleb called out. "How could you get back here, damnit, with all that ice to block the way?"

The tall, familiar figure did not seem to hear him. A flush of terror rose in Caleb. The shimmering heat that was coming off the try-pot was, like the Highlander, starting to fade in the morning light.

"Oh, Jesus!" Caleb called aloud. "Andrew, Andrewsikotak! Stay by me. Don't go!"

The frosted, iron try-pot was dead cold and the specter of the Highlander was gone. Caleb stumbled back inside and relit his stove. When he set his kettle on to boil, he heard his inner door open. He whirled around in terror, certain that Andrew's ghost had returned, then sighed, first with relief and then with pleasure, when he saw that it was Nilak, gently smiling.

"*Itiriit*, enter," he called softly as he went around and turned back her side of their eiderdown sleeping bag. "As usual, dear, you've come exactly when I need you most. I had a frightening vision . . . or was it a dream this morning?"

Caleb talked to Nilak in American as though she understood his every word, and she, too, comfortably expressed her thoughts to him in Inuktitut. He looked out toward the ships to check the pack ice before he made his usual hand signal, which he had long used to indicate that she should jump in bed beside him.

"*Aggai. Naalungmiuraluak.*" Nilak looked wistfully at him. "Excuse me much, but no, I can't do that."

"Why not?" asked Caleb in alarm.

"*Godee, Jesusee, Uvanni takunaatut* . . . They watching me." She looked up into the shadows of his loft to see if she could catch a glimpse of them, or worse, the horned, bat-winged *Sataanasi* spying down on her.

"Oh, don't worry!" Caleb laughed. "I'll say nothing to that little missionary about this farewell fling of ours."

Nilak turned away from him and stared out the window at Finn's house, beyond which she could see the huge pack of ice that barred the ships from leaving.

Caleb had forgotten the ice, forgotten that he was even going south. Stepping forward, he took Nilak gently around the waist and tried to draw her to him, blowing in her ear and slyly tickling her neck with one point of his moustache. She smiled, then hung her head before she politely pulled away and moved toward the door.

"Come on, dear girl, another hump won't lame the camel."

Nilak, sharing inside herself his feelings, slowly opened the door, for she hated the thought of hurting him.

"Where are you going, my dear?" he said as he pulled on his parka. "Wait. I'll come with you." He slung his long glass over his shoulder.

Outside, he pointed to the lookout. "I'm on my way up there. *Ivvitlu?* You, too? Let's go together and check that damned ice."

Nilak made no answer, but when he started along the path, she followed him.

Halfway up the hill, Caleb stopped to catch his breath. When she came up beside him, he clasped his arm around her waist. She smiled, but once more drew away from him. Caleb sighed and they continued up the hill until they reached the stone blind that was the lookout place. Caleb swept aside the sealskin cover, saying, "*Itiriit*, enter."

They studied the waters near the island's eastern shore. All was mirror-smooth, but out to the west, rogue gusts of wind were winnowing the surface of the Sound. This was the wind that Caleb and the crews had been waiting for.

"Look at that ice!" Caleb pointed. "It's opening over there near Niantelik. Come on, wind," he shouted, "show me how strong you are!"

At that moment, Nilak caught his arm, "*Taika! Taika!* Look! Look!" She pointed down to the calm waters.

There, a large bowhead whale was surfacing, blowing a high silver mist, then resting, taking in air.

"*Akviapik*, she's got a young one with her." Nilak pointed again. Caleb saw the small whale swimming close beside its mother.

Slowly, the whales started moving through a large, reflecting pond made oily by their traditional food. The cow's enormous head raised as she tipped it sideways and cruised majestically forward, her huge mouth gaping open as she sifted in tons of water swarming with tiny, shrimplike krill.

"She's teaching it to feed." Nilak clasped her hands to her cheeks in pleasure at this now rare sight of a bowhead with its young one.

They watched the cow and calf traveling slowly through the undulating slick of plankton, seeing the cow sluicing out the water from the sides of her featherlike, black baleen strainers until she reached the outer edge of her pasturing. The huge fish then rose slightly in the water, arched her back, and began her long, slow dive. The young calf tried to imitate its mother.

When the whale's enormous tail flukes rose, Caleb spread his arms and called, "Black butterfly!" For an instant, the whale's wide, winglike flukes were silhouetted in the air, shedding thin rivulets of water, before they, too, slipped beneath the reflecting surface of the sea.

Bowhead whale with calf

"We haven't killed them all!" the old man whispered proudly to Nilak. "That cow's got a new calf with her. Pray God these great fish will thrive again. I hope they'll have the power to increase."

Nilak smiled, knowing that he was talking about the whale and calf, feeling elated, yet somewhat saddened that everything had so quickly changed for them.

When Caleb looked again with his long glass, he could see that the white ice pack across the Sound was opening, spreading like angels' wings. He gave Nilak's rear a familiar pat. "*Atai!* Go ahead! *Tuavilaurit!* Hurry, please!"

Nilak laughed as she trotted down the rough, stone path.

Even before Caleb could see Finn's pointed roof, he could hear a hammer ringing, and as they rounded the last big rock, they saw the missionary kneeling at the roof's peak where he was trying to construct a small church spire.

"Good morning to ye, Mary, and ye as well, Captain. I've already forgotten Mary's old heathen name, and so will she soon enough. Won't ye, Mary?" he called cheerfully down to her. He pointed with his hammer out toward the ice that blocked the ships. "The Lord in His wrath has locked His icy gates against ye."

"Stand up, look sharp, Parson. You'll see He likes us well enough to blow open His gates for us today to get away from the likes of you."

Caleb could not bring himself to look up at McNab again, but smiled instead at Nilak. "Dear Nilak," he said, "I swear I'll never call you Mary." He glanced out at his whaleboat rowing in for him, then turned. "Nilak, let me give you my house for your own in memory of our loving friendship."

"Well, Captain Dooonston, that's a very decent gift ye've given Mary," McNab called down from above. "Isn't he the generous man, Mary? Remember, Captain, she is a Christian now and ye must call her Mary."

Caleb did not answer, but his shoulders sagged. "Nilak, dear Nilak . . ." He pointed to it. "I leave you my house and all its contents. You do with them as you please. But, Nilak, try not to forget that wonderful name your family gave to you. I promise I never shall."

"Och, Mary, this is splendid news!" McNab called down. "Yes, Captain, Mary will gladly give both wee houses to my mission, won't ye, Mary? *Iglussara*," he said, "that house will be my manse."

Nilak looked up at McNab, smiled, and nodded in agreement.

"You, McNab, hear this!" Caleb shouted up to him. "There's a big woman over at Niantelik, a great, heavy-chested, tricky creature. I don't know exactly what she can or cannot do. But I hope you two will have the chance to rough it up together, Pastor. I can only say I'd give anything to be there just to see your red hair fly!"

Caleb turned and marched off with Nilak following. They descended to the beach where the boat was waiting. He shook her hand, then waded out to climb into its bow.

"Caleboosi, *Tavvauvutit*, good-bye to you," she called out. "*Amerikamiutlu tavvauvusiilunasi*, Americans, good-bye to all of you." She waved.

Caleb, Jack Shannon, and all four oarsmen called back their farewells to Nilak. Then, looking up above Blacklead's rocky island bank, they saw standing on the tundra the ancient steersman from the umiak and that same silent group of kayakmen who had come ashore with their women and children beside them. Being hunters and hunters' kin, they stood motionless as stones. But when the whalemen waved and shouted, "*Tavvauvusiit*," many Inuit answered in American, "Goo-baay! Gooobaaay!"

The crewmen set their oars and stroked hard toward the ships. Caleb felt the sharpening of the breeze and ordered the stunsail raised. Coming alongside *Sea Horse*, they hooked the captain's boat to its hanging davit lines. Others drew it up and lashed it tight.

The wind was stronger now and the tide was swelling. The huge ice jam was audibly opening up before them, rumbling, splashing as great white slabs slipped into the sea. Crewmen and mates alike were shouting, each yelling to the opposite vessel, mad to break free and set sail south.

"Where is Caleboosi?" the old man demanded. "He's not in my cabin. Is he tween decks or in the hold?"

"No," said Dougal. "No, we cannot find him. We've searched everywhere below."

"Hell's bells," shouted Caleb, "I ordered Lukassi to keep a weather eye on my son. Where the devil is he? Where is Caleboosi?" The old man began to panic, striding back and forth along the deck.

"The lookout in the crow's-nest," said Mario, "told us that during the night he and the man on watch both saw a Yack making his way across that ice jam, heading toward Niantelik."

"Could it have been the boy?" Caleb bellowed. "What am I going to do? Where is Caleboosi?"

Lukassi came up out of the fo'c's'le looking drawn and desperate. "I can't find him." Lukassi spread his hands. "We've all been searching for him. He's not aboard."

Caleb's face furrowed with rage. "You're the one, Lukassi, you fuckin' well let him go. He's out on that ice, isn't he? Well, get your arse over that rail and onto the ice. You find him, damn you! Track him to Niantelik, Lukassi. Do you hear me? Bring him back to me. What the hell were you doing, you stupid bastard, sleeping like some dim-arsed twit while my son just walked away from you?"

"I couldn't help it, Captain. I'll go out on the ice right now and try to find his footprints." Lukassi started toward the rail.

Mario called to him, "You be damn careful, Lukassi, that ice is breaking up."

"You do as I tell you, Lukassi. Move your arse, lad! You bring my son back here on the run with you. I gave you the goddamned job of taking care of him and now you've gone and lost him. These two ships are leaving, mating south, the instant you bring him back. You'll get no fancy rifle from me until I see that son of mine aboard *Sea Horse*."

Lukassi climbed down off the side of *Sea Horse* and leaped onto the dangerous, spreading ice pack. Its widening cracks were tipping and hard to see beneath the crust, but he started running, jumping, desperately following a faint line of footprints that led toward Niantelik.

Both *Sea Horse* and *Lancer* were anchored a safe distance from each other, but the ever-changing shifting and grinding wall of ice made everything uncertain. The pack was opening faster now as the wind strengthened. The old man was dancing up and down, shouting orders to Dougal, demanding that he check the rudder chains and the whaleboats. Nothing suited him, for his mind was totally on Caleboosi.

"Damn that Lukassi, and damn you, too, Mr. Gibson!" Caleb roared. "How could the pair of you be so dim-witted as to let that boy of mine leave this ship?"

Several crewmen over on *Lancer* shouted, "Let's go, Captain Dunston. She'll close in and trap us for the winter if we wait."

"Shut up!" Finn ordered his crew. "Hard luck," Finn called over. "I hope Lukassi finds the boy before we have to raise anchor."

Finally, at 6:21 p.m. by Caleb's turnip watch, both crews gave another shout of triumph as the tide turned and they watched a riverlike passage open, offering *Sea Horse* and *Lancer* a widening channel south through the massive pack of ice.

The watch in the crow's-nest shouted down to the deck as he saw Lukassi running toward them, jumping across the ever-spreading cracks. He was alone.

"Where's the boy?" the old man hollered on his gamming horn. "Where's Caleboosi?"

304

"I can't find him," Lukassi gasped as he made his way closer to the side of *Sea Horse*. "Some at Niantelik say . . . they saw him . . . getting into . . . his father's new whaleboat . . . heading north . . . with his whole family."

"Oh, God!" cried Caleb, clasping his head in anguish. "What'll I do?"

"Pile on sail, Captain," Finn yelled across to him.

The mates agreed, but at that instant, Mario yelled a warning and they saw Lukassi plunge chest-deep through a widening crack. Spreading his arms to save himself, he managed to struggle quickly back onto the ice.

That sight seemed to bring back the decisiveness in the old man. "We can't stop now," he yelled . "This ice has opened and the wind's abaft of us. Who knows how fast it could shift again? Why did you have to lose my son, you ignorant, goddamned knuckle-head? I'll bet your father was Scotch," yelled Caleb.

Both ships raised their anchors and piled on sail. The yards creaked in the awesome silence.

"Good-bye, Lukassi, and thanks for everything," Finn shouted from *Lancer*'s bow.

"Good-bye! Good luck to you, Lukassi!" all the whalers called from the decks of both ships. "Good-bye."

Lukassi, shivering and dripping wet, walked slowly on the ice beside them and returned their wave.

"Get ready to stave off ice!" the mates shouted on both ships.

Finn called over to Caleb again, "Lukassi's worked hard as hell to help us this year and to educate your son. Aren't you going to give him that Sharps rifle that you promised?"

"Fuck him!" the old man yelled. "That useless bastard went and lost my son! Trim sail, Mr. Gibson! And, Mr. Shannon, keep your southern heading along this opening passage. Pray to God, men, that it lets us through."

Lukassi stopped and stood shivering, head bowed, on a huge slab of ice barely connected to the pack.

"Damn you, Lukassi, for losing my boy!" Caleb shook his fist at him.

Lukassi sagged down onto one knee on the ice, too exhausted from running to wave or grieve over the fancy rifle that had been for so long promised him. He had risked his life and fallen through the broken ice to earn it.

Pierre came running to Captain Finn.

"Here's my Sharps rifle," the ice master shouted to Lukassi, and he sent it slithering over the ice protected by its sealskin case. "And here's its ammunition." He flung his cartridge bag toward him.

Lukassi cupped his hands around his mouth. "Thank you so much, Captain Finnussi! You, Captain Dunston, can you hear me?" There was no answer, but Lukassi shouted, "Caleboosi, he's a lucky boy. Very, very lucky, Captain!"

Sea Horse's hull was moving further, its tall masts and sails beginning to fade in the ice fog.

"Caleboosi's lucky to be getting away from you, Captain, and back to his own family! You're no fuuuckin' good!" Lukassi yelled.

He turned his head away, not bothering to watch the fog-hung giants as they disappeared down the opening passage in the ice. These square-rigged whale ships were slowly sailing out of his life. Out of Inuit lives, he hoped, forever.

Chapter 19

Caleb leaned against the port rail staring at the ghostly blue-white giants that had calved off the Greenland ice cap and were drifting slowly south to meet their fate in the warmer waters of the Gulf Stream. Year after year, Dunston's memories of his Arctic voyages had seemed like icebergs, clear and sharp at first like the edges of broken ice, then melting like ice cream in the summer as they neared home port. Once there, he would begin to plan his next voyage while numbing his mind to the ponderous domestic life at Topsail House. Nilak, who had meant everything to him, was fading fast and his only son, Caleboosi, was lost to him forever. He turned and marched back to his cabin, feeling nothing but his need for rum and further calculations of his huge whaling profits. Why not end it now, while he was winning, Caleb thought. The big fish were all but gone. Wouldn't it be best to leave that son-of-a-bitch, Peapack, knowing that his own success as a Baffin whaling master would remain unrivaled?

Both ships lumbered slowly, oh so slowly, south. Their rounded bows made the heavily loaded vessels look like half-sunken bath-tubs. Both captains tried to remain in gamming range, and *Lancer* mated safe abaft of *Sea Horse* on their passage through the ever-changing pack ice. Finn sensed the fact that beneath *Lancer*'s felts and copper sheathing her whole hull had grown soggy during her long winter's slumber and was now disintegrating. But they had never found the time or place where the old man had promised to hove *Lancer* down and make thorough repairs. At night, Finn lay on the bed in his cabin, eyes open, staring through the dark, imagining that he and his anxious crew were holding old *Lancer* afloat with their stomach muscles.

One Sunday, Caleb's horn erupted without warning. "Ice Master!" the old man shouted. "You should row over and see old *Lancer* from my view. She's riding lower than a coal barge, with no freeboard . . . I'm telling you, Finn, if we get a storm, that old wreck will split open like a rotten watermelon and take your crew and cargo down faster than a load of bricks. Keep that in mind, Ice Master. Stay alert both night and fuckin' day. Can you hear me over there? . . . Acker, is Finn asleep?"

"Sure, I hear you," Finn yelled back in an angry voice. "You're the one who demanded that we leave nothing behind until we had to deck-load this old tub with corset bone." He paused. "I'm keeping all our whaleboats hung out on their davits, ready. Each boat has got in it a mast and jib sail, cask of water, a Bible, a compass, food rations, fish hooks, and a gun."

"Above all, you keep *Lancer* mating close by me," Caleb roared, "and stay clear of heavy ice."

"That's the way life goes." Chris Acker sighed as he leaned against the rail near Finn. "If we didn't have our hold jammed tight, he'd have us laying over another winter. Now both ships are overloaded. He's scared to death . . . and so am I."

They could hear Noel, Lester, and Everett with their caulking hammers thumping down below while the greenhands raised new raw blisters as they worked the Yankee bilge pump 700 strokes an hour, night and day.

"I got faith," said Everett, "this old grandmother might just have the strength to bear our treasure home to port."

"Aw, you've always been an op-to-mist," Noel said during the dogwatch. "The rest of us just pray to God we'll be awake and ready to get to the boats with our boots on when she dives. Even then, with every man rowing away strong, we could get sucked down with her when she goes."

When the watch changed at dawn, the men who had been on the pump staggered blank-eyed and humpty-backed into a line beside the cook shack to get their morning coffee and lumpy oatmeal porridge. Finn checked to see that the water in *Lancer*'s hold was still below the knees.

"We're holding our own!" Finn called back to Otto Kraus, who was standing at the wheel stem, steering.

"I got my cap turned inside out and I vashed my longjohns," Otto said. "That's all that's keeping this old *liebchen* afloat."

The ice master, who was taking a sun shot with his sextant at noon on the 28th of August, jumped up and grabbed his long glass when a voice from the crow's-nest called down, "Ice! Heavy ice ahead!"

"Son-of-a-bitch," said Acker. "We're a full nine days out of Cumberland Sound and here's more damned ice."

The ships were at 62° north latitude and 65°30' west longitude, still north of Labrador, off Resolution Island.

"Bad place, I've been told," said Finn. "That ice comes belching out of Hudson Strait this time of year."

"This stuff could hold us up," the old man called on his horn. "Is *Lancer* taking on much water?"

"She's doing not too bad," Finn answered. "But it's taking endless tar and caulking and pumping round the clock to keep her afloat."

Finn examined the sky, hoping for some sign of change of wind that might open up this shapeless mass and allow them to pass through.

For three endless days and nights, they hove to and drifted north of the pack ice. The conflicting temperatures shrouded them in fog. The ice creaked and groaned like old house floors as it met the warmer waters of the Gulf Stream.

Evenings during the dogwatch, both crews gathered near the foremast to smoke their pipes or chew tobacco and hold spitting contests, betting future beers on who could leave the furthest

tobacco stain on the accursed ice. Men's nerves grew jumpy. Boisterous tugs of war became shouting matches, then turned into
bloody fights that the old man and Finn were forced to settle. Caleb
played endless games of cribbage with his friend Gibson, then with
Shannon, but finally they got mad, slammed down their cards, and
gave up playing. Finn and Caleb, mates, and crews had long since
stopped trading visits. Then, one evening when they least expected
it, a northeast wind came off the Greenland ice cap and began to
open the jaws of ice.

"There's a lead opening in this mess," Finn shouted across to
Caleb. "*Lancer*'s closest to it so I'm going to start her through before
it closes. Follow me."

"You could get caught in there," the old man bellowed.

"Keep *Sea Horse* a safe distance off my stern," Finn yelled back,
"in case I am beset by ice."

The two huge, square-rigged ships reefed sail and glided heavily
into the lead. The lookouts in their crow's-nests could see the pack
ice ahead of them still opening, spreading out across the sea like a
scattered jigsaw puzzle. Several herds of walrus rested on the larger
pans, easy to smell and their grunting plain enough to hear, but
they were difficult to see as they lay motionless, close packed as
huge brown sacks of potatoes, half hidden in the drifting mists.

Finn climbed into the foremast rigging with his long glass to
gain a better view. There was only one main lead where the pans
were spreading, but no way yet that *Lancer*'s bulging hull could
slip through without being nipped by ice. The trick, of course, was
to know which light pans of ice would yield and which others
must be avoided. That was just the kind of judgment the ice
master had spent years learning during the spring seal hunt. His
skilled eyes were drawn to one growler three times the size of a
doryman's house. It was pumping slowly, heavily up, man-high,
then down, until it was almost completely submerged. Finn had
known growlers off northern Newfoundland. They worried him
the most, for he knew that even touching one of them could ring
Lancer's death knell.

The old man reset sail and followed *Lancer* further into the lead, carefully watching the overloaded ship as she nudged aside some lighter sheets of thigh-thick pan ice. A dozen of *Sea Horse*'s crew were standing nervously at her bow rails. They could now see a second growler bobbing dangerously as it drifted toward *Lancer*'s course.

"See dat mostly sunken devil just off to windward, Captain?" Otto warned. "Dat's de one scares the b'jesus out of me. She's only showing us her top skull. The big bulk of her weight is hiding down below!"

"See her make a whirlpool when she goes under?" said Acker.

"I know it," Finn said, trying to keep calm.

The wind forced *Lancer* along the lead toward this all-but-hidden, frozen threat.

"Ease to port," Finn called to Acker.

Caleb watched the old ship's frosted copper sheathing glistening just at the waterline as she forced aside wide pans of breaking ice to avoid the growler that continued plunging like a heavy piston as it moved into her path.

Growler

"This nor'easter's turning rowdy," Finn called to Angelo. "Shorten sail! And, Acker, watch that second, bigger growler coming at us off our larboard bow!"

"*Gott in Himmel*," shouted Otto, dancing on the deck. "Dat son-of-a-bitch is going to hit us!"

Finn ordered *Lancer*'s crew to lay out the long, iron-tipped ice staves. "Stand handy to them on the larboard rail."

"*Achtung, achtung,* watch dat second growler. She's pumping up, then sinking down," cried Otto. "We can't stand either of those devil's to even touch dis rotten hull!"

"Now," Finn ordered, "hard to starboard! Hard, hard! We've got to snake her through."

Acker, who was at the helm, responded.

"Oh, God, keep us swinging wide away from that second fucker," gasped Angelo. "*Lancer's* loaded like a thousand tons of lead. Do you think we're going to clear it, Otto?"

Finn ran to the rail. "Everybody, get set," he shouted. "That ice is moving in too close!" He looked at his whaleboat.

Frank Town was ready with his ice staff. Otto Kraus and the others were ready with theirs. Rafael Costa, the heavy cook, hoisted the longest pike pole. All in all, eight men stood balancing them against *Lancer's* rail, while the strongest of *Lancer's* seamen and greenhands ran to larboard with all the remaining ice staves.

"Angelo, lower number two boat!" the ice master shouted. "Fast, move fast! I want it down there as a buffer in case that second growler touches us."

Everett and Lester slipped the lines and lowered the thirty-foot whaleboat, keeping it in place beside *Lancer's* quarter with their long oak pikes.

"This second one's going to get us," Otto groaned as he used all his strength against the first and smaller growler.

"*Lancer's* too heavy," Acker shouted. "She won't swing away."

Alfonso Fernandes aboard *Sea Horse* could see *Lancer's* plight. He dropped to his knees and called out, "Hail, Mary, full of grace. The Lord is . . ."

Lancer's crew watched in horror as this deadly growler exposed its pocked, icy head, then submerged again to hide. It seemed to lie in wait for them, measuring the time when it should rise and strike. Those straining at the rail could now see the massive head of this blue-green terror shimmering, wallowing just beneath the surface like some rogue sea elephant. Its pale skull seemed to watch them from just below the waterline, waiting for the moment to rise and strike, to tear open and spill the precious guts of *Lancer.*

312

"Haul that number two boat around the stern," Finn shouted as he hung over the larboard rail in the icy wind, the sweat trickling from his armpits down his ribs. "Get the ice staves ready!" he yelled. "It's coming up!" Finn bellowed, "François, Sammy, and you, John, shove in the boat! Now! Right now!"

They could all hear the grinding, cracking sound as the cedar lath on the No. 2 boat buckled under the pressure. *Lancer's* staffmen pushed with all their might. All eight staves were out, forcing, stabbing at the growler's icy eyepits, trying desperately to find a hole to catch, then push. Otto and Rafael, together with Frank Town, did find strong pit holes in its icy nostrils, and, helped by others, pushed so hard that their oak staves bent like bows before they split.

The gunnels of the No. 2 boat were now breaking, still wedged in tight between *Lancer* and the head of the rising ice. The shattered whaleboat tipped slowly sideways, its oak ribs snapping, breaking with a sickening sound against *Lancer's* black scarred hull. The boat, almost flattened, still offered its tough oak keel as a last defense against the immense power of the rising tons of ice.

"Hard to larboard!" bellowed Finn. "Hard, Acker, hard!"

The waters around the giant growler swirled as it submerged, then it paused, waiting like an ominous blue shadow almost beneath them, before it rose again. This second grinding impact against *Lancer's* side caused her great weight to heave up, shudder, then roll away, creating a swoosh of wave. The ship hung there sickeningly off balance.

"Oh, Jesus, let her come back!"

"God, let her right herself!"

The crew cried out in terror, hanging onto any solid handholds they could find on the forty-five-degree angle of the deck.

Then, slowly, *Lancer* slipped, with a terrifying clatter of all her heavy oil casks shifting in her hold.

"Is she stoved?" yelled Otto. "Is she taking on water?"

"Get down and look," Finn ordered.

Otto drew back his broken oak staff and, aiming, flung it like a harpoon at the growler as it rose again off the stern. "*Verflucht nochmal!*" he yelled. "*Schweinehund!* Angelo, you start the praying again! Pray hard! We're going to know if *Lancer* stays afloat, or we all start running. Running for the fuckin' whaleboats."

Otto, helped by Acker, rushed aft and leapt down the ship's companionway into the hold.

"She's stove, yeah, she's stove hard. She's taking water," yelled Otto. "*Gott in Himmel* knows if she's going to stay afloat."

"Prepare to lower the boats!" called Finn. "Every man be ready to abandon ship!" He ran down into the after hold to take a look. Then he was up on deck again, hanging way out over *Lancer*'s larboard quarter rail, with Rory Decker gripping the ice master's belt so he wouldn't topple in.

"Lower number three boat," yelled Finn. "Drag it around by its painter to the place where that goddamned growler hit us."

Eager hands helped Finn and Noel Wotten hop down into the waiting boat.

Wotten shouted up to those on deck, "She took the worst of it just above the waterline."

"We're a bunch of lucky bastards that *Lancer*'s got that copper sheathing," Finn called up to the crew. "She's got an awful bash in her, probably broke the larboard knee frame, and she's bloody well taking water." He bit his lip and looked at Noel. They could hear Lester and Everett with others inside hammering. They were nailing up straw-filled, double-canvas mats which were blubber-greased to repel water. Spiking boards were nailed across them. The men yelled for others to help them to prop and jam oak beams against the damage.

"There's a helluva lot of water already in her hold," Acker shouted. "Get every man we need on both the Yankee and the Swedish pumps. Otto, help man those fuckin' pumps! Lead the Swedish pump hose down the companionway into the lower hold and feed it over the side."

"*Ja*, two pumps should make a difference," said Otto.

Finn, grim-faced, along with Noel, was helped back up over *Lancer*'s side. "It was a piece of Christly luck that growler had to break that whaleboat first before it struck on one of *Lancer*'s heaviest, live oak ribs. That's what's saved her up to now. Saved us all."

"Lord, God," said Everett, "they built ships strong in those old days."

"That Finn deserves the name ice master," Otto said. "Did you see how quick he gave dat hand signal to Acker, taking us to starboard, then to larboard, allowing *Lancer* to snake past that first growler, then drop the whaleboat in as a buffer? Now dat's what I call mastering ice!"

Acker saw the old man ease sail on *Sea Horse*. "He knows that we got hard struck," he told Angelo. "He's got all his boats out hanging free on their davits, waiting to see if we need help."

The strengthening west wind caught *Lancer*'s sails and moved her forward, but the waters remained almost calm around both ships, as it usually does in ice. The vessels were now close enough for everyone to talk.

"Well," the old man bellowed through cupped hands. "I would have thought an outport Newfie like you might have got stove in by that goddamned growler, but I'm surprised to see you're still afloat. Ice Master, I saw you out looking at your starboard quarter. Are you stoved hard? Are you taking too much water? Could you use some help?"

"Just hold there mating close with us, Captain," Finn yelled back. "I'll let you know damned soon. We're going to take the whaleboat around and protect the bash on the outside with some hickory boards."

The moon, nearly full, had risen above the jagged wall of pack ice east of them before Finn felt that they had done all that could be done to keep his ship afloat until they found a place to dock her.

When the old man boated over with Dougal, Shannon, and Chips Bell, Finn led them down into the hold to see the damage and repairs, then back up to his cabin.

"I guess you had *Lancer* too damned overloaded to answer to the wheel," Caleb sniffed. "It probably wouldn't have happened if you'd held back, like I told you, and I'd entered that lead first."

"Bullshit!" answered Finn. "I went into that lead first because the timing was everything. I was in position and you were nowhere near. Look behind us," Finn pointed, "it's closed."

"Don't try tossing the blame over onto me, lad. You're lucky that you, your crew, and *Lancer* are still up here looking at the moon. God knows," the old man said, "I'd hate to lose her just as much as you would, Finn, with all that oil below and all those tons of corset bone piled on her deck. Let's go below again and figure out what we can do to keep this poor old mother afloat."

"She'll hold up for now," said Finn, "if we can just keep going. The ice ahead is spreading out and those leads are opening wide."

Before dawn, Finn heard a tapping on his door. It was Lester and Noel with Everett. They looked dead tired.

"We've got her matted, propped, patched, and caulked up tight, and Otto's got the two pumps on deck working shifts with four men," Noel said.

"Good," said Finn. "Let's have some bannock and coffee, then I'll go below and look at her again."

"Maybe we could sail her as far south as St. Anthony in northern Newfoundland, or even St. John's," said Everett, "then offload her and heel her down for all the repairs she needs, or abandon her and hire two other ships to take her cargo safely to New London."

"I'd like to get as far as St. John's," said Finn. "There's no place to make repairs on the coast of Labrador."

"François La Flèche is on watch in the crow's-nest. He says there's still scattered drift ice to the south, but the whole sea could be clear by morning."

"Don't get overly hopeful," said Finn. "Warn the crew to keep their pants and boots on."

Both crews let up a cheer at noon next day as the mists were blown away and they saw the whole sea before them shining blue and cleared of ice. Everett and Noel began to build a new whaleboat to replace the one that had been crushed. They had all the help they needed, building it on deck between the fore and mainmast.

"Hopefully, we could sight the long arm of northern Newfoundland in a week or so," said Finn. "I long to see those lovely slopes again."

Three weeks of rising, dying winds and well-planned tacks carried both vessels to a point off southern Labrador near Indian Harbor. In another week, their slow-moving, overloaded ships were just off Battle Harbor. *Lancer* was leaking more and had taken on a list to starboard.

"Ice Master, do you want to go down the west coast or the east coast of Newfoundland?" called the old man on his gamming horn.

"The east coast," Finn answered. "The ocean winds are stronger in this season and there are inlets aplenty if we have to put ashore."

Acker slapped the wheel and sang "Blow ye winds hi-ho, blow ye winds that blow!" as *Lancer* led *Sea Horse* on their slow-moving tacks along Newfoundland's east coast. Both crews shouted out "God bless you" to the small vessels they passed.

Coming on the morning watch, Otto cupped his hands as usual and shouted up to the lookout, "Wake up, you lazy bastard! I can hear you snoring in that fuckin' crow's-nest."

"Sleeping, nothing," the lookout hollered down. "I'm eyeing a great gray foggy headland off our starboard bow."

"I'd say that's Joe Batt's Arm on Fogo Island," said a Newfoundland crewman. "Yeah, I saw it on the charts. It's not too far from Funk Island."

Finn ordered a new tack and the old man followed.

"*Sea Horse* is staying in our wake," said Acker, "because she wants to be abaft of *Lancer* if she founders."

Two days passed before they were in gamming range again.

Caleb hollered, "Finn, you want to put into Heart's Content or St. John's harbor?"

"*Lancer*'s doing far better than expected!" answered Finn. "Let's use this fair wind to carry us southwest to Lunenburg, Nova Scotia. They've got a boatyard famous for ship repairs. Our pumps are sucking out as much water as we're taking in. I'm for keeping under way."

317

In four days, they were off Halifax and *Lancer* was showing no troubles and the wind was blowing steady, carrying the mating ships south.

"I'm skipping Lunenburg and we're making our heading on Dover," Finn yelled over to the old man.

Acker laughed. "You can set a long tack for Dover, Maine. I've got a married sister living there named Dolly. She'll let us store all our oil and bone out back of her vegetable garden. She's got a market hunter's goose gun and God help any man who . . ."

The wind sheared off the mainsail and the rest of his words went scattering out to sea.

"I'd say Finn's a helluva lot different kind of man than this crew thought at first," said Angelo. "Imagine him passing up his own home port of St. John's and chancing sailing *Lancer* south?"

"*Ja*," said Otto, "I admit he's one helluva man in ice. I hope he's just as lucky with New England's autumn storms."

On September 27, 1876, the wind increased, and sooner than expected they were sailing into the enormous reaches of Passamaquoddy Bay, well off Portland, Maine. But their luck ran out and they were becalmed again and had to wait, pumping, cursing, and praying for three nights and days. *Lancer* stayed mating close beside the old man, but he seemed dispirited.

"I'm one unlucky son-of-a-bitch!" Caleb shouted wildly to any crewman who would listen. "Our logging wheel shows that this voyage north then south again has carried us 7,251 nautical miles. Now look at us, becalmed out here, just waiting for that poor old fuckin' wreck to sink."

While *Lancer* was becalmed this time, she had begun an unfamiliar kind of mournful groaning. Finn felt he must do something or the tension would drive him raving mad. He decided to try his hand at making a piece of scrimshaw, a ditty box that he might give his mother back in Heart's Content. He asked Everett to saw for him a long slab of whalebone the width and thickness of a playing card. Jacques Moreau volunteered to help polish the bone. Still nervous as a cat, Finn tried carefully to engrave their two ships on its surface, but he couldn't finish it. Everett did it for him in the end. When Everett was through carving, he rubbed his own tobacco juice into the engraved lines to darken them and help show them off. He then cut two oval pieces from a scrap of chestnut plank to form a top and a bottom of the box, and together they boiled the pliable whalebone, then bent it round the wood and pegged it into place. Onto the chestnut top of the sewing box, Finn pegged a small ivory carving of a whale given to him by Supa.

No sooner was that work done than a breeze came ruffling around them. That wind, as it increased, blew away the worst of the crews' worries. In these warmer waters, Finn and the crews, and even the old man, began to believe once more that *Lancer* might survive. Still, when all of them lay on their bunks in the dark, they thought of the enormous weight of all those tight-wedged casks of oil below and the drying sheaves of money bone, piled higher than the deck rails, lashed outside to dry, and their dreams turned to nightmares. They thought of themselves as men who had bet on a turtle race.

Ditty box

Finn studied the charts. "Mr. Acker," he shouted, "I'm going to take the chance and pass up your sister Dolly's place in Maine. We'll keep mating south, then try and reach home port."

"I'll feel a helluva lot better," Otto mumbled, "if he can get this old mother in off the ocean into the protection of Block Island Sound."

During the next three days, Finn changed tack often, now closely following *Sea Horse*. Both ships were careful to stay well beyond the outer reaches of the Nantucket shoals.

Angelo Daluz, usually on the bright side, stuck his head inside Finn's cabin and smiled. "Captain, can you believe it? We're off the Cape Cod light. If our luck keeps holding, we're going to get old *Lancer*'s big fat cargo back to port!"

"Don't get too hopeful yet," Finn warned him. "Have you been listening to the new way *Lancer* groans when she rolls and heels to port?"

"Sure, I hear her, Captain," said Otto, "but, still, I'm betting on her."

"The fog's lifting," the lookout called down to the deck. "*Sea Horse* is in sight again, less than a league off our bow."

"Well, I'd never have believed it, our two ships back mating in this Sound together, clear of all that goddamned ice and weather," said Acker.

"The barometer is falling a bit," said Everett. "But, hell, we've beaten the odds so far."

Finn called the mates and crew round him at the mainmast. "Believe me," he said, "I'm going to give a blowout at that Cock and Spur Tavern you talk about. The food and drinks will be on me. None of us will ever forget the backbreaking hours you've put in on those goddamned pumps and caulking hammers. Not one of you has ever let *Lancer* or me down during this whole troubled voyage, both north and south."

"Hey, Captain, we're all glad to be here," Rory Decker called out. "It weren't too bad sailing with an old man that's fair and square, and knows the ice the way you do."

Oh, Jesus, Finn's heart jumped inside. There it is! I heard it myself. They're calling me the old man, treating me like a real whaling captain, and it's my first Arctic voyage.

A dark, starless autumn night descended on them. Taking advantage of the warmish, fleeting winds, Finn set a new course, and at dawn they passed the Elizabeth Islands.

Over on *Sea Horse*, the younger seamen leapt like monkeys, gaily scaling the ratlines, then perching themselves along the cross stays, watching the new wind patterns shifting, spreading. Each man's toes were wriggling, eager to grip onto the cobbled streets of New London, Hartford, Groton, Mystic, Stonington, Pawcatuck, Westerly, and even far-off Providence. They saw two clouds of black smoke rising from locomotives on the shoreline, another from a paddle-wheel steamer headed toward New Bedford. They could smell the familiar scent of home.

A man along the cross stay laughed. "Oh, it'll be good to get back home next to some of that nice, thick 'cubic' hair, as our family doctor likes to call it."

From the laughter beneath, the ironsmith's voice came up to him. "It's pubic hair you're talking about, you dolt. Yeah, Yack girls have got no hair down there at all."

"Maybe some were just too young for that."

"No, no," yelled Norris, "they're different. But forget that now. It's not the kind of talk Connecticut women wish to hear. Tell them about the giant whales you've harpooned, the polar bears you've fought, and the high-priced corset bone you're bringing home. That's what they want to hear – and, God knows, that's all any of us should tell them. Get it?"

"Got it!" shouted many of the crew.

That same night, they saw the Cuttyhunk light off their starboard bow and, farther away, the lighthouse on Sakonnet Point. Then the wind dropped dead away.

In the morning, they warped both ships with all their whaleboats out. The men rowed hard, trying to tow both ships into a breeze. They cursed, sang, wiggled their toes, performed every trick they'd ever heard of. Nothing helped. *Lancer's* weathered sails hung slack. Finn felt glad of one thing – he was safely beyond the gamming range of *Sea Horse*. Nothing to do but sit and wait, and listen to *Lancer* groaning and the tired, sad sucking, wheezing noise of the bilge pumps. Block Island was a gray smudge on the horizon, five miles northwest of them. They should have a short run into New London, less than thirty-five miles – if only they could get some wind.

Two men on pumps

Leaning on *Lancer*'s rail, Sammy Douglas said to the third mate, "If I were feeling calm, I'd get out that walrus tusk and finish off the cribbage board I started for my dad, but I'm too goddamned excited to do any scrimshandering right now. I just want to see this load of oil and bone safe into port, get my share of the lay, and start living like a human being again. And I sure don't like the looks of that." He pointed to the sky in the south. It had turned a heavy, leaden silver, then higher up a darker, ominous gray.

Finn and the mates gathered, nervously talking about the falling barometer, remembering that October could be the most dangerous month of all. Long swells were starting to roll toward them out of the southeast, coming much quicker than they should. Then, without warning, the wind began a sudden frenzied gasping, gusting downward, causing *Lancer*'s sails to luff. The sea responded like the surface of a pail of water set atremble in a wagon. White caps swiftly appeared as the wind in a very few minutes rose to Force 4 and 5. Spray and foam flipped and turned in wild confusion.

All the ship's sails luffed noisily, then fattened with the wind. Now everyone knew that a vicious storm was brewing fast. Acker and Otto shouted orders to the crew, sending them scrambling into the rigging to tight-furl the topsails and shorten the fore-and mainsails.

Finn looked up, alarmed that the big black-backed gulls and herring gulls had disappeared. He had often watched these birds spread their wings and ride the strongest currents of air over Conception Bay, enjoying the power of the wind as they tipped to larboard, then to starboard, soaring, skimming just above the wave tops, laughing, perhaps screaming to each other, "What a perfect wind!" But now, all of them were gone, flocking inland, seeking shelter from the storm.

"Can *Lancer* stand a wind like this?" asked Acker. "It's bad because it's happening with the big moon tide."

"Too damn much vind coming on too fast now," said Otto. "This could be the beginning of a hurricane."

"Please, God, don't let that happen," Finn said aloud.

Lancer was rolling now enough to give off dull thuds below deck as her oil casks began to shift, and on deck her sheaves of baleen clattered in the wind. With each roll, the ship was all too slow in righting herself again. Beneath the racing stormclouds across Block Island Sound, Finn could see a bright, churning line of white between the darkened sea and sky. The sheaves of baleen were chattering now like black teeth in the wind.

"Take more line and lash the baleen tight," Finn ordered. "Do you hear, Acker? Tight!"

Bracing themselves on the heaving deck against the mounting gusts, the crew used long coils of harpoon line to lash the money bone against the midmast and main rails.

"That's a big bitch of a storm bearing down on us," Angelo warned. "I saw a blow like this once off Jamaica. Two French ships and one Portuguese were lost that day. *Valha-me Deus!*" He held his crucifix out against the rising wind. "*Vai la, vai la,* go down, go down. *Espiritos Santos!*"

"Stop moaning like dat, damn you," Otto yelled. "Take some men below and tight-jam some wood blocks between those casks. *Ja,* I know it's dangerous working around the casks, but you gotta stop dem shifting or they'll sink us."

Otto then ran back along the rain-splattered deck to check Acker at the wheel and ordered Rory Decker to share the task of fighting the waves with him. The wind was gusting now with enormous strength, forming dense streaks of foam and spray as it approached Force 10. On the Connecticut shore trees would soon be crashing down.

Finn cupped his hands and hollered orders to the rain-soaked seamen clinging above him in the rigging. They were aloft, trying desperately to climb down or hold on for their lives after they had done their best to reef all sails. But some sails had broken loose and now flapped furiously like giant flags. The sky was inky gray. Silver rain lashed against the ship.

"This storm is God's revenge," yelled Angelo just as an immense gust of wind and white torrent of water caught him and slammed him to the deck.

Blinding sheets of rain came driving at them, striking their oilskins hard as shot. It was clear now that *Lancer's* heavy cargo had shifted, and now her deck stayed heeled to larboard. This was doubly dangerous because of the rumbling, thumping casks smashing around below, and the relentless force of the wind battering the heeling ship. *Lancer* lost all ability to right herself, and those at the wheel could not bring her fully back in line to face the waves, in spite of the fact that her new rudder was still responding.

It was not yet noon, but few aboard *Lancer* dared to believe that they might survive this day. A flurry of violent wind sent Finn skidding sideways along the ancient deck, now completely awash with waves dashing over it. Fearing he would be carried overboard, he flung himself down flat just as a following gust of wind caught the new No. 3 boat, ripping it free of its davits and hurling it into the white and foaming seas, where it was instantly swallowed up.

The ice master was smashed against the scuppers. Slowly he grasped the pin rail and hauled himself painfully to his knees. Through the numbness in his side, he felt a sharp pain when he breathed. He wondered if he had broken ribs. The bumping, rubbing sound below had increased as the casks continued to move. He turned to face astern when he heard the mizzenmast come crashing down, its spanker pinning Lester Lewis to the deck. Lester had been struggling to help Rory and Chris hold the wheel.

When Finn reached him, he could see Lester's thigh bone thrust out, raw and white, through his oilskin trousers; half mad with pain, Lester was still reaching up, trying to help steady the wheel. Finn saw that the mast had fallen across the transom that protected the helm. Under his direction, crewmen cut the rigging and rolled it over the side, its jib and spars jutting crookedly at every angle as the yard lines stretched then broke, whiplashing back at Finn and Lester and others near the helm.

A giant wave rose beneath *Lancer*'s grossly overloaded hull, causing her to rear up and then pitch forward, her bowsprit disappearing in a thunderous mass of foaming water, tearing the foremast off in the enormous press of water, leaving its jagged butt stabbed through its sodden sails, a terrifying warning to the crew that *Lancer* was all but lost.

Clinging to a starboard belaying pin, Finn looked along the deck and saw but could not hear his desperate mates and crewmen shouting, their mouths agape, the sound of their voices choked off in the thunderous crash of waves. The ice master could do nothing but hang on as another heavy wall of water went boiling white along the deck and surged over him. He could see that *Lancer*'s bowsprit was now stripped of sail, but still pointing forward like a broken finger. Benoît St.-Onge was forced to abandon the bilge pump handle and somehow made his way abaft along the steep deck to *Lancer*'s helm, where Finn saw him tie himself beside the wheel. Then, struggling, using all the strength that he possessed, Benoît tried with Chris and Rory to keep the ship from yawling, from floundering in the deep troughs of the waves.

No men tried to work the bilge pumps now as the caulked deck seams opened and water flushed down tween decks. Every man was out on deck, believing that *Lancer*'s next roll would carry her too far, that an oncoming wave would cause her to flounder or turn turtle. All of them could see that *Lancer* was being driven toward Long Island's graveyard of ships near the end of Montauk Point. A giant wave flung a wall of water crashing against the tight-lashed baleen bone that was fluttering noisily on *Lancer*'s deck. Hard men screamed in fear, but no one heard them. They clung to the wreckage on the deck. Antoine, the steward, and Frankie Town were swept violently into the scuppers. Finn, like the others, believed that life was coming to an end for all of them.

Sea Horse was less than a cannon's shot away from *Lancer*, but she was a much newer, stronger ship, better able to carry her heavy cargo, and she was captained by a man of vast experience. Now, as *Sea Horse* rose, Caleb caught a glimpse of *Lancer's* woeful condition, with her foremast shattered and her mizzenmast down. Caleb saw *Lancer* heeled over for so long that he judged her casks had shifted and that she would never be able to right herself again. But another mountainous wave rose under *Lancer* and seemed to set her on an even keel again. Now seeing *Lancer* all but helpless, with two masts down, Caleb prayed to God that *Sea Horse* would not suffer that same fate.

In the very teeth of the hurricane, Caleb watched in fascination, knowing he was about to witness the loss of much more than half of his enormous, mated treasure while they were almost in sight of home port. He could see a pair of crewmen crawling forward along *Lancer's* deck between the steady rush of waves. One man carried the ship's fire axe and the other the cook's stove hatchet. Still kneeling, these two seamen reared up, chopping like foresters at the twisted mass of fallen lines and spars.

"Sweet Jesus," cried Caleb as he hung on, staring at *Lancer*, "does she have to go down now? Dear God, please keep her off Montauk Point and ease her into the safer waters of Long Island Sound."

The swirling might of the hurricane was quickly changing course, pressing both vessels south toward the sand-blowing bluffs of Montauk. *Sea Horse* was still responding. Caleb took courage from the knowledge that his vessel had new timbers and a limber, reinforced hull. She was a younger ship and he was still able to hold her running on a quartering tack, using only her reefed mainsail. It billowed violently, but was helping them to fight their way north around Plum Island and into the Sound. Jack Shannon and Mario Fayal had roped themselves to the wheel stem of *Sea Horse* and were struggling mightily to keep her on course, trying not to over-force their loaded ship, fearing that might damage her rudder.

Suddenly, *Sea Horse* was struck by another crippling blast of wind and all four whaleboats were torn off their davits and catapulted into the waves. The wind tore away her mainsail canvas and yards. Caleb watched in horror as the heavy mainmast and cross stays tore loose and toppled forward, crushing in the fo'c's'le hatch. The sails and cross stays, still caught by their shroud lines and rigging, trailed in the water, causing *Sea Horse* to pull back heavily, then pitch too far forward, twisting mightily. At that moment, Caleb and both helmsmen felt the awful wrench as the starboard rudder chain gave way. *Sea Horse*, now out of control, began to wallow in the rolling wave troughs, helpless, with her wheel stem useless. The wind and waves ruled her now. Slowly, inexorably, they lifted her, and rolled her broadside toward the lighthouse and the black-toothed rocks off Montauk Point.

Caleb swayed like a drunkard as he gripped the worthless wheel helm. Dougal and Shannon pulled him away, all of them helpless in the overwhelming power of the storm. Ricardo Moniz hauled himself toward them, staring out at the huge surf breaking on the rocks, its white spume mixing with the clouds of sand that blew like yellow smoke along the Montauk bluffs.

The rain had ended, and the clouds in the southwest were beginning to tear apart, while ragged patches of sunlight raked across the blue-green, heaving surface of the Sound. But still the wind and the waves drove them toward the rocks.

"Old *Lancer*'s still afloat!" shouted Dougal. "She's awash, but she's made it beyond the rocks. She's being driven into the Sound."

"Forget *Lancer!*" Caleb bellowed at him. "That rudder chain of ours is gone. We're licked. There is nothing we can do. There's no way we can keep this ship away from those fuckin' rocks."

The storm was driving huge swells upward over the rising sea floor. They were breaking into enormous combers that went foaming through the rocks standing like guards along the beach. The fine spray from the waves breaking over Blackfish Rock was drifting halfway to the top of Montauk Light. The drenched, exhausted crew aboard *Sea Horse* watched helplessly as the largest wave they'd seen went rolling, thundering in against the point. Great leaping chunks of sea foam whirled above it.

Caleb could hear nothing now except the deafening roar of wind and waves. An utter sense of hopelessness combined with terror gripped him. All thought of their twin cargoes of oil and money bone had been frightened out of his mind. His eyes, wide open, focused for the first time on the act of dying. Was he, were any of those aboard, prepared to die?

Even as their ship rolled helplessly toward Blackfish Rock, he took control again. "Throw off the main hatch cover," Caleb yelled over the gale. "Help me! Help me get it over the rail . . . then . . . jump in! Jump near enough to catch the hatch to . . . save your lives!"

Men strained, clinging to the rail like sea crabs, or scurried along the lurching deck on hands and knees, smashed flat sometimes as enormous waves dashed over *Sea Horse*. Many saw Orval Windtree rise up on a wave, striking the already broken monkey rail as he was flung overboard. No man there could have saved him.

The heavy wooden hatch top hung balanced on the larboard rail, the crew on deck pushing. A huge wave caught *Sea Horse* on the starboard quarter, lifted her, and thrust her hard on top of Blackfish Rock, and the hatch cover, with men still clinging to it, was hurled into the water. The ship stopped with a grinding, tearing jolt and hung there shuddering, her bottom ripped wide open. *Sea Horse* was defenseless against the power of the next incoming wave. This wall of water, when it struck her, broke *Sea Horse*'s spine.

Mario clung on as he watched the huge sheaves of costly corset bone break loose and shoot out like spears to sink in the foaming waves. From beneath his feet, Caleb could see the big oil casks come rolling out, breaking or spinning like brown corks through the gaping hole in her hull, spewing an oil slick over the churning whiteness of the sea. Seth Baker, one of the few whalemen aboard who knew how to swim, kicked off his boots and leapt over the side and dog-paddled hard toward a half-sunk whaleboat. He caught it. Heaving himself inside, he waved and yelled to others close by as he reached out to save them with the long steering oar.

Clutching some lines tangled around part of the foremast, Hammer Haden was almost the last to witness the death of *Sea Horse*. He was the last crewman over the side. The shuddering whale ship was now completely at the mercy of the waves. Her deck was half submerged. Her metal sheathing was being ripped asunder by every wave.

Only Caleb hung on. He watched the wreckage twisting, turning, shining in the waves. Her ribs now showed through her sides. Caleb stood alone on *Sea Horse's* wildly slanted deck, determined to stay with the ship. The next wave came crashing over him, shrouding the old man in foam and sweeping him overboard.

Dougal managed to raise himself and kneel on the swaying hatch, his eyes searching the sea for the captain. Suddenly, Dunston's whole body was thrust up atop the wave that was rolling him mercifully toward the shore. Then Dougal saw the old man's body stop abruptly, as though caught and held by some powerful force that dragged him slowly back. The undertow then buried him beneath the sea – forever.

The rain resumed, sweeping across the Sound in wind-driven patterns, striking the water like blasts of buckshot, stinging the faces of the men. Holding fast to the hatch top, Dougal could hear men around him in the water bellowing in terror, then see their heads disappearing in the churning whiteness of the tow. The hatch top gave a tremendous lurch as it struck a rock. Israel Steiner and another man were jolted away from the raftlike cover and disappeared. There was nothing anyone could do but try to cling to the hatch as it rode the waves.

Finn and his crew on *Lancer* watched in horror as they witnessed the final battering of *Sea Horse* and the drowning of her crew. Some turned away, unable to bear the sight of this sister ship rolling, dying on the rocks. As each rolling comber helped to demolish the ship, those left alive from *Sea Horse's* crew clung like rats to anything that floated, desperate to keep their heads above water.

"There's not a crewman left aboard her now."

"She's gone! And they're gone with her!"

"Sweet Jesus, protect those men of ours!"

"Please, God, help them!" cried Angelo, and he wept and cursed together with the others.

"Calm down, man!" Finn shouted. "We need your help with this line!"

Angelo blurted out in Portuguese, "*Ajuda aquele homen com a linha!* Help!" When he was excited, the words of both languages seemed to scramble as they leapt out of his throat.

"Come on!" cried Finn to everyone in hearing distance. "We've still got this ship and our own lives to try and save. Jump to it! Clear the wreckage off this deck!"

Luke Blais, a logger from Grand'Mère, was still doing good work with the fire axe, hacking away the tangled rigging. As the crew worked, they prayed that *Lancer*'s newer, heavier rudder chains would hold them on their course through the roaring hurricane. Finally, when that was done and the deck was free of tangled rigging and the sodden masses of fallen canvas, Finn looked up to see that the worst of the storm was veering off to the east. The skies in the south were clearing, showing bright blue breaks between flying clouds.

The ship's boy, Pierre, was trying to hold Lester steady against the pitching motion of the ship, to protect him from rolling onto his right side, where his ribs were broken and his thigh bone protruded. François and Rusty, with sweat and rainwater running down their faces, kept control of *Lancer*'s wheel helm.

Their fate had almost been the fate of *Sea Horse*, but *Lancer*'s rudder held. She lumbered on into the Long Island Sound, driven by the wind and waves. "What's the goddamn difference," Otto moaned to Angelo, "to be wrecked in there on the rock like *Sea Horse* or to swamp and drown out on the Sound?"

"We've got nothing but the main stick now to help guide this overloaded hull. Acker, have the men tight-reef the mainsail," Finn called to him, for it was their only canvas left aloft. "We're being washed into the Sound, and with God's help, we just might manage to cross it, 'cause this wind is turning north."

"Jesus, save us! Look up there," yelled Angelo. "The sky is clearing. Captain, I'll get four men working on the pumps again. The fuckin' hull's awash."

Finn looked north as he clutched the rail. "That wind is easing. Pray to God the worst of this hurricane has passed."

"I wish to *Gott* we hadn't lost all the chaseboats," Otto groaned.

A half hour later, the waves were beginning to swell bright green around *Lancer*'s hull as she rolled, almost quartering, and wallowed through the troughs. Montauk Point was fading far behind them, though they could still see and hear the huge surf raking the beach.

Noel rubbed his sodden oilskin sleeve across his bearded face. "Look! Look!" he shouted, pointing further west along the point. "Two teams of draught horses with heavy wagons are going along the lighthouse road to help them. That second wagon's got a lifeboat on it."

"Thank God they're going to try and save them." Finn clapped his hands together.

"*Nein, nein.*" Otto spat downwind. "Dem *schweinehunds* will be looking for salvage more than men. *Sea Horse* is lost, and her cargo will be up for grabbin'."

"There goes all her oil and money bone," said Acker. "It's fair now for anyone to grab."

"I don't care about the oil and bone," said Angelo. "But I pray to God there's some Long Islanders over there who's going to help to drag our friends ashore. I hope they get ahold of my cousin, Ricardo Moniz, and pull him out of the surf, for his wife's sake, and help any others they can. I don't care whether they got wives or kids or not."

Just before evening, the hurricane itself had passed inland, leaving only the long, mountainous swells that continued to roll *Lancer* like a half-sunk log westward across the Sound. Finn and his three mates each took their turn at the helm and on the wheezing pumps. The hold was waist-deep now in oily water and more was leaking in, for the endless coats of tar and oakum had been raked open. *Lancer* still rode dangerously heeled to port, with her cargo permanently shifted. But no one seemed to care, for they judged it a miracle that *Lancer* was still afloat.

A raging sense of thirst and hunger had returned to the crew, but their cook, Rafael, had fought off his fears of drowning with an unknown amount of rum and was useless when they needed him. The exhausted crew staggered to the water cask and drank before they shoved soggy hardtack biscuits in their mouths. They talked with each other and began to gather hope. To many it became like a game of high-stakes poker, a challenge to see if they could keep this slowly sinking hulk afloat. Men stood in line to work in relays on the pumps. Everett and Noel, with help from others, still worked like madmen, struggling in the hold, trying to plug the worst leaks by hammering in lengths of hemp. They worked for the most part silently, all of them aware of their nearness to death in this moaning, dying vessel. The water in the hold was chest-high now, and in spite of all the desperation and the praying, *Lancer* was slowly sinking with an almost ungovernable amount of water still seeping into her hold.

"I want to tell you all whilst I got the chance," yelled Finn, "not one of you is a greenhand anymore. You're all seasoned fuckin' seamen. I and the mates are proud of you!"

François shouted down the hatch to those below, "I can see Fishers Island off to starboard. It's only two miles off, maybe three."

Otto bellowed up to him, "There's no way that this old mother is going to stay afloat that far. And if she does, she'll wreck."

For once, Finn thought, Otto is looking on the bright side. That bronco's admitting she might reach shore.

Chapter 20

Opening the narrow door, Kate Dunston climbed the curving stairway that led to the cupola perched high on the roof of Topsail House in Mystic. She had always liked this windowed, octagonal room which had seemed, when she was young, to be her own small playhouse that some forefather had built for her. Kate's only sister, Abby, who now lived in California, had refused to set foot in the cupola, for she had a dreadful fear of heights.

Kate opened one of the slender windows that faced south over the Sound and adjusted the large brass telescope on its rosewood tripod. It gave her a high, clear view of Fishers Island and the Sound to Napatree Point and beyond to Watch Hill. Further to the east, she could see Block Island wrapped in haze. There was scarcely a breath of wind on this Tuesday morning of October 10th. A low white ground fog hung languidly above the lawns. Kate admired the flaming red and golden yellow of the maples lightly touched by frost. The streets beside the Mystic houses were bordered by well-trimmed yew and privet hedges and fancy, black iron gates and fences. Looking down along their street, Kate could see three white-painted churches. But it was the dark swathe of the Mystic River that dominated the town. It had glided slowly south through the Connecticut countryside to flow smoothly beneath the bridge in the heart of town. It eased past active docks and boatyards before it widened, spreading its fresh, clear waters into the brackish marshes that edged the Sound. There, in summer, red-winged blackbirds repeated high, sweet calls while swaying on tall, tawny cattails. Kate could see large V-shaped flocks of geese passing south across Long Island Sound.

She had climbed up this day as on most autumn mornings, for she longed to see Titus, her husband-to-be, on his return with *Lancer* and *Sea Horse*, mastered by her stepfather. If the hunt had gone well and the pack ice had not held them back, both ships could be expected home this month or next. She rejected the possibility that a poor catch, which had been the rule in recent years, might have forced them to remain in the Arctic for another year. Far off in the drifting sea smoke that hung near Fishers Island, she could see two sloops, a brigantine, and half a dozen other smaller fishing smacks, sails slack, becalmed like children's toys on a pond.

Kate looked down, then rubbed her feet in the deep groove of the wide pine flooring, worn there, she had been told, by numerous earlier female relatives' shoes. The small trench had apparently been made by Kate's chronically overanxious grandmother, Eliza de Alverado, and her Spanish great grandmother from Cadiz. Both these earlier women had lived and died in Topsail House. Somehow, Kate's own shoes, when she stood in those anxious grooves, always summoned up the image of her short, fussy grandmother, who swore during her last days that she had seen Confederate soldiers sneaking along the Mystic hedgerows and had heard their rebel yells as they charged into her bedroom.

Kate moved the eye of the telescope along the Sound. There were no three-masted ships in view. She closed the narrow window and hurried down the stairs to breakfast with her mother and her mother's friend living with them at Topsail House whom Kate called Aunt Melissa.

Two hours later, Kate was up in the cupola for another anxious look. The sky over the Sound had ominously changed color, and the earlier morning fog had disappeared. She opened the window again, noticing that the air outside seemed warm and thick. A strange gloom was gathering between the isolated Napatree Light and the jutting finger of Watch Hill.

At noontime, Kate again returned to the cupola. Short gusts of wind made moving patterns on the Sound and scattered the colored leaves off trees. The sky to the south had turned to a solid wall of gray. Small, dead twigs made rattling noises as the wind snatched them off the ends of trees and flung them against the house.

Kate turned when she heard her mother step inside the cupola.

"Just look at those waves that are starting to roll along the Sound," Arabella said. "Melissa's all atremble. She says she senses a terrible storm."

"Oh, I pray that those two ships of ours are far away from this," said Kate.

Arabella Dunston squared her shoulders. "There's been no warning. Overnight, the barometer in the captain's den has fallen to as low a point as I've ever seen. Could this be the beginning of a hurricane?"

Even as she spoke, a large gust of wind tore a limb from the garden maple and flung it violently against the house. Kate quickly placed her eye to the telescope for one last glance along the Sound, then closed and latched the window.

"It's hard to see out there with those rain squalls and rising waves," said Kate, "but I caught a glimpse of one ship coming toward us. Only her storm jibsail was set, but she may have been storm-tied or perhaps lost the rest of her canvas."

"It would hardly be one of ours," Arabella said. "Captain Dunston was counting on those two ships mating close together at all times, for he planned on easing *Lancer* through the Arctic ice, then mothering her safely back to port."

Kate frowned at her mother's remark, which belittled Titus.

"Oh, Lord! Look!" her mother cried. "Part of the roof is blowing off the Palmers' carriage house! Shingles are flying everywhere. This is a ghastly storm. Here comes the heavy rain. And look at the Mallorys' big elm tree! It's fallen right across the road."

They heard heavy rapping on the brass door knocker below, then the sound of Willie Kinney's nervous gait as he hurried up the stairs.

"Nellie told me you'd be here." Willie looked lean and haggard from a night of rum and riot. He was gasping as he closed the cupola door. "I don't think it's safe for you two being on this housetop with all this wind and broken limbs a-flying. Samson says he heard there's a ship out there in trouble." He bent forward and propped the south window narrowly open, then readjusted the glass. "Good God, it's blowing the top right off the Sound!"

"Can you see her?" Arabella asked.

"No," said Willie. "Wait. Yes, I can. She's a ship with only her mainsail tightly reefed, and her deck's awash. Oh, God, her foremast and her mizzenmast, they're down. And all her whaleboats, they're gone!"

"Oh, Willie, can it be either of our ships?" Kate's voice was trembling.

"I can't tell," said Willie, "with those damned rainsqualls hiding her most of the time. I can tell you one thing, that vessel out there ain't *Sea Horse*. I know her like the back of my hand. But it could be *Lancer*. She's an old one, built plump-sided. Their sterns are near the same. She's rolling heavy because her hold is flooded, or maybe she's heavy-loaded with oil."

"Pray God," said Kate, "she'll come through this storm."

"Yeah, the best thing for both of you is to pray," said Willie. "That ship's in awful trouble. She's got no freeboard left, she's mostly awash. It'll be a miracle if she stays afloat." Willie turned his pale, strained face away from the telescope and looked at them. "Kate, I hate to tell you this . . . but that old ship could be *Lancer*. Oh, God, I'm sick for all those friends of mine aboard. But I'm asking myself, where is *Sea Horse*? Where would she be now?"

An oak branch came hurtling against the cupola windows, breaking or cracking four of the glass panes.

"Come on, we're getting out of here," said Willie, herding them down the stairs. "This hurricane's about to come in off the Sound."

When they reached the eerie gloom of the lower floor, the whole

336

of Topsail House was shaking. Even the chimes of the tall hall clock continued to let off a stuttering, ringing sound after 4:00 p.m. was struck. Nellie and Samson had already closed and fastened all the upstairs and downstairs shutters on the windward sides of the house. Some of the others thumped and banged in the rising wind. Another chestnut tree came crashing down, whipping Topsail with its branches.

"Where will that ship come ashore," asked Kate, "if she can make it ashore?"

"I'm figuring," said Willie, "she'll pass just east of Fishers Island. If she still has a rudder and can steer off Catumb Rocks or Sugar Reef, that's what she'll be trying to do, if anyone's still mastering her. They'll be praying that the waves carry her between the shoals, past Lyddy Island, and into those salt marshes. That would be about the only place that might give her enough water to come near a beach. She's out there in the worst kind of distress, and no one but God can help her now."

"I'm bringing in hot water with the tea," called Nellie. "I've put the tray in the sitting room."

There was a flash of lightning and heavy rumble of thunder

"I hate that," screamed Melissa as she ran into a closet.

An hour later, the fury of the wind had passed inland, and the rain was slackening.

"Oh, I hope that marks the end of it," Arabella frowned. "Can you imagine how frightened poor Melissa must be? I must go soothe her."

Willie went out onto the porch, dead sober now. "Yes, the clouds are breaking, the sky's brightening, and most of the wind has passed."

"What can we do?" cried Kate.

"Samson, Samson!" Willie shouted. "Give us a hand here! The captain's rowboat is up in the rafters of the carriage shed. You get your son and haul it down and load it on the back of the cart. I'll tie it while you and the boy hitch Windy. If that crippled ship has any rudder left, they might be able to make their way through

Lord's Passage, which has maybe six fathoms of water, and if they can stay east of Wicopesset Rock, she should go on bottom somewhere near us among those smaller rocks."

Mrs. Dunston and Kate demanded to go. Both found a place to sit in the rowboat atop the cart.

"I'm taking my small long glass," said Willie. "We'll cross the Mystic Bridge and keep a watch along the shore road. If it's not too flooded, we'll try to reach Latimer Point. That should be near where she'll come aground – if she stays afloat."

Windy trotted out the drive of Topsail House and down the hill, heading for the bridge. They crossed to the coastal road. They were all shocked at the destruction that the hurricane had left all over town. Large trees had been split and torn up, barns had collapsed, and the roofs had been torn off many houses. All of the boats in the harbor now lay topsy-turvy on the shore.

"What a damnable mess!" Arabella cursed.

A half hour later, Willie stood upright in the cart, steadying himself against Samson, trying to use his glass.

"There she is," Willie yelled. "She's *Lancer* all right. God, that ship's been through a terrible pounding. But there's some crew alive aboard her. I can see three of them, no four, moving on her deck. There's still some huge swells coming in."

Samson was out of the trap now, holding Windy's halter, for large chunks of blown scud foam were tumbling across the darkened road, frightening the mare. Willie stood on tiptoe in the trap, straining to see the ship through the tall, swaying weeds and cattails of the marsh.

"We've got less than an hour's light," he said. "There's one of those small steam tugs out of the harbor; it's trying to get near *Lancer* and cast its spring, trying to get a hawser on her. Look, the crew's shifting and retying the baleen bone on deck. That means her hold and tween decks must be crammed with oil."

"Oh, I hope that tug can help them," Kate cried.

"I pray to God *Lancer*'s crew won't let that robbing tug so much as touch her!" Willie swore. "Those sharks who are circling her are trying to snatch *Lancer*'s cargo for themselves. If they can manage to take her in tow and move her, then all of *Lancer's* cargo will belong to them. It's the law of the sea."

They saw *Lancer* roll up on a swell and catch, then shudder from stem to stern. She hung on the foul, stony grounds not far from Latimer Point.

Willie stumbled out of the cart.

"Let me help you down, ladies. I'll untie that boat and we'll carry it to where we can slip it into the water. Hurry, it's getting dark."

When they slid the boat off, Windy reared in the shafts.

"I'll hold Windy's halter," Arabella called. "You three go ahead."

Samson took one side of the boat and Willie the other. Kate held the stern in one hand and lifted the hem of her long skirt with the other. They slipped the bow into the water. None of them could keep their eyes off *Lancer's* grounded hull, which now lay over on its side before them, its torn copper sheathing glinting in the dying, evening light.

"I'm in bad shape . . . I couldn't row a stroke," gasped Willie. "But Samson's strong."

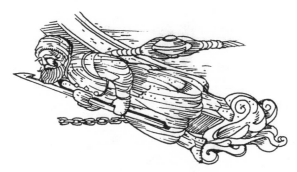

Lancer's figurehead

"I'm going with him," Kate announced. "I can help steer with the paddle. We'll bring Titus safely ashore." She climbed into the stern.

"Kate, you be damned careful. Don't do anything risky," Willie warned. "That wreck could shift and roll over on you."

Willie pushed them off, then stood peering through the gloom, listening to Otto Kraus bellow through *Lancer's* gamming horn, warning off the salvage crew. Willie saw them cast a towing hawser onto *Lancer*'s deck and watched the big German heave it back at them. By the grace of God, or by some helmsman's skill, that vessel had passed safely between Napatree Point and Fishers Island through all those shoals. Here she lay wrecked just off these salt marshes, heeled to port and hard aground with all her treasure, Willie hoped, intact.

Kate guided their small boat until they almost touched her hull. They could see someone waving a storm lantern on *Lancer*'s deck above them.

"We're all right!" Kate heard a voice yelling. "This vessel is not up for salvage! Stand off, stay clear! I'm master here. This ship is under my command."

Could that be Titus's voice, Kate wondered.

"Careful, Miss Kate," Samson warned her. "I'm going to move this boat along her hull. You call up and tell them who you are."

Kate cupped her hands around her mouth. "Can you hear me, Titus?" she called. "This is Kate . . . Kate Dunston! Can you hear me, Titus?"

There was no answer, but she caught a glimpse of a tall man in the lantern light. Kate held her hand out against the cold and battered copper-sheathing. The ship's side bulked enormously above them, for it was now almost entirely out of the water.

"Titus, can you hear me?" Kate again called loudly.

"Can that be you, Miss Dunston?" Chris Acker's voice called down from the deck that was tilted away from shore.

"Yes, Mr. Acker, it's me . . . Kate Dunston. I'm here with Samson just below you. Where is Titus? Where is he, Mr. Acker?"

There was an ominous silence above her.

"Is he all right? Has he been hurt?" she asked. "We've got a small boat down here. We'll take him, take anyone who's hurt, ashore. Are some of you in need of help?"

"We're going to try and get Lester Lewis down to you right now," Acker's voice called. "His leg is badly broken and probably his ribs. Be careful with him. His thigh bone's sticking out. I trust you're not alone or overcrowded in that boat."

"No, no, we're ready," Kate answered.

She heard leather boots climbing *Lancer*'s sloping deck and then the round beam of a bull's-eye lantern searched the water.

"The crew is staying to protect the ship until we can turn her over to Fisheries," said Acker.

"We're putting a rope sling around Lester and we're going to try and ease him down to you," another voice shouted. "Come further forward, lady. Otto is going to lay Lester in your boat."

"You got someone strong down there with you?" called Otto.

"Samson's here with me," Kate answered.

Otto was roped down *Lancer*'s side like a mountaineer, guiding Lester in the sling.

"Samson's got ahold of him beneath his shoulders and I've got his legs," called Kate. "We'll rest Mr. Lewis safe here in the boat."

Samson started rowing ashore while Lester lay shuddering on the bottom with Kate trying to steady his twisted, bleeding leg.

"Miss Dunston, can you hear me?" Acker shouted. "We've got to get word to Fisheries in New London. You warn them to come right away and help us save *Lancer*'s cargo."

"I'll try to telegraph them from the station," Kate called. "If the lines are down, I'll send somebody to them." She put an encouraging hand on Lester's side as she said, "We're almost ashore. I can see our cart on the side of the road. Willie Kinney and my mother are waiting by the cart to take you to the doctor."

Lester tried to smile at her, but he was in too much pain.

Willie waded out and helped to ease the boat through the reeds. Samson's great strength allowed the four of them to raise the small boat onto the cart while Lester was still lying in it. Willie lashed it expertly. Samson and Kate's mother sat up front, while Willie perched on the boat's bow and Kate crouched in the boat beside Lester.

"I've got my Paisley shawl around him," Kate told her mother.

"And I'm keeping his leg steady. Hurry, Samson. He's shivering terribly."

"Samson, you try not to let this cart bump too hard," ordered Arabella.

"I'll do my best," the big man answered.

The going was slow because of darkness and fallen trees.

Arabella turned, her deep voice questioning Lester. "Where is *Sea Horse* now? Do you know?"

There was a long pause before he answered. "Yes. Yes, I do know, ma'am."

"Where is he?" Arabella asked.

"They're over on . . . over near the end of Montauk Point."

"Why there?" asked Kate. "Were they able to take shelter in Fort Pond Bay?"

"No, they couldn't do that." Lester took a deep breath. "Because *Sea Horse* was . . . wrecked," he sighed. "Wrecked hard." He began to weep. "We all watched *Sea Horse* being smashed to pieces. We saw her whole bottom and larboard side get torn out. Her three masts went down. Her whaleboats blown away and swamped, the same as ours. Jesus, save them!" Lester wept. "As many as you can, God help them. You wouldn't have believed it, Willie. She must have broken her rudder chain, and those big seas were bothering her so hard. They drove her right into Blackfish Rock on Montauk Point and busted her back and split her keel, smashed her to pieces. Oh, Jesus, save her crew! *Sea Horse* is gone!"

"Did you see any of her crew get ashore?" Arabella demanded.

"I don't know, ma'am," Lester gasped. "Some say they saw a few heads struggling in the water. I saw one man floating not far off shore, but the undertow was sucking hard, dragging him back out to sea. I'd say he was already drowned."

"Oh," Kate gasped. "That's terrible!"

"You stay strong, Kate," Arabella's deep voice commanded her daughter. "We're needed now. More news will come tomorrow or the next day."

"Where's Captain Kildeer?" Kate bent and whispered desperately to Lester. "Is he aboard *Lancer*?"

"No. Sorry to tell you, we lost him a long, long time ago, Miss Dunston." As he spoke, the cart wheel hit a bump and Lester bit his lip in pain. Kate tried to straighten his knee. "There's a new captain now. He's out there aboard *Lancer*. It's better if someone else tells you everything . . . later."

Kate felt her face flush and her throat swell until she could not speak.

That night, hundreds of folks from Mystic and the nearby villages, wives with their families and other relatives of the crew, who did not know yet whether they were widows or had lost sons, clutched onto their small children and rushed to the scene. Along with many seafaring men, they waded out to Latimer's salt marshes carrying lanterns to see if they could lend a hand, and to marvel at this ancient, wooden giant that had somehow managed to survive for ninety-seven years, and then to best this hurricane. But beneath any feeling of triumph by *Lancer*'s crew remained the sickening knowledge that *Sea Horse* was lost with all her cargo and probably many of her crew. How many friends of theirs, they wondered, had lost their lives that day?

Sometime well before dawn, a gray Fisheries tugboat with barge in tow arrived from New London and anchored near their heavily loaded wreck. Three of the partners climbed aboard *Lancer* and heard frightful details concerning the loss of *Sea Horse*. They ordered half a dozen Fisheries men to remain aboard the ship and protect her cargo with shotguns.

Finn joined all of *Lancer*'s exhausted, nerve-wracked crew as they helped each other go ashore, shuddering in the pre-dawn cold. There they were quickly draped in warm woolen blankets and helped to board several farm wagons that took them to the nearby Seamen's Mission in Mystic. Once inside, they were warmed with hot beef broth heavily laced with rum, followed by home-baked bread with slices of beef, and blue cheese, sausages, and chasers of ale, and those famous Mystic green prick pickles that the crew had dreamed of for so long. Tom Finn, walking stiffly because of his damaged ribs, was invited by his friend Captain Shirley to share his home in Mystic until the difficulties cleared. He went to sleep in the attic bedroom and slept for fourteen hours.

When the New London Fisheries had first heard news of the disaster, the yacht `Hector` had been dispatched immediately across Long Island Sound to do what she could for any of *Sea Horse*'s survivors, and to try to salvage anything of her cargo. But in the rush and confusion that always accompanies disasters and hurricanes, those aboard *Hector* were misinformed by two men in a small fishing smack who were themselves out searching for storm salvage. This caused the partners aboard to redirect *Hector* to Sag Harbor, only to discover that while *Sea Horse* did have some survivors, those men were no longer there. Some believed they had been taken to Greenport, but most agreed they'd gone to Orient Point to board the delayed ferry on its first passage across the Sound to New London since the hurricane. It was dark before *Hector*'s skipper finally received a telegraph message, and by the time the Fisheries yacht did reach Orient Point on the following day, the morning ferry to New London was already halfway across the Sound.

Since pirate days, then later privateering days when booty was shared with the government, the excitement generated by any news of captures or of shipwrecks always caused a flood of rumors to race along the Connecticut and Long Island coastlines. Scores of relatives, friends, and acquaintances of *Sea Horse*'s crew, as well as shameless curiosity seekers, were waiting as the ferry finally pulled into the New London dock. Many Mystic and Westerly families had crowded into the small coastal steamer to get there, as did Mrs. Dunston, Kate, and Captain Finn, who had been offered the privacy of the master's cabin.

When they let the gangplank down, the crowd on the ferry dock watched in wide-eyed horror as the survivors off *Sea Horse* emerged. Rafael Costa led them, his head wound bandaged with a printed cotton torn from the hem of a woman's apron, now heavily stained with dried brown blood. Then came two of the three boat steerers. Buffalo Munro had two short, handmade splints holding his head upright and his throat bound with bandages, for they feared he'd suffered whiplash. He was followed by

Ricardo Moniz, looking shy, his broken arm supported in a sling. His best friend, Hammer Haden, led the cooper, Ezra Morse, a big man, who was shaking and weeping and could not bear to raise his head. Ezra hesitated with each step, his eyes covered with his best friend's dark blue neckerchief.

The wives and relatives of each man let out sobs or wailed "Thank God" and heaved sighs and hugged their children as they saw their kin step off alive. Down the gangway walked Chips Bell, still trembling from shock, but nodding sociably to those he thought he recognized. Next came Charlie Flender, hobbling between two ferry men, trying to smile, not meaning to show that his nose was broken and two of his upper front teeth had been broken off at the gums.

After a long pause, Dougal Gibson appeared, shaking and confused. Rudi Haas had Dougal's arm, carefully easing him down the gangway. Dougal's ribs had been broken and his face was ashen gray with pain. His friend, Tom Finn, and Dr. Greeley were on the dock to help him as he stumbled at the bottom. Finn stared at him aghast. Could this be the same cheerful Dougal he remembered? Finn had now counted all twelve men who had survived the wreck of Sea Horse.

Kate clutched her mother's arm, for Captain Dunston was not among them.

There was a painful, sickening silence, then the thirteen drowned bodies of Sea Horse's crew, the ones who had been washed in by the waves, were carried down on rough-made stretchers, each body tightly wrapped and scarf-tied inside a length of weathered sailcloth. Gripped by rigor mortis, they lay rigid as cut birch logs. A moan of anguish went up from the crowd that waited at the dock. Hardened sailing men, parents, grandparents, sisters, brothers, wives, and children broke into tears when the last to appear was the thin, half-sized body of Jose Pasco, tight-bound in his small shroud.

A large high-sided wagon that was passing had stopped, and its driver had climbed down to join the many who had gathered at the ferry dock. "You're welcome to put those poor, dead sailing men inside this wagon," he said after he, too, had waited awhile. "I'll take 'em anywhere you want. I got my barrels delivered and I've got the time, if this team can be of help to you."

The partner and the lawyer who had arrived from Fisheries had been up all night and naturally looked exhausted. They asked Finn and Dougal to take over their duties and were told that the bodies of Captain Dunston and several others had not been recovered. It was Finn who accepted the driver's offer and directed the crewmen from *Lancer* and other male passengers to stack the remaining bodies carefully in this makeshift cortege wagon. Finn helped Dougal up beside the driver, who gently slapped his reins on the haunches of the pair of heavy, feather-footed Clydesdales, and the sturdy rig began to move.

Captain Dunston's wife and daughter offered space to two of the newly widowed wives as they climbed into the smaller cart provided for them by Fisheries and followed.

In the soft sunlight, the wagon driver eased his team up the cobbled street, heading away from the water that now lay flat and calm. Finn quietly spoke to him. "These shipmates of ours should be taken to an undertaker's parlor. But I don't know New London."

"I'll show you where to go," the driver replied.

Only now did *Sea Horse*'s survivors and those sailors who had come from *Lancer* start to take an interest in the streets around them. They were stunned at the devastation that the hurricane had wrought. Hundreds of trees had been blown down, their branches torn and scattered everywhere among thousands of roof shingles. Some older wooden houses, sheds, and stables had given way before the winds and now lay in various swaybacked stages of collapse.

A dozen men in one of New London's work disaster parties had come along the road with their axes and crosscut saws and hacked away the largest limbs from a fallen oak. When they had cleared space for the wagon to ease past them, the wood cutters all removed their hats and bowed their heads.

The driver halted the team in front of the undertaker's parlor. Finn climbed down among the walking group of mourners, then went with Dougal to the entrance. Its door was drawn slightly open just prior to their knock. A short, gentle-faced woman dressed in black, wearing a small, gray Dutch bonnet atop her tight-drawn hair, appeared.

"We would like to speak to the undertaker," Finn said in an uncertain voice as he tipped his cap, remembering that it was a borrowed one.

The undertaker's wife looked out at the wagon with so many white shrouded feet protruding, and the crowd that was gathered behind. She thought a moment, choosing her words. "Sorry am I, sirs, Mr. Voorsanger, here . . . he is not. Work to do he had . . . in Waterford yester eve. Could I . . . of any help be . . . to you, sirs?"

"Thank you, ma'am," said Finn. "We have the bodies of eleven of our shipmates in that cart, and also the body of a small ship's boy. They're all from that wreck on Montauk Point two, no three, days ago. These men have all been friends of ours. Most of them are from these parts, save some from the colony of Newfoundland and others from Lower Canada. We brought them all here for your husband to prepare for burial."

"That many crewmen and a boy? Oh, Lord, have mercy on them all!" cried the undertaker's wife. "*Mein* husband has not tables, no space, here enough to handle deceased, so many." Her eyes were shining.

"Have you a carriage house behind?" asked Dougal gently.

"No, sir, no," said the wife. "Mr. Voorsanger keeps the funeral carriage over in the livery stable." Then, hiding her face in her apron, she began to weep.

After a moment, Finn said, "Excuse me, ma'am. Is there some other place? We've got to take those men out of the wagon and put them somewhere . . . soon. We can't let them lie in the sun and . . ."

"You might, sir, do what some others did six years before . . . when a big ship sank . . . right out there." She pointed to the mouth of the Thames estuary. "You must ask . . . the pastor if he let you lay them men and that poor little boy in his church. It's dark and cool in there. *Mein* husband . . . he moves them later when he and our son gets back."

Finn and Dougal looked around behind them. They could see four churches, none of them far away.

"Which church does you choose, sir?" asked the undertaker's wife. "Do you know which faith these seamen is belonging?"

"The Portuguese will all be Roman Catholics," Finn answered, "and others are Baptists, Episcopalians, Presbyterians, Quakers, Congregationalists . . . I think one's a Lutheran. We don't know which are which right now. Maybe," Finn said pointing, "we could ask permission from that church because it's closest. I don't think these men, all of them being shipmates, would mind which faith we choose right now, as long as all of them could stay together."

That church's clergyman was nowhere to be found. Every man there offered a hand as they carefully drew each stiffened body from the wagon and carried it inside the church and up the center aisle until they reached the step before the altar. There they started to lay the dead men down two by two in their canvas shrouds, all heads placed toward the bow-shaped pulpit. And at the end, the body of the ship's boy, Jose Pasco, half the size of all the others, lay alone.

A nervous young man came hurrying in from the rectory. "I'm sorry, sirs, our pastor has gone to attend a person who is gravely ill. But I'm sure he would agree that our church should welcome the bodies of all these brave, seafaring men until more final arrangements may be made. I shall remain here in the church with you, Captain, until the reverend returns."

"I am not a captain," said Dougal, "but I will stay here with them, for these men are all shipmates and friends of mine."

"Of mine as well," said Finn. "I would also like to stay."

Nervous and shaken, they both sat down beside each other in the nearest pew and rested. In a little while, Dougal's head tipped forward and he fell asleep.

Arabella Dunston and her daughter, Katherine, felt too shaken to take the coastal steamer back to Mystic that day, but stayed in New London with another widowed captain's wife they knew. That evening, they had a visit from the minister, then next morning were driven to the ferry dock to catch the eleven o'clock to Mystic. Kate and her mother were slowly recovering from their shock, trying to imagine all the different plans that they'd have to make with both men gone. On that chilly October day, Kate was still trying somehow to reckon with the death of Titus, and now her stepfather's death as well.

Tom Finn, who had also remained in New London overnight, looked grim-faced in the morning. Yet beneath that he had some cause for satisfaction, having just left a somber meeting with Amos Peapack and the Fisheries partners where they had congratulated him for his masterly prowess in saving *Lancer*'s cargo, and their ship and crew.

Finn was already in the line to board the 11:00 a.m. Mystic ferry when he saw Kate and her widowed mother approaching. He nodded and stepped respectfully back, giving them his place in the line. Both women were so shocked and saddened by recent events that they barely nodded at Finn. They huddled together, their mourning veils quivering in the chill autumn breeze. Finn remained quietly behind them as they moved slowly forward to board the ferry home.

Captain John Shirley, one of the few ships' masters Finn had remembered from the Captains' Rest in New London, was a well-mannered man originally from Chesapeake Bay. Because he and his wife knew Topsail House and the Dunston family well, he offered to escort Finn there and present him, since Finn had had so much to do with both the late Captain Dunston and with Kate's fiancé, Captain Kildeer, who had lost his life the year before.

Finn recognized Topsail House from the oval silver print of it that hung on Dunston's wall at Blacklead. What Finn had not expected was that Topsail House would be freshly painted a star-tling white and of such huge proportions.

Captain Shirley quietly explained to Finn, as he opened the ornate iron gate, "This great white elephant of a house was inherited by Captain Dunston's wife, Arabella. May I warn you, Finn, of Señora Dunston. She is very manly, very determined, and she bites!"

Nellie, who had been watching them approach, opened the wide front door on the captain's first knock.

"Captain Shirley here. Is Mrs. Dunston receiving today? Please tell her that I have Captain Thomas Finn with me, most recent master of the whale ship *Lancer*."

"Step in, please, sirs," said Nellie. "I'll inform the Missus that you're here."

She hurried down the hall, and in a moment, Arabella Dunston and Kate came out of the parlor where they had been examining family documents. Both ladies were dressed in black, and they quickly squared away their veils.

"It's thoughtful of you to come, Captain Shirley, and with Captain Finn."

"Ma'am, we were wondering if we could be of any service to you ladies during these most stressful days," said Captain Shirley.

"Thank you, gentlemen," Arabella nodded. "My daughter and companion, Miss Melissa Shore, share with me the anguish for both captains and their crews. Poor Kate has lost her dear friend, Captain Titus Kildeer, whom you must have known as *Lancer*'s former master."

"I knew him but a little," said Finn as he looked directly at Katherine Dunston. My God, he thought, how beautiful she is, even through that gray veil. She's nothing at all like her stepfather. She has her mother's manly way of standing, her fine skin, jet-black hair and oh, those round, dark eyes.

Mrs. Dunston straightened her back like an admiral. "Would you care to stay to tea, gentlemen?"

Kate began to speak with the new, young captain who had on this morning managed a much-needed shave and haircut in Mystic's Main Street barber shop. He smelled strongly of lilac cologne. They spoke of their brief former meeting on *Lancer*'s deck at the moment of departure. She noticed that his borrowed jacket fitted badly, but for Kate the expression on Finn's lean, sea-tanned face made up for everything.

Chapter 21

Nellie brought in three daily papers and laid them on the sideboard in the dining room. Ten days had passed since the terrible event had occurred. Kate rose and read their front pages, then hurried into the hallway.

"Mother! The weekend newspapers have arrived from New York, Boston, and Hartford. The *New York Herald* proclaims, 'Captain Thomas Finn, a genuine American hero.' They call him 'the dauntless young master of New London's Arctic whale ship, *Lancer*, . . . who exhibited heroic skill and courage in saving his valuable cargo and all of his crew during the worst hurricane in living memory.' The *Hartford Courant* has run an engraved portrait of the young hero, Captain Finn, and his ship, *Lancer*. Mr. Peapack says the news has put New London Fisheries and the town of Mystic on the map." Kate did a quick dance step. "Oh, Mother and Aunt Melissa, I'm so very proud of Tom."

Kate now called him "Tom" because they had met each day for more than a week – with Aunt Melissa acting as their chaperone.

"These papers only mention the Dunston name once." Arabella frowned. "They've written about the tragic loss of *Sea Horse* and only listed Captain Dunston among those drowned. They don't mention that they haven't found his . . . Well, I wonder, could that man possibly be alive? He was always a tricky one. He enjoyed living a double life. Oh, I've known that for years. And there's little or no mention of Captain Titus Kildeer. Nevertheless, Kate, you must cut out and save these news accounts. Here's a very favorable article in the *New London Evening Journal*. It's almost entirely about Captain Thomas Finn's bravery."

Kate had experienced a great loss in Titus, but her mind rallied when she thought of Captain Finn. It seemed miraculous that at the very moment of her learning of the mutiny and Titus's brutal murder, this strong, young ice master had appeared – capable, kindly, and decisive, a successful captain who had brought his valuable cargo home. An American hero, the papers said. Well, he was a North American, thought Kate, if not a genuine American of the New England breed. Thomas, she noticed, was somewhat shy in public, but a good bit more animated on those occasions when he and Kate found themselves in almost private conversation. At some point in Kate's mind, Titus Kildeer and Thomas Finn seemed to blend together, as though they had always been one and the same person.

As he sat with the partners at the boardroom table, Finn said, "For my part, I want Fisheries to fairly distribute one-half of all my lay to those good, honest families whose loved ones were lost off *Sea Horse*."

There was a murmuring around the table, with some nods of approval and some raised eyebrows.

Later, when they sat together in the front parlor of Topsail House, with the tall double doors wide open and Aunt Melissa sitting in the corner listening while she did her needlework, Finn tried to console Kate.

Finn received a letter and showed it to Kate on Sunday after church. "It's from O. S. Elliott, a retired admiral from the Civil War. He's president of the Eagle Packet Line of Boston. His firm is offering me employment." Finn's face was flushed. "Admiral Elliott writes that articles in the major newspapers have caused them to admire my determination and success, and asks if I would like to discuss a captaincy in the Eagle Packet Line. He requests that I immediately send my résumé to him by Special Delivery. He says he will personally present it to his board. Kate, if I get that job, I'll become master of one of their fast passenger ships sailing from Boston to Liverpool and Spain."

"That sounds thrilling, Tom! I hope you'll accept their offer. Whaling keeps you men away too long."

"Accept it? I'll jump at it!" Finn danced a series of double pigeon-wings along the hall. Laughing, he explained, "Those sleek, fast packets sail east across the North Atlantic on the westerlies. It only takes a month to Liverpool. Sailing men refer to that as shipping downhill. Then the ships sail south to Spain to catch the favorable tradewinds back to Boston by way of the West Indies. Sometimes, if the winds hold right, those whole round trips take less than eighty days. The masters of those vessels are able to relax with their families between sailings, sometimes for several weeks, and all on full pay.

"By God!" Finn told her. "This isn't Newfoundland. Only in America would they try to make a hero out of a man like me, then offer such a job to him. Why, in Newfoundland or Great Britain, they wouldn't dream of such a thing. Those places hate to even hear of anyone who dares to raise his head above the ordinary level, unless, of course, they're dead. Yes, they sometimes admire the dead up there."

"Oh, Tom!" Kate laughed. "Come, let's tell Mother your incredible news!"

"What a well-deserved honor, Captain," Kate's mother said in a hearty voice. "It's a chance to free yourself from that wretched whaling trade. Let's celebrate by sitting outdoors. It's such a lovely autumn day. Come, Melissa." She smiled at Finn and added, "This news calls for a toast and now that Sunday service is over, as the Bible says, 'They thirst after righteousness.'"

Melissa giggled as Arabella Dunston turned her head and whispered, "Tell Nellie to bring the rum decanter for Captain Finn and some sherry for dear Kate. There'll be a small breeze on the front porch. Melissa, don't you think some of that medicinal gin will help raise our sails?"

"Mother!" Kate raised her eyebrows. "Don't even think of imbibing on this porch with all the neighbors strolling past our gate."

"Well, I'm determined to celebrate this red-letter day," her mother said. "Melissa, tell Nellie to bring out the tea tray instead. Tell her to put the captain's rum into the teapot, our hygienic gin into the hot water pitcher, and Kate's sherry in her teacup. Then we can all drink at our leisure, using that best tea service – the Limoges. My grandfather acquired that when he captured a French supply vessel.

"Grandfather was a loyal privateer," she explained to Finn, "with a topsail schooner christened *Lightning*. Fishers Island was his favorite place to hide. What a time he must have had. A young man with nerve and a fast schooner with a good crew could make a quick fortune in those days." She looked up at the tall, white Ionic columns that so grandly supported the porch of Topsail House.

"We've been forced to learn sly tricks around this town," Arabella said as she watched Nellie bringing out the tray. "Notice old Mrs. Smithers over there across the street, Captain? Her father was my father's first officer before he bought himself a fast schooner to go privateering on his own. I once watched her doing a joyful solo waltz under that wisteria on her side porch before she fell off into the lilac bushes."

Pouring from the teapot, Kate's mother filled Finn's cup with rum, then from the hot water pitcher Melissa's and her own with what was widely known as "mother's ruin."

"Fair winds!" Arabella's voice boomed across the lawn as they raised their teacups, drank, and gasped, recovering just in time to nod at two shawled and bonneted members of the Mystic Abstinence Society.

"Phew!" said Tom, "that reminds me of home. I'm off for Boston at dawn tomorrow to have my interview with the admiral, but I'll be back in less than a week."

Six days later, Finn returned. Clutching Kate's hands, he said, "They've hired me! I've got the job with the Eagle Packet Line. They plan to send me on a trial voyage to Liverpool as an apprentice captain under one of their experienced masters to show me the ways of the Eagle Line. I'll be leaving next week. But I'll write you,

Kate, from Liverpool and bring you a souvenir from Spain. I expect to return to Mystic in . . . give or take a week or so . . . mid-March. Kate, don't take on any other beaus whilst I'm abroad. I've come to love you very much."

"I'll be waiting for you, Tom," Kate promised. "I'll be on pins and needles until I have you safe back here beside me."

The grass was greening and the first new, earthy smell of spring hung in the air when Finn bounded up the steps of Topsail House again and Kate was there to greet him. A good number of Mystic families asked Captain Finn to dinner to welcome him now that he had become a famous sailing man. Arabella Dunston gave a party in Captain Finn's honor on the day after the proper six-month period of mourning ended.

Finn had to make another trip to Boston in early April, but he did not dawdle there. He now felt that with Kate and other new friends in Mystic, it really had become his town, his home.

"In Boston, it's all new sailing schedules and passenger lists and talk of profits," Finn told Kate, "boardrooms gray with cigar smoke, baggy eyes, and walrus moustaches. It's good to be back here with you, Kate! I dreamed about you while I was gone. Will you marry me?"

Kate threw her arms around his neck.

Arabella was delighted when Tom Finn asked for Kate's hand in marriage. They all agreed to pick an early date for the ceremony.

Tom was trembling with excitement when he kissed Kate good-night. "Someday we'll travel north and you can meet my mother and sisters. You'll enjoy Heart's Content."

Next morning early, Finn returned to Boston, but four days later, a letter from him arrived at Topsail House. Kate opened it at the breakfast table and read it, then looked up, her face flushed. "Tom's schedule's been set. He sails from Boston as master of *Shenandoah*. She departs on Tuesday, May 15, 1877."

Arabella took command in her deep, authoritative voice. "That leaves us just a decent length of time to post the church banns and plan your forthcoming wedding."

Kate read on. "The line has offered as a wedding gift my free passage with Tom on our first voyage together!"

"How heavenly!" said Aunt Melissa.

"We must invite the admiral from the Eagle Packet Line," Kate's mother said. "I admire our famous Navy men."

"And add the Widow Smithers," said Melissa. "I hate to see her studying our arriving guests through her late husband's long glass."

"Kate, you can wear your grandmother's Spanish wedding dress and lace," said Arabella. "And Captain Thomas Finn will look so handsome in his new uniform, with that white wave collar and black stock close-hauled around his neck, and all those gold stripes and shining buttons!"

The long-awaited day dawned with clouds in the morning that cleared by noon into bright sunshine. Finn's best man was a captain from the Labrador named John Bockstoce who had his brig hove down in Mallory's Boatyard. Kate's maid of honor was her school friend, Louise Dyer. The wedding ceremony at the church went off without a hitch.

Back in Topsail House, Finn looked around at the gathering of more than seventy guests, which, Finn reflected, was about the male population of Blacklead Island. Many of the guests now gathered on the sunlit porch and lawn. The huge white house had been freshly painted and the fruit trees were in bloom. Everything that Finn could see was polished until it gleamed and his new wife, Kate, looked more beautiful than ever. Even Arabella, his mother-in-law, conjured up a smile as she made a saluting gesture toward the admiral, introducing him to all those gathered. He and the captains Shirley and Bockstoce made amusing champagne toasts as they wished the newlyweds a long and happy life.

In the dining room, the table and sideboard were arrayed with food of every kind. Maids wearing fresh-starched white caps and aprons demurely served plate after plate of delicious little cheese and green prick pickle canapés and rum cakes while whisking away still half-filled champagne glasses which they planned to share together in the pantry. Crowding around the punch bowl, the five mates – all save Angelo, who was off at sea – whispered among themselves that the whole affair was too damned stuffy and needed the old man, the Highlander, and a good Yack woman on an accordion to liven it up.

When Kate had changed her costume and it was time to leave for the Wadawanuck Hotel for their wedding night, the couple was showered with rice as they hurried down the path to the waiting buggy. Finn got hit square on the back of the neck with an affectionate hand-packed ball of fruitcake thrown by one of the mates, but when he turned to identify the culprit he found that his nautical groomsmen had gathered into a swaying, red-faced naval body that defied all rank or reason. The admiral warned the womenfolk to stand back as this crew of men in blue began to run, lurch, and stagger down toward the river's dock, cheering, singing, and pausing now and then to drink from their personal flasks. Their journey was only five short blocks. Kate and Finn looked back and waved and laughed, pretending to cheer them on.

"Don't worry, Kate," Finn whispered as he took her hand. "They're slowing down."

"I'm not worried about them," said Kate. "They're only coming to see us aboard *Hector* and wave good-bye from the dock. Being seamen, I know they all love boats."

Finn laughed. "That Admiral Elliott's a damned good sport. Were you in the parlor when big Otto Kraus shouted him down and climbed up on your mother's skinny-legged piano bench to make his wedding speech in German? Rum can sometimes do that to him."

The yacht *Hector* was waiting at the Mystic dock ready to sail in the afternoon breeze that had set all her pennants flying. Finn and Kate quickly left the carriage amid joyous shouts from the rear. They rushed up *Hector*'s gangway, turned, and tried to wave farewell to all their followers, who came leaping and jumping toward them.

"Good-bye! We're leaving! Don't fall in!" Finn shouted, wishing he had his gamming horn.

"We're all coming with you," shouted the admiral as he and the others scrambled aboard *Hector*.

"These mates say there could be heavy ice, growlers, or bergie bits ahead. They say it's their duty to see you safe to Stonington," *Hector*'s captain yelled to Finn. "They don't look or sound like the kind of men I could order ashore."

"They're not." Finn laughed. "Don't try it. I guess they've made up their minds to come with us. Kate says it's less than five miles." He came close to *Hector*'s master and shouted above the din, "For God's sake, Captain, don't give that crowd another drop to drink. My wife and I are going forward to the bow to catch that breeze. Will you try to keep the lot of them aft, Captain? And don't let any of them touch the wheel."

Finn saw Mario still working on a pocketful of cheese and green prick pickles. He took Kate's hand and they hurried to *Hector*'s elegant bow, where they tried to ignore the shouting, jokes, and laughter from the stern.

"Kate, you look so beautiful . . ." Finn placed a daring hand on his new wife's bustle and sprung it in and out.

"Careful, sailor." Kate laughed nervously. "You could break those expensive corset stays."

"They won't break." Finn beamed at her. "They're made of bowhead baleen. They'll bend like fishing rods."

"This is the most exciting moment of my life," said Kate.

Finn didn't actually kiss Kate but rubbed noses with her very gently.

"Listen, listen!" Finn held up his hand. "Hear those Blacklead mates? They learned that song from me."

We'll rant and we'll roar
Like true New-found-landers.
We'll rant and we'll roar
On decks and below,
Until we find shelter
Inside of two sounders,
Then straight through the channel
To Toslow we'll go.

Finn felt *Hector* give a lurch to starboard then swing back on course again. His best man, Bockstoce, and Captain Shirley had joined in with the admiral, who was singing at the wheel.

"God, lucky for us this is a short voyage in fair weather," Finn told Kate. "If there had been one piece of ice around here, we'd have hit it square."

"Tom, I've been wondering. Do you still have trouble with your side? Does it pain you when . . . you roll over in bed?"

"No, no," said Finn. "Don't worry about my ribs. They're fine." He smiled. "And I've got powerful forces ready to work for us, especially, well, especially . . . in bed."

"What do you mean by that, Tom?"

"It's kind of hard to explain to an innocent girl like you, Kate. But, well, there are lots of men, fast-sailing men, who take off at the starting gun and cross the finish line alone."

Kate considered this, gazing across the Sound. "My grandmother told me that it – the act of procreation – was often very disappointing for that reason. Do you mean you're that way, Tom?"

"I used to be," said Finn. "But, look. See this?" He reached into his side pocket and held out the precious amulet, its hard shank so neatly bound with sinew. "This amulet should make all the difference for us. There was a female *angakuk* in the Arctic . . . the big woman, your stepfather used to call her. She got mad first at the Highlander, and then at him. I believe it was that same big woman who brought so many whales to me. And to your father, at first. She didn't give a single one of them to the Highlander. It was that big woman who gave me this amulet . . . to ease my ribs . . . and to help me overcome another little problem I used to have."

"Wait, wait, dear Tom, you're all mixed up. You didn't crack your ribs in the Arctic. You did that during the hurricane out across this Sound near Montauk Point, remember?"

"Be that as it may," said Finn, "I guess it's turning out to be a wedding gift from her to . . . well, let's say . . . to the three of us."

"You mean including my stepfather?"

"No, it doesn't include your stepfather because he made a big mistake with her."

"How?"

"Well, even before we had our ships' holds filled, your stepfather got his mind dead set against her. He insulted that big woman during our farewell frolic. I believe that was when she decided to go after him. Not me, thank God. She brought me luck. She waited until that hurricane struck near Montauk Point. That was the last day of our voyage but she decided to avenge those whales." Finn pointed out across the Sound. "That's where she settled the score with him."

Dougal had wandered forward and now stood behind them. "Captain, I think you've got that exactly right."

"Tom, tell me, did you and Dougal drink a gallon of that rum punch and champagne during that reception?"

"Probably." Finn laughed. "But I never felt less drunk in my whole life, though I can't speak for Gibson. But I will say that this new job gives me the chance to wash my hands of both the sealing and the whaling trades."

Dougal spread his arms. "Just today, Captain Shirley has offered me a mate's birth aboard his clipper in the China trade. And, by God, I'm going to take it."

It was almost sundown, as *Hector* eased in close to the Stonington wharf. Tom hopped up onto the rail then took a flying leap onto the dock.

"Come on, Kate, jump! I'll catch you," shouted Finn.

Kate caught up her long skirt, then, helped by Dougal, leapt across into her husband's arms.

Hector's captain wisely grabbed the wheel and swung his yacht just far enough away so that none of the earnest wellwishers could make a jump for the dock.

"Good-bye! Good luck!" the excited knot of seagoers shouted.

Finn and his new bride waved then ran up the street, wildly eager to begin their new life together.

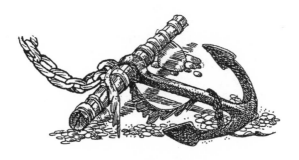

Ship's anchor

AUTHOR'S NOTE

In the 1870s, whaling was North America's biggest business. Successful sailing voyages into southern oceans for sperm whales and into the more dangerous ice-strewn waters of the north for larger bowhead whales provided oil for the lamps of North America and Europe and whale baleen to stiffen ladies' corsets. Many of the fortune seekers in this blood-soaked trade lost their lives while others became very wealthy.

I have made three sea journeys from the Outer Hebrides to Greenland then west back to Blacklead Island, the former whaling station of the Americans and Scots in Cumberland Sound for half a century. Lying almost on the Arctic Circle, this small island is a lonely place, now very difficult to reach. Its shores remain ice-bound for almost ten months of the year. The whalers' secret charts plotting a safe course into harbor have long since vanished, although traces of the old houses, and try-pots and barrel hoops, still remain.

Blacklead Island has had a remarkable history. At the height of the shamelessly destructive quest for oil, whalers from New England and Scotland eagerly joined with Inuit/Eskimos in the hunt, which almost totally destroyed the bowhead whales, until John D. Rockefeller with his development of Ohio and Pennsylvania rock oil all but ended the grim Arctic whaling trade. These three very different cultures were all desperate to accumulate more and more new ships, new houses, and endless gadgets, no matter at what cost.

This story is based on facts (yes, even mutineers in barrels!) that I gleaned from whaling journals and museums in Mystic, New London, New Bedford, Dundee, and Hull following the dozen years I spent living in the Canadian eastern Arctic with Baffin Island Inuit where some of the elders, men and women, remembered hunting and bedding, respectively, with the whalers.

I have cast this story as a work of fiction. Any similarity to Eskimo names in the Far North, or family names in Scotland or New England, is a matter of pure coincidence. My son, John Houston, Jonasikudlik, who was raised in the language of Baffin Island and schooled at Yale, helped me to arrive at the newer forms of Inuktitut spelling in this book that better suit these times. In earlier Arctic days, the word "Eskimo" was recognized and respected around the world. That term recently has fallen out of favor in Canada and now "Inuit" (the people) and "Inuk" (the person) are most frequently used.

ABOUT THE AUTHOR

As with his best-selling autobiography, *Confessions of an Igloo Dweller*, the strength of *The Ice Master* lies in **James Houston's** familiarity with the land, the Inuit, and their customs.

Raised in Toronto and trained as an artist, he spent World War 11 with the Toronto Scottish Regiment, after which he studied life drawing in France before wandering into the Arctic on a sketching whim in 1948. That visit changed Canadian history: "Largely owing to the insights and promotional energy of James A. Houston, a young artist from Toronto, 'Eskimo art,' or 'Inuit art' as we know it today, came into existence in 1948-49." *The Canadian Encyclopedia*

His years in the North – recounted in *Confessions of an Igloo Dweller* – lasted until 1962 when he left the West Baffin Eskimo co-operative in Cape Dorset running smoothly to move to Manhattan, where he designed glass sculptures for Steuben. He and his second wife, Alice, now divide their time between the Connecticut shore portrayed in *The Ice Master* and a writing retreat in the Queen Charlotte Islands in British Columbia.

An Officer of the Order of Canada, James Houston is the author of many books for adults and children, most notably the novels *The White Dawn*, *Spirit Wrestler*, and *Running West*. In June 1997 he received the Royal Canadian Geographical Society's award for life-time achievement, the Massey Medal.

SELECTED STORIES *by* Alice Munro
"The collection of the year," said *Kirkus Reviews* of these 28 superb stories representing Alice Munro's best. "The whole volume makes one believe anew in fiction's power to transfigure." *Washington Post*

Fiction, $6^{1}/_{4} \times 9^{1}/_{4}$, 560 pages, hardcover

THE MACKEN CHARM: A novel *by* Jack Hodgins
When the rowdy Mackens gather for a family funeral on Vancouver Island in the 1950s, the result is "fine, funny, sad and readable, a great yarn, the kind only an expert storyteller can produce." *Ottawa Citizen*

Fiction, 6×9, 320 pages, trade paperback

THE MERRY HEART: Selections 1980-1995 *by* Robertson Davies
"A marvellous array of Davies' speeches and reviews, interspersed with bits of his personal diaries." *Hamilton Spectator* "It's a happy thing that the voice from the attic is still being heard." *Montreal Gazette*

Non-fiction, 6×9, 400 pages, hardcover

THE SELECTED STORIES OF MAVIS GALLANT *by* Mavis Gallant
"A volume to hold and to treasure" said the *Globe and Mail* of the 52 marvellous stories selected from Mavis Gallant's life's work. "It should be in every reader's library."

Fiction, $6^{1}/_{8} \times 9^{1}/_{4}$, 900 pages, hardcover

HITLER VERSUS ME: The Return of Bartholomew Bandy *by* Donald Jack
Bandy ("a national treasure" according to a Saskatoon reviewer) is back in the RCAF, fighting Nazis and superior officers, and trying to keep his age and his toupee as secret as the plans for D-Day.

Fiction/Humour, 6×9, 360 pages, hardcover

THE ASTOUNDING LONG-LOST LETTERS OF DICKENS OF THE MOUNTED *edited by* Eric Nicol
The "letters" from Charles Dickens's son, a Mountie from 1874 to 1886, are "a glorious hoax . . . so cleverly crafted, so subtly hilarious." *Vancouver Sun*

Fiction, $4^{1}/_{4} \times 7$, 296 pages, paperback

BACK TALK: A Book for Bad Back Sufferers and Those Who Put Up With Them *by* Eric Nicol *illustrated by* Graham Pilsworth
This "little gem" (*Quill and Quire*) caused one reader – Mrs. E. Nicol – to write: "Laughing at this book cured my bad back. It's a miracle!"

Humour, $5^{1}/_{2} \times 8^{1}/_{2}$, 136 pages, illustrations, trade paperback

PADDLE TO THE AMAZON: The Ultimate 12,000-Mile Canoe Adventure
by Don Starkell *edited by* Charles Wilkins
From Winnipeg to the mouth of the Amazon by canoe! "This real-life adven-
ture book . . . must be ranked among the classics of the literature of survival."
Montreal Gazette "Fantastic" *Bill Mason*
Adventure, 6 × 9, 320 pages, maps, photos, trade paperback

THE HONORARY PATRON: A novel *by* Jack Hodgins
The Governor General's Award-winner's thoughtful and satisfying third
novel of a celebrity's return home to Vancouver Island mixes comedy and
wisdom "and it's magic." *Ottawa Citizen*
Fiction, 4 1/4 × 7, 336 pages, paperback

INNOCENT CITIES: A novel *by* Jack Hodgins
Victorian in time and place, this delightful new novel by the author of *The
Invention of the World* proves once again that "as a writer, Hodgins is unique
among his Canadian contemporaries." *Globe and Mail*
Fiction, 4 1/4 × 7, 416 pages, paperback

THE CUNNING MAN: A novel *by* Robertson Davies
This "sparkling history of the erudite and amusing Dr. Hullah who knows the
souls of his patients as well as he knows their bodies" *London Free Press* is "wise,
humane and constantly entertaining." *The New York Times*
Fiction, 6 × 9, 480 pages, hardcover

OPEN SECRETS: Stories *by* Alice Munro
Eight marvellous stories, ranging in time from 1850 to the present and from
Albania to "Alice Munro Country." "There may not be a better collection of
stories until her next one." *Chicago Tribune*
Fiction, 6 × 9, 304 pages, hardcover

THE BLACK BONSPIEL OF WILLIE MACCRIMMON *by* W.O. Mitchell
illustrated by Wesley W. Bates
A devil of a good tale about curling – W.O. Mitchell's most successful comic
play now appears as a story, fully illustrated, for the first time, and it is "a true
Canadian classic." *Western Report*
Fiction, 4 5/8 × 7 1/2, 144 pages with 10 wood engravings, hardcover

FOR ART'S SAKE: A new novel *by* W.O. Mitchell
"*For Art's Sake* shows the familiar Mitchell brand of subtle humour in this tale
of an aging artist who takes matters into his own hands in bringing pictures
to the people." *Calgary Sun*
Fiction, 6 × 9, 240 pages, hardcover

LADYBUG, LADYBUG . . . by W.O. Mitchell
"Mitchell slowly and subtly threads together the elements of this richly detailed and wonderful tale . . . the outcome is spectacular . . . *Ladybug, Ladybug* is certainly among the great ones!" *Windsor Star*

Fiction, $4^{1}/_{4} \times 7$, 288 pages, paperback

ROSES ARE DIFFICULT HERE *by* W.O.Mitchell
"Mitchell's newest novel is a classic, capturing the richness of the small town, and delving into moments that really count in the lives of its people . . ." *Windsor Star*   Fiction, 6×9, 328 pages, hardcover

WHO HAS SEEN THE WIND *by* W.O. Mitchell *illustrated by* William Kurelek
For the first time since 1947, this well-loved Canadian classic of childhood on the prairies is presented in its full, unexpurgated edition, and is "gorgeously illustrated." *Calgary Herald*

Fiction, $8^{1}/_{2} \times 10$, 320 pages, numerous colour and black-and-white illustrations, hardcover

FRIEND OF MY YOUTH *by* Alice Munro
"I want to list every story in this collection as my favourite . . . Ms. Munro is a writer of extraordinary richness and texture." Bharati Mukherjee, *The New York Times*   Fiction, 6×9, 288 pages, hardcover

THE PROGRESS OF LOVE *by* Alice Munro
"Probably the best collection of stories – the most confident and, at the same time, the most adventurous – ever written by a Canadian." *Saturday Night*

Fiction, 6×9, 320 pages, hardcover

THE PRIVATE VOICE: A Journal of Reflections *by* Peter Gzowski
"A fascinating book that is cheerfully anecdotal, painfully honest, agonizingly self-doubting and compulsively readable." *Toronto Sun*

Autobiography, $5^{1}/_{2} \times 8^{1}/_{2}$, 320 pages, photos, trade paperback

A PASSION FOR NARRATIVE: A Guide for Writing Fiction *by* Jack Hodgins
"One excellent path from original to marketable manuscript. . . . It would take a beginning writer years to work her way through all the goodies Hodgins offers." *Globe and Mail*

Non-fiction/Writing guide, $5^{1}/_{4} \times 8^{1}/_{2}$, 216 pages, trade paperback

OVER FORTY IN BROKEN HILL: Unusual Encounters in the Australian Outback *by* Jack Hodgins
"Australia described with wit, wonder and affection by a bemused visitor with Canadian sensibilities." *Canadian Press* "Damned fine writing." *Books in Canada*   *Travel, 5¹/₂ × 8¹/₂, 216 pages, trade paperback*

DANCING ON THE SHORE: A Celebration of Life at Annapolis Basin *by* Harold Horwood, *Foreword by* Farley Mowat
"A Canadian *Walden*" *Windsor Star* that "will reward, provoke, challenge and enchant its readers." *Books in Canada*
                    Nature/Ecology, 5¹/₈ × 8¹/₄, 224 pages, 16 wood engravings, trade paperback

HUGH MACLENNAN'S BEST: An anthology *selected by* Douglas Gibson
This selection from all of the works of the witty essayist and famous novelist is "wonderful . . . It's refreshing to discover again MacLennan's formative influence on our national character." *Edmonton Journal*
                                        Anthology, 6 × 9, 352 pages, trade paperback

UNDERCOVER AGENT: How One Honest Man Took On the Drug Mob . . . And Then the Mounties *by* Leonard Mitchell and Peter Rehak
"It's the stuff of spy novels – only for real . . . how a family man in a tiny fishing community helped make what at the time was North America's biggest drug bust." Saint John *Telegraph-Journal*
                        Non-fiction/Criminology, 4¹/₄ × 7, 176 pages, paperback

ACCORDING TO JAKE AND THE KID: A Collection of New Stories *by* W.O. Mitchell
"This one's classic Mitchell. Humorous, gentle, wistful, it's 16 new short stories about life through the eyes of Jake, a farmhand, and the kid, whose mom owns the farm." *Saskatoon Star-Phoenix*
                                        Fiction, 5 × 7³/₄, 280 pages, trade paperback

NEXT-YEAR COUNTRY: Voices of Prairie People *by* Barry Broadfoot
"There's something mesmerizing about these authentic Canadian voices." *Globe and Mail* "A good book, a joy to read." *Books in Canada*
                        Oral history, 5³/₈ × 8³/₄, 400 pages, trade paperback

WELCOME TO FLANDERS FIELDS: The First Canadian Battle of the Great War – Ypres, 1915 *by* Daniel G. Dancocks
"A magnificent chronicle of a terrible battle . . . Daniel Dancocks is spellbinding throughout." *Globe and Mail*
                        Military/History, 4¹/₄ × 7, 304 pages, photos, maps, paperback

MURTHER & WALKING SPIRITS: A novel *by* Robertson Davies
"Brilliant" was the *Ottawa Citizen's* description of the sweeping tale of a
Canadian family through the generations. "It will recruit huge numbers of
new readers to the Davies fan club." *Observer* (London)

Fiction, 6¹/₄ × 9¹/₂, 368 pages, hardcover

THE RADIANT WAY *by* Margaret Drabble
"*The Radiant Way* does for Thatcher's England what *Middlemarch* did for
Victorian England . . . Essential reading!" *Margaret Atwood*

Fiction, 6 × 9, 400 pages, hardcover

ACROSS THE BRIDGE: Stories *by* Mavis Gallant
These eleven stories, set mostly in Montreal or in Paris, were described as
"Vintage Gallant – urbane, witty, absorbing." *Winnipeg Free Press* "We come
away from it both thoughtful and enriched." *Globe and Mail*

Fiction, 6 × 9, 208 pages, trade paperback

AT THE COTTAGE: A Fearless Look at Canada's Summer Obsession *by*
Charles Gordon *illustrated by* Graham Pilsworth
This perennial best-selling book of gentle humour is "a delightful reminder of
why none of us addicted to cottage life will ever give it up." *Hamilton Spectator*

Humour, 6 × 9, 224 pages, illustrations, trade paperback

HOW TO BE NOT TOO BAD: A Canadian Guide to Superior Behaviour
by Charles Gordon *illustrated by* Graham Pilsworth
This "very fine and funny book" *Ottawa Citizen* "updates the etiquette menu,
making mincemeat of Miss Manners." *Toronto Star*

Humour, 6 × 9, 248 pages, illustrations, trade paperback